Deborah Durant

Edie Meidav is the author of *The Far Field: A Novel of Ceylon*. Winner of the Janet Heidinger Kafka Prize for Fiction by an American Woman, she teaches at the New College of California and is currently in residence at Bard College.

www.ediemeidav.com

A score for *Crawl Space* is available at:
www.savagerobotrecords.xbuild.com/collaborations

Crawl Space
An *Electric Review* Best Book of the Year
A *ReadySteadyBook* Best Book of the Year

Praise for Edie Meidav's *Crawl Space* and *The Far Field*

"Poulquet is, he says, 'one more unjew jewed by history.' Such a fellow should not be good company for the substantial pilgrimage we undertake with him in Edie Meidav's troubling new novel, *Crawl Space*. But he is quite a creation indeed, this aging anti-Quixote with his residual windmills to tilt at. . . . It might have been tempting for a novelist to show Poulquet crumbling with guilt, self-accusation, and awareness; the quality of his whimsical hauteur is not the least of Meidav's triumphs as a storyteller."
—Thomas Keneally, author of *Schindler's List*

"A new school of international women writers is among us, in the wake of Janet Frame, including Jane Alison, Delia Falconer, and now Edie Meidav. Meidav's huge panorama of Ceylon is not only stylish but reveals a rare intensity of imagination. *The Far Field* grows on several levels with a patient, incisive amplitude that works wonders. The novel reads like an orchestration of André Malraux's *The Temptation of the West*."
—Paul West, author of *The Tent of Orange Mist*

"Meidav's style is subtle and sophisticated, resembling that of Marcel Proust."
—*J.* (the Jewish news weekly of Northern California) on *Crawl Space*

"Edie Meidav's brave novel about an aged French Nazi who has slipped between the cracks of the legal system, and, with unreconstructed prejudices, seeks shelter in his hometown now."
—Robert Kelly, author of *Lapis*, on *Crawl Space*

"*The Far Field* is ambitious, capacious, and a good deal of fun."
—Emily Barton, *San Francisco Chronicle*

"Unfailingly interesting."
—*San Francisco* magazine on *Crawl Space*

"[*The Far Field* is] a richly detailed and lyrical epic. . . . Despite its imaginative scope and intellectual heft, the book moves as rapidly as a thriller, propelling the reader toward a heart-stopping conclusion both unexpected and inevitable."

—*Harper's Bazaar*

"Meidav has the ability to tackle the huge, unanswerable questions of history with breathtaking skill and daring. She goes deep into The Other and brings into focus the complex interrelations among beauty, cruelty, sympathy, and brutality. The profundity of her moral and philosophical probing is matched by the strikingness of her imagery and the lyricism of her prose. She surveys the most reprehensible moral landscape and elicits from her reader, in that miraculous act of grace that only fiction can provide, a sympathy, as well as a repugnance for that very sympathy. A masterful manipulator, she milks every nuance of vulnerability and shamelessness, delusion and contrition. Like Penelope weaving and unweaving her tapestry, Meidav heals and rips apart the wounds of history nearly simultaneously. She forces us to interrogate the very nature of memory. Her vision is vast, global, uncompromising, risk taking. Thus it is no surprise that her brilliant career is fast evolving."

—Mary Caponegro on *Crawl Space*

"An original, new novel about the Holocaust . . . A provocative and compelling second novel."

—*Jewish Woman* magazine on *Crawl Space*

"Meidav embeds the reader in the mind of a narcissistic, self-loathing, obsessive, vengeful narrator, a French Nazi collaborator, whose oddly compelling voice is the achievement of this complex novel (after *The Far Field*). . . . With a tale both chilling and comical, Meidav considers the struggle to define history."

—*Publishers Weekly*

"A deep character study of an octogenarian who knows that even death will not eliminate the guilt that haunts him. His need to 'go home' grips readers. . . . Meidav does the impossible."

—*Midwest Book Review* on *Crawl Space*

"[*The Far Field* is] an ambitious and distinguished first novel . . . luminous, perceptive, lyrical, poignant, powerful."
—Chitra Divakaruni, *Los Angeles Times* (a Best Book of the Year)

"It's the high-voltage prose and thematic intensity—involving sophisticated observations about idealism and culture clash—that set [*The Far Field*] apart from the crowd. Images coil around ideas in Meidav's sentences."
—*The Village Voice Literary Supplement*

"Edie Meidav writes with Melvillean exuberance and dramatically conjures an extraordinary and unfamiliar world. In its ambition, vitality, and scope, *The Far Field* is a remarkable first novel."
—Claire Messud, author of *The Last Life*

"Another jewel inspired by Ceylon. Brilliant, dazzling, spraying light far and wide. Meidav's first novel is a rare and precious treasure."
—Martha McPhee, author of *Bright Angel Time*, on *The Far Field*

"A delightful first novel of infatuation by a promising young writer."
—Walter Abish, author of *How German Is It*, on *The Far Field*

CRAWL SPACE

PICADOR

FARRAR, STRAUS AND GIROUX

NEW YORK

CRAWL SPACE

EDIE MEIDAV

CRAWL SPACE. Copyright © 2005 by Edie Meidav. All rights reserved. Printed in the United States of America. No part of this book may be used or reproduced in any manner whatsoever without written permission except in the case of brief quotations embodied in critical articles or reviews. For information, address Picador, 175 Fifth Avenue, New York, N.Y. 10010.

www.picadorusa.com

Picador® is a U.S. registered trademark and is used by Farrar, Straus and Giroux under license from Pan Books Limited.

For information on Picador Reading Group Guides, as well as ordering, please contact Picador.
Phone: 646-307-5629
Fax: 212-253-9627
E-mail: readinggroupguides@picadorusa.com

Design by Gretchen Achilles

Library of Congress Cataloging-in-Publication Data

Meidav, Edie, 1967-
 Crawl space / Edie Meidav.
   p. cm.
 ISBN-13: 978-0-312-42575-3
 ISBN-10: 0-312-42575-9
 1. Men—Fiction. 2. Memory—Fiction. I. Title.

PS3563.E3447C73 2005
813'.6—dc22
                                                        2004029121

First published in the United States by Farrar, Straus and Giroux

First Picador Edition: July 2006

P1

To the alephs BC and EC, CC, SS, RB, JC, CD, RM, MR, MH, JS, SB, LBA, AB, DD, LJ, LW, BD, PJ, SA, CM. JTMM. SS and ESM. Marleen.

I'll build you a house you won't destroy,
without blueprint or cement.
—HENRI MICHAUX

For to him that is joined to all the living there is hope: for a living dog is better than a dead lion. For the living know that they shall die: but the dead know not any thing, neither have they any more a reward; for the memory of them is forgotten. Also their love, and their hatred, and their envy, is now perished; neither have they any more a portion for ever in any thing that is done under the sun.
—ECCLESIASTES 9:4–6

PART ONE

ONE

You think you know me and still my name slips away on your tongue. You've probably seen me countless times, but you never noticed. There has been surgery on my face, yes, to disguise me. Yet I live in your pile of clippings, I exist in your mind as a niggling question, a thing troubling your sleep certain nights. I understand your dilemma. You would not give it the importance of a dilemma but having been on your side, I understand how denial becomes an easier route.

In school, they taught us that the ninth century considered the devil to be in charge of bad timing. Here at the end of the twentieth century, people say the devil is capable of taking up permanent residence in certain people, thousands simultaneously, including within my former colleagues. Many have also hinted that the devil lives in me, just as my own father believed.

What I mean is that if my father still lived and you had the chance to ask him, he would say the hump on my face, no longer there of course, was the first sign of badness—my hump which caused such suffering in my early years, even after my father grew quite obsessed with my disfigurement and had the thing sliced off, believing the hump both caused and flaunted my innate evil.

Hump or no hump, I still think timing matters most when *deciding* what is evil. You can't have a belief without having been influenced by timing. My father was influenced by his era, I by mine. If nowadays anyone thinks the devil is in charge of bad timing, wouldn't I at this late date be excused for having been born too early or too late? An accident: can a lone human misfire, timing his birth wrong? My guess is the ninth century might have been kinder to me. Now people tend to think the devil is in charge of many departments. As they say, the devil is a *multitasker*. Despite my advanced age, I have heard that word, as I have heard so many words, all those young and unhappy modern words used against me.

I MEANT TO LEAVE the café but I could not stop listening to the men discussing their ideas about timing and immorality, all of which sparked my own thoughts. The inspector—the others called him Louzange—thought the Turkish biker they'd found fornicating with a local girl on the side of the road was merely a victim of bad timing. Louzange had pretended to issue the biker a summons for *unlawful congress in public spaces*. Of course, this was an invented ticket. Louzange had considered how to phrase the infraction while walking toward the twosome, as the local girl ran away and the biker tried to zip up the leather britches which covered only one leg, the other one swathed in a shocking hiplength plaster cast.

"I walked toward him," said Louzange. He had the thick accent of someone who had rarely fled the eastern valleys of our region, his French a guttural burr. "Already his oddness struck me." Louzange had thought, at first, that the back in its heaving was caught in the terror of an epileptic fit.

His associate, more rough-hewn, sniggered at this. "When you got out of the car, you asked for a tongue-guard."

Louzange was a neatly calibrated man, a man I might have worked with in my heyday. "It was not wrong for me to have thought that, Tissan."

"Okay," said his associate. "But an epileptic fit it was not. More like Bronco Bill, you know?"

"I gave him a fake ticket. He should have gotten a real ticket," said Louzange. "Not because he had bad timing and we happened to see him. It is that people should not think that France can be the playground for their immorality. We French have never been prudes, yes, but we cannot be the toilet for all Europe!"

They had opened the man's briefcase. Predictably, the biker had sworn at them. His French had been quite capable. In the man's briefcase were letters neatly addressed to and received from the one hotel in the region, which tended to suck all visitors toward its ancient heart.

"What would you expect?" asked the bartender, his first words, such an attentive listener that he'd already dropped and broken one wineglass.

Indeed, what would one expect? The hotel—the Hotel Fauret in Finier, or, rather, the lady who'd married into the Fauret family—had played too large a role in my life, not to mention in my current trek. It appeared that once again I wasn't going to be able to choose the details of our encounter. Never mind how sweet the town of Finier was to me and how long it had lurked, whether as backdrop to my childhood dreams, student years in Paris, or my more recent time in a holding cell. This hovering (the town's, yes, but also the Fauret lady's) had made me decide I needed, for once and for all, to return to the arena for those dreams. I would give that lady something she wouldn't forget, presenting myself as I am: one more unjew jewed by history.

It is much harder to stay and fight than it is to merely flee. If I could just get into those pale hands my last will and testament, which would amount to the correct version of history, this heroism alone would, I thought, accomplish something. Anyone could see how much the Fauret lady had done. Worse than bad timing, almost my whole life, she had distorted my prospects.

Poulquet, come back. It was not Arianne Fauret's voice that spoke to me but the voice of the place, ever since my first exile and return. What was there not to like about Finier? The town with its chateau and two rivers: one a lisping froth, stinging the mountains, a viper's reddish tongue, the other rolling toward Spain, far more ripe and calm. In the early mornings the whole setting was so pristine that it is little wonder our town was so frequently compared to the Rhineland.

IT WAS FROM 1940 until 1945 that I'd overseen the prefecture of Finier, the offices which manage the entire region. Though I felt myself to be something of a partial suicide, I had decided to return to Finier in 1960 for a brief spell. Disguised by some minor surgery on my face, I thought my return a feasible solution to being in exile. For a month, long as I could bear it, I served as janitor at the prefecture, before I needed again to flee into a new and more waterproof series of aliases, disguises, noms de guerre, the slippery welcome of other nations.

Here in 1999, I was back again in Finier, having traveled, having been only briefly imprisoned, released on a technicality, face operated upon again, and having lost only a bit of what many had long called my unusual physical heartiness. For despite everything, I remained, at eighty-four years of age, a time when most set their dimming eyes upon some horizon of diminished movement, failed kidneys and sluggish circulation, *a hearty physical specimen*, one still complimented (if I ever came to having much discourse with others) as being cool-tempered, iron-nerved, articulate, strangely able to summon help from aristocratic quarters. I was still a man with an elegance others called, if spruced up a bit, patrician.

I may have been born with a lump on my face, but my genes had played a fool's game with me, composing me of an appallingly strong stock. This—in addition to my half-century's practice of choosing all food via the swing of a pendulum, a trusty device which I kept in my pocket, a bit grime-covered but nonetheless a pendulum capable of steering me toward both correct comestibles and decisions—has kept me intact.

Admittedly, it sounds odd, but there is a wonderful simplicity to the pendulum: one direction swings toward YES, one toward NO. Thus, one knows not only what to eat, but what to do, whom to consider an ally and so forth. One might find it strange that I have trusted such a simple device, but mortality statistics state the case. My wartime colleagues had long died out, either at their own hands or succumbing to that strange catalogue, the ills of senescence a flipped mirror of a baby's development: loss of speech and dignity, the slide toward drooling dementia. Or else they'd surrendered to ills taken from a catalogue asymmetrical to a baby's: catarrh and hemorrhoids, cirrhosis or dependence, pneumonia, incontinence, despair. And there I was, thanks to the pendulum. True, not robust anymore, but undemented, fairly undespairing. At times, one might even find me lamenting how whole body and mind remained, how unabated remained my instinct for self-preservation. Most recently, I'd witnessed my own surprising ability to perform some fancy footwork, escaping from my trial virtually unchallenged (if one didn't examine certain protesters too closely).

Perhaps now, yes, at eighty-four I was a bit less impervious to cold, slower up a hill, and then more likely to doze off wherever I arrived, enduring both sore bones and a startle of memory as I awoke. It is also true that whenever I slept the night in an odd boîte, I could tend toward insomnia, leaving me a wreck of a human the next day. Worst of all, my eyesight had begun to turn life's lovelier sights into watery dabblings, doubled, lacking firm outline. But still! No need for any of those accoutrements of old age, the hearing aid, bottle-thick spectacles, a decorated cane, a catheter somewhat hidden, the diapers fairly unignorable. Since I was a child first hearing the sphinx's question about the four ages of man, I'd hoped to escape the terminus: there was the baby who crawls on all fours, the whimsical adult moving about on two, the dodderer with three legs, one of them being his cane, and the last, the dead man, lacking need for legs. And my childish fears seemed to have borne fruit. By some whimsical moral organizing force—I do not say God—I seemed destined to remain, indefinitely, in the age of the bipedal.

And though some have said I must have been born with a questionable morality, if vim had been sapped in one particular department, other vigor must have then been rewarded to my physical being and opportunism, as well as to whatever force my pendulum channeled. It was also true that I had a pacemaker, which, to use the parlance of this age, kept my heart unnaturally hopped up. And further, that because I had upon me what would probably be my ultimate disguise, the scars of my most recent operation, I may have looked younger than I am, the hypodermic collagen and suturing of this era one of its sole advantages. Yet it was true that the sheer melancholy of being myself at eighty-four couldn't wholly escape me.

For all that, if appetite is what defines the young, and the tempering of appetite is what defines the aged, I remained a young man most especially in this regard: ridiculous and foolhardy as it was, I starved for the town of Finier, I thirsted for it. About Finier I cannot be agnostic. It is a fact of our land, as much as our rivers flowing down from the Pyrénées.

SO IT WAS that at the Bomont station café, eavesdropping on the inspector and his cronies and the foreigner they'd stumbled across, I could not help but lean in to listen to the men speaking of the biker's destination: my old hotel, the Hotel Fauret.

Here the bartender interrupted them again. "Your Turkish biker? You're wrong about him, by the way. That guy in the leather pants and the huge leg-cast? He comes in here sometimes. Doesn't leave a crumb behind. Some people think he's a journalist. Or I've heard he works out of some institute in Paris. But I think—"

Louzange cut in. "Well," drawling, a consider-the-facts tone, one I would've commended had he worked in my bureau. "Who did you hear talking about him? Journalists? Common people? Civil servants?"

"All." The bartender ducked his head as if to assuage Louzange that no oneupmanship had been intended. "This isn't my field, you know. Get me on the subject of fingerprints on glasses, though, I'm your man."

Louzange nodded, serve taken, sliding smoothly on, turning to the topic of the biker's passport. Samuel Varden Panir's occupation ostensibly that of a journalist, the pages impregnated with the inks of many countries. Turkey. Also the United States, Israel, Bosnia, Nicaragua. It was an American passport, though the man, to Louzange's mind, was clearly Turkish, given his name.

"Samuel Varden Panir? I'd say just a careless man," said Louzange, a professional, summing up the case. "The guy must be a travel writer. We're used to these fellows, aren't we? They come for our beautiful Pyrénéenne roads. Or he's from one of those American biker clubs."

"They only know their *j'aime les femmes* and *j'aime les frites*," his associate breathed, performing a passable imitation of the bikers' bad cowboy French, this man who'd been called Tissan as he'd entered, who'd announced that he was on to vermouth before ten in the morning on a Saturday and was proud of this fact. Not only did my situation prohibit me from looking at these men too directly, I didn't want to. Over one of Tissan's eyes was a whitened caul, a disfigurement I found as unattractive as prominent veins under a rolled-up tongue. "Bikers like to stand outside our markets drinking warm orangina and beer. Mixed."

"Basically, if I may?" said Louzange. "They are outlaws. They think that in our mountains, our solitude, if they can just look out on our farmland and breathe our good air, they're going to find something." He went on to describe the bikes, so adolescent and bulging, as if the bikes themselves were made up of Adam's apples.

"The biking clubs attract outlaws but you know," said the bartender, clearly fancying himself a barroom egghead, "those types just want to feel they can get in on some family will. They like to think nature belongs to them."

"No," said Louzange. "They like to think *France* belongs to them."

He withdrew from his satchel a notebook, neatly imprinted with the insignia of the Bomont football team, and notated his insight.

"That girl," Tissan was sniggering again. "The brunette with the Turkish biker? Barely legal. Not half-bad." And with his fingers formed a circle which I found rather crude.

FOR ALL THEIR TALK of identity, none of the men had made much note of me as they'd entered the café. To them, whatever hostesses and superiors had once frequently seen in me (elegant, iron-nerved Emile), I was just a Saturday-morning drifter, one of many grizzled bushels one sees in France. The bushels are men who brandish certain talismans to show they belong. They wear special raincoats, favor certain cafés, smoke fancy cigarettes. When it rains in Paris, the bushels frequent late-afternoon cinemas. In my own day, I too would have ignored the man I have become. I believed no Saturday-morning café denizen would recognize me, given all the work done on my face since the time I had to go undercover, not to mention the most recent work, still smarting at the seams. First off, as I said, I looked much younger than I was. To these people, priding themselves on their perspicacity, I was just a bushel with a bad sunburn, flared veins, imminent skin cancers. Thus, when Louzange began to speak of the Turkish biker, of the bike stickers proclaiming I LOVE TRUCKEE, USA, I began to feel self-disgust, unable to hide how my smell had become noxious even to me. For days, ever since I'd decided to flee my Paris doctor friend's apartment (a choice which also stripped me of the comfortable alias of a man named David Modine), I had been unable to shave. So in their gaze, these fellows shared breathing space with a random old man, nothing to which one had to pay too much attention. While my own sense was that I was made of the same decent tissue and bones as they were. Haunted by a particular lady, yes, wanting to lay history on her doorstep, a man recently tending to err on the side of sincerity—but a human constituted as they were, a fellow wishing to get home to set a few things straight.

TWO

The night before all this café discussion, sleep had been stolen from me. With the last will and testament I'd almost finished crumpled in my coat pocket, I'd sat in a lavatory on the super jet train from Paris, heading toward Toulouse and then on toward the Spanish border. I'd run out of the pills which had helped tremendously during my recent courtroom ordeal, the entire basketful of medicine bottles whose contents had lent me at least the interior sensation of elegance, a basket handed me by my doctor friend back in Paris. "Freeze-dried alcohol," he'd explained. "Keeps you calm. But it disinhibits people. You'll have to stay on top of it, clear about what you ordinarily *wouldn't* say." Somewhere between the trial and the train, pills still flushing my system with their ferocious tranquility, I'd decided to hand Arianne the will, the first time I'd have a face-to-face interview with her since I'd been prefect. Now that I'd run out of pills, I marveled at the decision. A different man had made it, yet I seemed obedient to the older regime. Though this is not to say that the will didn't possess its own degree of forethought, having taken me more than a year to write. It was something I had begun without naming its executor. Its writing had given me a sense of industry and meaning, whether as a free man, lawfully forgotten citizen, or, now, fugitive.

It was what one might call a will of rectification, written to be portable, stretching over only a few pages, composed in tiny handwriting, employing inks both blue and black, oyster-hued where rain had blurred it, near the left crease. I told myself in the lavatory that if anyone could decipher it, Arianne could, as its prime executor (and instigator). This is not to say that she had asked for the role of executor. Rather, what was required was that I would foist the document upon her. All night long the thing had crumpled further as I'd tried to hold the faulty lavatory-door latch shut—I could not be discovered by the train inspectors—and so I'd been forced to breathe in the confessional stink of diverse kidneys. Sometimes the strands of the stench became one, which was bad, mitigated only when I could make them diverge, each smell sniffed out of context, becoming almost pleasant: butter, lemons, straw, vinegar. Still, one could not help but remark how maintenance standards had fallen since my era.

Unfortunately, when you are fleeing from what everyone else calls justice, when you are practically an escaped convict, you must live above complaint. You end up being held to a higher standard, even if no one ever identifies you.

Through the lavatory window, at the Bomont station, I'd detected an army of cleaners marching toward the train with determination, their mops like national-pride-day flags of sanitation stating that eventually I would be dislodged from my refuge. One of those cleaners would find me out and force me into the corridor to confront an inspector. Realizing this probability, I'd decided to take a little breath in the village of Bomont. Quickly, not wishing to make trouble for anyone, before the troops advanced, I'd gotten off the train and headed for the succor of the station café. My aim was to get to Finier, some twelve kilometers away, but I'd thought it wouldn't hurt to use the last of my francs for a coffee—what the pendulum always chose for me, steering me away from the pernod and pastis I truly desired. Waiting for the next train, au lait before me, I'd found myself in the café listening to Louzange and his colleagues discuss morality and the problem of timing which seeped into everything, including train schedules.

Though the trains had never betrayed me. Near my childhood home in Esfauret, there'd been a federation of train workers and a train graveyard, and I'd often peeked through the yard's wooden slats just to glimpse those engineers with lanterns, headlamps, and toolboxes, men in full-blown camaraderie, all ruddy men I'd envied and admired, deploying a genie's magic resuscitating dead machines and steam.

You know that being a fugitive from others' ideas eventually makes you into a sort of eternal child, forever peeking through slats. My modern-day eavesdropping imposed similar rigors. I'd sorely needed to break into the conversation about the biker, wishing to ask the inspectors about the nature of the fellow's correspondence with the Hotel Fauret. Or was such an urge the pills' aftereffect? My goal in heading toward the hotel at that point had to do with Arianne Fauret (though I recall telling myself, silently, that I should not confess anything about her to anybody. This desire to spill the beans, as they say, was already a bad sign). My plan was to set her straight so that she would stop thinking solely *her* whim had let me survive. At least in certain precincts, the name of Emile Poulquet would be absolved.

He shows no remorse, they had said in court. *He would've continued his naked careerism had the occupation not come to an end.* As I always say, though I lacked the chance to say this in court: I did not know how many would be affected, I did not ask for others to manipulate me as they did, and I too once had been a young man making a young man's choices.

Whatever the case, any information the café men might have offered about Arianne's hotel would have been useful. Instead, again I had to stay mum. And when I saw the ten-car local chug into the station, I had to finish the last of the au lait, place seven francs on the counter and sidle out.

But rather than getting on the train toward Finier, I stood like an ancient tree, held in place, watching the peasant ambition of a lone older woman. Her baskets hungry for better markets closer to the Spanish border, she mounted the train, her thick stockinged calves strangely beautiful. As I paused, the conductor looked straight at and then through me. We both waited. He then signaled the train could leave, a departure always more compelling than arrival, the Andorra train caterpillaring over the mountains, fog thread low among those rocky crags. Having heard the inspector and his cronies discuss the calm of our Pyrénées, our roads curved up to the place where you answered only the treetops and your conscience, I had longed to be any old man, walking the roads again.

Those twelve kilometers would end up being the first of many mistakes I was starting to make. Later I would think that at least the walk led me toward Moses. Because when I did meet that unassuming boy, though I had serious doubts, yes, a few, I'd soon find myself thinking he was something like the friend I'd waited for my whole life, despite the unlikeliness of his affect. Hours before Moses and I found each other, however, I first had to surrender the station's temporary shelter and just start walking. In my current state, permanence does exist, if solely as a refuge for everyone else.

THREE

I began to pick my way through the ghost town of Bomont, a town practically land-mined with memories. But at least the roads were the same as they'd been in my time, straightforward and lacking pretension, and since the roads had not changed as much as road signs had, since they showed the courtesy of staying exactly the same as they'd been during my time, all while ladies' hairstyles and the rate of penetration of foreign phrases into our French and the general speed of life had turned traitor, though these roads were not my roads, too far from Finier for that, they were at least halfway loyal to the era of Emile Poulquet.

Just recently our government had needed to admit it had been wrong about a man. The man in particular—I'd known him—had overseen a certain bureau which collected our region's card indices. So what, one might say, *card indices*. And indeed, who really bothers about cards and the census unless they happen to strike the lightning rod of popular imagination (bad timing again) and become a celebrated cause? In other words, right now, in some region of France, in the Algerian suburbs for example, in the outer boroughs of Paris, someone is preparing what will get called an ill-conceived census. But what concerns me most is my era, and the fate of the man who'd been responsible for overseeing our card index bureau. A beetle-browed individual, not a bad type, a man who'd said hello to everyone and who'd spoken a few degrees deeper to me, going just beyond the niceties of *how are you* and *how was the train, it always runs slow, doesn't it?* This fellow was friendly enough that whenever official business (now already a half-century old!) had brought me to the Bordeaux prefecture for the delivery and discussion of special cards and papers and files, he'd blathered through halitosis to me of his mushrooms and wine. Five years ago, the officials had gone so far as to have had this unfortunate colleague hunted down, arraigned, dragged to court and arrested, sentenced for life. My old friend had made the mistake of a plea bargain, and hence the officials, wily personages, had been able to elicit a false confession. Yes, all this was by definition fine for the sentencers; damn the man, seal the coffin, go about one's duties with a dim memory of some beetle-like Vichy fellow left to wither in a cell. Let the scapegoat off into the wilderness. If a ghost one day crosses your vision in a mirror, that's fine, serves the fellow right, smack of satisfaction on everyone's lips. Only that this year, new facts had emerged which made it appear that they had sentenced the wrong man! Incredible but true. The beetle man released, apologies left and right, a former employee of the state left to dwindle in the countryside, ending up a clerk in a cheap pension, alliances left over from the war enforced by children and grandchildren. The man trying to taste his wine and mushrooms with a prison-scalded tongue. Let bygones be bygones, sure, even governments make mistakes. But the incident could not die. The dying-out leagues of veterans, the church groups and secret groups, those younger politicians with family pasts stretching back, people from the left and the right and beyond the seas had mobilized an international hoopla. The judges could not have foreseen the size of the protest. Yes, people were used to wrongful convictions in the case of, say, a pedestrian affair, the jealous boyfriend who murders a lover, the trafficker or bigamist, the pornographer. But that they had wrongly sentenced an *official* when surely the very definition of a good bureaucracy is that paper abounds, enough to craft a three-dimensional box around the *right* man, enough to contain identity or at least to make sure the right man gets caught. An unbelievable mistake made by the prosecution! As one might imagine, I followed these stories with great interest, the articles and counter-articles raising the question of France and favoritism, of special-interest groups spearheading witch-hunts, and then all the articles regarding backlash to the witch-hunts.

The sole clarity to this was that we in France could not bury our wartime ghosts. Both victim and oppressor have an awful tendency to rise like wraiths from the rich earth, wafting up from our official Days of Patrimony, our annual day when no one, whatever their facial features or hair texture, has to pay a sou to be admitted to our tourist sites, at which little engraved plaques detail our history, the one we like to pass on: the burnt baby carriage at Oradour-sur-Glane near that livid, vitalistic apple tree. The noble shed where a strategy to unseat the occupiers had been fashioned. The hotel where the liberating general had issued his first radio address. Of course I knew all these sites, or rather, I'd sniffed out what they promised for my own future. The scent of wartime memory is a much better aroma when it rises from our multicolored textbooks, not wholly unpleasant. I'd seen my own name barely mentioned in a few, the name Emile Poulquet in books now mouldering in secondhand stores along the Seine.

I had often thought it would help the moral development of those experts, so mired in the past, if someone could prevent them from pillaging history's chapters, keep them from escaping with lives folded into simple black and white answers, all that ends up being hoisted like some precious valise. When most recently they made my own case pop up again, like a dreadfully repetitive jack-in-the-box, rather than letting them slam me back down into whatever destiny would soothe everyone else's unclear conscience, I thought I should instead be allowed to walk out of that courtroom a free man. One can see how little anyone really wants Emile Poulquet around much longer: Emile as a living man serves no one.

Along these lines, it had been suggested to me—and I thought it a rather brilliant stratagem—that I walk out of that courtroom as *not-*Emile. This maneuver, inspired to its core, had been outlined for me during a few weeks of discussion with one of my Paris lawyer friends, a man now in retirement, as well as with the surgeon whose many efforts on my face have kept me alive and not, paradoxically, cut to bits by all the sharks wanting pieces of me.

At first, as anyone might have, I'd scoffed at the idea that, prior to the trial, I would not be able to accomplish some hackneyed escape-from-prison action. Like any unfree man might, I'd imagined myself vaulting over cinderblocks, chicken wire, barbed wire, all into some gravity-free beyond. I still had my friends, however dwindling, people who remembered me as elegant, patrician, et cetera, friends here and there, old colleagues with younger friends able to craft passports fitting with various aliases. My lawyer's counterposed idea, that I *avoid* being identified, had seemed beyond the pale, so to speak. For them to release me on the basis of *not being recognized* sounded at first like a tactic drawn from the kind of novel I'd once favored.

Who among the chorus of my naysayers could truly, if forced to look closely, *fail* to recognize me?

"But you see," my lawyer friend had said, having questioned me extensively about the nature of the documents I'd signed (or not signed) as prefect so many years ago, documents I'd unwittingly delegated, "given what's happened so recently to your fellow, that wrongly accused Bordeaux friend of yours—"

"Not a friend—"

"The colleague, whomever, now the evidence against you must be absolutely solid." And it wasn't. "Most witnesses have died out," he offered, rather unhelpfully, I thought. "No one will even want to begin the quagmire of DNA testing."

"No?" I said, wishing to believe the new fable.

"A bureaucracy, my friend. Too many papers handled by far too many. So there's that. Not to mention the sheer fact that we've lived long, Emile, we're among the lucky ones."

"This is luck?"

"Your job," my lawyer friend had remonstrated, "is to keep me inspired. Please. Don't make my motivation falter." And he'd given me a long look, his face so much like a horse's, the length so humorously accentuated, I had to stifle a nervous laugh. After all, like all of us, he wanted to believe he was doing good for another, for the greater good of society.

One can see that my survival had become less of a preference, mostly a habit. At times it seemed as trivial as preferring that one's sugar-pot spoon point toward one rather than toward the wall. And then there was no escaping the fact that so many years ago, I had escaped inscribing my delicate signature

Emile Poulquet

on certain incriminatory documents. One might call me successful in having delegated the worst of these papers to others, or one might call me a coward, and not because I had the foresight to imagine that later history would judge me. Rather, and this is my explanation, one which has satisfied me, it has always been my tendency to stay hidden on all fronts. This aspect has made people call me elegant. I have become a fugitive, you might say, because almost from the beginning I approached my existence—because of Arianne, yes, but before that because of the huge hump on my face—as a crab might, slantwise. As if I'd always been practicing to be a convict, a future fugitive, lacking desire to engage too much with the messy stuff of life.

So it was that I employed the counsel of my lawyer friend and decided not to testify on my own behalf. Such avoidance was harder than it might seem, given that I had frequently been praised for my ability to lend grandeur to the most mundane situations, to speak my way out of a foxhole, as it were, though I'd never served in any actual battle, and had just narrowly missed being appointed to a post in Algiers. But most people had failed to assess my elocutionary skills accurately: I was not such a terrific speaker as they made me out to be. Rather, my success in my career, as functionary and fugitive, has relied upon my avoidance of the cardinal sins I'd seen in certain colleagues.

Five main sins as far as I am concerned:

1. Being convinced of one's indispensability
2. Megalomania

3. Quarrelsomeness
4. Hot-headedness
5. Indiscretion

I have succeeded merely by sidestepping these five, although it is true that, in the past, among certain audiences, my favorite defense once lay in outlining the parallels between my case and the man history loved, the allegedly wrongfully convicted jew journalist Dreyfus, which surely must qualify as some form of #2, and perhaps of #5.

So at my own trial I stayed mute and in this manner, strange as it may seem, I avoided self-incrimination. And because of the attention which had been showered on my wrongfully convicted colleague (his five wrong years in prison really did absorb any sin anyone might have imputed to me, just as the proverbial scapegoat had done for the children of Israel), my case had to be treated with, beg pardon, kid gloves. They just could not prove I was the same man as the Emile Poulquet who had committed what everyone kept calling dastardly acts. Back in the early eighties, first act of this charade, some newspaperman had accused me of crimes against humanity, which made a special honor jury investigate my credentials, which then led to the most recent prosecution's strategy of having me tried for the smaller *complicity in arrests and internment.* What about any of this was not outdated? When I looked up the word *dastardly* in the dictionary, I saw no evidence that the word had been used since 1969.

Meanwhile, of roughly the same vintage as my defense lawyer, the prosecution was led by the famous mother-and-daughter team, the two who'd fattened themselves on the lean years of my distress. I felt as compelled by their charisma as everyone else was, these two figures who would've collapsed without their public. To me, their faults were glaringly obvious. The daughter had been born into an age which had assigned sincerity to its interior, where it festered, growing into an authentic violence, returning to the outside world as a scabbed, ironic style of speech. Perhaps no one had ever asked her to imagine what she might have done had *she* been born in 1915, when our bistronnaise peasants had just begun to use all the abandoned tanks littering our landscape as tractors. No one had asked what she might have believed had she been born only some years after the unfortunate case of Dreyfus, whom I and my colleagues had dubbed Tropied, when people had seen how our republic was in danger of having too many states form within itself. States of rich bank-controlling jews or revolutionary society-defying jews. Not to mention the law-defying foreign hebrews who kept to their own laws and languages. Or, far worse, like Tropied, those insidious israelites who were cosmopolitan, intellectual rootless jews lacking loyalty to our France, to any *land*, jews who'd pretend to be French enough that our France could easily lose its borders. Not to mention all the colonies of depraved sexual jews, or the occult groups of jews linked with freemasons and worse. These were known truths when I was coming up, and to say where one learned them is as hard as to say where one learned the letter Q. Can most people remember where they learned the letter Q? I should say not.

To her credit, however, the daughter lawyer did appear far less obedient than I have been. Defiant in a certain lanky upturned-chin way, possessor of great coolth, apart from the moment when she had been forced to stand not far from me in the hidden chamber of the court, when she clearly failed to restrain her inner violence. *Aren't you ashamed?* she whispered to me with a girl's peppermint-lacquered breath, just before she was called to the bench. What did that mean, anyway, *ashamed*? Shame depends wholly on others. Who cared if I toted shame around like some battered private trophy, proof of my inner good, my bewildered soul? Wasn't it more heroic to wander the world lacking an audience, the society of brothers and sisters which shame and its absolutions automatically offer the renegade?

I whispered back: *What I am is ashamed of you.* Of course, at that point she couldn't hear me. In contrast, the mother, by virtue of her generation or her age, in both speech and bearing possessed a greater ambiguity, seeming to know more about the purgatories involved in all choice.

Together, however, these two were a well-lubricated machine, capable of producing a great obfuscatory fog, moving the case along in a flurry of public statements, none of which hurt me. However, what nothing could erase from my own internal record, acting as a scar no operation could remove, what I was now forced to remember from the many weeks in court—all the depositions and presentations of faulty evidence and reliance on secondhand evidence—were not the accounts of my dastardly deeds, with which I was already boringly familiar, the papers having long painted me as an archvillain in the opera of history, but rather the few points at which two people were invoked and called forth, people with whom one could say I had been at least somewhat intimate.

IF I SOUND AT ALL blasé in recounting all this, it is only in order to avoid the omnivorousness of those few moments: they have seized me, refusing to let me go. The first of those called to testify against me was Odile, my former secretary at the prefecture, Odile who had gone sadly brittle in both edge and substance. She'd entered the court as a collapsible, mechanical bird might have, all wound-up, painted and studied.

She was one of a remaining few who could still summon enough knowledge of my quirks—my left-handedness, the port-wine mark on my right wrist left untouched despite all these years of surgical intervention, the fleck of miscalculated color near one iris, the note on which my voice broke into falsetto if I sang an ascending scale—to have claimed me as Emile Poulquet.

And yet she did not. She swore that she was sane, that for what it was worth, her sympathies had always been with the general, not the marshal, all while standing near enough for the scent to impress itself upon me, that certain lilac perfume which had been antique upon her even when she'd been a young lady with all the world before her. The daughter lawyer then asked Odile whether the man standing before her was Emile Poulquet, her former employer.

A hush, yes, the warped hush in such moments is long enough for one's bones to turn into fish-hooks. No, she said, so softly the judge made her repeat it. No, not Mister Poulquet.

The stand-in for my lawyer friend, the young reddish bear too new at the legal game to be discreet, a fellow named Duhamel, immediately raised his clasped hands toward me in some aborted, miniature power salute, though I find all salutes repellent and insulting. But it was true—fragile Odile had advanced the cause of Emile just a bit. And she did not lock eyes with mine. Not for a second.

Because the prosecution had found it hard—who wouldn't?—to contact any of my old familiars, it seemed Odile had offered the kind of moment on which my destiny would turn. I'd be able to walk out *on the basis of the prosecution's witness*. Apparently, and how could any lawyer predict these things, the instant Odile had entered the courtroom, she had changed colors and had decided not to recognize me. I felt protective of Odile, wanting to take her by her frail arm and say *you know, my dear, the cost of perjury? The remainder of your life behind bars. No more lilac perfume.* At the last moment, had she found some inner mettle? *Fraud*, I'd tell her, avuncular, protective, *is always worse for the protectors, better for the protected.* Silent, however, I watched the ripples of Odile's comments. The lawyers eyed one another, pivoted back and forth, finally called for an adjournment.

You see, said the reddish bear, his face glowing with a triumphant sweat, they'll come back, our game'll be done. But he was too young and impatient to declare a verdict when none existed. There's always a hitch, I wanted to tell him, and it came during their lunch recess. The court chatter had it that a statement had come from somewhere far beyond our left bank. At the last minute, a document was to be admitted, a bit of bootlegged evidence, based on a long screed the prosecutor had received, one strong enough to drag me back to the realm of culpability. We'd thought, of course, that all available witnesses had been called. Now one who'd been thought to be unreachable had floated up.

Who'd been thought unreachable. Causing something of an internal nostalgia blitz in me, bits and pieces of memory floating up, old neighborhoods I had walked through, all the cold potato soup I'd ignored, the velvet trim I'd sat upon, smoke-tarred people or calloused hands brushed against, wax seals used, carbon paper smeared, onionskin paper torn, pencil nibs I'd broken by pressing too hard. The cabinets containing notebooks and ink blotters, the telephones resembling octopi, gargling their underwater ringing tone. There was no one left from that world, I could think of no one.

Meanwhile, you would've thought smugness a shared gene, the way that mother-and-daughter lawyer team could not wipe self-righteousness off their faces. Those ladies were announcing they had *in their hands*—they used that barbarous phrase—in their hands someone alive and well. Someone who'd come to Paris from abroad with the express purpose of attending the trial. Their courtroom audience shivered, I thought, with the same self-satisfaction emitted by the mother and daughter, savoring the idea of someone *from abroad*, someone with an *express purpose*. They treated me as their whodunit. If they could have worn anonymous masks, they would've chosen to stone me. Their witness had been persuaded, by internal or external pressure, this part they hazed over, to produce a document that would raise serious questions about the identity of Emile Poulquet, questions that might place Mister Poulquet away behind bars forever.

And yet. This same witness had expressed a preference to avoid being in the courtroom with Emile Poulquet. This *witness from abroad* had chosen (and how fitting this seems, in retrospect, how in character) to look down on the courtroom through a one-way mirror. Now, earlier I'd noted the portico, taking it merely to be one of those odd architectural features left in our older buildings, but no, it turned out that it proffered means to an even more awful end. This *witness from abroad with an express purpose*, listening from the safety of the perch, had overheard me speaking, had identified me positively as Emile Poulquet, and this statement had already been entered into the official record.

I wondered at first if this whole charade was a fabrication of the court. *The witness from abroad.* It had too much of the fairytale to it. I scribbled a note to this effect and forwarded it to the red bear, whose face had splotched into a dismay which I found neither very professionally becoming nor reassuring. I asked him to check with his sources on the actuality of this new deposee. Because, as I wrote in my second note, feeling a haughty calm in this act of notewriting, as much as I could search my memory, there really remained no one who could have succeeded in unseating what had been established by Odile. What I wanted to restore to the lawyer Duhamel was the jolliness of his ugly power salute, the optimism it had contained. WHO IS THIS

CLOWN? I wrote in my third note, SOMEONE REFUSING TO APPEAR IN COURT? I wanted to laugh it off. Duhamel had begun to search through a spindled dossier, one I'd never found quite so organized as it should have been, given that he was officially chief counsel on a case *gripping the national imagination*, as the most liberal of the newspapers had phrased my captivity.

IS IT EMILE POULQUET? the headlines had read. (Foolish headlines, taking the bait we'd laid. Who else could it have been? An imposter Emile?) Yet my alias, my most recent life, one I'd lived mutedly, abstemiously, almost joyfully on the margins in both Paris and Buenos Aires, had been to my benefit. Just as my lawyer friend had foreseen, there were born-and-bred Parisian apartment dwellers and storeowners, citizens whose credentials would go over well in the court, lawful citizens, transparent republicans, believers in liberal ideals with no vested interest in Vichy anything who had proven eager to testify that "my" life as David Modine, my most recent alias, had been one of quiet helpfulness, that "I" had bothered no one, that "I" had been kind to neighborhood pets and small children. David Modine had even been known for being especially kind to Moroccan gas workers and older people left to wither in the city's summers while their children went off on package holidays to our former tropical islands.

We retired then, I and my red bear, the two of us forced to share breathing space in a claustrophobic chamber off the main courtroom. Duhamel was quite unlawyerly, slamming his belongings down on a metal chair but making as if to ignore me, studious in rifling through a new sheaf of papers. As if this act alone could keep at bay any more unexpected witnesses. Yet Duhamel, alleged genius of the countermeasure, the young, undisputed king of spinning evidence so it could be rendered inadmissible, was finding it hard to locate the name of the new deposee.

"Ah, I'm mistaken," said Duhamel, angling his jaw so it cracked. "Not Suzanne Robineau?"

"No," I said, sifting through memory. Hems, lines of wind-whipped trees, morning coffee on the bedside table.

"Ah, sorry, not her. That's the recording clerk. Okay. Vic Gradis?"

"No one I know," I muttered.

"Here we are! You're in luck. The fellow won't appear in court with you, so it doesn't count as the kind of testimony the prosecution needs. Here's the fax from my main clerk. We got it. A special case in 1974. We can block them. We take the appropriate measures, they can't admit new testimony."

My hands were shaking. I didn't care about *appropriate measures*. "But who?" I almost wrung that bear's neck, such was my edginess.

He cracked his jaw again. The bear was reading, failing to do me the courtesy of raising his gaze.

"Not to mention," he almost simpered, "your guy's legally blind. Funny, right?"

"Funny." I considered. "But then I couldn't be identified. I didn't speak. Unless he overheard us in the corridors. Or in this chamber?"

"I believe that may be the case. He overheard you." Duhamel raised a finger. "Just give me a minute."

I was ready to storm out, but what better fate awaited me outside? My whole world had sickled into that tight little chamber. I fortified myself to stay: Emile an idiot in waiting, looking nowhere, nowhere to look but at myself waiting. So that when the red bear finally found the depositioner's name, I felt I'd already salted myself anywhere but there.

Not far enough away. Not far enough that I couldn't hear Duhamel mispronouncing the name. "Funny," said the bear. "You don't happen to know an Israel Horwitz Lisson?"

FOUR

How little I like to remember what followed, two weeks in a cell, almost forgotten by a coarse if not uneducated guard, glued to the one luxury, the television set, forced to watch the mother and daughter mewling out their statements, while the same exterior shot of the court continued in endless replay. Two weeks while the lawyers were left like hounds to yawp over what counted as admissible evidence and what was mere gambit and divide, desperate countermeasures. On the thirteenth day, my old-guard lawyer friend had signaled me through the increasingly flat-toned Duhamel that something marvelous had happened.

"Marvelous," the young bear told me through the plastic viewing panel. For multiple reasons, I wasn't inclined to trust him. Besides, next to me, in a long parallel line, other citizens were shouting out their own banalities. Further, I was sleep-deprived, having been kept awake for much of the previous night by what had been described as a routine cleaning of the upper cell-block though it had sounded more like a lynching. "Really," added the lawyer, flat-toned, flat-footed, this ridiculous advocate of me. "You'll be happy."

"What's happy?" I asked, hoping he wouldn't answer but sorry when he didn't.

IN COURT, wearing my old oversize tweed suit which in the prison guard's closet seemed to have accrued the dirt of entire eras, I sat on the poorly cushioned seats, numb as could be, tired beyond belief, since another cleaning had taken place the previous night, this time with what had sounded like rather more enthusiastic participants.

It was then that I saw her brought in, my protectoress, wearing a cherry-red suit. Flanked, as always, by an entourage. Would she have it any other way? A beautiful young man with curly blond hair was with her, what we used to call a strapping young man. Someone who, may it be said, was aryan in his look, perhaps a bit of slav blood in those thick lips as well, who by his very being seemed to testify not just to the woman's indestructibility but to her lifelong commitment to a certain pragmatic candor of the flesh, the hard physical facts as they presented themselves.

I saw her full on: my breath stopped.

I tried to get the two images to reconcile: the one who had ruled me and the older woman pared from her younger self, Arianne who now seemed a bit desperate about holding on to whatever beauty had been allotted her at birth. Her once-black hair dyed platinum, short in the manner of film idols of our postwar era, her cheeks splotched red as her stiff jacket. She looked at me like a falcon sighting prey, her breed far sharper than gentle Odile's, her lips parted as if to say something, showing the slight gap between the teeth, and then closed again.

Arianne: did she recognize me?

She took the witness stand. With a determined voice, she swore she would not perjure, and then spoke what would change my fortunes. Of course she would be far more eloquent than Odile, her station in life warranting as much.

While she spoke, unreeling what was essentially her curriculum vitae, an unnecessary list, which she however seemed to enjoy recounting, my head spun.

What had compelled her to come forward? Was it that she wanted merely to demonstrate, once again, how much power she retained over me? Or, again and painfully again—did she not recognize me? Perversely, I wanted her to claim me as Emile, to call me her own. I wanted her to know how successfully I had managed my life in the postwar years, which also meant my post-Arianne years.

"Is this Emile Poulquet?" the daughter lawyer finally asked, her voice a screech, the question just as redundant as most branches of the law.

"No," said Arianne.

This was all that was needed. *No.*

Not her curriculum vitae but the all-important, I-refuse moment. She said no. For a second, I loved her all over again, *merely because I knew her.* This was my Arianne, who could not overlook an opportunity for drama. "No," she repeated, just as Odile had, though she did trail off on that second response. It was probably salutary that she stopped when she did.

Afterward, Arianne acted far more like Odile, refusing even to turn her head in my direction. She had said at the beginning of her speech—which had sounded, after all, a bit scripted, but what might one expect from someone who'd always performed her own life?—that she spoke as a woman of principle, concerned with justice, and I will also say that during her speech, so caught up was I that for a second, and I know this sounds a bit loony, but for a brief flash, I almost began to think I was not Emile Poulquet, or at least not the Emile who could have done the dastardly deeds of which he was accused. The weight of the two speeches made on my behalf, and one can call it a moral weight, sat upon me. Doughty Odile and dramatic Arianne: both had stood by me in my hour of need, both had chosen to fail to recognize me.

In the afternoon session, all the jurors appeared shapeless and lethargic from the stretching out of the case, the second longest in France's history. Perhaps they were tired from trivialities, from too much proximity to one another's faces, too much time spent hearing the judge's monotone or smelling the waft of the refectory's overcooked cabbage and burnt meat sneaking under the heavy doors. Or perhaps their fatigue came from the generally vitiating air of ethical debate, from too great an intimacy with the question of *Emile Poulquet vs. the Jews*, which was my name for the trial, though officialdom had dubbed it with a different euphemism. Perhaps the prosecution had assessed the jurors' fatigue, because after lunch, in a strange turn, its lawyers doubled back and declared the testimony of blind Israel Horwitz Lisson to be inadmissible. They recused Izzy's words, withdrew their final charge. Was this a result of Arianne having interceded during the lunch recess? Not even the red bear fully understood why the prosecution had made these preliminary moves toward withdrawing its entire case. Had the accuser from abroad asked (and been allowed to ask) that his words not be used? Or had Arianne yanked my destiny again? Did she have some special pull with the mother-and-daughter lawyers—or with the judge? All of these possibilities were equally likely, which is to say, not at all probable. However fortunate, to my mind the whole thing offered more of a strange turn than a flare of hope. As one can imagine, I slept that night as a fitful baby might, awakening to the slightest creak outside my cell, unsure what morning would bring.

I DID NOT WISH to entertain overmuch any hope that I would be released on the basis of Arianne's protection. Outside the courtroom, the protest grew in size and decibel, all the children of survivors and deportees gathering every day outside the courtroom sporting their arcana of deprivation, their yellow six-pointed stars in ostentatious position on their lapels.

Waking in my cramped holding cell, I was not sure after all that my lawyer friend's strategy had been correct. I consulted my little silver pendulum on its pocket chain that morning over the prison's breakfast offering, a triumvirate of herring, a slice of Rome apple, and a dried crust of bread. The pendulum was a bit sticky that morning as well, cramped and swinging in a wobbly arc, finally settling into the direction of YES only over the herring, so though I was hungry, I was forced to ignore the other items, a decision which may have made me a bit more light-headed than usual, which may have also been why, later in court, when I heard the almost unbelievable sentence pronounced, I was unable to disguise my relief.

They said I was free.

Inability to authenticate identification of the defendant.

In an era when it seems your thumbprint alone identifies your genetic code? But it was so, and it would serve nobody were I to second-guess the court. When no one was looking, I consulted the pendulum again. IS THIS A GOOD TURN? I asked. My friend hovered uncertainly for a moment and then swung again in the direction of YES. I had to take this as reassurance, though I would have asked the pendulum more had my reverie not been broken by the red bear. Clearly he wished to be rid of me. Though surely he had seen me withdraw the pendulum at crucial moments, now he ignored it, taking my right hand in his. His eyes half-closed, I could see how drained he was, especially after all the charges which the press had levied against him. Some reporter had gone digging and had found, actually, that the bear was related to the great Duhamel, defender of republican justice and all that et cetera. Hence his defense of me—David Modine, the name I'd gone by in Paris—had defamed the name of his great liberal family. I understood how this could deplete a man, siphon off his legacy.

"You've weathered this well," he offered, a parting and unnecessary generosity, also a sally.

"You too." I would not be outdone in courtesy.

"Poulquet the cat," the red bear said to me, forgetting to use my alias in public.

"Who's Poulquet?" I asked.

"Our friend told me at the very beginning that you'd get through. He said you had nine lives."

"Despite my detractors."

"Granted another life. Amazing."

"I try never to misplace optimism," I demurred.

"We'll be in touch." He barely pumped my hand before already beginning to melt away.

"Through our friend."

"Yes," said Duhamel, paces away, though he seemed uncertain about sharing anything further with me. "I'm sure he'll want to be in touch with you soon."

After all these turns and twists, which had required intestinal fortitude on my part, I was released on the basis of insufficient evidence. And you might think that as I left the courtroom in my fuzzy suit, some glee pumped my heart—and I say glee despite the hisses of the group which forever seeks reparations, its members with their resplendently virtuous lapel stars, the group flanking me down the marble corridor, its scent of lunchtime cabbage notwithstanding, its columns immaculate, its walls blank of the frames which had once held pictures of the grandfatherly marshal whose goat eyes had twinkled at so many of us. The group followed me, hissing *shame on Poulquet!* and the like. There might have been glee in my heart, you might have thought, from the way I neatly smiled at those yellow-starred sons and daughters of deportees, from the manner in which I sidestepped their anger as politely as if they had stepped onto the wrong bus and needed redirecting.

I made my way out to where the Paris boulevards had never looked more crisp, the sky never more heavy and open, the city's color that I loved, not rose at all but a fulminating gray. Without considering, I turned left to go to the Marais, that infested neighborhood right across the Seine from the court, which used to be called something that sounded to me like Plaisir but was perhaps Pletzl. It may seem natural that I found the Marais, a customary warren of jews, never more charming. In the Marais, where I thought I might not be followed (if I operated out of the counterintuitive logic which has kept me hidden all these years, a sheep among wolves, you might say), I sat out the shocked particles of a summer thunderstorm by lingering over acrid coffee in a little bistro owned by someone I thought must have been, at the very least, an Alsatian jew, who might therefore have been fond of the fact that Edith Piaf's lover was a jew, and thus kept playing the same record over and over as if to supply any happenstance tourists or himself with a spot of gaudy energy. One might have thought from my exterior guise—and a guise it had remained—that at least I was not downtrodden.

Yet though I'd been released, I had the instinct that the endless boomerang of law—not to mention those yellow-starred reparations people, and that dreadful mother-and-daughter team—would find another way to get me back, within less than a week if they were lucky. A hearing would be called. The deposition of a blind man would be admitted after all. The testimony of my protectoress would be disallowed. Too much momentum had been amassed. Some wily someone would turn up some new worms.

Operating solely on this instinct, in the Marais café, fairly certain of the future, I made the decision to skip any hearing, to give up all connection to my old-guard lawyer, my youngish red-bear lawyer. I wouldn't use any of my false passports but would instead plead a last favor from my retired surgeon, submit to his knife again, aiming for a final disguise. Then I would flee Paris. Fatigue weighed upon me, but I saw I would have to pick up, start a snappy new life somewhere.

Yes, a better man than I might not have sworn softly to himself just then. How to make it easier? In that cozy café, it came to me. Having tried for civilized strategies for so long, now I was to obey the sheerly animal. Return home, home to Finier.

It was easy to rationalize: Finier was where perhaps I could find a way to retrieve a bit of money, a small sum of gold ingots once hidden for me behind a pissoir near our old stablehand's quarters, more than a quarter-century ago. My own coffers were almost depleted. Perhaps I might even find some domicile there, on our old land, lost in those woods which had afforded me the bit of boyhood pleasure I could claim as my own. There I could be an old man like any older man. *Deliquesce*—the word suited me—back into the earth from which I had sprung. Pick up, give up the dual identity I'd maintained recently, David Modine, a Parisian pensioner often vacationing in Buenos Aires. This would be hard, yes, but why stay in Paris awaiting the wolves?

Monsieur Deliquescent.

I lacked the stamina to sit out another court ordeal, no matter how fortunate its potential end. What else could be done? I tried to console myself with a thought of the pleasures of Finier that might soon be mine. Its air, the cleanest in Europe; its rivers, the most sparkling to be found on perhaps any continent.

Afternoon approached evening and the proprietor turned off Piaf. He started to grumble in a certain wedged-gorge manner as he washed his cups, indicating his wish that the old bushel would leave the premises, wanting the old man dawdling over a single cup to realize life had a rhythm which excluded him. I saw how impossible it would be to go to Finier without seeking out Arianne. I didn't want to seek her out. No, far from it. No one in his right mind wishes to seek out his tormentor.

But I had to admit that as much as she'd tyrannized my life, she remained an itch. Some kind of reckoning was necessary. If I were to be in Finier, it would be incumbent upon me to make her come to grips with her own relation to the truth. First, I had not been so vile during the war, if one were to compare my actions to those of her resistance-hero husband. Also, as she might have guessed, I was curious, compelled to find out why she had jumped up to protect me. Perhaps her action had been, in essence, a veiled love letter.

That she had jumped up when for years she had been part of *the cabal hunting for me*; that she had jumped up when she'd long ago made her name as a *forthright woman rooting out wartime injustices.* Amazing. For years, she had been almost as big a hunter as she'd been an altruist, and almost as big an altruist as she'd been a publicist regarding such altruism. For years she had given shelter to the homeless and the downtrodden spawn of many nations, furbishing her reputation so that Finier had become synonymous in the nation's mind— whenever our little village did appear in the national papers—as this: a place for the polyglot, the dispossessed, those suffering injustices. Arianne had started her Society for the Restitution of Memory, her Foundation for the Homeless in Finier. Her Creative Living experiment for those lacking a full complement of wits. She was a powerful figure in her little kingdom; I'd kept tabs on her, after all, and any village bumpkin could have seen how well she had ensured her notation in Finier and history, all while grabbing up rights to various agencies and securing her goodwill among contemporary politicians in our prefecture, the end result being that many people surely owed her favors. From the bounty of her reputation, banking upon her lifetime pursuits, she had come forward to misidentify me.

But how could I know she hadn't jumped forward merely to slight me?

I decided I would go to Finier for my own peace of mind. I would seek her out, reckon with her, and as a last challenge (I would not call it an insult), I'd hand over my will, the last testament of Emile Poulquet.

Odile, yes, it had been a tinny buzz in the heart, where a pacemaker keeps me regulated, to have seen her. Odile and her lilac perfume, Odile now funneled down into the spinster her young self had predicted. And seeing Arianne—and to have stood nearby, in the same room—had, again as the modern parlance would put it, just about done me in. But the clincher, of course, I found it hard to admit, right as the café owner turned me out onto that purpled Marais street, was the name appearing out of nowhere. Someone I'd forgotten about. Israel Horwitz Lisson. Izzy.

Forget that he was now said to be blind, I had long ago called him dead.

FIVE

The current-day town of Bomont remains faithful to its past. You find essentially the same houses as were around in my era (if somewhat boarded up), the same footbridges (a bit crumbling), and the same faded Coca-Cola sign. Bomont has always been a sad tongue stretching toward the mountains and has always attracted brusque farmers with a penchant for inbreeding. Bomont has also always been jealous of its cosmopolitan neighbor, Finier gifted with the prefecture, Finier the seat of the region, Finier attracting money from the entire region of La Bistronne, enough to give handsome wages to its bureaucrats, enough so that they could butter their croissants on *four* sides; that is, if they chose to spend their salary in such a reckless manner.

Though I'm no prophet, I predict that Bomont will always play second fiddle to Finier. Bomont the stalwart, Bomont the almost picturesque, starting off most of what I later came to regret. There was that night more than a half-century ago, when the houses had given zero clue that one day they'd be boarded up, when I'd been invited to a special dinner in Bomont. It was Arianne who'd invited me, in an official manner, just as if she and I hadn't recently spent so many private hours during and after our vegetable marketing. Her resolute little face had been dolled up (those clumsy red splotches, those glittering sapphire eyes) as if to silence me. All the hours we'd so recently spent shopping together for her hotel or sitting alone by the river had postulated a denial of her husband. We had fingered polished riverstones, something moving between us, puckering my skin. All our time together had, I thought, added up to a sum of possibilities and shared private wishes.

Once her Paul returned from his important, valorous job, however, we didn't see each other for months. When we met in Bomont, the three of us, she'd laughed a little as we'd met by the main footbridge in the town. That laugh terrified me in its way, something transparently hostile to it, as if she were half-swallowing a toad (how others failed to remark this aspect of her still baffles me). She could see, I'm sure, how surprised I was that she'd brought along Paul, whom I hadn't seen for enough years that I had almost succeeded in doubting his existence, believing him her imaginary friend, a shape in the clouds. Beyond my annoyance at her laugh (how easily she could get to me), I could not help noticing how Paul, our local hero, had bloomed. At first glance, you could see he'd taken well to manhood, having become someone who raises the stakes for other men, younger or older. Despite myself, he made my spine lengthen, my chin lift.

At that point, she and Paul had been married some eight years, their coupling more like two turnstiles in parallel, as he often traveled, working in Algiers and up north: my guess was that he perhaps worked alongside the communists. Though it was I who had so recently kept Arianne from falling into some dusky disappointment, since he'd returned from his most recent business there had grown between them a whole wealth of gesture and intimacy, every breed of exclusion.

The meal itself, held in the home of a chic proprietor, was memorable as much for its company as for its discretion and ambience, or one could say its dodging and veering. Soon after the fig lamb but long before the cheese tart, Arianne decided to mention to me a certain possibility. Why she chose to do this in front of Paul, in such an official context, I was not sure. She was lobbying for me.

At that time, I was only months into the job as sub-sub-prefect. My education in Paris had been entirely theoretical, leaving me unqualified to deal with all the queries and priorities of a small administration, not to mention the pressures put upon us. Though Paris had not been invaded, already we had a flood of refugees with tattered valises and suspect politics streaming into the Bistronne. Our prefecture saw fit to send many of these packing into neighboring regions where superior holding camps with better facilities had been set up. Only later did people start to call them camps de concentration. At the time, we thought we displayed great humanity, given the security and health risk such foreigners posed. Still on my table was the execution and enforcement of Paris' fresh restrictions over our foreigners' cultural associations.

As a student, I had written a thesis on a topic my mentors considered important—*L'Ideé de Francisation*, regarding the citizenship process for immigrants who wished to take on becoming French—and whatever I'd written had evidently knocked upon all the chambers of their hearts. Because of this, I'd graduated with honors, and because of these honors, after my exams, my main mentor had been the one to arrange for me not a posting in Algiers but what was supposed to have been a two-year, clean-shot and superior posting in the regional prefecture of Finier. After that, a posting in Paris had practically been guaranteed, if I didn't have to pass through the midway station of Bordeaux first.

Above me in the small prefecture of Finier was Manterre, an insufferable type very much like a whippet, and above Manterre was the prefect himself, Sirouve, a genial man with lopsided, indulgent eyes. What Arianne indicated that night in the restaurant was that Paul's family had a certain pull with Manterre, and had heard that Sirouve soon planned to leave the job. Having tired of the mess being deposited on our doorstep, the prefect wished to devote himself to a deer park he'd created outside Finier, where he might bloody the fauna at leisure. What Arianne suggested was that the sub-prefect,

Manterre, might be persuaded to leave, or would even stay in his position, if the right candidate could be found.

"*Right* candidate?" I had asked, naïvely.

"You see the mess we're in," she said, and only later did I figure out the wrong assumption she had made. She thought, for one thing, that we had been speaking in political code during our months of marketing, assuming therefore that we shared opinions, dwelt on the same side of things. Later I realized the extent to which she'd misunderstood my habit of exaggerating my importance at the prefecture: she had taken it as a moral stance, unable to believe that someone in her thrall would not share her ideas. When I reflected on this, years later, I remembered once, after marketing, having described the sorry state of our internment camp. At the outset of our difficulties, as I've mentioned, the Bistronne truly lacked any sort of internment camp. What we did have was a single makeshift facility, poorly equipped, lacking water or the most basic facilities. In the years before our problems, this bruised and splintering lean-to had been used to house, briefly, men from Senegal or Morocco. When our problems began, we used it as a merely temporary waystation for international refugees before we were required to send them off to other regions.

I remembered much later how I'd told Arianne it was my sworn duty to release certain refugees from this lean-to: those said to be politically innocuous or who had children born in France. At this, her eyes had taken on a night-cat aspect, glowing as if we shared a secret. Far too late I understood that she must have believed I took some initiative, risking something rather than merely following orders. It must have been in light of this crucial misunderstanding that she'd asked me to meet in Bomont.

"We're saying you could leapfrog over Manterre," said Arianne that night over dinner. "We think you should become prefect." Nor did I understand immediately that she'd been cooking up this scheme in the back of her mind all those months marketing. Hours spent by the river's stunted plane trees, she'd considered this possibility, offering me the false bait of her affections. On a few occasions we had ventured into the forest and its cold gray mist, and at such moments, her talk had not been political. No, those months she'd plied me with the confessions of a married woman. "This promotion will help you," she said in Bomont, a trace of that old aggression in her voice, a flake of tart suspended off her lower lip, hanging on a second before dropping off.

She now meant to bribe Manterre, offering him some genial rural allowance, the chance for him to annex some of the Fauret land for his horses, and therefore the opportunity for him to bequeath his homely son and daughter something of real value. Manterre would, of course, like any good bistronnaise man, prefer land to position. In her schema, he would end up taking orders from me. By quirk of her will, by dint of her force, *merely because she could*, Arianne had chosen to have the sub-prefect become my underling, reversing the current state in which I had to answer to him. "That will save you many headaches, no?" This was her only reference to the conversations she and I had entertained, alone by the river. She leaned toward me then, so close her hair could have caught fire from the painted candles.

"Be careful," I said, and they both misunderstood.

"We wouldn't say this if we didn't think you possessed the necessary qualities," Paul added, as if he had some say. He'd always appeared to lack a most basic sense of humor or nuance, and it was this which Arianne must have found attractive. Every cell of Paul screamed strength and solidity, mud formed into blocks, a literal mind bent on completion. Whereas whatever I had to say was too unfinished to emerge into the light. I looked at Arianne, her cold eyes which could flicker with such promise, as they did then. I thought about it, not long enough.

"I'll do it," I said, too ready, again her pawn. Pinioned. There was no way to meet her behind the curtain; Paul was with us. When I reflected on the dinner a few days later, I saw she had sized me up correctly. As I'd once been a victim to her play, for sport and frolic, she'd decided to have this dinner, to have me hoisted on my own petard, victim of my own ambition, an ambition warmed and coddled in the university, excited by the admiration others had shown for my smooth talk. Arianne herself had once told me I was a master tactician, sure to rise (when my main skill had been, as I said, that I knew not to get in the way of my superiors' wrath). But already I was digesting the compliment of her confidence, telling myself that during all our riverside talks she had admired my gift of gab, the ridiculous palaver which I'd learned from Izzy but which my superiors took to be my birthright.

OF COURSE, becoming prefect after only a year was a terrible mistake. If I had been overwhelmed as sub-sub-prefect, I now wandered in a labyrinth. We worked with names and lists, natives from fifty-nine nations to sort out, the masses who would not stop landing within our Bistronne. We had before us the new task of ridding our military of both these foreigners and israelites, of sending these newly demobilized men to other regions' internment camps or, much more difficult, requiring many more carbon copies, to Algeria. Not to mention that during this, the period when we'd thought this would be someone else's short war, our own hexagon's borders secure, our army gave in up north. The armistice provisions that came down to us made us realize the extent that even our new commanding town, Vichy, saw our region as a remote backwater, a younger sibling. Who was considering us when they asked, for example, that the Bistronne give up a portion of its onion and wheat crop for German soldiers? Everyone's morale was sapped. Odile, my secretary at the prefecture, followed me into the maze of my new duties, and I quickly put her in charge of finding the five most important priorities in one day. It was Odile who began to determine with whom I should meet, Odile who culled from the infinite women and men milling in our corridors, all the immigrants with their ravenous faces yearning for francisation, for citizenship. They waited for us, for Odile and me, and then waited some more, often displaying the serenity of centuries. It is true there were also those who would occasionally exhibit fidgetiness, the impotent irritation of slaves, grumbling a few sidewords to me as I closed up my office, jacket neatly buttoned and ready for my lunch hour. But mostly those immigrants, in their various costumes, summoned up stamina. For one thing, many bore children in pulpy clusters, children who looked at me with crossed eyes, hanging off the adults' shoulders in unseemly, monkeylike manner, while old kerchiefed grandmothers watched from the chairs, speaking a clotted French if able to speak our tongue at all. All these nomads appeared to breed generations more quickly than we French could. Perhaps it was this profligate, unperishable tendency which most helped their inner vigor when facing the state. For it seemed that many could have waited forever for signatures, whether twitching or impassive, displaying despair or hope or mothlike stasis, leaning against the cool stone walls of our sacred building, which had once housed Catholic prelates but which now housed us, new bishops of the bureaucracy. When the prefecture had been born, a few centuries ago, holes had been drilled into the uppermost naves of the neighboring church so that Catholic bureaucrats who dared attend noontime Mass next door could be spied upon, and it was into these holes that the children of immigrants now stuck their overactive little thumbs or pressed their noses.

Some applicants, I'd understood from Bordeaux and Vichy, were to be considered priorities; others would have to keep fighting upward, trying to stay afloat despite the quicksand of our procedures, our documents in triplicate. "War of attrition," Sirouve had commanded me. To make sure I was paying attention, he'd sliced the air with a marionette-like hand, a jerky cut. "War of attrition, Poulquet! These people multiply!"

In a box under her desk, Odile held the extraneous bounty we received from those who waited: papers in foreign tongues, photographs of families who wished to be reunited dressed in garb meant to suggest dignity, expired visas, valiant pleas and murky confessions. Not to mention all the strangely knowing gifts (those far surpassing the usual veils, carved sandalwood boxes, and incense resembling blackened turds), gifts which recognized *us*, such as a good bistronnaise wine or a runny cheese. In that era, Odile had begun to favor her particular perfume, and as she leaned over me, asking me to please sign this document and overlook another, I was forced to inhale lilac, so that to this day I have not been able to pass even the most unhealthy purple trellis without breathing in the air of obligation, of duty under fire.

Odile happened to be a young lady with the misfortune of having arrived at the utmost brink of her competence early in life and so had found there was nowhere else to go. Thus her competence bristled with frustration, the blandness of desire deferred. Waiting perhaps was what had turned the key and had entered her into wholly uninvited, electric realms of imagination. In those days, however, I didn't give her existential quandary that much thought. Mainly what penetrated my bachelor's mind was how sadly capable she was, hipbones broad for a girl whose overall impression was of being slight, those bones a false promise and probably better suited on another, promising serviceability as a childbearer and wife, a burnisher of heirlooms. In a second, Odile could arrange citizenship for those found worthy, in a wink could write up a visa for those whose fate we couldn't decide. Yet in the great method of her pearl-drop earrings and unwrinkled snub nose, her disappointed chin, her oft-patted bowl of hair, she was untouchable and ageless. She could have been a crone or, as she was, diffidently unmarried in her late twenties. I should not disparage her—at the time, I found Odile indispensable regarding the smallest detail.

For example, when I needed her to arrange with the janitor Cagnon the uprooting of geraniums and the laying-in of golden nasturtiums outside my office window, she proved excellent. She alone of all of us knew how to speak to the surly-lipped Cagnon, an intractable janitor if I'd ever met one. Odile could get him to do exactly what no one else could.

In all things, therefore, Odile was my mouthpiece, my right hand. I must say here that I was also not blind to the fact that she had fallen in love with me. It was late at night when she would sometimes lose grip of her behavior. I would feel this in the leading way she'd ask me to inspect such and such a folder, her tones honeyed. Even if someone else had not already colonized my peculiar heart, Odile was milquetoast to me, despite all her efforts. She carried herself like someone who would not be shocked by the air of cities, but for all that she had a good village head on her shoulders. On certain days she wore a flowered frock, and I would note how hungry and alert she seemed, enough to have scrambled me into a marriage proposal. It did not take a genius to know that Odile could have been my proper mate.

Yet all the time I was prefect, I was trapped into contemplating

Arianne, who, once Paul had returned, behaved with a crazed circumspection toward me. Was it my promotion or Paul's return (or was it after all the beginning of our region's end as the pure Bistronne) that made the two of us unable to recapture intimacy? In intervening years, I have often thought how much easier life might have been had I ignored Arianne altogether, conceded defeat early on to Odile. Who knows? I might not have been compelled to act as I did.

Perhaps in Odile's way, she'd intuited my destiny and tried to spare me much of what would come. Or perhaps, like me, she was just another lonely soul, a bird lost in the rolling countryside, watching others. So easily union with her could have spared me my current lot: an old man escaped from a sentence, a man skipping out from the courts, but yes, admittedly, returned to being a *bushel*, walking from Bomont to Finier in the last year of our century.

SIX

Somewhere before Bomont gives up hope altogether, the roads screw themselves into the approach toward Finier. Thirsty and tired, almost ready to call an end to my journey, I saw a scarecrow which jarred me, making me remember a certain comment Odile had once made about Izzy, during the days when he was still nominally my friend. The scarecrow was wearing a very wrong shirt, similar to the blue-and-white striped croupier's shirt Izzy had worn when he'd returned like a hero to Finier, after he'd decided to give up his apprenticeship and return to his law studies. Natty and serious, evidently pleased with his renewed direction, Izzy had come to visit me at the prefecture to get my signature on some petition or another.

Your Izzy's a generous man, my secretary had said afterward, *maybe the most generous man I've ever met.* As I think she'd intended, Odile's remark had smoldered upon me, the remark of a spurned girl. She had persisted: *don't you find Izzy's generosity special?*

"If being a martyr makes one special," I'd said, closing the topic. All these years I had chosen to forget this conversation, but now it came back as clearly as if it had happened the day before. What had already made Izzy a martyr? I tried to recall but couldn't evoke the exact circumstances.

I did remember that Izzy had meant to be in public service, but his lofty ideals hadn't prevented him, not long after his heroic return, from giving up his studies and keeping his head low, getting ensnared in a job which entailed mainly the passing and burying of papers. "Not so different from my job, eh?" I used to like to rib him, when we were still on speaking terms. We had shared so much, most of boyhood in Finier and then our university time at the École Polytechnique, even if it was also true that during our Paris years Izzy had elected to live in a different universe than mine, one where his comrades were overfond of bandying about ideas of justice. Early on, he'd reconstituted himself into noble stuff, wearing a beret like a newfound aphrodisiac. His primary tactic had been to buttonhole any young lady who would listen to him ponder the lessons of history and the truth of the dialectic. At the outset of our student years, his social stamina for such discussions had been infinite, staggering, wine-fueled, overbearing, though all this would soon harden into a charismatic, mysterious shell. Back then, I'd had the correct hunch that once he was done with school, he might wish to return to Finier, perhaps to be near Arianne, perhaps with a fantasy of nattering communist ideas into her translucent ear, but unlike me, he never breathed a hint of the power she might have held over him.

In that brief spell between Izzy's time as a student and his becoming someone remarked upon by my secretary for his *generosity*, while he and I still had the habit of acknowledging each other's existence, I do remember how awful I'd found one of his characteristics, the way his face would take on an aggrieved look if I dared mention some of our school pranks, starting with our years in Paris and moving backwards. He especially did not want to be reminded of our seventeenth summer when we'd worked as waiters in the Hotel Fauret, with Arianne our manager. Though this did not occur to me, he may have been considering the threat of being put on the wrong list. Somewhat blind to this apprehension, I found him too serious, far too married to the Izzy whom he wanted to become, *an indispensable, inconspicuous clerk*, it seemed, a man busily divorcing himself from his ludicrous and swaggering prior self.

Heading toward Finier but still in Bomont, thinking of Izzy, I was half of a mind to enter the field and steal the shirt, one which from a distance did after all resemble Izzy's croupier shirt—or was this an illusion made up of the shimmering field, the dew still clinging to the tips of the recently harvested crop, all lit from behind with the virginal freshness of our countryside?

It was at this crossroads, gazing at the shirt, that I first heard the rattle and creak of a bicycle, and the syncopated wheeze of an older man uneven upon it.

In the basket-front of the man's bicycle were two baguettes, crisscrossed, fresh from whatever bakery had managed to survive in Bomont. On his head the man wore the houndstooth cap typical of men from our region, the bistronnaise, tipped back with a certain defiance, and had the stern inward stare of our Bistronne. Still a hundred paces from him, my awareness slow as a wool-gatherer's, I also noted a car approaching from the other direction. Already its way of driving down these roads was wrong, already a foreign accent tainted the driving.

We French know there are roads to drive quickly upon and roads to be careful upon. On country roads, one must be prepared for moony lovers, risk taking children, farm animals desiring better pastures across the road. And instead of taking this into account, this car drove incorrectly on a Saturday morning, a time when contingency generally has a happier hand. And this may seem a minute point, but for those of us with memory enough to remember the old clean Citroëns, the car was an abomination, its lines almost buxom. I was caught in these thoughts—it was not inaction but rather a whirl of impression—so that though I was walking toward the car and could see, on my left, the old man approaching the main road, cycling, preparing to turn left, I could do no more than flinch.

He actually flew in the air. His mouth in that *O* I knew I had seen before, but where? His bike standing a phantom second before it wavered, suspended a half-moment like a schoolboy's joke before it crashed into the narrow roadside ditch.

He still flew, arms outstretched, taking in the horizon, and then tumbled.

Down.

Rather than do what my condition requires of me, which is to bound away like a deer back into the forest, hide from scrutiny, I suppose I must have run to the fellow. Perhaps I felt for his pulse, I cannot say for sure. Some scrappy instinct had intruded. What I remember is how this country man's face softened so immediately from its hammerlock, how an opalescent skein of saliva stretched between his lips before popping like some perfect bubble. I'd heard somewhere that at death the body immediately weighs two hundred grams less, lacking the weight of the soul, but all I could see in the victim was how in death he looked just as alive as any ornery older man quick at weighing vegetables in our markets.

I GLANCED UP to see that after a long, not unimportant moment of hesitation, the culprit had decided to exit his car. I will say he looked caught between the panic which makes someone escape and the guilt which makes someone stay.

"Shit," he said, in the same broad cowboy English I'd heard on so many rainy afternoons spent as a bushel among other bushels in Parisian cinema halls. "Shit shit shit." Yet he did not then run toward me or the victim. This was a function of his in-betweenness. On his feet he wore shoes which looked like a high-rise mix of melted tropical fruit, mini-mattresses, plastics. With these shoes, he kicked a wheel on his Citroën (rented, I saw from the license plates). "God," he was saying then. "Goddamn shit."

"Hello," I said, not rising.

His spongy loud shoes already a mark, he did run then, toward the crime. *Toward.* One might say he wasn't such a terrible person: he ran toward the crime. However caught between guilt and panic he may have been, he came to stand by me, where I believe my hand found itself gripping the dead man's wrist. Again there arose an opportunity for me to run. Instead I was noting the creases in the victim's hands, suggesting a farmer for whom even udder balm could not soothe years of hard work. I had the ridiculous urge to share with the culprit this observation about farmers' hands. The culprit, however, was so clearly distraught, hissing between his teeth, speaking in that cowboy American English, pulling the collar of his own shirt which had the greenish pattern, earnest or ironic, of a Scottish tartan.

He knelt by me, ran his hands through his hair.

One might think many ladies had tousled that hair, had stared into those eyes. Green eyes on a dark-haired man, a cool glade in the forest. He had probably been the kind to, as they say, believe his own reviews. One could almost see the phantom shape of all the ladies who'd ever come to that glade, who'd entwined themselves to share his bliss, ladies like wood nymphs locked around his thighs, wraiths carving out his waist and arms, loving the uneven teeth showing in his nervous smile. I cannot explain how I knew all this but I did. It would turn out later that I was far from wrong.

At that moment I also knew how easily I could tell the culprit that down the road he could find an inspector, a man named Louzange, a man drinking morning coffee while discussing bikers in the train station's café. The culprit could head there and explain to the inspector some of what had happened. Perhaps the inspector might be moved to exculpate the visitor. To come tend to the victim, to bring victim to family, to follow through and seal the case with waxy satisfaction, stamping the state's seductive, potent insignia upon the dead farmer's life.

Instead, I found myself acting as inspector in residence. I automatically rifled through the victim's coat's chest-pocket, pulling a folded receipt out, an invoice for chimney-sweeping performed on such and such a date, and then, with a certain tenderness, folded and replaced the paper.

AS IT HAPPENED, it would take at least a week for the papers to report on the victim, and how differently I'd be living my life in a week. When I finally saw his obituary, the farmer's life would strike me as so quaint that it had become what other people might call *avant-garde*.

For sixty-four of his sixty-nine years, Bruno Somport had been bicycling the same path between his home and the church, the bakery a convenient stop midway. Somport was a man who'd favored steak tartare on his birthdays, which until recently he'd enjoyed with his wife and his childless daughter. He was, as I'd guessed, a small-time farmer, probably someone who had in my day sold me baby mâche leaves in the Finier market, where he sometimes moonlighted, someone who'd undoubtedly cultivated discerning customers for his escarole and fennel, his beets and onions. Somport was survived by a sister, a lawyer in Finier—was it my destiny to be surrounded by lawyers?— a sister with whom he'd sustained little contact these last years. His wife and his only daughter had died a few years apart (some cancer in the female organs). The only time that Somport had ever raised any kind of public ruckus had been the year he'd protested the church's replacement of the organist with a music student from Paris, a young man with a tendency to improvise during the bridges. Since then, however, Somport had slowly gone deaf, as I'd half-suspected.

OF COURSE we did not know any of this then, the American and I, in the moments after the accident. The only thing I ever know with any certainty is that one always gets thrown some role to play, and whether one gets to be judge, actor, witness, victim, or fugitive, no role is fully rewarding. In life, yes, it has come more easily to me to play fugitive. I could see how easy it would be for me to leave—victim could remain victim, fugitive could stay fugitive. But I noted a certain likability to the American, however much the fellow was in shock, unable to stop shuddering.

We began to converse. This was my fault. I stayed because unfurling in my head was a parallel scene. I saw the American brought before court, in a time when anti-American sentiment has never been higher, a time when McDonald's restaurants are being blown up. The American's clumsy French would bring him no respect with judges, juries, or cellmates. He'd have a worse time in his holding cell than I'd had in mine, he'd be incapable of the kind of word-games which can soften our hearts, he'd probably have awful routine cleanings performed *on* him. He'd had no intention, he was a blundering goose.

The commandment came to mind, *thou shalt not murder.* The American had hardly murdered, since the sin of murder, as I've had to contemplate far too many times, requires intention.

He seemed reduced to speaking in single-word sentences, and from these I surmised he was a filmmaker, officially invited to come document the reunion of refugees organized by Arianne Fah-ray just outside of Finier, part of her Society for the Restitution of Memory—

"Fauret?" I asked. The name offered its familiar and pleasurable shame.

"That's right," he said in a dullard's tone. "Foh-ray."

He did let me know that he'd lived not far from here, only for a year during secondary school, that his father had been a refugee, and that he hoped to learn more about him. He brightened at my interest. "Refugee too?" he asked in his cowboy French.

I hated having to answer on the side I did. "No," I said, "sorry," the word so unpracticed on my tongue as it came out. "Sorry," I said again. I had the idea of walking down the road with the fellow, arm chummy around his shoulder, like a distant French uncle come long distances solely to comfort him. It was somewhere in this vision that the command came. "Just go," I said. "Head out. Go document your refugees."

"What?" And the tips of his fingers outlined something which might as well have been the fleeing ghost of the fallen farmer.

"You'll be better off. It won't serve anyone if you turn him in." I was at a loss to explain this concept. "If you turn yourself in, I mean. A man like this was due for a heart attack. A return of childhood measles. Something like that. Why should you be considered any worse than *that* sort of accident?"

He stared at me long enough that I thought he might not have understood. I had to look away, take in the farmer and his baguettes crossed in the front basket, all of which had taken on a certain glow. I was aware that I risked the hallucination I'd had before when staring at someone dead. You think the head will turn, the chest will rise and fall with restored breath, the eyes will open and wink. I'd first had this hallucination at the deathbed of my beloved stablehand Charlot, whom as a child I'd loved down to his cracked fingernails. So I forced myself to look directly into the American's eyes.

"You might see me in Finier," I said, trying to stay on track, "but probably better not to make a big fuss about it. You understand. A gentlemen's agreement."

"Right," he said. "Cooperation."

"We don't know each other."

His way of assenting was to push off his knees and go to the back of his car, where he opened the trunk and began to rummage for something. He brought out a large camera case, eyed it, held it up and then close to his chest, the arbitrary fussy gestures of a parent wishing to confirm a child's good health. Once he'd replaced the camera in the trunk, he chirped, in the tone of a salesman at a convention. "Right you are."

He came back to me, held his hand out to me and shook mine. I almost expected him to say what I'd heard his countrymen say. *Have a nice day.* "Soon," he said instead, already heading back to the offending car. I was too stymied to say anything back. The American exuded good fortune, practicality, relaxation. He was ready to head in reverse, as if one might always reverse away from the more unfair colors of life. I will say that for a second I envied the American: his ease, or whatever it was, thwarted me.

SEVEN

My first thwarting, or upset, or whatever we wish to call the kind of event which sets one on a certain unrecoverable course, came during my eighth birthday (which I'd thought I would celebrate by finally being able to ride our stablehand's gray mare). Instead of sending me off on a horse, my father had sent for the barber of Milazzo, a man I'd known about for years. The barber was a Sicilian with a penciled-in moustache, a man who traveled through our region and whom all the children of Esfauret thought of as a stinkfish ogre. I will admit that I'd heard such scary tales about the barber that, as he pulled out his towel and needle, his matchbox and lye and alcohol, beginning the operation procedures, I could not keep myself from shuddering, which of course helped nothing. At one point I cried openly. Only the fear of being beaten made me restrain myself. For all that, the barber was deft enough. He said something that sounded like gumbo-gumba as he iced my cheek, he said ravanissimo as he injected a numbing solution near my ear. Using one of the great shiny curved knives which had already starred prominently in my nightmares, he sliced the hump off in one fell swoop.

It was not my father's fault that the man was not the most scrupulous. My father could not have foreseen that gangrene would set in, the darkly poisoned vein leading down my neck toward my heart. How, in the week after the operation, I lay feverish in our carriage, usually reserved for fancier occasions, watching our stablehand's sturdy back, hearing him urge the horses on as we traveled a rutted shortcut to the Bordeaux hospital, where the name Poulquet made the nurses admit me immediately. When the doctors saw my infection, they grew excited about trying a newfangled, bitter sulfa cure on me and, the next morning, pronouncing its success, they dismissed me. Home at last, exhausted, traumatized by the sulfa and all the amputees we'd seen at the hospital, I stood at the woodpile, my innards boiling and heaving. How to say this delicately? Charlot and I emptied the contents of our stomachs. That he was as trustworthy as a mother, that he had not let me down, sealed us together. As he later soothed me with a weak bouillon, treating it with a snap of wine to help it go down better, I felt all the more sure he was not just someone to count on but also my first true friend.

If a child is left to raise himself mostly alone, it is easy for him to develop the certainty that he has gifts both fantastic and real. During my childhood with the hump, Charlot and his folk wisdoms had aided this certainty, often telling me that the albatross of my deformity was an asset. He believed I'd carried clairvoyance in my hump, and that this gift enabled me, for example, to bring home the cows at night. Not a dim man, but certainly never called a genius, Charlot would often bring in his own dreams for me to parse, dreams in which large animals figured, dreams which, if I squeezed my eyes tight enough, could make a message appear. I would tell him what I saw, whether it was that a distant cousin might soon pay an unexpected visit, or that my father would decide, in some unprecedented show of beneficence, highly uncharacteristic, to offer a raise in the stablehand's annual retainership. And more often than not, these events would come to pass, and so my confidence in that moment of squeezing my eyes would grow. Because of Charlot's belief in the hump's magic, both of us were afraid that some good fortune would leave after the barber had sliced it off. Yet, humpless, I thought I might still find a way to channel some mysterious force, and I banked upon this possibility, even though Charlot stopped asking me to interpret his dreams, and though my travails at school continued. And one day long after, fortunately or not, when dust was starting to settle on our war, the hump's force must have been taken over by the regime the pendulum imposed, a pendulum hungry enough to swallow most of my potential for independent thought.

WHEN, AS A CHILD, I returned to school, my face shorn of its hump, a raised shirring the fingerprint showing where the adults had cut, sewn, and unstitched me, I did not imagine that I'd stand to be taunted in such a callous fashion by Arianne.

Five years older than I was, she was smart enough (even back then) to focus on the vanity of my operation. *As if he thinks this makes him normal*, she called out. Faithful to doctrine, her tribe of followers echoed this in girlish cacophony. One can understand if I say here that children's shrieks, especially those of girls, are still as painful a noise to me as it is for someone else to hear, say, nails scratching across a blackboard, an insect scrabbling across a floor, a cell-door slamming shut, or let us say the rattle of keys on the guard's belt as he walks away, all of these lonely noises I do not wish on my worst enemies.

The shock of her tyranny rested in the main fact that for years before the removal of the hump, Arianne—she was then still just Ari—had been adept at ignoring me. Who had I been to her? Just another six-year-old, a seven-year-old, another boy in short pants. Though she was much older, she was only a couple of classes ahead of mine. For what *this* is worth, I had never paid too much attention to her, beyond shivering whenever I saw her glassy blue, slightly bulging eyes, thinking her eyes could see through walls. But mostly, I did not think about her eyes and I did nothing outlandish, too busy adapting myself to my life circumstances. Like any boy, if within a fairly limited sphere, I'd learned how to line up various comforts for myself, all good as marbles. I had my friendship with Charlot, for one thing, and also the opportunity to spy on the Polish nursemaid next door. For a certain kind of boy, such pleasures can be enough: their limits are never questioned.

Once, before my operation, among her friends, but without showing the specific malice she possessed later on, Ari had thrown pebbles at my feet, making me dance away from the girls. In her defense, this was not an extreme act. Conceivably, she might have been cruel to any boy. After that, however, I kept a careful distance from Ari, tabs on her whereabouts. When she was alone as we passed each other on the road, she ignored me as if I were a bit of stray tumbleweed, yet when I first learned the word *cruelty*, somewhere in my seventh year, I imagined Ari. The heedless economy of the girl who'd thrown stones at my feet, her braids bouncing about on her shoulders.

It was true that after the stones-at-the-feet episode there had been another moment, in the year before I'd had the operation, when she'd been especially cruel. One arbitrary day, she'd accosted me, in front of her friends, chasing me until she was victorious. She sat upon me, holding my wrists down. Is that such trauma? I must have been seven or so, and though she was not a big girl, she had the strength or will to keep me down in a corner of the schoolyard where none of our teachers could see. Surprise worked in her favor. Plus, she had the gift of an actress in a gaslit theater. In front of her friends, she knew how to suspend the moment to its maximum, how to lean forward slowly, the same lean forward she would perform on my desk at the prefecture years later. Finally—a young girl with flair—she kissed the hump on my face. This had the desired effect. The laughter around me was like tangling river-grass, immobilizing me until I came to, enough to push her off. Of course, this moment was hardly the worst of the humiliations she wished to visit upon me in life, only among the first.

But my childish hope was that the surgery would grant me an invisibility suit I could wear, good enough to hide me from all the girls of the world. I'd hoped the hump's removal would leave me free to travel everywhere without friction.

It was, however, this admission of weakness or vanity which must have marked me, I suppose, so that I became her fabulous favorite.

Once Ari saw me in the schoolyard, a boy with hump removed, the scar its only memory, I seem to have entered into a lifelong slavery to the girl.

In front of everyone in the schoolyard, she began talking, her voice hypnotic and enthralling. Though I stood next to Izzy, my shock must have made me amnesiac, so that later only he could recount the moment's details, his damnable perspective stripping me of all rights to my own recall. So I don't know whether I am the one who remembered Ari's gray socks falling, or if it was Izzy who saw the coffee stain on her white pinafore. Or whether Izzy was the one to note how her eyes were so determinedly blue, you'd think the sky had entered into a pact with her.

She started as a genius would, in a roundabout way, with patience to spare. "Doesn't Emile's face," she asked a group of girls and smaller boys at a break in a breathless game of tag, "doesn't it make him look like Luc?"

"Luc," exhaled one of the smaller boys admiringly. "The village idiot Luc."

She was smart. She mentioned Luc to trigger me to respond. That was Izzy's later theory. But when I looked at her (or as I remember looking at her, according to Izzy's telling), she was such a potentate in front of the salmon-colored bricks of our schoolhouse. Her nostrils—such imperious, fluttering slits—and her chin—so high—carried authority. I stood paralyzed as if waiting for a bell's final chime. I think I felt a strange prickle of happiness in the moment when I recognized her power.

Because the understanding came in a flash—to give in to her would be like entering a warm bath, a defeat pleasurable in its ease, a fate fulfilled and thus not without its delights. Later some would say our France fell in a similar way, but I had no truck with any of those ideas. We didn't mean to give in.

Anyway, what I knew about Luc the village idiot was common knowledge, Luc being an overgrown teenager already grotesque to us: he had a special fondness for running his hands up inside the skirts of girls in church. We all knew this was bad, if not exactly why. He liked to lay belly-up on the wooden platform under the pews, hands going wild. But he'd been spared jail because of his parents and their slobbery ways, parents who were our local butchers and hence useful, whom even my father deemed expert with a side of ham. Since they were the only butchers in Couzac—our village outside the big town of Finier—and the parents loved their idiot boy, his behavior mostly went ignored. Most people forgave the butchers for Luc, as Izzy's mother did, as my own father did, calling the son an unfortunate curse. Strangest of all was that because of his perversity, Luc had received a special pew in which to sit while in church. His name was engraved on a bronze plaque, and anyone who saw him stationed elsewhere was to gently lead him back to his rightful place. In this way, we tolerated our idiots.

BUT BEING COMPARED to Luc, in front of everyone, the scar still smarting on my cheek, stumped me. I may have thought myself evil—it made the world into a more orderly and trustworthy place if I thought my hump the logical outcome of some badness lodged in my core—but no one had ever called me an idiot. A concealed devil pushed my chest right then, paralyzing me, making it harder to breathe. Ari was going on about my vain attempts to look normal. And there (not at all far from me) were boys I knew. You know how it is with an old man. Yesterday's memories feel like today's. So here it is where my memory returns full force. I'm able to remember how strange I found it that my erstwhile friends did not become one boy-arrow of uprising, rushing her in defense of me. And I knew these boys, had skipped stones along the river with them, tortured flies, played at war. Now, as if they barely knew how to pronounce my name, they stood by, no smidgen of action left in any of them. I tried to concentrate on the boy I'd thought both most friendly and popular, Denis, certain he would step forward, come to my aid. But Denis had gone feeble, hiding under his cap, hands clenching and unclenching.

And was Ari such a priestess because her father was the schoolmaster? It seemed the sun hung with greater significance behind her. Her words that noon held and threw me down as if I were a broken toy. We all waited for a clue to fall in our midst, to tell us how to react. But she was the moral cue, too great a force to withstand. Everyone knew you were never supposed to make fun of a cripple and there she had done it openly. *The great martyrs of France have died for lesser causes*, we often prated forth unthinkingly in our history and civics lessons. And there I was, some kind of composting of both invalid and cripple. Boys could tease one another, but for Ari to point out my deformity, and also Luc's—this ordinarily would be called a fishwife's bad manners. So it was understandable that no one offered a defense of me. What she said was simply too low and it took our tongues.

Ari squealed with disgust. "Look at him!" she said, breaking our trance. "He cut the thing off his cheek. Emile thinks he can be normal now." Her hand held the jut of her hip, a cipher just beginning to hint of the future. Some of the other girls took up her words, and, if I can still see their faces correctly, they looked relieved. There was a rhythm to such moments and the curtain was falling on this one. We'd had a culmination, a cycle of disgrace closed, a sentence pronounced. *As if Emile thinks he can be normal now*, they chanted, skipping away happily enough.

FROM THIS ACCOUNT, it is probably already clear how Ari was one of those prodigies of cruelty. Her genius lived in what seemed to be her impartiality, though as a child, of course, I felt all her force directed solely at me. And only Izzy said anything. Only he came forward. It was the mark of how outcast I was, that only the jew with his stupid grin and interloper's bravery, someone I'd ignored, would want to protect me. If I believe his later story, Izzy took my hand once the girls started to skip away. If his story is true at all, Izzy's was the only hand offered for me to take. What I do remember without Izzy's telling of it is how heavy the slingshot in my pocket suddenly became, one I'd whittled and planned on giving as a gift to that perfect boy Denis, a slingshot I would end up giving to the highly imperfect Izzy.

■ ■ ■

Later that afternoon, Charlot the stablehand said to me, when I told him the story: "Ah, but did you cry?"

I said I hadn't.

"You stayed without running away." He was in the business of establishing facts and I did not mind. His facts always led somewhere, so I told him I had stayed.

During all this, Izzy stood right by me. "I heard everything," volunteered Izzy. "Emile didn't cry."

"Then you were brave," concluded the stablehand. He had his own burly logic and it had served him well in life. That logic, along with my new friendship with the jew, the only part Charlot couldn't understand, made up my consolation prize. And the prize was almost enough. I took comfort in it, held it close as an infant does with a favored rag. *Then you were brave*, a simple enough statement.

IN REMEMBERING this story, I see Arianne's action created the room for some good. Supposing for an instant that she had never singled me out for my hump, would Izzy then have gotten a chance to exercise his courage? Although I became the playing field for a wrong (hers), I also enabled someone else (Izzy) to act out a right. Izzy was the first to save me from Arianne.

Also, I have to credit Arianne with this: she had an accurate historical sensibility, being no dummy about the stories that reigned over our little village of Couzac. Because no one forgave my father anything. Certainly not for my hump, not for his actions in the village, not for the death of my mother, which they all blamed on something awful. Had my father been *neglecting* my mother, hence my hump had appeared? Or had he been *paying her too much attention*? These were the two things that I'd heard said about my father, more statements than questions. *Neglect* versus *paying too much attention*. Both implied legacies beyond my comprehension, implications I could not bridge.

One day my mother had died. There'd been little explanation. We'd gone to a funeral. After that, the stablehand had started to help a little more around the house. At that time, I began to play a game that had to do with spying on the Polish nursemaid next door, which is a completely different story. I found new ways of keeping myself cleanish behind the ears and occupied, having taken the gossip about my father as one more sign of the world's unfairness. No one knew the truth of him. My father's main failing was that once he entered our house, he'd go on a rampage asking *who left this bucket here? who left crumbs there?* and I would cower from that unpredictable god, knowing I could get boxed on my ears for both the telling or distortion of the truth. It was best to say nothing, obey his whimsical regime, follow him around like an innocent. At least on the home front, behind closed doors, when he wasn't in a rage, my father could have moments of vast sentiment. No one knew this as I did. Out in the world, those he encountered thought him a severe, hard-hearted man, a good breeder of horses if erratic with his laborers' pay. A hard bargainer, someone you wouldn't want to get tangled up with. *Old Poulquet is a terror*—I did hear them say that often enough. In its way, this was no worse an insult than hearing that the goat-milk woman had cuckolded her husband or that the butchers were decent with a side of ham. It was known, something one could almost lean upon in our village, just as if it were a sun-warmed post. People never changed much. If someone did something surprising, like run away with the goat-milk woman, people would say *it was always in him to do such a thing, he just lacked the right opportunity*. And they would search for evidence to support this conclusion, and in this search they were rarely disappointed.

So far as the village was concerned, my father was a stable quantity. He himself had a great-grandfather who'd come down from Paris, a failed courtier of sorts, one who nonetheless had some tie to the shipping industry. But my father preferred to be landlocked. He'd several times told me the story of his grandfather, tired of the watery horizon, the shape-shifting waters, who'd bought for a sou the count's castle that came to be known simply as Roc de Poulquet. This was back in the era when many counts were deserting their country estates and taking to the cities, trying hard to imitate Versailles and all its Bourbon esperance. But the particular count who had sold my father's family the castle had gone bankrupt, and my great-great-grandfather, such as he was, a stubborn man, had refused to sell back to the count even a small portion of the land once they'd come back into a bit of money. He'd said, according to my father, a phrase carried down over the generations: *No one will cross me.* Once he made up his mind to do something, it stuck.

And for this reason, though we Poulquets had stayed on our land, we were resented not just by the pauperish descendents of the count, those who for generations continue even now to live in the outbuildings bordering the very perimeter of our forty acres, but resented also by their caretakers, and their caretakers' children. So it was that among the insults I received at school were not just those occasioned by the monstrous hump protruding from my face, but also the accusations that, rather than being an heir to a rightful legacy, I had inherited larceny, though my father had told me we rightfully owned the surrounding forests. Thus, Ari had been somewhat correct to pick me out, having sensed the disparity between who I thought of myself as being (the internally evil but externally honorable son of Poulquet) and who I really was (a son of thieves).

AFTER THE JEWISH boy befriended me, his mother, who favored tall feathered caps toppling over her slight self, a giant vertical crease carved into her forehead between her amused eyebrows, would nod with the barest feint at politeness toward my father if the two happened to meet in the street. Even she knew to beware of my father, the first Emile Poulquet, who, true enough, didn't spare the bamboo cane on either horses or his son. For his jaundiced look and sternness, his workers had nicknamed him Yellow Flypaper, and this was the name which, beg pardon, also happened to stick to me. Or at least it was one of the names Ari chose to call me the week after the schoolyard humiliation.

WHEN SHE CAME to seek me out again, that following week, I had nobody to protect me from her malice, not my new jewish friend and not even my fake friends arrayed around like frightened rabbits. "Come look at Yellow Flypaper!" was what she called out. She and her girlfriends had ambushed me behind my father's woodpile. Smart girls, to have arrived at my house when Charlot was gone. Could Ari already have known and controlled so much? Quicker than I could think, she had pinned me down by the shoulders, again sitting astride me as if I were her tame pony. She called to the others. "Come look at Hump!" Then looked down, rich with excitement. "Or what should we call you?" And there was a tenderness to her, which took me aback, thrilling me terribly, a feeling which I tried to diminish by focusing on two falcons circling overhead.

It was as if she'd been crowned by the friends who appeared around her, girls as curious as I was. Was she really so strong? Was I not going to fight back? I could have, undoubtedly, I could have thrown her off. I was not a strong boy, but left-handed, using that advantage, I could often beat others at arm-wrestling. I did think that going limp could work in my favor, since Charlot had told me that was what you were supposed to do if a bear ever attacked. So I did not cry, but also did not move, summoning forces beyond myself to go limp.

Then they held me down, pecked however they could, took off my shoes, my belt, then my pants. And the whole time it was their sticks but also their hands which prodded. Mainly it is their eyes that I remember, hard bird eyes unmoving but relentlessly curious, looking at how my body involuntarily responded, twitching, rigid, releasing. As if on pain of death, I kept still whatever I could. The main thing that helped was focusing upon the falcons and, once they flew off, the two black swaying braids, Ari's braids shiny in the last of the day's sun.

NINE YEARS, but only nine years later, an unseasonably hot June day, Charlot got in my father's new sedan to drive Izzy and me to the town of Finier. Charlot had a friend who'd once worked in the hotel's kitchen, and it was through this friend that we'd known about Maman Fauret's illness and what you might call Ari's promotion. We two boys would apply for the hotel's summer jobs. But at the interview—in the cool smoky light of the café, its dank heaviness holding all things fried, served, forgotten—I found it strange that Ari accepted us so quickly. I tried to see in her 1932 self the cruel girl of my childhood but she had remade herself. Talking to her made me feel I stood before a soot-covered mirror in which only occasionally could I catch sight of an image, fleeting backward. After every sentence, her laugh followed, a riotous explosion like a startle of birds, flattering but unsettling. For a second at the beginning, as we came in sweaty and covered with road-dust, she'd stared as if we were specimens brought in for her delectation. Then came that laugh of hers, a remarkable laugh, and then she reached out and held my hand gently, as if we were meeting for the first time. Charming. Was it possible that she was a new person? Could a person be remade? From the slight curl in her short black hair, from the paleness of her skin and the alert angle of her nose, her eyes still blue but condensed into something like warmth, from the way she sat, fatigued, as we stood before her, she announced it was possible for a person to be reconstituted. She did not let on she had ever seen us before. But still I found it strange that Arianne—she insisted that we call her Arianne and not Ari—would accept my jewish friend and me. Perhaps in her isolation she was happy to see people she knew, however poorly she had once treated them.

EIGHT

It was important to her that Izzy and I understand exactly how long she'd been building a monument to Paul in her heart. When Arianne was seven (a few years before the time she'd decided to make me her plaything, I thought ruefully, but stayed mum), Paul had moved into our school. He'd commanded any room he stood in, she said, you'd think he'd been born tall. Only seven years older than she was but he'd looked eons older. She'd liked him from the get-go, had sized him up while the teacher took him around. Paul Esfauret or Fauret. Hard to hear the name perfectly, though later she'd enunciate it like a life sentence: *Fauret*. Back then she'd seen how he'd bowed his squarish head, a nod breaking off importantly as if already he were an adult eager to dispense with protocol, a boy with adult-size reasons to be impatient.

In the midmorning break, everyone tore into their buttered rolls, but in the schoolyard she was industrious, setting up a stall out of two boulders and a plank. Atop the plank she laid three mud creations. As the new older boy passed by, she called out: "Fresh crepes for ten francs each, Mister Paul!"

With a crumbling mud-coin he fashioned quickly, Paul Fauret bought a crepe from her. (Listening, I wondered where I was during their first exchange, a little boy at the periphery, soon to cower in shame.) She saw the perfection of Paul, how thoroughly he could pretend, eating her mud-crepe. I can see now, all too easily, how this act forged Paul's fate, many years later, when all there was for him to eat came from Arianne's hand, and his beautiful dusky reputation rested solely on what issued from her ingenious mouth: who he was, what he'd done. After the mud but before the lies, she mimed this for us, how boy Paul had eaten until his face was smudged with dirt, and told us how she could not stop laughing, his act was so perfect. Did she laugh at the recognition or collapse of destiny?

She did not know. It was merely the first transaction. One day Paul would tell her he too remembered that moment. There'd been that strand of hair falling over her face, he'd say, the sly look in her eye. "That's what he liked, I guess," Arianne told us in the hotel's café.

"That wasn't the end of it," said Izzy.

I was his love stooge that summer, practically a brother to him, signed on to nod agreement to most of what he said. So I nodded. Because my inner world was so confused. What I wanted in relation to Arianne was amorphous, a sea monster made of vengeance and gratification, its flaccid wet tentacles barely visible to me. Hence it was easier to go along with Izzy's script, as I felt prone to cravings a world apart from others' inner life. The lust was for something big enough to redeem lack: a bubble with an unnameable interior, painful in its contours. In my fantasy life, something like a vast dragon or a lost, real father would come reclaim me, declaring in Emile the superiority Arianne claimed for Paul.

Arianne contended she'd found Paul upstanding from the start. As a child she'd easily seen Paul's sense of honor; the stiffness had intrigued her. Who was he? A new boy, new to the schoolyard, born of more solid stuff.

Someone at any rate not to be afraid of. On the schoolyard, returning to her mud-crepe stall, he'd said he'd throw some flowers into the bargain. (And as she related this story, I had the unrequested memory of myself, fleeing from her sightlines, only a few years after her mud-crepe moment. If only I could have guessed back then how distracted she could be by her penchant for romance, I might have had an easier time.) From a forgotten childish bouquet of flowers drying on the ground nearby, Paul withdrew with care a long-stemmed daisy. The flower was still white and yellow, she said, but the stalk had begun to turn milky green, already dying.

"Amazing memory," sighed Izzy in the hotel café, playing her out.

For this gift, Ari had given Paul one more mud-crepe, the bargain simple. Paul pronounced the last crepe even better than the first. She pocketed his daisy in her smock-front. There *was* something perfect in all this. Later she would relive the moment, searching for clues, giving us the impression that it was gratifying to search in our company. Fifteen years past that first meeting with Paul, we'd become her jug-eared audience, Izzy and I, bathed in that strangely forgiving Hotel Fauret light, a light swarming through dust motes in front of the café window. It was our favorite time, a restful ease after we'd put away all the lunch plates. Was it the nimbus around her? Was it the gap in her front teeth? Was it that laugh which could startle away the past?

THAT SUMMER we boys probably spent more time listening to Arianne's stories about Paul (Paul off on an internship leading to an apprenticeship, heading for his life of frequent travel) than we did actually working. Arianne clearly loved holding the title of being *interim hotel manager*, twenty-two years old and with a strong sense of herself, we two boys playing the roles of her willing waiters. Izzy and I never intended to stiff the Faurets by spending so many hours listening to the future Fauret bride rather than, say, mopping the kitchen floor. In truth, we were a bit stupefied that we'd found our jobs so easily, without training, and we subscribed, somewhat lazily, to the idea of reverencing the absent Faurets. We made decent money and listened well. Anyway, for us to listen to tales of Paul, Arianne implied, honored both the Faurets and ourselves. When speaking, she always kept her apron on, as if forgetting that Izzy and I were not her intimates.

What was most curious was how casually she treated me, so capable of forgetting those schoolyard years. I alone was burdened with memory. What struck me most, listening to the story of Paul and Arianne, unable to stop the seventeen-year-old's rage in my loins, was how enviable her amnesia was. Perhaps one could truly forget an entire history.

Yet her treatment of an old scapegoat as a new stranger also suited me. For one, it gave me latitude for a certain self-creation. I could become anyone. It also told me that her former being must have been so distasteful to her that she had vanquished *Ari*. She apparently needed the full trisyllabic dignity of Arianne. With that single extra trill, she'd banished her former self, the one who liked taking little boys down a peg. Finally, it told me that not only can people forget who you are—sometimes everyone feels more comfortable with the arrangement. She offered me the flower of her amnesia, yet if one is used to perceiving life as a battlefield, even the offer of a flower can feel like an attack.

In the middle of one of her tales she'd turn on me. "You're listening, Emile?" she'd ask. "If you're not handing out ribbons, I'll give myself one." I knew she was still diddling me, making a joke for someone's benefit—but whose? not Izzy's, and if I listened well enough, my boyhood self thought, I could become so conversant and savvy in *the art of diddling Emile* that I would be able to laugh at earnest Emile and hence grow. In humiliation was education, a dull toothache, nothing more, making room for the new. So in this way she lured me into listening all the more, becoming her prey all over again. In the private closet of my heart (I never dared tell this to Izzy) I thought she must love me, perhaps even more than she loved Paul: I must have been important for her to exert such effort. To not recognize me. And why would she extend such interest, making sure I hung on her every word in the hotel café? And why would she have wished to humiliate me all those years before?

You're listening, Emile?

"But of course," I'd say, sitting up straight, as if at fault. *She loves me*, I kept thinking. Though this may sound irrational, in my honor, I thought, she'd refashioned herself into a kinder Arianne. I tried to do as we learned to do in school when studying homologies, butterflies and elephants, proboscis and trunk, comparing and contrasting bits of evidence, but could never come up with a single truth about her, enough to satisfy my literal adolescent mind. There were too many Ariannes. Thoughtful Arianne showed concern, inquiring after our rooms. Considerate Arianne asked about the mildew from the previous year which needed to be washed out of our curtains. Savior Arianne inquired about the blind beggar by the river. Mindful Arianne asked which days of the week we'd prefer to have off. When Izzy asked for Saturday, she paused just a second, as if her mind could cradle his entire tribal history. Then his wish was granted: he could have his sabbath. For him, she'd play being a wish-granting sprite. As for me, she told me that I'd need to take only one day off, and it would have to be Monday, the day the restaurant was closed. (Because she wouldn't be caught dead on Sundays without two boys, managing the kitchen alone—Sunday guests were the worst, dining at an hour when they substituted for their lack of family by harassing the help. In my delirium, I hazarded the guess that she pined for more time with me even after our shared Saturday alone.)

Only rarely could I find irrefutable traces of old-time Arianne. Certainly, there was controlling Arianne, who evidently felt happy jolts of electricity in the exercise of power over us. *Don't tell me you're not listening, Emile.* This was all right, though; everyone's desire was fulfilled. If she spoke of how she'd wished to lure Paul, disingenuously, pretending unawareness of how incendiary an adolescent would find any tale of seduction and conquest, I was nonetheless as entranced as her fiancé must have been.

She must have known she *had* us, as she'd once had us, as she'd later continue to grip my every adult action. Even her smallest gesture, running her fingers through her short black hair, captivated me. Lacking nerve, how could I have brought up the past with her? By stating the obvious. *Arianne, you seem to be a different person now but.* Or something more interrogative: *Arianne, how do you look upon those years when.* Sometimes I thought a gentle opening would be best, complimenting her current sophisticated facade: *Arianne, undoubtedly you've had a change of heart since.* Yet how to end the sentence? Because what did I want in the hotel—her apology?

No. What I wanted had to do with the sea creature, the embrace of the monster. Pure libido, one could say, though I'm prone to thinking my desire surpassed libido. Because years later, when no one had much libido left to speak of, I would still find my tongue stymied. I would wander with Moses, an old doddering don't-mind-me shell of myself, only to feel it again, Arianne's proximity turning my tongue into a mute lizard corpse.

She had a gift for robbing speech from others. All that summer in the hotel she wore dresses, those she'd had a local lady make for her, skimming her calves, and they were all part of the statement Arianne was making to Paul's mother, Maman, about her elegance and good posture. One can see how caught up I was in her drama, how it imprisoned my breath, as it must have for others. Details, dresses, posture, the future mother-in-law, I suffered as keenly as if they were my own. Another question that scratched at my inner being had to do with what I'll call intention. For instance, did she mean for us to see her underclothes? I thought it might be called a bustier or brassiere, the thing I'd peeped between the buttons of her shirtfront dress an unknown contraption, like a prosthetic you could imagine hanging disembodied from the ceiling of the chemist's, some hollow surgical device both alluring and nauseating. She'd never let you guess if you were meant to glimpse all this: only her most obvious of cantilevers.

ONE NIGHT after work she asked Izzy, who liked cataloguing breeds of beauty, to describe hers. "Of course, yours is an innocent beauty," said Izzy, agreeably. He was half-right. I too could, in allowing myself to dwell on her face, impute to its bones and planes a purity. As if, rather than being punished, she'd gotten to pay with the coin of a childhood nastiness for her clean adult beauty.

In her stories about Paul, the theme remained—she loved controlling someone's movements, especially those of a man seven years her senior. What I hated was that she could make me laugh, unwillingly, a laughter teased out just as if I were being prodded. She may have wanted my laugh as much as I wanted her gaze to rest on me, then hated when it came, uncomfortable in its spotlight. Sometimes I would have to take a break from our restaurant labors and go in the full heat of hormonal confusion to a spot by the river closest to the hotel, trying to remember the world beyond Arianne. I'd watch rivulets pour over stone, straining into braids and then facets, both facile and eternal, and once even penned an anonymous poem comparing at first her own braids and then her gaze to those rivulets, cold shallows protecting a depth. An awful poem, really, riddled with inconsistent imagery and brutish figures, and I left it carefully inscribed on a folded piece of paper on the doily shelf, but I never knew whether she read it or not, the thing just disappeared.

"Later, Paul said I'd bewitched him," she'd say, casting a wayward enough glance at Izzy and me. "Because of that, we're all here. What other manager would've hired you types?" And we knew we were supposed to feel complimented by the insult. *You types.*

HER FATHER had given her an odd middle name—Verité—she'd said it was an old family legacy. And for what it's worth, at times I forgave her all previous insults by thinking of her as Truth. She blurts things out, I told myself, she may love to control others but probably can't help it, and this allowance made her past mistreatments a shade more tolerable. She was explosive in laughter and speech, especially proud of telling us things she'd spat out in a righteous heat to her future mother-in-law. *And I couldn't help myself but I told Maman there was no way in the world that we could do that*, she'd explain, after any dispute about the hotel's workings. There'd been a disappeared workman or a clogged drain, an important guest mistreated or silver pilfered. *It wasn't my intention*, she'd say. *Why should I do this to an old woman? But I ended up shouting into her hearing aid. Her idea was ludicrous, out of the question.*

The *ideas* didn't matter. Because what was important in these stories was that Arianne was always victim, a martyr forced to the outermost brim of endurance and hence roused to activism, the theme being that she had not been raised to do things the way Maman preferred. Already Arianne probably had a slight clue that she'd entered into a lifelong wrestling match with the name Fauret, with the meaning of the Faurets in our region, and that this struggle would consume most of her life energy, conquering not just the connection to her future mother-in-law, but also her romance with Paul and her own self.

THE PARADOX of it was that I too began to feel I awaited Paul's return from his apprenticeship, which, from what I could understand, was to a master linguist. Despite the protestations of Paul's mother, Arianne had already won the first battle. She had gotten engaged, hadn't she? Not only that, when Maman had fallen ill, in the spring, Arianne had been asked to come manage the hotel restaurant. Now she was the one to order her future mother-in-law's morning coffee for her. And she was the one, saint and savior Arianne, who ensured that the nurse attendant maintained the schedule of morphine injections flowing straight into Maman's veins.

Arianne managed this so well that Paul's mother was known to me mainly as a kind of flimsy, opiated ghost in a nightdress, wandering the halls requesting a glass of water, or worse, a hot-water bladder, or much worse, a frail woman asking me to scratch her back in certain spots she couldn't reach.

WHAT WE LEARNED from Arianne's stories was that Maman had initially shown concern that Arianne's stock might not be strong enough. She had not seen the young girl as an appropriate *breeder* for the family Fauret, Maman had confided to the family physician. After the first meeting with her son's intended, Maman had inquired first of her son and then of the girl herself—wasn't there a strange tilt to Arianne's shoulders? After this, Maman had taken the fianceé to see all the region's doctors and specialists. They'd thumped Arianne's spine, asking the girl to touch her toes. Unfortunately, even the most sympathetic doctor had found it hard to discover anything unfitting about Arianne's skeleton, so they'd prescribed more morphine for Maman's nervous tension, assuring her that not only were the bones of her potential daughter-in-law essentially sound, she would certainly produce milk enough for good strong Fauret children.

At this Maman had discovered another concern: was there not after all a golden halo around the iris of Arianne's eyes? Wouldn't this signify a tendency toward blindness or else mental incapacity? The doctors, paid by Maman, nonetheless failed to give a satisfying answer. At the root of it, Maman admitted to her son, who immediately—with a certain queasiness—relayed to his bride-to-be that Maman had a deep question about Arianne's father's origins, or rather, his orientation. Arianne's father Vado was a schoolteacher, of course, respected enough in the town of Esfauret; but what exactly had he been doing up in Amiens during the great war? Yes, Vado had helped the war effort, Paul knew all about that, he himself had been involved peripherally with Vado's work, but had Vado also been involved with something more shadowy during those years? What exactly had Arianne done for the men whom her father trained? Did Vado have some connection perhaps to Spain or Germany? Was there a hint of counterespionage to his work?

"OF COURSE Paul didn't doubt me," Arianne stated flatly. "He just had to ask. His mother, you know."

It was Izzy who was best at wheedling out of Arianne the most revealing stories. He was comfortable with girls, calling himself a romantic. I hoped to be a romantic myself one day, whatever that entailed, but for the time being, Izzy was the one who knew how to butter Arianne up, saying how much he respected her candor and honesty, her generosity of spirit.

I could never name myself enough to know how to name—let alone flatter—another. Whenever Izzy complimented Arianne, I had the sense that honesty and candor were the most important attributes one could possess, qualities sorely lacking in me. Upon waking, I often lingered in bed, enumerating my bad qualities as if I stumbled about in a medieval allegory: my Deceit and Secrecy, or the portmanteau that seemed to contain the worst, Selfishness. I was not good and simple like Charlot, nor was I half so useful. I had eaten my father's food, for which he worked hard, overseeing his holdings and estates. I had taken mushrooms in the forest from other foragers, and had stolen baby animals—ducklings, goslings, baby rabbits—from their mothers, solely for the purpose of having pets of my own. Not to mention that I often peeked upon the Polish nursemaid next door as she bathed, and that I'd often burnt flies and ants with my magnifying lens until their lives flashed to an end with a hellish sizzle. If I were a better person, love would have come more easily to me. Not to mention that my mother would not have died.

Ugly, deformed, a sneerer: others had called me these names. Yet even my own father had never called me evil. It was rather the voice of my hump, continuing to channel its mysterious force through the scar, which confirmed Emile as someone barely deserving to live. So as Izzy flattered Arianne, using words like *candid* and *generous* for his own motives, gaining footing, my shame silenced me, my heart exploding.

Arianne would accept anything Izzy said, so heartfelt were his eyes—brown, fringed with soft lashes. "You should have been a girl," she often told him, covetous.

"It's you with beautiful eyes," Izzy would purr back.

"No!" as if in a fit of self-loathing. "My eyes are a shark's," she'd say, not half-wrong. Her stare was so dead. It may have been the coldness which affected me the most: when it flickered toward warmth, I felt the hope that I might be getting closer to her. And in this too I lost all rudder, for now, seeing with some vantage the events of that summer, it was clearly Izzy, morning, noon, and evening Izzy whom she favored, no matter his murky tribal origins.

OF COURSE, when I was alone in my room, down the hall from her, I practiced speeches I would thrust upon her, discourses to banish the sea monster, all on the same topic: how difficult it was to forgive her. Had she any idea how permanently she had scarred me? She, not the hump. I would be eloquent as a lawyer, telling her that I could not have a nightmare without her name on my lips as I awoke, *Arianne* always floating above me. Nor could I have a waking thought about a girl or older lady without seeing her braids swinging above me behind the woodpile. Blurry adult love, I felt, would spell out only more of this same humiliation.

The twinned image to my eloquence was a scenario in which Arianne knelt before me by the willow tree outside our house. She would apologize for the eternal filter that she had set before my eyes. *I never meant to humiliate you in the school yard*, she would plead. *I was cowardly, can you forgive me now?*

I would consider a long pendulous moment before granting her my pardon. Somewhere on a hill a crowd would cheer, she would dissolve in tears, rise up, and then my mind would go a bit misty: the crowd vanished and she succumbed to me, finally, but how? The sea creature did not allow for details. My mind stopped somewhere at her white calves, tightly balled, and the way one could steal a look, when she raised her arms to put away the special platters in the cabinet, at those horrifically exciting beige underclothes.

AT ONE POINT that summer, she uttered what I now consider to have been the hex of my life. She told us that neither Izzy nor I would ever care truly about anyone but her, heedlessly speaking what would later become my obsession. I will stand by this—her influence led me into certain acts which then exiled me into the desert, far from the comforts of civilization. She meddled with my one chance at love, puppetting me into what identified me as an "inarguably" evil man, turning my days and years into those of a convict, a fugitive, a bushel.

Is it so wrong that I blame her?

And is there a person alive who can explain to me how words said so lightly can slam into one's being, become one's heart's tattoo, taking on a life of their own? *You will never care about anyone but me.*

NINE

Arianne's stories hinged on missed opportunities. Every action she had taken defied other actions, each choice bore great consequence, spinning off into unknowable losses. To us there was no grander heroine, and perhaps this is the danger of small, isolated places like Couzac or what I thought of as the big town of Finier, Finier with its smallness I could not apprehend as a young man: all such places birth grande dames who weave tragic stories for their audiences. What defines the audience in such a town is the degree to which they believe they are not stuck.

Izzy and I might as well have been lunatics. Only in recounting her stories can I begin to see how trivial her regrets were. For example, she told us that Paul's family had moved to the coast when his father took ill. What she lamented was that while Paul was gone, she might have struck up a correspondence with him, and that this correspondence might have developed their romance. They would have a private code with a stronger history corded between them. She referred to letters they might have shared when they'd been more innocent. What weight her imagination gave these unsent, unwritten letters! How I mourned with her, weirdly enough, as if Paul had been my suitor. What these imagined letters would have rectified was a mystery. But she longed for them, a watermark of intimacy. Everything would be better, she'd sigh, and we with her.

During his first childhood absence, after the mud-crepe incident, she'd asked someone about Paul's last name. Already, asking, she'd understood a greater truth. Paul's name—Fauret—formed the root of our village's name, Esfauret. She would go on to have the kind of epiphany children have when figuring out status on one of those ladders borrowed from the world of adults. *Paul Fauret is from an old family*, she realized. His family had returned to the Pyrénées to reclaim its lawful ancestral lands. A town possessed his name. *He is an important person.*

The Faurets came from Esfauret. Naturally, she responded to Izzy's daring ribbing, yes, she would have preferred if *her* father had such a neat connection between name and village. Yes, she said, Izzy's impertinence verging on what sounded like insolence to me, her father was something of a big man in the village of Esfauret: he'd been appointed schoolmaster some twenty years earlier. He and his bachelor brother lived next to each other in houses set back from the main road, many safe acres away from the road, and while the brothers had made money from what remained of the family's various businesses, both of them were teachers. Teaching was not a default position—she asserted this with some flush to her cheeks—it came out of a desire to be honest, public-spirited men, to do good! It was however also true that some prospects up north had failed. Near Amiens and some generations ago, they'd been in some kind of import business. Her father had told her that once, expecting her to remember it, and ordering her to never fret him with questions, to never discuss the business with anyone else. She swore us to secrecy. He'd said that he hated to remember much about his family, that he'd run away from several generations of kitchen-sink and fireside tyranny, a latent Prussian strain coloring the family's routines.

■ ■ ■

In Esfauret, when I'd studied with her father, in the tenth form for Latin, despite my fear of Arianne, I had liked his eager nature. No one called him Mister Vadet but rather Vado, because he taught Latin and favored puns. He was a natural teacher, I thought, also a leader, given the charismatic rigidity of his principles. No one begrudged him the power he'd begun to hold in the village, as Vado was a republican, known for incorruptibility and will.

And if Vadet was considered new to Esfauret, he was still counted among Esfauret's most conservative citizens. For example, I remembered Vado leading a fight against outsiders who came to buy up vacant lots in the village, outsiders who would eventually drive up land prices and buy out old-time farmers. Vado was equally active in organizing to ban lorries. He helped keep a crucial bridge—one which would have linked Esfauret with the main Toulouse road—unbuilt.

BUT VADO, such a republican, ended up working as a cryptographer in Amiens. In 1916, he moved the entire family north for a few years. This part she didn't mind telling us. *War* was one of the first words Arianne understood to mean adulthood. She'd had no siblings and her parents had doted on her, making up a private home of amusements, seeing her as a lovable reminder of their own infancy. They'd kept their own childhood toys, and by the time she came around, they rolled those same wooden horses and silver bells out, trying to keep her as young as they could. Her only elder sibling, she felt, was the war.

So she'd begged to join the effort with her father. You could hear the report of rifles in the forest, not the usual muffled shots of poachers. She wanted to participate in her father's secret life, to help hide packets for the passeurs across the water. She ended up getting to risk long walks at night past the guards, just so she could place bread-filled knapsacks for the passeurs near the quay on the Somme. And she was good; no one would stop a little girl. The passeurs, her father's colleagues, each became known as Mister Redon once they entered the village not far from the Somme, and all the Redons had expressions that might as well have been hammered by mallets. They showed up after midnight, the Redons, seated at her mother's table refusing coffee and tea, looking surprised at their vigor in the face of what history had thrown up. No one could doubt their lives' difficulty.

Though by the time they arrived, from Antwerp or Barcelona, the Redons had usually encased themselves within their embassy personas, wearing white shirts, stiff bodies. Their passage had civilized them. They had just enjoyed the relative luxury of an overnight train, and kept asserting how happy they were to have arrived at the Vadets' table. The Redon alias was, of course, just one small part of the firewall her father offered them, one more of Vado's many moments of thoughtfulness.

Arianne's efforts to help the Redons came easily, she admitted, answering Izzy's sycophancy. She leaned forward and confessed she'd entertained crushes on all of them. If her father had said it would have helped the Redons, in their honor she would have lain breathless under an elephant's foot, tied herself to dynamite, awaited fate in a white nightgown atop a fuming volcano. The ideas came too easily, she claimed, because she'd been weaned on tales of exotic cultures.

And though the Redons wore the outer marks of civilization by the time they showed up in her mother's kitchen, you could sense something else. The brutality and sadness of bad choices made somewhere across a river, in the mountains, on slippery rocks at night, chased by the forest-flank patrols. Moments they could remember but wouldn't disclose, not even to Vado—Vado the octopus head, who kept them together, Vado whom they could trust.

There were moments in the mountains, clearly, when all you had to hold on to was your idea of someone. This was her favorite topic. She'd heard all of them mention this. Sometimes all you had to depend on was someone who would (no matter what) return to find you, bearing water or bandages, encouragement, a stretcher. Someone who represented enough of a lodestar to get you through. Quickly the inner stuff of a man would fade. All you would have to hold on to, inside the forest, would be the shimmer around someone. The barest line, like what hunting dogs must see, all movement and contour, the substance itself dark. You'd have an idea of a person who, even if not especially a hero himself, nonetheless believed in your heroism.

She'd learned this from the Redons so that later in life, it was easy to claim Paul as her own star. A pilot star could be enough to help you get to the other side. Otherwise you'd give up hope, stumble forever, allow yourself to make the first bad decision which would ramify into a thousand other bad decisions. In the lives of the Redons, one bad decision could lead to whole nights spent clinging to trees deep in the forest and its many extortions.

If, back in civilization, you asked any of the Redons how they were, they wouldn't respond in our regional dialect that they were fine. No, they'd say, *I'm getting by, I'm defending myself.* Sometimes at the kitchen table the Redons made allusion to their particular testing moments. One would mention the time he'd caught himself going in a bad direction, and how abhorrent it had been that he'd needed to backtrack. Corrective moments they called *equilibriums*; backtracking was an equilibrium. So were the moments at Vado's kitchen table when the Redons required a spot of luxury, a balancing measure. They'd beset Arianne with tiny requests. A tablespoonful of a certain blackberry liqueur, please mademoiselle, a small plate of goat cheese if it wouldn't be a bother. No sir, not a bother. Because how could it be a bother? When she remembered these moments, she grew quite heated. She knew *then* how much she wanted to help people, she said, straightening up.

"Like Joan of Arc," Izzy said, his knee nudging mine under the table.

"I love Joan of Arc!" she said, triumphant, as if Izzy had read her soul.

She'd beg her father to let her go find supplies from a neighbor's, from somewhere, even after midnight, though Vado forbade his daughter such missions. She was not allowed to give neighbors reason to guess whom her family harbored; let the Redons instead find blackberry wine from a farmer in another village, the next morning. She should let Mister Redon—or les Messieurs Redons—sleep it off, as the Redons were used to having one more need left unfilled, ignored, eh? And the passeurs would exchange their knowing laughs at Vado's words, having all left wives and betrothed women behind them at the threshold of war.

Don't risk too much for others, Ari! her father would later tell her, hypocritically. You're too young. You can only afford risking your name once you've built up something to lose! That's when it becomes worthwhile to risk something for another person!

And when her father said her name she felt all the patrimony vested in her and thus obeyed. "I could've resisted him but I didn't think of it," she said.

"You kept your independence within," said Izzy, not making complete sense. "Like Joan of Arc."

"Exactly," and she flashed him great approval. "Now you remind me a little of a Redon."

She'd liked the way the Redons had sat in the kitchen, so drawn, cracking their knuckles, their grim jokes. Soon they'd return to the truth of their grizzlement. A few weeks later they'd show up again in the kitchen, a notch more drawn, two notches sadder. There were also those who never showed up again. Never mentioned again. Fates everyone was aware of: lost to the front, the patrols, the forest. After the war she kept busy studying their fates, learned about those who spent a couple of years as prisoners of war until they couldn't digest anything more than a potato. Only to die after the war from starvation. Killed by potatoes: the fate seemed inglorious.

"You wanted them to die from something greater," said Izzy.

"Yes, a cause." Instead, some were sent on peculiar death marches in Russia.

"Like a card game," hazarded Izzy. "All cards get thrown down. Only some get played."

"He knows too much!" she said. "How does your friend know so much, Emile? You're listening, Emile? But it's true. I found it strange that some would survive. Then they'd lose it all later."

They could go mad later, quietly, their families calling them strange. She heard reports from her mother about the families who came whispering to Vado, saying *he never used to act this way*. It was only later that she learned what it meant to find a newspaper article on a table reporting on one of the Redons, another soldier of conscience who'd hanged himself in a maid's chamber or in the Trastevere, in sight of the Vatican. Another who'd thrown himself into the Seine. The only pattern Arianne could discern was that the Redons favored waterways. She tried to see how choosing death—and particularly death by water—might feel superior to death in the mountains, where the conquest would be too total.

"I've always thought *I'd* like to die by drowning," said Izzy, and for this he received an explosion of respect from Arianne. "The most peaceful way."

"You'd give in," she said dreamily.

"Hunger or fire would be the worst," he said, suddenly expert.

"Or loneliness." And there came a great pause.

"So what happened then?" I said, wanting to break up any game which inexplicably ruled me out. Even at that age, I felt myself to be too hardy, too much a survivor for my own liking.

LEFT BEHIND, having returned to Esfauret with her father, Arianne had no waterway. Instead she had a scrapbook and black felt corners, glue and good penmanship. She carefully placed all the news items that came, one page dedicated to each passeur she had known, with a little couplet she would write for each.

Jean-Paul, bravest of men, you conquered them all/Now a maid's chamber spies on your fall.

Each of the passeurs continued to live on in her book. That was, anyway, her hope. She loved their gravity. It impressed her irreparably. After that, her whole life needed to live up to this moment, to this degree of seriousness. "Maybe that's why I like Paul," she said, twirling a strand of hair. "He's pretty serious."

"Or maybe that's why he likes you," said Izzy, incorrigible to the last. "You learned to be serious from your Redons."

"I did?" she said, and laughed again, finally homing in. "You're flattering me. Your little friend, Emile, was he always such a flirt?"

"I don't know," I said, diplomatic.

"It's impossible," intoned Izzy, "to flatter something one believes to be real. Right, Emile?" only to make her blush all over.

. . .

LATER I TEASED him about that. *Something one believes to be real.*

"You're crazy about her," I said. We were standing in the hallway between our rooms, lit by gaslamps mottled from dead moths, as the maid had been on vacation. "You'd say anything. *Something one believes to be real,*" in a high-pitched imitation.

"I like her enough," said Izzy, faux casual, flicking away one of the flittering moths.

"You think she remembers you from the schoolyard?" I asked. We hadn't broached this subject between us. It was as taboo as talking about Izzy's religion. Only now do I realize Izzy may have avoided the subject of her cruelty toward me out of greater tact than I'd granted him. Arianne had as a schoolgirl always ignored Izzy's semitic origins, but whether she did so out of convenience, pity, disgust, or because she had desired to single me out was unknowable, another part of our black unspoken, a silence capable of swallowing one entirely. I wished he would have been the first to speak about her schoolyard deeds toward me. Why should I have to bring it up? Instead what I asked was whether or not he thought she liked him.

He laughed. "Who can tell how ladies are?" But we both knew he was just as painful a virgin as I was and hadn't earned this savvy tone. "I don't know," he backtracked, "you think she *could* like me?" The meaning was well-understood between us, and didn't need to be stated: *could* Arianne like someone named Israel Horwitz Lisson?

ONCE ARIANNE and her family had returned to Esfauret in 1919, with a surge of relief and patriotism in the air, which Arianne childishly linked to the damp ink on the Versailles treaty, she kept an eye on Paul. He had returned to school as a teacher. She was nine years old, just past the age of selling mud-crepes, and her eye stayed studious upon him. When she mentioned the treaty, I figured out the years, and could see the reentry of Paul marked the time when she'd started to slight me, when she'd started to make my back tremble, when she'd thrown stones, assembling her cronies to make fun of me, later to prod me. She'd been merely a girl, yet what power she already possessed. My tongue so thick, I listened, there in the hotel café where only the pendulum of the corridor's grandfather clock carved the space within her story. I wanted to insist on my importance to her legends, insert myself into all her yearning, but I was irrelevant, apparently, a footnote in her history.

Paul had come through a fire, she could see that much, one which had made him even more earnest. He'd served bravely, she thought, almost as if he'd been a Redon. She'd heard he'd lied about his age to serve on the western front, but he was reticent about his year among soldiers. All this meant that he was wiser and more distant, so he seemed even more destined for her, not at all an arbitrary person. Though one day she'd learn a bit about *arbitrary* teenage loves, she hinted, as she would have a few.

"Who?" Izzy couldn't let that go. "That's not allowed. You have to tell us." He busied himself with a boyish prank, spinning an ashtray across the tabletop toward Arianne. "Who did you like? Before you met us, I mean."

She wouldn't say. But Paul's solemnity—it had spoken to her. You could hear in her account what grandeur she thought should be hers. She tried to ignore that Paul seemed diminished, no longer commanding any room he entered. As if he were a Redon, his shadowy soldier duties had shrunk something inside him. "War scars," she sighed, aiming for sophistication, almost achieving it. To us, such a glamorous older lady in her early twenties. She kept wondering what had Paul survived? He'd gotten meningitis from wartime shock at one point, that's what her father had hinted, but seemed to have recovered enough, joking in the backroom with Roger, a brotherly friend he'd met and brought back with him. Though she'd heard that other towns slighted teachers, the town of Esfauret deemed teaching a noble position, perhaps because of Vado. It was considered an accession to a certain throne when Paul started to teach algebra to the village children, while his friend Roger taught history. Paul, however, might as well have been teaching the art of staying mum. He would not mention his family unless pressed, while his friend Roger, far more haunted, carried the same silence to an extreme.

"What was Roger like?" crowed Izzy, a detective at the end of his case.

"Exotic. Dark hair, green eyes," stopping herself from going further. Paul, however, she could tell he was cut out for high pursuits. She thought of him as a king, caught in the body of an algebra teacher for students in the fifth form, and so she asked her father whether, after her own classes were finished for the day, she could volunteer as a teacher's aide, moving between rooms with a silky footfall, charged with important tasks, inventing duties, finding the perfect excuse to watch the hidden king teach.

My memory of Paul was different: an abstracted presence, his parrot-blue eyes scanning you, small eyes positioned too high in that lengthy face so he always seemed about to tumble over, despite the way his stride bisected the corridors with method. Older kids dubbed him Professor Head-in-the-Clouds or sometimes the Contemplative Cricket, but such palaver didn't affect Arianne, apparently, as she refilled the chalk bins or arranged books in order of ascending size.

Mainly she listened to Paul's gravelly voice, how he spoke to students as if they were fascinating objects of study, a bit removed, as though all words were being uttered for the first time in history. When she read about the great philosophers, she thought of Paul's sober face and how it made her pay attention to all the more susceptible parts of his body, the joints of his squarish hands, stabbing the air, making some point about a variable. How red he turned when playing his trumpet, attempting the new music called jazz, and how feminine and beguiling was this vulnerability. Or his laugh, so genial it surprised everyone. She was good at imitating this laugh.

"I don't get it. Why's that so great?" asked Izzy, perhaps snubbed by the *exotic* comment.

"It's the contrast. Paul's a solid person. But then he has this certain lightness," said Arianne.

"Lightness?" I asked, my favor to Izzy.

"If you surprise him, or—" She smiled, making both Izzy and I cringe at her private savoring. "Like a child you see with trousers rolled up, you know, like a child heading into a river for the first time."

"That's one kind of lightness," said Izzy.

"You know others?" she asked. "Oh, shush. You're just making up stories."

"I'm not. We'll discuss this later. If you're good." Izzy had regained his poise. "Go on with your story."

So she'd watched Paul's gravity, trying to tug his attentiveness toward her. But Paul was apparently such an upstanding citizen he'd do nothing to jeopardize his position by courting the schoolmaster's underage daughter. For eight years all of them stayed stuck in their positions, Roger the history teacher, Paul in algebra, Ari serving as Paul's aide, slowly taking on tasks, tutoring the slow. One day she was seventeen, almost a decade after having sold him the mud-crepe, and Paul was already twenty-four. He still seemed to ignore her, treating Vado like a father, occasionally eating dinner at the Vadet house, discussing unions and labor strikes in hushed tones after dinner. Who knew? Everyone was getting older and nothing had happened. Speaking in other tongues became necessary.

Unfortunately, it was Roger who would notice, Roger who complimented her while Paul wouldn't let on. She'd started to put her hair up and let it down, perfumed herself. A flower in a sweater's buttonhole, but how *little* such efforts had to remain for no one else to notice. She wanted Paul to consider her serious. She'd wear her mother's lace-trimmed blouses, an animal stirring inside, wanting, in some inchoate way, to get him to think of the bedroom. She couldn't name all this exactly, the girl instinct awaking after so many years dormant. It had something to do with the seductively filmy waxy veil, easily crinkled, used to protect wedding photographs in their neat black felt corners. Her mother delighted that her tomboy, her only child, would suddenly let herself be dressed properly. She warned Ari away from Roger and meanwhile put her sewing skills to new use.

I CAN STILL imagine Arianne now, how she must have waited for Paul. For years, in the filtered classroom light, with every possible sense available to her, she waited. Her breathing high in her chest, a hummingbird caught in her throat, colors too vivid, the world contracted, spiraling around this desire. She wanted to link herself with a hero. She felt waiting would, or could, win the game. It was a tactic she had at her disposal.

And then she must have had hazy, fantastical desires (much like my own unhappy sea monster that summer) involving his smile. She imagined that if she could interest him, if he were to listen to her in the way that he listened to his students stumbling through theorems, she would never have to preen again. She would just flower, put forth unimaginable shoots. At least, this is what I imagined.

All she said to Izzy and me was this: she knew he was *it* for her.

MEANWHILE, her own father had wanted Ari to develop her mind. He'd been unable to come up with an appropriate direction for his little hoyden, while her mother had been upset over the direction of Vado's political work and stopped her flurry of lace-making, taking to bed with neurasthenic complaints and an admiration of the virtues of morning claret. There was so much Ari didn't know. For one thing, over the years, Ari had begun to see how little Paul actually knew about algebra. Once, over midnight soup in the kitchen, she asked her father why he'd hired the boy and Vado did not shame Ari for her transparent interest. Paul was a kind of avatar, he said, a promising boy who'd been in the Lorraine right before the evacuation to Bordeaux. A fellow who'd shown himself to be a natural cryptographer. Not to mention how brilliant he was at writing in miniature script.

She had burst out laughing. "Who cares?" she'd said. "*Miniature* script?" Arianne was still so young, to her it was as though her father had said the boy was good at clipping hedges, and that clipping hedges could aid patriotism. She would have preferred him to have been a stretcher-bearer, a cannon-cleaner, anything else. But the boy was a born codifier. Once they got engaged, he (finally!) wrote her love letters, each time using a different base from which to create both code and key, employing slogans, popular radio songs, stock reports. But he'd been best at what the information services prized most—his tiny script depicted all manner of military movements, information the Redons gathered from Berlin.

"You skipped so much. How did it all heat up?" Izzy pressed her. "Between you and him."

Paul could write a whole battle plan in script on a piece of paper no bigger than the circumference of an egg, waddable into an ear or hatband. In war, her father said, you must be grateful for small talents, as they make your luck. While the Redons had sat tight at the kitchen table, like *natures morts*, it turned out it had been Paul's tiny script which had brought all of them, which meant he had managed to get himself behind enemy lines.

"We don't want to know all that," said Izzy.

When she was still his aide, she sometimes studied Paul parsing text with his exacting movements. You'd think his hand was shrugging off flydust, because he used a pen with a nib so narrow you could cut yourself on it. One time, she did, accidentally, in his presence, cut her finger on his pen. Then Paul brought his lips to the cut.

"Then what?" asked Izzy.

"Problem is, I've had too much wine," she laughed.

"You haven't had enough," said Izzy, refilling her glass. "Allow me, Mademoiselle."

"Soon Madame."

"But still Mademoiselle. So what happened?" said Izzy.

They were alone, she explained. She and Paul. He pressed in. That night, he walked with her and she described the spot where she'd hid supplies.

"Oh, the spot!" laughed Izzy.

"What?"

"You're leaving out the most important part!" Izzy almost yelped.

"There were indiscretions."

"We forgive you," said Izzy, daring beyond all prior darings, "our child," anointing her with drops of water from his glass.

"Why do I tell you lagabouts so much?" she said, laughing.

"Because you want to," he said. He turned a pious look at her. "Secretly."

"We want to hear." My weak voice an echo, everything about me an echo, Emile the echo of his hollow core.

"You won't work well tomorrow," she said.

"No, we'll work better," promised Izzy. "Your stories give us strength. Right, Emile?"

"Right," I echoed.

The next morning, Paul finally asked Vado for the hand of his daughter. And Vado, the great Vado, gave his consent. She's difficult, he warned Paul. Ari overheard this and resented it but the truth was, she agreed.

"I am difficult," she said.

"One of your charms," said Izzy, incurable.

"It's true," I said. Shrugging. What did I know about *difficult*?

She was almost spinster age. The morning Vado consented, she was still wearing the yellowed lace camisole she'd worn the previous night. The look in Paul's eyes, uncertain but fierce, had reminded her of that David picture of Napoleon during the Marengo campaign, the soulful eyes of a man who could conquer the Alps on a mule, depicted as having crossed on a beautiful white horse, his arm aloft, pointing toward the heavens.

"Does that painting show Napoleon with dark eyes?" asked Izzy.

"Dark as yours," she said.

Izzy thanked her by kissing her hand. I looked away, my only minor recompense the thought about Napoleon's tirades against jews, a flicker in my mind, just as the letter O might have shimmered and vanished.

The war had been over for many years, she said, wanting to continue, so Paul would be hers soon enough. Then she got up from the table and almost ran away, muttering something about kitchen cleanup. She didn't know how to stop talking to us, I thought, astounded by the possibility. She had embarrassed herself.

"That girl's a huge liar," Izzy whispered to me. "Those inconsistencies. You believe them? But a charming liar, right?"

"Right," I said. I had no clue about lies, nor could I say where charm began. I only knew I was Emile, Emile serving mainly as a ricochet, and that Izzy had gained the advantage. "Absolutely right."

■ ■ ■

THAT NIGHT in our hallway, Izzy and I worked over a few of the details together, figuring that at least thirty percent of what she'd said must have been somewhat true.

"I bet Paul was her first lover," Izzy said with his shrewd air. I didn't know how anyone our age could summon up such precocious tones. He used words like *lover* and *liaisons* as if he really knew their meaning. "But he won't be her last." He mock-jousted with me.

"Big shot," I said, evading his fancy footwork. "Her last," imitating him.

"Not if I have any say in it."

I didn't want to admit my gratitude for having a spy as committed as Izzy, someone who would at least give me vicarious knowledge. "You're crazy," I told him, thrusting my invisible sword forward.

"Maybe," he said. "Call me crazy if it makes you feel better. I'm also right."

I wanted to warn him she could turn on us. But he knew this as well as I did. She had chosen to be a new person. Not remembering the past was different from forgetting. *Not remembering* was almost a mistake, like failing to button one's sweater outside because one failed to notice one had left the cozy precincts of one's own home, while *forgetting* was a paradox, requiring greater resolve and greater passivity. Arianne had chosen not to remember, I thought, to not notice who was around her. "At least she won't throw stones at you," I said, though she'd never turned that breed of ire on Izzy. "You're safe that way."

The barest of grimaces crossed his face. He had, more than I, chosen to go along with the new version of Arianne. Now I saw that, for whatever reason, he didn't like to be forced to remember anything of her prior self, or that he'd once protected me.

What I really wanted to tell him was that I was glad we'd be together for another month, working at the Hotel Fauret before we went up to Paris and our futures as students and all the unknown. In that era, his strongest ambition was to make it past the hurdles and become a judge, while I yearned to become a civil servant. We had discussed such ideas without looking at each other. But instead of saying any of this, I punched him in the gut when he least expected it. He ran down the hall after me until I slammed the door in his face. This was how most boys were back then. I don't know how they are now. Perhaps they are exactly the same.

THERE WAS SOMETHING else I wanted to tell Izzy but found it hard to say.

Once, after a chilly Sunday in which every seat in the restaurant had been filled until after closing, fatigued into some mindless moment, I'd been standing in my room as I imagined, from reproductions, Michelangelo's David might have stood.

My body bared just after the bath, steaming from the cold.

In that seventeenth summer, I barely recognized myself in mirrors, a long skinny boy with a heavy thatch of black hair, the sneer—left over from my botched operation years earlier—now just a bit relaxed.

I turned slightly away from the mirror so the sneer could relax completely into shadow. The light in the room was a cold blue, just before dusk, despite the curious golden panels which divided the room, panels painted over with dancing rosy women. These were useless, given my narrow room, made up of a single bed and a table and writing desk, yet I couldn't fold the panels. To get to the bed, therefore, one was compelled to walk a mini-labyrinth. There was also a sputtering wall lamp with a frame made of iron pincers sticking out rather menacingly, and something like an ancient lady's fake pearl-studded handbag hanging from it.

Faintly illuminated, therefore, but illuminated nonetheless, I stood in my room, number 410: holding nothing over my bare self. And she walked in. Just as though she'd made a mistake. As though she'd thought my room was hers down the hall, in the alcove by the stairs. When this was hardly possible. Hardly something she would have done. She would not have made such a mistake.

She came in (or rather her reflection did) carrying nothing. There was no letter to deliver, no excuse. Was she going to pretend I had summoned her? She wore one of her flowered dresses and the dress still bore the imprint of the day's apron, pressed to her body by what

I had come to know, from small errands in proximity, as a tender sweat.

    She hovered within my room's dusk, just inside the open door, assessing her old prey Emile through the slit made by the golden panels. She waited some more, appraising. Minutes or hours later (how can I judge anymore, the memory has played so often in my head it no longer looks like truth), she left.

TEN

As I walked down the main station road, along the eastern border of the river Nodaire, before one enters Finier proper, I could not help the shiver. This was my third return to the town. The first had been as a graduated student, a pretend-sophisticate, a self-branded Parisian, a return which had begun the moment I'd stepped onto the shuttle train headed back to Toulouse. At the time, I'd been literal as any newly minted graduate, ready to go home, turn over old stones, expose worms, take charge. In my leather valise, between tissue paper, I'd held the embossed document which had hired me to be sub-sub-prefect.

In my student years before that first return, I had successfully suppressed homesickness until my first impatient step onto that shuttle. On the train, I smelled the Bistronne onions which had journeyed north in the burlap sacks of all the villagers jostling by me, disembarking. With their harsh laughter and sunburnt round heads, their baggage banging against their legs, these provincials struck me as pitiful, their onions serving as passport, enabling them to sell in the haute Paris market-stalls. And yet our onion scent stung. I too was a child of the Bistronne.

The second return to Finier had been in July 1960, long after the war. My doctor friend had performed some minor surgery on my face in his Swiss clinic, to ensure that anyone *offended* by my return could pretend not to recognize me. Back then, his was an experimental clinic, his breed of surgery really quite primitive. Nonetheless, I had enjoyed the laughing gas, only disappointed that my doctor friend could not erase the sneer left on me by that long-ago barber of Milazzo. Mostly, however, I'd appreciated the relative artistry of my friend, along with the fact that no gangrene had set in. For all those postwar years, I'd lived out versions of myself, more than a card deck of names, having dwelled in so many small towns in France and elsewhere that it remains hard for me to keep track of each biography. The sole constancy in this particularly active period was my robustness, which was twinned during the similarly active and mobile period following my second return to Finier. Perhaps these two epochs, along with the pendulum, have most aided my singular longevity. Before my second return, any given year could have seen me doing all of the following: milking goats, clerking in any variety of small forgotten dusty places, ushering theater patrons, shining shoes, selling antiques. Some of my old associates from my time at the prefecture, however dispersed, retained the habit of *looking out for me*. This string of connections, radiating outward, finally helped me find something which I hoped would be my terminal employment—I returned to Finier's prefecture as a different man named Roland Molton, janitor of the prefecture. On my belt I bore keys to all doors and filing cabinets, and could walk ignored down halls where once my whistle had raised a wake of power, while enjoying the great, private joke of being a sheep disguised among wolves. Once, in those same halls, underlings had made nonsensical chitchat with me about the weather, laughing politely after any anecdote I told. *Very good, sir.* In this second, albeit brief, Finier era, I was Roland Molton, swabber of halls, a janitor forced to smile at each of the unfunny jokes, however infrequent, made by the new prefect, Gilbert Galtimer, a tone-deaf man lacking any clue about the past.

At the start of my third return to Finier, I'd wanted to choose a name possessing greater weight than all my previous aliases. I hit upon Raoul Tavelle: *Raoul* bore a desirable moral authority, what with its various connotations, and *Tavelle* had the fine word-pleasure of meaning, in various dialects, either *your city* or *your old man*. In this most recent fugitive period, before that crummy Paris jail with its fuzz and rats, its guards and routine cleanings, I had of course cycled through names, all of which had held their own private sound-magic for me: I'd been Vincent de Mirepoix during my long Paris period, Rodolphe Honsecker in Buenos Aires, François Lespinau in Barcelona, Jacques Montluc in Provence, and most recently David Modine. There were other names, true, but why should they hinder the futures of those associated with me while I lived under those aliases? Why should my names clutter anyone else's life? I have no interest anymore in leaving such a wide wake behind me.

WHAT STRUCK ME as I approached Finier was how unnecessary I'd become to the life of the town. In contrast to the permanent dereliction of Bomont, in Finier you could practically scent change from the cobblestones up—a bland rubbery smell, hygienic, not at all the old perfume of Finier, our fine-tuned mélange of cigars and turpentine, hatters' glue, mouse fur, spilled wine, mold-veined cheese. The new soulless change, of course, was not my doing. Once, far too long ago, I'd considered myself practically master of the town and then, for a brief spell, I'd been the town's janitor (while now I was merely the town's parentheses).

Not only did the town smell clean, ammoniated, there were no men playing boule. Zero. I'd begun listening for them as I'd descended the old station road, unable to quell my longing. The fading voice from the train station saying *attention, attention* had a plummy accent which halfway soothed me. But no boule-players, not yet. Had I been able to hear their cackle, the crack of their mallets, I would've known without a doubt that Finier could take me in a last time, embrace Emile Poulquet, a prodigal and not wholly errant lover. There'd be a chance of redemption.

I stared across one of our two rivers, rivers which accomplished many things and dared you to do the same. They defined the town, as necessary to its guts as to its contour, rivers which, on many past Augusts, had been fast and impressive, spinning whitely over rocks. Their course had been echoed by the town wall's almondine design, a great medieval perimeter, though for many years now, all that was left of that wall was a remnant crumbled near where cheese-makers and booksellers used to congregate on Fridays. And all that was left of the river Nodaire at this point in the summer was a shallow, oily flow.

"You look the same," I whispered to the town, more as reassurance to myself. I cut in over the bridge to town, seeing the familiar lion-faced flags flying from the Hotel Fauret, the bulge of its lemon-hued restaurant set out on stilts, but still without hearing any boule-players. After the bridge, to my dismay, I found two new tourist photo shops, a pharmacy advertising, as if after a harvest, a seasonal sale on medications (FIFTY PERCENT OFF ANTIDEPRESSANTS WITH NEW GOVERNMENT COUPONS!) and one new bakery, a needless addition if the bakery I'd favored still survived. It was Saturday afternoon, an hour when shopkeepers used to linger at home over the cheese course and the Moroccans in the outflanking government apartments used to slumber, but still, the ghostliness of the town made me shiver.

Never had I felt so criminal as on this third return to Finier. Such a solitary return. It would have felt better to be saluted by someone, anyone, but all windows were shuttered. As I continued on, shoes loud on the cobblestones, only my climbing offered the thinnest of illusions, that our mansard roofs leaned toward me as if in consolation. It was then that I started to truly mourn the absence of the boule-players. Give me just a few men wasting time over a hard heavy ball and a set of markers, I would have been happy. Not that I had ever played with them; I had never understood how to belong to the boule-players. I merely watched, as others did, often ending up in a makeshift team of spectators. As I neared the small southern square where the majority of players used to congregate, certainly on a Saturday afternoon, I still heard nothing. They used to stand there, no matter the excuses they had to give their families, old men and young challengers, their heights and girths already a visual point of dispute.

All wearing our bistronnaise, a cap owing dual allegiance to both the beret and the sailor's cap, the bistronnaise as typical of our region as our sweaters, made from our sheep and patched by our women. Soon after lunch the boule-players began their pretense—that the game required a degree of serious dedication—when what the men in the square really had come to do was bicker. They could spend their lives bickering in guttural tones because their arguments, in form and content, grasped at something of the eternal, all their topics revolving around lack. Territory, the shade a tree made over another's property, crop seasons, the noise of a neighbor's poultry, what is mine versus what is yours. If a laugh rang out, it was tinged with malice, each laugher assured of his place in the scheme of lack, each assured of rightness. It was understood—we all understood—that the world beyond the game was unfair. Also understood was that each man had many selves: the peasant self and the regal self, the tribal self and the martyred boule-player. So there was no excuse for the disappearance of our players, because their absence made the town ugly and Finier used to know how to treasure beauty.

It is also true that our beauty has always lacked the bold spontaneous risk you'd see in, say, the shadow of an adolescent blundering toward his new love, or the speed of a shadow beneath a dancer's slipper, pirouetting over a lit stage. Rather, we've had the beauty you might find in the crevices of a tight fist, or, under a bench, a shadow which extends itself from a fixed position, belatedly, at day's end. In Finier, our only generous beauty used to come from the mountains or if you listened to the endless looping arguments of the boule-players, and this beauty had vanished.

"You're peaceful now?" I asked the phantoms, wishing to badger just one. If I squinted my eyes, I could practically see the men arrayed around the square, frowning until their laughter broke out, a result of that Finier cocktail of hard cider, mountain air, inwardness. People used to tell me that though I'd been born in Couzac, and hence wasn't truly a native son of Finier, I'd also possessed the Finier laugh. You live here long enough and it is easy to swallow this laughter about lack. You always sense greater abundance beyond the mountains and the fact turns troublesome, it starts to stick in your gullet and you laugh around this lack. Lack is the horizon and abundance is where men fall off the edge of Paris.

I had felt this way as a young man, before I'd left for my studies in Paris. Much later in life, I understood why in Finier storekeepers never touch your hand as they give you change or take your coins. If a Finier man or woman is too personal when dealing with money, it admits to our lack.

And because people generally prefer to avoid the personal, a town the middling size of Finier has its advantages. In towns like this, where old men bicker, where no one touches your hand unless required, one could be a leopard-spotted fugitive and still pass easily in a crowd—the bickering occupies everyone that much.

I was passing the shuttered street where I'd lived in the years when I'd been not merely a rising star in the prefecture but its firmament. It was here that I'd had a dalliance with a jewish lady, one who'd helped me decorate my apartment. Here she'd tried to get me to leave my bachelor existence behind. Once I'd waited for her in my bare kitchen, recalling her slim throat, how lovely it was, back when she was still known to me only as the young lady from the notions store. On my second return to Finier, as janitor Roland Molton, I had resolved to forget the lady I call Natalie.

Now, unfortunately, on my third return, this internal prohibition seemed to have collapsed. As I walked in, I was suddenly troubled by forgetfulness in general, unable to recall whether or not I had, in my second brief period as janitor, been *bothered* by Natalie's absence from Finier. Further, for the life of me, I could not remember what sort of store had replaced hers. In my season of mops and brooms, had I tried to find out anything more than I already knew about her fate? It seemed that for too many years I'd lived as if in a fog, so obsessed with identity that disguise alone had crafted my internal landscape.

How much easier to remember, in relation to that brief second return, the keys I'd worn, their jangle off my beltloop, the quick but ineradicable degrees which had led me to became Mister Molton, janitor of the prefecture. It had hardly been the world's most humiliating position. I could have stayed on. I'd loved to pity the new prefect Galtimer, with his Bavarian chin and dandruff-specked coat, the camphorous despair hovering in his office. Galtimer had a voice everyone praised, saying about him that he could have sung opera had it not been for his administrative talents. Meanwhile, he was stricken with what must have been chronic catarrh, constantly coughing up awful memoranda from his insides. Further, he lacked all capacity to recognize the man who brought him coffee. To him, I was an underling of the genus eternus, the fellow carrying in his early-morning tray. Late at night, I mopped the prefecture's halls using what had been recommended, diluted peppermint oil larded with animal-fat soap. Occasionally, when alone at night, I had the opportunity to search in the archives and cut into blunt childish little figures, ring-around-the-rosy shapes, party decorations or confetti, certain records of my era which had escaped being seized by the central courts. All the while, Galtimer never cared to guess what had led me to the moment where I served him. Never once in his wispy-haired head did he consider asking who my family was, or where I was from; never did he dream that the shuffling man I'd become had arisen from the prefectorial species.

He would not have fathomed, such is the benefit of his generation—born too late, anti-feudal but lacking all the old restraints, with its slippery hierarchies and segregations far more insidious than my own—how as prefect I myself had been considered an innovator. He would never know it was I, for example, who'd devised the morning coffee ritual, my ensuring of the happiness of all who worked in the exquisite prefecture.

WHILE PLACING Galtimer's cup on his desk, studying his scalp pattern, hearing his quick thanks, I would feel a terrible irony strike me, the kind I say lawyers these days possess. From firsthand experience, I testify that such irony hides violence. Day after day, every pore in me screamed as I stood by, replacing Galtimer's empty dirtied cup with a full one. What I imagined was something that could never take place in the physical realm—were Galtimer a peg, I would easily screw him down into the seat, one also squeaky during my time. It was a wooden rolling chair with a generous indent for the back of whomever occupied and then grew large in the job.

This seething was almost worse than my proximity to Arianne.

During one of the morning rituals, unable to control the furies, I happened to make the comment to him: "It's a terrible chair, isn't it?" He, barely looking at me, history wholly on his side, confirmed this. Suddenly all I wanted was for him to recognize me, if at an oblique angle. "I don't find it that comfortable," I added.

This was an error, an error beyond sarcasm. I immediately realized my mistake. From the way that Galtimer's brows shot up and his eyes squinted into two hawks, I saw the question behind the scrutiny. Did I amuse myself in the off-hours rolling back and forth in his chair before all the locked cabinets?

"I am speaking visually, sir," I said, before retreating back. "Not that I would know how your chair feels. To one who might sit in it."

Naturally, at a certain point, I'd taken a look at Galtimer's tedious correspondence, filed neatly within his locked cabinets, and had found the man to be stultifyingly proper. He paid such careful attention to etiquette, he would have made an awful opera singer. Underneath, you could see he was the kind of man scared to wonder whether he'd ordered the life that had been served up to him. That much was clear. But better that he should have been a failed opera singer in Paris than what he was, a line-obeying prefect in Finier with the habit of ignoring Emile Poulquet.

Having read Galtimer's correspondence, I could almost feel myself in his bulk, the new appointee to the prefecture of Finier, scared to behave improperly.

"Glad you like the chair," he answered, though this didn't make sense.

On my way out, I smiled at his big cherub face. "I don't," I said.

Though Galtimer was an awful cross to bear, at least Emile Poulquet had a solace. Had I not had to read the paper the day the Allies rolled into Paris, had I not been forced to flee for several months of repose at a friend's deer park, had the mania for correcting the past not started with the force of a witch-hunt, had I not had to undergo surgery to disguise me almost from myself, had I not had to spend years incognito—well, though that is a plummeting pile of *hads*, conceivably I might have been occupying the very chair Galtimer did. Or I would be considering taking a late retirement, and Galtimer would be exerting every brand of sycophancy to gain inside knowledge of our workings. Once I'd possessed a power like Galtimer's, greater than his perhaps, more like that which monks had held over their novitiates centuries earlier, in the very same halls. These days, people don't like to admit their need to cling together under the umbrella of hierarchy. Or let me correct that by saying that modern people are masked snobs, individuals whose hierarchy is maintained within, an endoskeleton safe from the threats of the outside world. I had all these consoling thoughts while acting as Finier's janitor. Unfortunately, being Roland would prove an untenable satisfaction.

For one thing, the alcoholic concierge who used to work the Hotel Fauret's night shift appeared not only to suspect my wartime identity but also seemed keen on making it public. As she left work in the early mornings, on the streets, she would dog my heels—an amateur historian and professional pest—shouting out *Emile Poulquet!* to which I never turned my head. But more significantly, I could not last more than some six weeks as janitor, because it was far too hard on me to be so close to Arianne with such a unilateral regard, the lady not once showing any recognition of me.

THIS THIRD TIME I entered Finier, disguised by the iterations of surgery on my face, surgeries performed in unidentical triplicate upon my face, one erasure over another, I actually was my most naked self, stripped of designs on the prefecture. A native son, a fugitive with a purpose, if my purpose had sprouted a few branches. Originally, I'd meant the return to Finier as a way to find an easy abode. Later, I'd thought to give Arianne my last will and testament. Yet now, as I walked in, I thought that perhaps I should try to find something of Natalie, and by this lay everything, finally, all of it to rest. Let that whole cloud not continue to master me.

After overhearing the police inspectors in the station café, after the little roadside problem with the American, easily I might have boarded a train and continued on to Barcelona. Easily I might have settled into some fleabag wharfside residence, made friends with a whore, for instance, shared a bottle and spent my remaining days slouching on a central bench, judging the relative merits of pigeons versus street performers. I'd performed similar functions at various periods, and had found it a not-bad existence, doing such things as collecting coins for street musicians playing on cathedral stairs. But Finier's magic had lured me, and my disguise kept me safe enough that reentry was simple enough, requiring me merely to hunch a bit, hat pulled down.

ELEVEN

In the café on Finier's main square, just before the television started to show pictures of me, it was playing clips of what I believe would be classified as American action films, the volume down low. There were karate geniuses and skyscraper-vaulting fiends. Also pregnant ladies clinging to stalwart men, knives brandished through broken windows.

In between, commentators stitched the whole mess together by speaking tranquilly out from under unimpeachable hairdos. Without fully thinking things through, I found a seat for myself at my old favorite table by the small gas fireplace. It was not difficult for me to hide in the obscurity, stooped over a cognac, watching the television play out its footage.

During my second period in Finier, I'd favored this café, Café de la Place. I'd liked it partly because it made me feel I was out in the open, a man like any man, a janitor at the prefecture, gainfully employed, possessing every right to drink across from my place of employment. And partly because I'd liked the fellow who had owned it,

Louis, evidently now replaced by a new owner, Olivier, as deft a cafetier in his own way.

In that brief janitorial period, if officials did happen to recognize my face, disguised by the broken nose, the thigh-meat paddings and z-shaped sutures, courtesy of my doctor friend's Swiss clinic, none let on. Perhaps a few may have recognized me but they wisely stayed silent. They let me play out being good old Roland the janitor. It was also true that once we all left the walls of the prefecture, no one ever made too big a show of saying good evening to me.

Content to be back, or as content as could be, I sat in the bosom of the café, enjoying the cognac's warmth. Perhaps it turned my head a bit, drinking on an empty stomach, because when the television moved to a new subject, I did not feel fully surprised. The television was playing my memories in a way I'd never quite seen, and this was just the introduction. Immediately, a newly unimpeachable commentator came out to jabber before a handsome wall of books.

After he was done, the special news program began, which seemed to concern details of my past career. A man at the bar shouted to the cafetier to turn the sound up. So I heard for the first time a report on what the newsman kept calling my flight from justice. The disembodied male voice spoke of the chaos at the Paris court where, had I not been released that third week of June, I would surely have been condemned. Another mentioned the fact that I had failed to appear at Friday's hearing—back in the Marais, I'd predicted there'd be another hearing, hadn't I?—to determine whether my case could go ahead, on the basis of documents initially recused from the court.

Is Poulquet on the loose? the voice asked, so false that one could practically hear behind it the rustle of a toupee being adjusted, while a cameraman resorted to the same shot of the well-columned Cour de Cassation, the same angle they all liked, panning hallways I had known so recently. Of course the camera showed nothing of the disappointed judge, quite obviously a man thirsting for my blood. Nor did it reveal the beatific moments when Odile and Arianne had testified on my behalf, nor the oddness of Izzy, hidden by a partition, trying to doom me. No, instead, in front of the court, the cameraman now turned to film the contemporary group I had just escaped, its members amassed with yellow stars on their lapels, teeth bared for reparations and justice, now behaving with an unusual aplomb, the respect of stillness. I soon saw why. In front of them stood the famous pair, the mother-and-daughter lawyers who finished each other's sentences. The ironic daughter lawyer had just said there was a slim chance that, on seeing this footage, Emile Poulquet might feel guilty enough to make a public confession, identify himself, show up at the court.

He may have gotten through our fingers, she added, but he might choose to return.

"Right," I laughed to myself, making a fellow café dweller, a man who'd slid into the next table while I hadn't been looking, a man somewhat carbuncular himself, nonetheless take a peek at me.

Who had time for distraction? Seeing the two ladies again was like receiving a letter from a difficult friend. How well I knew their wailing voices, even if what they said was abhorrent.

"You like this café?" the carbuncular man suddenly asked me, looking out from the recesses of a lowslung bistronnaise. What I mainly saw was the tetragonal jaw, spittle stringing from one corner of the mouth.

"It suits me," I said, hunching lower, unable to keep myself from watching the two ladies on television. Both were owners of unusually sturdy mounds of brown hair, tufted and arranged to make one see them as figures of seduction. But also as persons of control, authority, redemption. Depending on whether you looked at them through your left eye or your right, which I experimented with, you could practically see them in a medieval painting. They would play every single role—queen, king, virgin, martyr, infidel, avenger.

"I actually hate cafés where the television takes over everything, you know?" the carbuncular man said, his accent unsettling, thick with our bistronnaise gargle.

"Sometimes it's better than at other times," I said, turning away to make my point. I could not stop watching.

For all her self-righteousness, most of the time the daughter lawyer did come off as a paragon of virtue. Not medieval, rather, but as if she'd borrowed her ovaline youthful face from some of those old figures-in-landscapes of Corot. Her face so French and yet she was sheer hypocrisy.

WHEN I'D BEEN held in that awful jail before this most recent time in court, when those lawyer ladies had been my spectral window out into the *eyes of the world upon the Poulquet case,* as the newspeople kept saying, when they'd been beamed in nightly, I'd wanted to pull their masks off them. That was the urge. And when I'd finally stood near the daughter lawyer in court, her little shameless whisper hadn't helped matters.

"You're from Toulouse, right?" said the dark-skinned man nearby. "Mind if I?" He came to sit at my table so that I had to look over his unruly head to see the television.

"I'm sorry," I said. Should I move tables? Or would this cause more of a scene? "I've been sick. You probably don't want to breathe my germs."

"That's okay," said the man, laughing broadly. "I take all vermin as friends. You're interested in that television, aren't you?"

"Sometimes," I said.

"Pretty interested, huh? Pretty fucking interested?"

I looked up at the bar, where the cafetier was occupied.

My new tablemate let out his sawing laugh. He waved at me, hands strangely young-looking yet as bulky as the rest of him. "Don't get scared, I'm safe." And, fortunately or not, he fell to watching the television with me.

The problem was how spellbinding the two lawyers were, and perhaps this is the problem of television. You look upon its actors all you want. No matter how much you look, its subjects are caught, as much as I once was, in a self-prescribed duty to *present the hard facts,* to live on the unilateral side of rightness, while the screen is forever pliant and gullible, a silly lover accepting all currencies. You watch with a shrinking sense of your own importance: those who appear on television know their calling and what is wrong with you, watching them? Sad-happiness, gloating, Schadenfreude: whatever you call it, the two lawyers possessed that gloating gene in spades. Also, because they triumphed at peculiar facts, their public statements always composed of a dripping irony, I was fairly sure the daughter had crafted them, and thought it strange that no one else ever noted the violence in their irony.

"The one on the right's a real looker, don't you think?" the man asked me, more companionable.

"She's good enough," I said.

"She'd never have the time of day for someone like me, don't you think?" he asked.

"Maybe." I didn't want to commit, nor did I want to make a scene. He was big and squarish but probably remained, after all, a harmless specimen.

His tongue lolled in one corner of his mouth like a lazy beast and then came to action again. "You're agreeing then?"

"It might be worth a try," I said, mild but watchful. "Why not?"

"Yeah, but Paris," he said. He winced, pulling one of his legs so it torqued at a strange angle to the table, his boot near the tabletop. "How we getting to Paris?"

The two lawyer-scourge ladies in their statements favored certain facts about my case, especially that when the police laid hands on me recently, I was in the middle of a tango lesson in an outer suburb of Buenos Aires. They loved this tango idea, and so the French press also came to cherish this fact. All of them were childlike, their favorite occupation being to exile me to some Elba of otherness, loving to make me into a child, a silly shameful child Poulquet wearing a polka-dot hat, one which makes the adults laugh all the more shame into the child. They depicted me as having had, during the war, such an enunciated disdain against foreigners coming into France. And now, haha, here is that Nazi Poulquet, the insult far from accurate. Here that old racist Vichy bastard had been forced to hide in a Latin American country, where he'd been compelled to take up dancing.

VICHY'S POULQUET LOVES TANGO, the headlines had simpered.

They trafficked in stereotypes! What they all failed to realize was that it was my love for humanity which had brought me to tango. Would they prefer for me to have been found in some remote misanthropic mountain abbey begging for sheep milk? But then there would be no delectable news for them. Or perhaps they would have preferred me to be a mute penitent, bartering for beads? Blessing peasants, fixing leather sandal soles. But I made no pretense in my fugitive life: I have never pretended to be greater than what I am.

"We could take the quick train to Paris?" said the carbuncular man. "Or a night train."

"A brilliant thought," I said. "Maybe some other time."

"I'm serious, though," and he reached out to take my hands. "You probably never got enough adventure in your life." He smelled, strangely, of foreign tobacco, and I pulled away. "Forgive me," he said. "I'm the kind gets excited when an idea comes."

"Don't worry," I said. "I'd just like to watch a little more."

Apart from the work done on my face, I have exercised the bare minimum of self-disguise. I never imposed on anyone a superior résumé. Rather, I have disparaged myself. I have claimed at various times to have had a Spanish mother, an Irish aunt, a Belgian father, even an American cousin. I have given myself all sorts of aquarelle origins.

But I have never presented myself as superior. Not spiritually superior, not intellectually superior, not even by dint of the richness of the French culture which has so lifted our nation above all others, giving us a prospect view, lending us insight into all other cultures, such as those of the noble American Indians.

"I bet you're the kind likes more skinny nervous girls like the one at the bar," the man said.

"I'm a widower," I lied. "Pardon me," I said, rising to go to the men's room.

Through the door, I heard the television continue, and when I returned, my companion had left his seat, which was fortunate: I lacked all power to have had him removed.

■ ■ ■

TO EXPLAIN THE mystery of Emile Poulquet, the television was presenting wartime footage with the important subtitle SHOT AT LIBERATION. There were sunken-eyed skeletons stirring about like crushed insects on straw mats in the internment camps. Then there were more talking heads who were experts on me and my era. Clearly my era had passed. Now I was living in the era of experts about my era. The experts were even worse than the mother-and-daughter lawyers. Because these experts robbed me of my past—they practically brandished titles to my era. They knew more about my era than I could ever hope to know. They were multiple and confident, could speak from the milieu of easy gains.

Young and untouched, old and wizened, all of them intoned from the succor of their safe libraries, containing such beautiful leather-bound books. One could only presume their books were not vacant sets. These newly minted experts spoke with knowledge and their knowledge was not nothing. It was something. I was the nothing. I sat in a café watching them, forced to speak with lowlifes. I was the fish swimming outside of the correct bowl. I knew them from one another's footnotes in their many expert books, which I had often tried to read, trying to understand my life in retrospect. Although no expert cared whether I read their books; to such people, I was the real footnote. No matter how much knowledge I might have of my era, I was condemned to live outside the bowl made by the specialists and their libraries. I would love to be asked to tea by an expert, to sit expectantly, browsing in one of their safe, beautiful libraries, without fearing for my head, yet this was impossible. The books and the experts rejected me in all my strange and messy current self, preferring me as a story, their unicorn fable and monster. They would not really wish to meet me.

This is why so many fugitives, negated, try to live in nondescript fashion but fail. In my experience, fugitives end up asserting the value of their own beliefs, carving out a flamboyant, unmoored era unto itself, a life apart from the stingy stories of the authorities.

Certain fugitives, as did Honsecker in Buenos Aires (whose identity I assumed when I arrived there), specialize in rare treatises, such as on medieval antisemitism. They trump the experts by going several roots deeper. They befriend fringe experts, develop their own theories and skills, make their lives into algebraic proofs, all to establish that they are not confined to an era, as the experts are, but are rather from one overarching era capable of gulping all time and expertise.

And the fugitives' fancy habits, their caviar on toast points on purloined heirloom silver, prove their carnality. The caviar claims that they too have flesh and presence. They too can still grip what is of this moment, what is contemporary, urgent, of the passions, fleeting. We all have some kind of right to belong to life, even if our version of it ends up possessing a morality equivalent to that of a fishbowl: aggressive yet arbitrary, transparent and eternally replaceable.

I WATCHED the television and the experts. But what I was really watching was how the experts lived in places where they were probably called to dinner at regular times. They lived in places where neighbors greeted them with formulas of politeness. They had places where their children were allowed to play with other people's children. They could conjecture with persuasiveness about my lifelong pattern of ambition and escape, as if they weren't prone to the same pattern themselves. Every now and then, between experts, the television showed pictures of my young self, just before a liver crisis (the officially stated cause for my promotion) had bumped me up from being sub-sub-prefect to prefect.

Forgive the vanity, but what startled me was the contrast between the young person I remembered myself being and the actual person in the photos, as if I had already been in disguise to myself.

There was, for example, Emile Poulquet looking not exactly ruthless but determined, as if an important conscript, a patriot and hero. Here, on a dais, I bowed my head with a good measure of self-respect. There I looked out at a crowd from a platform. Generally, I was flanked by other people of significance. There were streamlined men in suits, a few ladies with strong chins. Often my neighbors were people of forthright brow, possessing motivation and drive, many of them among the more valuable personages to have passed through Finier and our region of La Bistronne.

The television's sound was dialed too high—the stirring music played as a backdrop came out like a whiny, distorted Wagnerian march. This was not such a terrible fault. I could not hear the commentators' words any longer but I watched because it was impossible not to watch. These were talking heads in their important libraries.

Yet I knew not to seem too avid. Therefore, I scrutinized the beautiful scratchings in the zinc table I sat at, the zinc a palimpsest, scratched so many times by all the habitués who had slid coffee cups or ashtrays closer, the tabletop now possessing the shattered beauty of fire. But it was hard to stay fixated on zinc, to avoid looking up at the television where my own face sneered back.

To dodge having to look at my younger self, I got up to order a café au lait, though I had ordered the cognac before this. And one should never have the coffee after the cognac: this is the wrong sequence, like locking before loading, impossible to accomplish even with the most unsafe rifle. My pendulum practically buzzed in my pocket, protesting the wrongness, though it was not the most opportune moment for me to take it out for a quick consult.

I told myself the order of things didn't matter. All was possible and fluid. I then managed to order and retrieve the au lait without fully meeting the cafetier's eyes. While waiting at the bar, I found a bit of good fortune awaiting me in my pocket: the forgotten last of the pills from my friend, a bit of freeze-dried alcohol, wrapped in tinfoil, the last of the bounty bequeathed me. I popped the acrid thing in my mouth without so much as a how-do-you-do, even without water, wanting it to start work immediately.

RETURNED TO MY SPOT in the back of Olivier's café, I found the au lait an incredible treat, my first real nourishment since morning in Bomont. What comes at the end of the cup is always the best, but one must be careful not to slurp or otherwise call attention. I bent over the cup, hat still on, mainly remarking to myself about Olivier. An admirable café man, as good in his way as Louis had been.

You could tell no guilt had ever besmirched Olivier's professional practices, the fellow expert at whipping his rag smartly along the top of the counter, his neck straining up out of the high-collared shirt and pinstriped vest. A man resembling a well-trained circus seal, both comfortable in his skin and ready to serve, energetic and ageless, connected to the zinc counters and his customers by invisible lines, lacking the false haughtiness you'd find in the equivalent cafetier up north. He communicated to his wife with glances, a solid lady with curls framing her face who stood behind the vitrine making bar sandwiches, her skin a thick silent layer laid over the usual human impulses. She must have earned from life a pair of suffering dark eyes. When she looked over the vitrine just once at me, I cringed, thinking it was the Look.

Though I doubted anyone could have recognized me, given my current disfigurement, it was still true that in the provinces, despite all the intervening years, you could never predict on which side of the war people would fall.

Was I once Emile Poulquet? the Look asked.

But the wife of the cafetier gave me no special look. Instead, she was just taking me in to assess the holding capacity of her café. There were to be some new arrivals.

TWELVE

Out in the square, a group of people was amassing. At first I took it to be a rather unusual tourist group. Then I realized this must be the commencement of activities, organized presumably by Arianne, the reunion of refugees toward which the American had been rushing.

I saw them, like a bad dream recurring, the refugees returning to town, now with lippy smiles and a desperation to show how flush with success they were. How untouched by the years, good or bad. They wore coats which reminded me of the stripings and spottings of fish dredged up from the sea, and more of these fish now flopped onto the plaza, shivering despite the brightness of the afternoon, dregs coming in droves, schools, movements. Shouldn't their survival be proof that I alone could not have been such a monster?

Those who came clearly wanted to triumph over the past, with as much vengeance as history had shown them, wanting to play slave-master over their past selves who'd been well herded.

■ ■ ■

I REMEMBERED from my young schooling how Plato had Socrates saying that a just man conforms, in practice, to a just city. Should I have been so singled out, having so married my fortunes to Finier? Our schooling trained us to be bureaucrats; our position as bureaucrats trained us to be obedient to our schooling, and I was obedient to Finier. One was ostensibly free to question anything from an intellectual standpoint, and yet one was also compelled by the nature of the whole system to obey. Any Frenchman trained for the bureaucracy, as I had been, might have done what I did: shouldn't Finier be considered the real culprit?

You might think that with my young face looking out at me from the television, its Wagnerian march playing bass to the café's contralto, I might have felt something like remorse. At the very least, fear. You might think that my whole life stretched and attenuated like putty stuck to a gavel, muffling the sound without delaying the eventual judgment.

"Look at the clown!" one of the men at the bar said, and I flinched. But the man in his long burnoose, maybe a Moroccan, just wanted Olivier to raise the sound on the television even higher.

To his credit, Olivier did not like a loud café and shrugged. "Isn't it better not to offend people who need moderation?" and he smiled in my general direction. Being around Olivier may have endowed me with an unnatural hope: that the Look might not be turned my way here. Could it have been that my little coffee had been poisoned so that I was fantasizing, ready to keel over? Yet anyone would feel safe in Olivier's café. He was an old-style café proprietor, a cafetier who understood what it meant for a customer to come under the auspices of his leadership, and was just now explaining his café manifesto. He spoke almost without moving his lips to a young lady in a fur-trimmed coat, her hair so platinum it looked congealed. A lady who'd been sitting, denim legs twisted around the chairlegs, at a sliver of bar farthest from the solid wife. And to her Olivier boomed out his creed: he supervised his café differently than others do. For this reason, said Olivier, many single women felt safe coming to this café alone, away from the boors who congregated at some of the other cafés in town.

"Because if any man misbehaves," he said, "I myself take him by the ear and throw him out."

To which the young lady shuddered a flirtatious thanks, then smiled a bright recompense at the cafetier's wife. Everyone was interested in compensation around here and in such safe environs I watched the refugees arrive. They greeted each other with various atavisms upon entering the square, with salutes and embraces, laughter.

Some were cheery if unable to hide their bedraggled souls. Most gave the impression of having arrived directly from the train station. Some showed themselves unable to relinquish the refugee habit of overwrapping valises in tape and twine. One held a violin case. Few had facial hair. Many emerged from a chartered bus that had chugged up, spitting fumes, to the street north of the square. One of the refugees disturbed me more than the others, a slight woman with dark curly hair, made smaller by the inappropriately thick woolen jacket she wore, what we used to call a canadienne: an apparition soon obscured by the mass of others. I moved one seat closer to the window to study their greetings. From my perch in the café, I saw a thin man and woman walking empty-handed but as if paralyzed until I realized their tears were what loaded them down. Now this pair entered Olivier's café with tentative ownership. They said they wanted a quick pick-me-up, speaking like stooped and ancient shuffleboard players. Others shoved past, explaining they needed an aperitif at the bar before pushing off.

I saw the thin man look into the woman's eyes, counseling her to get some rest. He then showed off his shoes, extending his foot and saying: A far cry from the day when we had to paste rubber tubing on the heels so no one could hear our escape, eh? She then swallowed her drink as if it were cough syrup, and he looked away as if she were relieving herself. Once she was done, he kissed her goodbye, led her to the door, staying on to down a drink in similar manner, albeit privately.

A few women announced where they were quartered, listing various hotels and rooms, making a show out of reading aloud. They hoisted their itineraries like winning lottery tickets and victory flags, slips of paper showing how well they had controlled their postwar lives. I hated their banal certainty; at the same time, I begrudged them their pride, how these women made it seem that good fate could rest in little slips and reunions of refugees. All of it organized for them and their permanently high status, so much so that I felt compelled to recall a certain story. Years ago in Paris I'd met a whiskery, garrulous man, a survivor of the concentration camps, whose age and speech style alone could have made him my grandfather. Though ignorant of my identity, perhaps the fellow had sensed my interest in the topic of war, because after only one bottle of wine the fellow confessed, in a tone carrying the harshness of a private self-condemnation: *Understand, it is not always the best people who survive.* Could he have guessed how his words would help ease the pressure on a man who would still endure all too many years as a fugitive?

IN THE CORNER of the square, opposite the café, the American had positioned himself. He seemed to be interviewing a small clump of refugees, his camera light beaming straight into their eyes. They spoke into it before tottering away as if top-heavy with memory. He was a pure professional, unhampered. I had suspected we would meet again in Finier, and though I didn't want his camera to address its ministrations toward me, I was safe for now, able to watch him bring survivors into his camera's trap, its hypothesis and conclusion neatly joined.

New arrivals coming off the bus shoved into the café with greater confidence, more casual, needing less to put a fearless face on things as their very beings shrieked valor. Frank and well-fed, wearing the brighter colors of another nation, brighter than I would have seen on any of them during the war. Of course I did not recognize any. They had been names, unknown, and so many had been children during the years of my service.

This latter group spoke that American cowboy French and moved through the crowd like energetic salesmen, trying to pick through the years to recognize someone they might have known. Some shouted from one wall of the café out into the square; a few shouted back. One actually leaned over my head through the open window, smelling of mothballs and victory, screeching *hello, hello!* into the café, and bad as it is to admit, I could not hide my cowering.

"Sorry," the screecher said to me. "One gets excited."

"Of course," I murmured. But I will be honest and say here that seeing these people filled me with the worst claustrophobia I've ever known, one no pill could counteract. Because these people did not stop. The curly-haired woman in the canadienne had vanished, while others kept cramming into the café, well-fed or defeated, cheery or choked-up, overscented with aftershave, lavender, thyme oil. A few smelled to me like a hospital's combination of ethyl alcohol and disinfectant. You'd think none had rid themselves of the taste for small, crowded places.

They probably also liked the Frenchness of the place, having returned to find Frenchness eternally awaiting them. They liked the zinc bar and the comradely assurance of Olivier, Olivier nodding professionally to each visitor to his café, their swelling numbers speeding his movements, his quid-pro-quo nod as if each customer were a quantifiable investment, about to commence a lifelong habit of drinking coffee under his roof and no one else's.

Some refugees commandeered a big table in the center of the café, drawing forth chairs and side-tables, legs screeching on the tiles. One said loudly *you still can't believe what could happen here*, waving around at the café's civilized interior. In short, they showed little of that refinement which usually marks a group of northern French. Had Arianne handpicked these rustic southern prodigals?

AND THOUGH I didn't realize it at first, one of the refugees presented, as you will understand, a terrific problem, one I probably would not have been able to countenance had I not found the last of the freeze-dried alcohol pills. He'd come into the café when I'd been distracted and now appeared to lead a round of reminiscences, wearing goggle-like sunglasses so broad and dark they made him into an aviator of the interior. My old friend Izzy right there in the flesh, Israel Horwitz Lisson.

Someone whose wartime fate I could have prevented but did not; a name I might have held back from the detention camps; a name I might have kept from becoming inscribed with the epithet that wipes the slate clean for everyone. A survivor, whose name I'd forgotten for many years. Yes, conveniently forgotten. As a child, I'd already had the life sentence thrust upon me regarding how grateful I was supposed to remain to him—his backbone, comradeliness, et cetera. And gratitude as a life sentence makes for a terrible prison. Now I had the mischance to look upon my friend, weathered and grayed, a man who had *come from abroad* only a few weeks earlier, a month earlier, with the *express purpose* of testifying against me, from his safe portico above the Paris court. Perhaps I should have made a bolt for the café door, as the law of survival demanded, but his blindness, combined with curiosity or the last of the pills freeze-drying my bloodstream, made me want to stay.

Izzy was still a handsome man, or at least stately, do I have to admit as much? His hair tamed from its former brambles-and-bushes look, yet the same broad nose threatened to engulf the face, the same soup-warmer lips dominated. Still a Frenchman only in name, as I'd thought once while looking at him, having felt the advantage of not being born a jew.

Izzy now an old man but not undignified, his voice carrying a remnant of its former boom, if just a bit cracked and feathery at the edges, all of which conspired to make it all the more genteel.

YOU COULD SAY he'd stuck with me through thick and thin until, as I saw it, his own guilt got the better of him. When Izzy had determined to remake himself as a clerk, he had once dined with me at my Bordeaux mentor's house, Honsecker's seaside retreat. This was during the time that our leaders were approaching a certain precipice, forced to make certain choices. It was my guess that recently Izzy may have been the one to lead them toward Honsecker's mansion in Buenos Aires, Izzy smart enough to figure out that when my situation grew the most dire, I might run for the villa of my late old mentor in

Buenos Aires, where the authorities sniffed me out, sheltered by Honsecker's widow.

I put the pieces together, yet the question remains: despite my mistakes, why would someone turn against an old friend after all these years? Could we not have gone our separate ways?

He was speaking French with a broad American accent, speaking of life in America with the blandness of those with nothing to hide, quietly but with enough volume that anyone in that café could have heard. Banality, banality, I told myself, trying not to hear. A wife had died and he had two grown kids. O, great banality. He'd once been what he called a character actor in Hollywood but had most recently been in a profession I could not have predicted for a blind man: real estate. You could see he was flush with a particular American success but also that a worm had eaten out his innards. Even without his testimony against me, my guess was that he might have liked me to rot in jail, turning dry and pocked as an old lemon peel. He probably would have liked me to pray for the embrace of either the guillotine or his religion. Which fate would have been worse? I could have forgiven him for withholding pardon of me long ago, but how much harder to forgive this figurative blindness, that he'd gone on the attack now, blind to how the war had splintered all of us, leaving some shards bigger than others, with Emile Poulquet, of course, turning out to be one of the smaller shards. Not much left of me after so many years in hiding. With Izzy's understanding of my early life, wouldn't he have known how everyone else had forever possessed more of a sense of themselves upon which to hang, hold, survive?

"They're calling the reunion off," he was telling the other refugees with a quiet charisma. Something about him made people listen. I abhorred Izzy as much as I envied him: he had grown into what he had shown every sign of becoming early on. A sensitive, admirable man. Izzy had *gravity*. "We don't know why yet."

I hid deeper in the shadows. After his first schoolyard bravery, we'd been friends until that summer we were both seventeen, when in different ways we'd both fallen for Arianne at her hotel. Was this latter-day, reconstructed Arianne our first real rupture? Afterward, we'd been friends of convenience, finding apartments together as students in Paris, watching couples on the bridges, so many fingers and thimbles. It was only back in Finier, during the various arrangements that had to be made, at the outset of both my career and the war, that Izzy and I had started to show fissures.

If I were trying to be in the right, I would say he was the one who had betrayed me. However, let me be candid. Even back in our schoolyard days, I was a traitor toward him. When given the opportunity, rare as it was, I would speak of him in a less-than-positive light. I'd long sensed his foreign name gave me an advantage, and each time I'd smeared it, I'd felt a little jolt, which made being Emile Poulquet just a bit more bearable.

A few weeks earlier, during my brief time in that Parisian prison cell, I had created a program of self-rehabilitation, having found a few timeworn ways of repenting, most drawn from the familiar privations of Lent. For several nights running, I made much of my announcement to the prison guard: I wished to forego the usual crust of bread that came with dinner. When the guard showed little surprise at this, I made a different announcement, upping the stakes. I told him I wanted to forego all meals.

"Hunger strike, chief?" the guard asked, bored and stoic.

He was the son of a wartime relic like me, that much he'd relayed, and had said he was staying on mainly to ensure his pension. "Okay, boss," was his usual riposte.

That I'd been bad to Izzy *while still a boy* weighed on me. Then again, when I'd had a chance to alter Izzy's fate, when the lists started to cleanse France, I did not lift a finger in his aid. This, one might say, could have been the arrival of my chance to redeem him or myself, but, as I've said, gratitude had already imposed a life sentence.

I thought my prison discipline, exerted during such a difficult time, had been an original idea. Going hungry could serve as a hair shirt. Hungry, I would feel what they came to know in the internment camps, something of what Izzy had experienced, what all of them felt, including the jewish lady I'd thought I'd cared for, all stomachs burning in camps surrounded by unharvested wheat fields. In penance, I believed, I might yet emerge with my skin clean. One of my friends in

Buenos Aires had been a retired brain scientist who, after every good steak we enjoyed together, would inform me that our neural circuitry linked our sense of hunger to our sense of injustice. I believed that such wiring went back to our ancestral Lascaux cavemen fighting over bison brought back from the kill, cavemen peevish about who got what portion, but whenever I voiced this, my friend would always politely differ, explaining that the sense of injustice could not be an acquired characteristic, but rather merely linked all mammals' genes.

Whatever the case (I still thought our cavemen had influenced us), in the wee hours of my first morning fasting, the prison guard tried to sneak me two servings of the wheat-shaft gruel which was the local staple. He turned eloquent, actually tossed around a few polysyllables, telling me the shafts came from remains which a local farmer's hogs had refused to eat. We had extra that day, why should it go to waste? But this may have been his fabrication. Wherever the gruel came from, I stood staunch, would not accept his unjust attempt to foil my penance. *Okay, boss.* Though I could have eaten his fist and he knew it.

Each time over that first day of my fast, every time my stomach rumbled, I forced myself to think of Izzy, remembering my earliest schoolyard betrayals of him, the most trivial of boyhood slights. For example, that I had bad-mouthed him to the popular Denis, or that I'd gone through inexplicable periods where I'd shunned being seen in public with Izzy. After these episodes, I'd return to being his friend, grateful for his lack of complaint, though his readiness was a mark against him.

What did Izzy see in me? A temperament of mercury, flesh trumping bone, a fellow pariah. Perhaps someone whom, given the schoolyard's pecking order, he could impress, craft in his image.

After my preliminary sacrament of prison hunger was completed, I thought I'd move on to the more difficult question, one that had nothing to do with Izzy. But first I had to cleanse myself of my slights against Izzy—you see I do not say crimes against humanity, that overused phrase, I say *slights against Izzy*, because every slight is personal, every bit of humanity is particular, and to pretend otherwise is to raise the criminal above punishment, to raise him to the lofty status of someone who cannot be prosecuted but by some divinelike dispenser of justice. I laugh when I hear that lawyers' phrase *crimes against humanity*, because I think people who use such a phrase don't admit to their own lifetime of petty and particular slights against their mothers and friends and acquaintances. One commits the worst crime against humanity against one's friend, I say, not against one's unknowable enemy.

I never said I would deliver an account of all this without its contradictions. So it was that I stayed quite fixed to my discipline in prison. Every time my mind flitted elsewhere, I dragged it back to contemplate Izzy. This might seem simplistic, but it felt like survival. *Okay, boss*.

By the fourth day, however, mainly to stop *okay, boss* from coming my way, I gave in and accepted the guard's hogfeed.

BECAUSE OF MY ZEAL to repent of my crimes against Izzy, I did not get to begin the particular cleansing I'd wished to do in honor of my jewish lady, Natalie. My court time had begun. Before I could do the necessary acts, before I could say Constantinople, I was already on the lam, heading out to the Marais, escaping again. A bit of surgery and I was heading toward Finier, avoiding my hearing, fleeing toward Arianne, not knowing that, in one of those great unfairnesses life serves up, the great *okay, boss* of life, I was going to get Izzy to boot.

> In later years, it has become clear to me that history is hardly a static entity, but rather that it requires vigilance, like a tender-spined plant to be forever tweaked and pruned.
> —from the opening of *The Last Will and Testament of Emile Poulquet (with an Addendum of a Corrected Version of History Regarding Paul Fauret)*

OF COURSE, Izzy was mentioned in my will; in this way, I would hand off the eternity of me to Arianne. Izzy had no clue that his future benefactor was watching him in the café. None of them did. I was forced to be the eye; they were forced to be my entertainment. "They're going to have to call off a few of our events," said Izzy, speaking with his quiet significance to the refugees. "Perhaps even the concert."

I could see that, despite his carapace of Banal, Successful American Man, Izzy's core remained that of a refugee. More than his vision had been lost. In the cell, first night of my penance, I had considered Izzy's ladies'-man aspect and its contradictions. Even when he'd pressed his courtship upon Arianne that summer, for instance, he'd always possessed a moral conscience greater than mine, though I called it, in my secretive heart, the slave-morality of the jew, a phrase I didn't fully understand but which was satisfying to the taste.

Something in the war, it seemed, had made what I'd found to be Izzy's insufferable moral superiority surface. Perhaps it had something to do with the loss of sight. When he took off his goggle glasses, for a second, as he rubbed the bridge of his nose, I saw the eyes, weak and watering. One turned toward me, orphic and limpid, but skimmed off my mug without recognition. Someone must have beaten him for that eye to revolve so blindly and for the other to offer such a deadfish glare. Here was where something awful began to wash over me and I do not call it guilt exactly. Not guilt! After the war, all of us who'd performed our service to the state had known what we felt was not the permeable membrane of guilt. It was rather guilt's opposite, a hardening—we returned to lives in our quiet rural villages or even quieter foreign countries, working at being clerks, gardeners, retirees. In the sanctity of our preserves, we began forming our counterattack, seeing the deviltry of the small minds now occupying all our former seats of power. After De Gaulle, so many nonentities ruled our France, truly the meaningless paving-stones of history. Now, Mitterand, his was another story, and an amusing one. But I digress. What I found was this: you had to make a sanctuary away from guilt.

Honsecker had first told me this and I believe he was right. He had foresight, saying guilt could do a man in, lead to bitterness, madness, or what he happened to call, ironically enough, *backtracking*—and for what good purpose? Does recognition of a wrong really help the future? Or does it just bog people down in the past, blinding them, beg pardon, to the present? And who can say whether later history will judge us as having acted incorrectly? Because we were trying to preserve France, old Honsecker would say. Because the left had indulged in wishful thinking by opposing our defense budget. Because the left and its megaphone jews had weakened France by supporting the jew Tropied against the honor of our army, the guilt or innocence of one jew trumping the maintenance of stability and respect for our institutions. In all these words of Honsecker, I heard the ring of truth. One makes certain choices under pressure. Of course, later I had the unfortunate but salutary example of Honsecker's own suicide.

It had not escaped me that right before his dreadful self-hanging, the man had begun to ignore his own advice. That bulldog had started to look so tortured that his very neck had started to swell, as if too much had gone unexpressed, a swelling beyond the reach of all his pill bottles and special muscle relaxants, the sleep aids and brown-labeled painkillers bought in the wide-open Argentinian farmacias. Whatever it was, it ended up strangling him long before he finished the job off with his own hands.

After the war, following Honsecker's original advice, I had been fanatical in one important respect, proving masterly in running far from guilt. It was from Honsecker that I'd learned the tactic of focusing upon the immediate particulars of each new day, upon the exigencies of survival, cigarettes and coffees to be numbered off, houses to be invited to, people to be met or avoided. I could identify the demon from a distance, knowing guilt to be the dry rot of the soul which Honsecker had once described. We took refuge in our admiration of the philosopher (yes, he was German) who said that there were no absolutes, but that the strong are fearless, and guilt is only for the weak. True, in prison, I had grown weak, succumbing to a template Christian in origin, the penances and absolutions of Lent, but after all, my hunger strike had served no one, least of all me, before my guard's unimpressed gaze.

As I watched earnest Izzy, I saw a rationale start to foam in over what a lesser man might call guilt. The foam was revulsion, and the sight of Izzy was abhorrent. He'd just gotten up from his café perch, and with his cane before him, a slight accent to it, he swung it left, skating it between chair and table, skimming half-arcs over the café floor, LEFT and right, LEFT and right, leaning forward as if the cane were magnetized toward events down the road. He made his way out the café door in the direction of what must have been familiar voices, a pair of refugees whose hug in the square he interrupted. I saw it all: Izzy opening his big lion mouth and laughing, his arm comradely around the shoulders of each of his friends. The small, violet-eyed woman in her oversize canadienne. That bald man. These people loved to laugh and hug: this could burn a hole in a person forced to watch such a charade for too long.

While Arianne had never minded Izzy's big-toothed zealot's laugh, I had, and some of the justification for my deeds came back to me, lending only brief relief to my spirits, reminding me of Talleyrand's axiom that a true Frenchman should never betray too much zeal. Funny that despite those refugees whose cases I followed during my time as janitor of Finier, looking into—or tearing up—records after hours, my bucket and mop a stiff-necked bride awaiting me in the corridor, I had surely been quite French in my understanding of Talleyrand. Not once had I searched for Izzy's case.

IZZY DECIDED to return to the café with his two friends, including the one who could have been a hallucination of a certain jewess. Though I tried to distract myself, nursing along the last of my little nothing, watching these visitors ignoring pastries or slinging back their pernods and beers, my mouth watered uncontrollably.

"Pardon me, none of us are perfect," said Izzy, voice breaking a little. He was answering someone who had said something rude, actually, a slight pertaining to me. It was in reference to the honor of my late mother, something implying that Emile Poulquet had been born out of wedlock to a female dog, and that Emile Poulquet was a female organ to boot. "We like calling other people monsters," he said. "Without preaching, isn't it too easy? Calling him any name lets him off the hook."

This defense of Emile apparently compelled him to start in with a story he had no business to tell and the café shushed. Even the cafetier slowed down, listening without appearing to be. It would have been more in Izzy's interests *not* to have told his story. At one point the violet-eyed woman put her hand on his, as if to help him place a lid on it. But it seemed he could not help himself—it was as if the story of his mother told him. He let them know he'd made excuses for many years. He was young, he'd say, justifying. He didn't know how the infernal machinery worked. Worse, a sheer survival instinct had come into play, not to mention denial and a desire to protect the family. But with flight-or-fight impulses manning the deck, overcoming reason, he too had relinquished all rights to a blameless conscience. Now he could only tell the facts, giving no excuses for himself. How he'd thought it right if he'd obey the requests of the central authorities, having gone to register his mother on a special German form. How because of this the police had surrounded him and his mother and had failed to recognize Izzy. They had taken away his mother despite all his useless protests. Because of his belief that the government would treat them fairly, he had served up his young pretty mother who'd been shining the hotel's silver. A mother who had sacrificed her own life to bring up Izzy in Couzac and its fresh country air, with her perfect face, in Couzac where no one would know that Izzy was, in fact (this he also admitted publicly, to my surprise), a bastard.

I had never thought Izzy was this thing, a bastard, but when he said it now, it made sense. He'd always cherished a peculiar concealment about his origins, occasionally claiming his real father to be a descendent of a family active in our revolution, or saying he'd come from the line of a fallen count. However he used to tell it, his mother had sacrificed for him, and however much she had sacrificed, she ended up being condemned by her bastard boy.

Izzy, to his credit or not, failed to mention a couple of important details. He didn't say that Emile Poulquet had helped Vichy. A stand-in for the Nazis, his friend Emile had distributed the decree that all jewish families had to register. He didn't mention how Emile had stood by as Izzy had made a useless protest to the police. Nor did he say how a few weeks later this same Emile (had he been judicious enough) could have saved Izzy's mother from Izzy's mistake.

Toward the end of the story, Galtimer came in, surrounded by a crowd of unctuous underlings. I was not thrilled. It was not that I wanted to hear the end of Izzy's story. It killed me to hear it from Izzy's perspective. Call it claustrophobia which had set in with a vengeance, burning my gizzards. But worse was that Galtimer had not aged as much as I might have hoped. He still possessed about his head an aureole of unbroken good fortune, a cloud of sandy hair whose wispiness betrayed his vanity. He still had the same elitist face which would see right through you if you were the janitor, the same face which spoke of having eaten too much sauerbraten at some formative point.

When he spoke to the cafetier, you could actually hear in Galtimer's voice a kind of ticking, as though he'd swallowed whole a tiny clock that now insisted on burring metronomically, a little clock forever going back and forth within that man's successful chest, reminding him exactly how many minutes he was away from achieving his ambition. Yet he worked hard to project an air of leisure, of someone to whom things come. Being prefect of Finier, in charge of the Bistronne, had been good to him. There should have been a mandatory limit to service in the prefecture, to prevent this kind of haughtiness from setting in.

His underlings gathered around, noses dipping eagerly, nodding at any absurdity he said, like ducks ready to dive into whatever he suggested. Is it exaggerating to say I wanted to shoot them all? My finger itched, my back rounded, I sank deeper into my corner, pulling the hat lower over my eyes. I wondered what I'd do if Galtimer, for all these years the Finier prefect, recognized me as his former janitor. For, yes, on the television right now, without sound, they'd returned to the second part of the special program on me, showing pictures of me in Finier before my brief custodial period.

APPARENTLY, and for this I owed my continued existence as a free man, no one had photographed me as Monsieur Molton the janitor, a handler of scouring agents and bleaches, skilled at maneuvering a large bucket on wheels, a long-handled brush, the massive set of keys; nor had they photographed me in any of my other guises.

I only existed for the media in my years as a rising official in the

Vichy administration. This anonymity carried a certain sting. For no good reason, succumbing to the childishness I had apparently kept well-preserved all these years, I wanted Galtimer to come pay his respects. He should thank me for the seat I'd warmed for him and for being his straw man, just by dint of having existed in a prior age which rendered everyone of my age suspect, everyone of a later age superior.

On the screen I saw myself now striding dapper in Paris and Bordeaux, one photograph bleeding into another. Bleed bleed bleed. I left fifteen well-counted francs on the counter and tried to leave. Izzy had resumed his story, his tone low and commanding, insidious. Unfortunately, I managed to escape only at the point where he had arrived at the camp himself and was trying to see if his mother had been subscribed on a train heading toward Poland: the details were too clear. I could not pretend he was inventing. I knew the exact camp, exactly which trip he'd taken.

AS I OPENED the door, I almost bumped into a dark-faced man in a leather jacket, a tall foreigner with small eyes and a square jaw, somewhat familiar, leaning on crutches and wearing a massive plaster cast all the way up one thigh. Was this the Turkish biker in a cast whom I'd overheard Louzange and his associates discussing in the station café? For all his encumbrances, the fellow was untroubled. Or could he be another refugee? He finished his cigarette, stubbed it out with the point of his crutch, and held the door for me as I exited.

I should not have looked back, but I did, I looked back like Lot's wife, and the man was saluting me, the sole gesture which to this day (though I've never served in the military) compels me to raise a tiny, limp imitation.

FLEEING THE SQUARE, I headed for the river, where I thought I might find a private landing, flanked by trees, which I'd once thought of as my outdoors office. There I hoped to nap under a willow. But unfortunately, the landing had since been converted into some kind of guesthouse, done up with a gaudy, lopsided neon sign advertising a vacancy. Instead, among the dogwalkers and casual bicyclists, I paced some of my old length of the river, as former habits dictated.

When I returned to the square, perhaps an hour later, the big man on crutches was still smoking by the café door, now wearing an out-of-season army anorak, bearing on its shoulder a flag from some unknown nation. He was probably another lover of our French quaintness, a tourist passing through, wishing to state his own flavor even as he absorbed ours. He saluted me again, I thought, but I wasn't sure of this until he started hitch-poking himself toward me. I stood, unsure whether it would look more suspect for me to turn my back to him or just to wait, gazing around the square as if I too were a newly returned refugee.

Once he reached me, he sucked his cigarette and handed me that morning's paper. "You'll enjoy this," he said out the side of his mouth, in cowboy French.

"What's that?" I asked without thinking. "Which—?"

But already he'd pivoted away from me, leaving me his newspaper. He started to hobble away in the general direction of the Hotel Fauret's annex, stopping once as if to relieve pressure on the leg made massive by its cast. He had the air of an old-time military man. You will understand that I found his whole battery of gestures odd, especially when he cocked his head back toward the square and let out a high whistle. Yet I could not see him signaling anyone, nor did he look back at me.

He worried me, but I felt as if I were driving an unsteady vehicle, and had to keep my attention on the road ahead, not looking too long at any obstacles which could force my crash. This was not, assuredly, the way I'd lived my life; but if I let my mind linger too long on that disturbing fellow, I believed all the momentum I'd been amassing could make me teeter and burn.

I also knew that, had the Look been in the fellow, it would have come as he'd handed me the paper. Yet his whole being had been seamed shut, lacking any recognition of me, especially for an American or Turk or whatever he was. The face he wore had no more expression than a blank piece of paper.

· · ·

ONCE THE MAN on crutches had turned the corner, I threw his newspaper into an ornate Empire-style green wastecan. These were heavy and straight-lined, courtesies I'd instituted during my most powerful period in the prefecture. It was my choice not to read the paper, whatever the hobbled man's intention had been. I generally made it a principle to stay on a news fast. Being forced to see the faces of the two lady lawyers had not been my choice—that itself had seemed to be indirectly controlled by Arianne. While reading the news required choice, one I could exercise with small acts of resistance.

YET PERHAPS the man's paper had been a show of charity toward a vagrant. Whatever the gift, needing a moment to gather forces, I entered the gloomy foyer of the church. A small chorus practice was in progress. In the back, a brunette with a heart-shaped face conversed urgently with the priest, and I sat not far from them, on one of the tall rosewood chairs facing the pews, where important officials used to sit. I found my hands on the armrests and hand-knobs rubbing strange carvings in the rosewood, crowned pagan beasts with rounded bodies, delicious clefts and furrows: this was what the notables' hands had felt while Mass was being served. I had never noticed these and now almost jumped from the seat. In church, whatever my beliefs, it was wrong to let such lusciousness, an affliction, enter my hand.

THE GIRL in the foyer continued to talk urgently with the priest and the chorus went on undisturbed. No one noticed me and in this not-noticing, one might think there would have been room enough for me to pray. Not that I thought anyone's god was paying attention to me. Because whenever I thought of my fellow patriots' god, I always felt that too much bureaucracy intruded. Too many layers of church hierarchy, angels, and saints to penetrate before my petition would be heard, and for too long have I lived with this sense of being thwarted.

I did find myself wanting to send up a flare—had the priest been free, I might have approached him. Not for absolution, hardly that, but rather for a hint of what he might call a divine pattern, just one clue which might bring me a step closer to reckoning or to Arianne. Once I saw her, I might tote up whatever I needed, deliver my sum, be free to leave. I could avoid staying here where I would undoubtedly continue to bump into Izzy. Perhaps a fleabag wharf hotel in Barcelona was preferable, lighter in its metaphysical weight. Surely I could not last long in Finier. Not only did it feel too strange to be back here, in virtually a third skin, there was no accounting for this reunion of refugees, whether or not it had been postponed. These sorry creatures had not figured into the landscape I'd planned.

Unfortunately, the girl didn't interrupt her audience with the priest, not for a second, and I couldn't approach the barest semblance of prayer. Soon as I tried to think any worshipful words, they fell back on me like blank shots. After pretending to read the hand-posted flyers about community events on the bulletin board, I sauntered out, needing a safe place in which to catch my bearings.

WHEN I RETURNED to the square, I made the first decision which would turn my luck that Saturday. All I did was sit upon the square's raised stage, the one which held vendor booths on market days. Flare sent up or not, there I found that someone or something must have been looking out for me.

On that stage, I was to meet Moses, the only mixed kindness the world wished to show me that day. At least, I would find someone, friend or comrade, who would take me on as both his liege and responsibility. This boon was, as one can easily see, nothing that I could take for granted, nothing to have taken with as light a heart as I did.

THIRTEEN

"I appreciate you!" I told Moses early on. "Seriously."

"Go easy, man," he said, this being his customary response.

"You found me. I appreciate that."

"No biggie," he said. "Don't get twisted. Hey, it's not like a one-shot deal. Maybe I'm looking for a father figure, you know?" He saw I didn't buy this. "I mean it. You got a lot of courtesy. For an old guy."

Moses *had* found me. I thought he'd become my liberation. This was not unimportant. Moses approached me, asking for change for a ten-franc bill. Moses of a sort I'd once considered the very lowest of humanity. Sub-beetle scrabbling scum, drift and dirt. The unemployed youth of our well-employed nation, tepid sons and daughters of our patrimony who squander our wealth, specks existing in their gravity-free, guiltless world. And yet he had enough magnetism that, initial misgivings aside, I eventually let him become my protector.

I will put it up to this: I have always enjoyed charismatic individuals, from many unlikely corners, and despite his tribe's schemes, which in my right mind I might have found off-putting, this charismatic seemed willing to make me the newest member of his circle.

Moses and his lion's bright hazel eyes, his wild hair fashioned like that of people from certain Caribbean nations, Moses with his two mongrels scuffling behind. Moses whose own easy personality acted as both tonic and command upon the nerves of Emile Poulquet, worlds apart from Arianne and the reincarnated horror of Izzy: Moses was my boon.

I MET HIM not far from the church, the last of the sun favoring only the buildings' tips so they became the scene's radiant actors, tableaux vivants outshining the gentry and refugees milling about in dwindling numbers. And while I was taken aback by Moses' appearance, and though in years past I could afford a vestige of my former snobbery, now my circumstances forced me to appraise his virtues. Moses was even-tempered. After I'd told him I lacked change, he returned to the task at hand, feeding his two dogs chunks of wet meat from his leather vest-pocket. Without getting distracted, he sized up my homeless situation as quickly as a veteran caseworker might have, as if he could have been one of our state's functionaries. Strangely, I didn't take offense in his calling me grandpa—*nice to meet you, grandpa*—a familiar but polite acknowledgment of my bushelness. More importantly, the phrase promised candor. I forthwith introduced myself as Raoul Tavelle. Almost immediately the boy offered to take me up away from the city, grandpa Raoul.

Why? I asked, the pendulum gathering questions deep in my own pocket.

No reason, he said. It's getting dark soon. We need more of a reason?

Seeing the circles of refugees joining only to disperse further, circles upon circles of natives and foreigners with live-wire connections, I had to weigh the worth of the offer. Hardly unhappy to be included in this strange boy's *we*, in anyone's *we*. To be called away. It must have been at least a few hours that I had sat in place, growing cold near my old prefecture, paralyzed watching circles swirling in and out with my mind chilled by the simpleton's thought that *most people know how to connect to other people of any stripe*. I told myself to proceed with caution, but a large majority of Emile Poulquet was uncharacteristically voting for the boy and not without some enthusiasm. Still, it took me more than a few minutes to rid my limbs of their stiffness, enough so that I could walk with that boy and his fleabitten mongrels into the end of what anyone would have called a long day.

THE RHYTHM of so many previous evenings in Finier, one into which I had often tried to fit myself, was starting up, a lovely hammock of calm, always an illusion—you felt the pink could go on forever and you were always betrayed. Dusk in Finier was for me a preamble more familiar than throat-clearing, more beautiful than an orchestra's tuning. Before dusk, there was always that last twinge, the rose-gold hour unfolding just after I met Moses, the hour when strollers and diners were made up of equal parts anticipation and the dulling of wishful thinking with wine. I too had once dwelled among these people and the nostalgia stung. No one knows memory as I do, no one has had to learn, as I have needed to, how one must establish a bureaucracy of memory, delegating and supervising, reshuffling and padlocking, just to keep the institution on its forward-seeming course.

"Started without me?" a panting lady declared in a restaurant's patio, arriving in a cloud of astonishment, brushing dust off her seat.

"We should consider you more important than wine?" her dinnermate gibbered back.

Struck by the wrongness of the choices most people make, I wanted to tell these types how mistaken they were. They didn't recognize the essentials. All of them, friends and lovers, family members in the golden hour, were settling onto their verandas and terraces, into the comfort of restaurants and homes. They were good at keeping themselves busy, as I had once been, good at projecting into a future in which they had amassed more things—objects, foods, stories, dwellings, significance. Because I was with Moses, for once I didn't mind being outside of them, outside their gestures toward banishing ghosts and terrors. On the streets, the refugees had either blended in with the others or disappeared. True to what the American had said about Arianne's event taking place on the outskirts, so few refugees remained that one might think another scourge had chased them out. Perhaps some greater refugee amusement was just then starting up in a rented ballroom, elsewhere, somewhere night would enter with all the impatience of war.

As we walked, Moses started up an agreeable prattle, explaining a genial life philosophy, one with a certain charm, touching on issues quite dear to me, but it was Izzy who conquered my attention and surveillance. We passed homes and restaurants, schools and the bank, the once-grand park like a navel of the town, sunken at its center where a field grew weeds, its bordering billboards like householders' faces, sun-faded, the paint of old advertisements peeling off in lovely strips. Nowhere did I catch a glimpse of Izzy or his particular entourage.

This I considered auspicious, as reassuring as the Finier residents, in age and manner distinct from the refugees, diners who sat in pairs at outdoor cafés like sober barbarians, diligent at spearing bits of sizzling meat on their tables' hot stone pierrades, the act managing to swallow all their words.

"When I was in Italy, people practically threw money at me," Moses was saying. "Here we don't have an idea of generosity unless we're religious. I'm saying people only *give* if they feel like they'll get to be part of some kind of big-deal organization." He told me he saw himself offering his fellow countrymen the chance to be philanthropic beyond their own tight lineages. "I used to wonder about my purpose. Now I get it." Cosmic rays had alerted him to his calling: to remind others of their own generosity. This was partly why he'd taken on the name Moses, he said—he'd wanted to let the French be generous toward someone with the name Moses. Give people a challenge. Same with the hair, the whole outfit, the dogs he took in, his whole *gig*.

"You're brave," I told him, meaning it, yet also trying to discern holes in the boy's story, leakages, hints that he was not the proper guide for old Emile. My pendulum was amassing a strong energy, yet the opportunity to withdraw it from my pocket and determine its valence had not appeared. So I tried to listen as deeply as I could, thinking that if my own story were half so coherent as this boy's, I too could walk with ease, limbs oiled if not by youth at least by integrity.

"You see, it's sort of like," he was saying, "I'm not totally brave." He asked where I'd been staying, misunderstanding me enough to think I'd been sleeping in the riverside homeless shelter run by the Ursuline nuns. "You look clean enough," swabbing one finger rather experimentally behind my ear. "That place jumps with bugs, right?"

It was I who jumped at his touch but in fact did not truly mind the intrusion—his crude humor had the same degree of sophistication as that of certain long cocktail hours I'd spent as prefect. Now Moses was telling me we had an urgent appointment at his evening ritual—*it's calming, grandpa, like archery*. He wanted to engage in a kind of bottle-target practice with stones by the river wall before the light went. *We're losing it*, he said, though at first I failed to understand he was referring solely to daylight.

WHAT OTHER RECOURSE was there for me? Or: how can I explain the combination of calm and excitement the boy provided? He was both peaceable and intent, off-kilter. The distraction he offered was respite, salve for an old man's bones and a mind which had run on tight, repetitive tracks ever since my bad night on the train. Let us say that in the space of a minute I have made far worse decisions than I did in obeying Moses, and I wanted to obey something beyond myself. All too easily I might have flitted around Finier like a ghoul, seeking Arianne, avoiding Izzy.

The truth was, I had entertained such poor luck for so long that the boy's friendliness made me want to think him an ally. Call it a tingling in the pendulum, but my urge surpassed that. A child will impulsively lean across a table toward a toy spinning away, and will risk falling off the table to grab the toy. In my long seasons of calculation, I hadn't had much leisure to act impulsively. In my reaching across the table, I assured myself the boy would lead to Arianne, even if the road toward her could prove one of the more unpredictable paths in my life—unpredictability was part of his appeal. Where I would sleep (or spend a few insomniac hours) had not yet been solved, but how much better it seemed to allow someone else to make the decisions, if just for an interlude.

■ ■ ■

HIS THROWING ARM was that of a young man, perhaps a young man the age I'd been when I'd entered the prefecture, while mine had been around for all of eighty-four years. It took all my powers to keep myself from saying *once I used to be able to*, though the phrase kept wanting to tumble from my tongue. When I finally managed to hit a single bottle with a stone, I received a clap on the shoulder. It was the first time in a long spell anyone had touched me with something approaching warmth. "You're not as old as you think, Gramps!" he said. One of his dogs nuzzled my hand as further compensation.

This marked the end of our bottle game. It had become night in the most natural way, and I was starting to feel how time in Moses' life functioned differently than it does in a fugitive's: the boy was full with his moment, not seeking ways to slice up time. At night birds are tiny, sparrows fly quickly for cover. You walk down streets where shadows lengthen and something of the night lengthens inside you too. I remembered from childhood how proud people were: they built dovecotes, eaves for sparrows, holdings within the edifice itself, and once the birds started to nest at the top of your building the birds, through rights of habitation, became yours and yours alone. Now they started to flutter past, rushing to find a home within our Finier night.

Then we were back on the main streets, hearing music floating down from one of the halls where young musicians must have been hard at work restoring an idea of French nationhood, using old-fashioned zithers and accordions. Their effect was soothing, unironic, a rasping melody true to our Finier stones. Beyond that were the government doorways where small maghrebin children called to one another from stucco doorways and stony corridors connecting the houses—*achi, mais oui, c'est ca que j'avais dit, inty akroot akbar mini, achi*, shooting and ricocheting down and between. Enough to make anyone feel sentimental about a boyhood those boys didn't get to live: no mushroom hunts, no cows to care for, no deep dwelling in our Bistronne mountains and forests. The few other colleagues surviving from my time tended to lack sympathy for our nation's rapidly proliferating Arab families, for the banlieues that had spread like a giant moorish apron out from Paris, but whenever I saw the camaraderie of those boys, the verve they brought to their underdog existence, in my current state, I felt touched by their situation, almost scorched by it, though I'm supposedly Poulquet the monster.

Walking with Moses toward the outskirts of town, toward the eastern rim along the highway, I found myself telling him about the hunting expeditions Charlot and I had gone on. "Young people have their topics," I apologized. "You won't be interested in this."

He told me he was, though I have often cautioned others regarding the importance of just letting young people be. Young people have their things and activities; what do they want with an old man? "Listen, I'll tell you what age is," I said to Moses. "I went to a bank to see if I could obtain a safe-deposit box. I got off the elevator. I was walking and saw a man walking toward me. I came close, he came close. I was going to say to him, beg pardon, *you rude bastard!* Excuse me. But he didn't stop. I almost wanted to punch him. Something to stop the fellow. Only then I realized who was walking toward me. That's what age is. You don't recognize yourself."

"Wow," said Moses. His receptivity did me in, making me wish to tell him more. Before the time of mirrored banks, I'd had signposts, stability. "I used to be a big hunter," I told him.

"Game?" he asked.

"Mushrooms." It might as well have been game, mushrooms that seemed more alive than their hunters. You foraged for cèpes in the mountains, cèpes the meatiest of mushrooms, three days after a rain and cèpes came out, coupled, near trees. You had to tramp through savageries of undergrowth to find them. The best cèpes were fat-stalked, elephant-legged, the opposite of poison, found in the ancient trees' shadows. You found a champion and you'd trumpet it. You'd add yours triumphantly into the large basket.

"Cool," said Moses, continuing his soft whistle to the dogs. "Keep it up, guys."

"I'm boring you," I said. "Who cares what an old man once did?"

"No, man, I *like* this shit. I'm all about it. I live that way too."

On your family's land, neighbors who paid rent to your father called you little Cèpe since you were so good at the hunt. You'd have a transitory fame until the next person found the next cèpe and perhaps a bigger one. The risk that you could find poison made the whole endeavor more delirious. You had terrific responsibility, as good cèpes could be indistinguishable from poison mushrooms, and you were the one to accept and reject, allowing only good ones into the basket. You'd know you'd once again saved your family from certain deaths and yet also that you'd reserved the most special treat for them. Actually, foraging is probably one reason vigilance prevails in our Bistronne mountain households—we have a long history of knowing no discovery can ever escape a parallel menace, and our patriotic nature lets us know that no truth lacks its contrary argument.

Moses beat a little rhythm on his chest in time with my talk, spitting a bit. "Kachung, chungchung," he said, or some similar tribal nonsense.

"I'm not the first to say beauty and death are linked," I backtracked. "It's just that my circumstances make strange things beautiful. Does that sound funny?"

"I feel you," said Moses. "Kachungchungchung!"

At home, noon the same day of the hunt, you'd watch mother's hands working, each slice a decision. "Fuss over a fungus," she'd say, frying your harvest in butter and garlic. If garlic turned green, you knew the test and its results: the mushroom was poisoned (but the thing never turned green). She'd only use parsley to mask the point when cèpe season was almost over. Then you'd have that moment as you sat down at the table, when your father eyed you with a silent, rivalrous caution, just before, together for once, the three of you would eat your labors.

The only bad thing about hunts was that whatever you hunted for began to multiply all around in a thousand and one mirages—fakes everywhere, false friends. After I reached my first decade, it was my chore before dinner to bring my family's cows home, and there I'd be, after nightfall, trying to hear cowbells amid fields and forest: even the branches' creaking transmogrified into the low-high clank of cowbells. I knew that if I failed in my hunting task, if I couldn't bring the cows home, even after dark, I would be beaten by my father, wealthy enough but a dullard, who'd married my mother (according to our stablehand, well-attuned to village gossip) not because he could bring her into the era of the electric iron, but only because I was the possibility growing in her belly.

As a child, it would have been unthinkable for me to call my father a hopeless case. Only once I started speaking with the stablehand did I get a bit of perspective on the family Poulquet. That perhaps my mother had coveted my father's ancestral land, land which always disoriented me, acres of forests in which one could hunt not just for mushrooms and cows but, in the right seasons, for deer and fox. If she didn't love him for his talents, perhaps she'd loved his arrival on her threshold, a man armed with provisions.

That first Saturday night back in Finier, soothed by the presence of Moses if nonetheless somewhat alarmed by the flow of speech he excited in me, I told him of our land, mushroom hunts, and a bit about my father (without once saying his name, of course). Enough to say that I walked in something close to peace, having stopped, for a blessed second, worrying about being recognized.

Near the new shoe and clothing stores, a man argued with a woman, blocking the sidewalk, the two defining themselves by constraint, each delivering hostility in packets more civilized than the other. You're a cold castrating bitch! the man politely hissed at the woman. You can't live without being constantly angry! she enunciated, stopping a few crucial decibels short of yelling before turning on her heel. These were other people's problems, however, the usual atmosphere of our streets only fueling the peace between my new companion and myself. Just beyond the arguing man, who'd been left befuddled and solitary at the corner, Moses approached a newspaper kiosk to speak in a hush to the seller sitting inside. The fellow eyed me over his long truffle-like nose but I was unafraid, sensing the newspaperman gave me no Look but rather merely scented on me one of the larger things in life: money, status, former badges of honor. I stood at a distance, watching the fellow exaggerating his gestures, arms dramatic, confiscating whatever calm we had.

Moses confirmed afterward to me: "Me, I have little to do with such types. A real bourgeois!" I was glad he shared my opinion, confirming our affinity: we had no need for such distracting people, we were to continue on. Above us, profiled in an open second-story window, a hawklike woman with a tight bun commanded her assistant, a bent man employing a long pole to straighten the backs of young ballerinas. The pole itself danced, tapping a wrist or neck crooked at the wrong angle, turning a leg out, reminding an errant toe to point. The piano music fell upon us, a three-legged elephant clumping out chords. "Beautiful," Moses said, either in relation to the dancers or the man's pole. We were rapt in what I believed was shared appreciation for that room's particular complexities. "You thirsty, man?" asked Moses, breaking the moment. "We're near this place where the bartender's kind of a friend. Guy used to sell with me in the market."

FINIER, it said when we got to his kind-of-friend's place, aglow, the town's name a neon red sign outside a bar, a Finier with music thrumming inside, so loud my pacemaker vibrated. And though nothing of this was my place, having habitated none of this under any guise, I walked into the bar with that wild-haired boy, feeling woven to some joy courtesy of the night or what we'd seen of the ballet's cruel tenderness or merely because I'd spoken too much. It was a bizarre escape from gravity: hence freedom.

"You hear, Moses?" asked the bartender, a man with something of a pinhead floating above his massive torso, too much in demand to chat much. Refilling people's glasses and carafes, speaking over his shoulder. "Something strange happening down the way. Should check it out, no-good types starting a big bonfire."

"Bonfires," said Moses to me, herding me outside. "I know who's doing that. The anarchists. We don't need distraction now, don't you think? Let's get you settled first and take it from there."

I told him he was rapidly proving to be a reasonable man. What I wanted more than anything was to rest somewhere, and after that, I had a thirst to return to my story, though the urge was poorly timed, as it wasn't in my interests to speak volubly to anyone. I was tired but as we resumed, I held up my end of our bargain, walking alongside the crazy-looking boy, boots loud on the cobblestoned streets, streets emptied of last-minute shoppers and workers on their way home. Both of us felt, I thought, the lull in the night's blandishments. I nodded my assent to his plan. "The thing about foxhunts—"

But here Moses shushed me. "That bartender. You can tell, the guy tries to be respectable but he used to get pretty crazy." He grabbed my arm. "What's this like for you, old Raoul? Don't tell me I'm not doing my job."

I must have appeared quizzical.

"I'm showing you life," and did a little hipless dance to demonstrate. "Life!"

"We just met," I said mildly, but obscurely hurt. I hadn't thought it a unilateral exchange. I'd thought we'd already established rapport, sharing stories, appreciating the evening, the diners, the bad little ballerinas. "You don't think I know something of life?"

"Got to educate you a little," he said. "If you're not handing out stars, I'll give myself one. Many stars," without intending to, he echoed something Arianne had said to me years ago.

I told him he was a genial fellow, and further, that I thought he was many stripes above most of my former colleagues.

"That's interesting!" he said. "Like what?" Then caught himself. "You're just saying that."

"Believe me," I said, surprised at my seriousness, "whatever bad luck may have been mine in my life, I've always been a good judge of character. I've never been forced into saying something I didn't mean. I have principles." I did not love how my voice broke.

"Whoa. We just met," said Moses. "Maybe get to know me."

"But I do mean it," I said. I had never felt so sincere, though I didn't know the source of all this uncouth emotion. That I'd talked so much? It wasn't the pill; I wanted to grip the boy's hands.

"You sound like someone who gets hard on himself, man," said Moses gently. "Slow down. Easy." We were walking back toward the first of Finier's two rivers, as he said he had to check something out at the Ursuline shelter where he still assumed I'd spent the night. I was worried I'd get caught in my lie, but then told myself the boy wouldn't notice any small inconsistencies.

We came to it, a pretty clapboarded place, its shutters half-open, restraining an interior brightness. He was saying how funny it was that the place used to be a convent before the sisters went common-law. These ladies didn't even wear habits, they tried to be too modern for his taste, what did I think about that? "Some things should stay old, you know?" giving me his long look.

"They shouldn't be called nuns at all," I agreed.

He said he thought it cool that they took in people even if the state paid them for it, and then asked what I'd thought of the scratchy blankets; I gave a little knowing sigh. He told me to wait outside, *to avoid confusion*: this was a nice turn of events. "But don't go fleeing on me," he said, holding up a finger. "Wait up. Please. We got places to go to."

Charming, I told myself, but don't get sucked in, Emile.

I had learned to trust no one fully. No one really wants to befriend an old bushel; why would this Moses character? His dogs sighed as they sat near me, equally compliant, noses alert. It was strange to admit that Emile Poulquet, who may it be said had never fully heeded orders from anyone, Emile Poulquet who had always inserted snakey little transgressions into the most trivial of exchanges, whether it was the petite rebellion of a requisitions order filled out in code, a bouquet missing a few flowers, or a delaying tactic inserted into protocol, Emile Poulquet who used to spin out official apologies while handing back to petitioners their documents with significant information missing, enjoying the ball of consequence and omissions rolling out, that this same Emile Poulquet now found himself obedient. That Emile relished his complete obedience to this boy, to this *stranger*, Emile as acquiescent as the two mongrels sniffing the air next to him. Maybe it was the new persona of Raoul Tavelle—a patient, biddable man, more in step with others' schedules and needs than with his own.

Hidden, semi-hidden, I enjoyed hearing the stillness along the river, torn only by the distant three-note computerized melody preceding the distant train station announcements which were given to the world by a plummy mechanized voice. *Attention, attention.* I startled a bit when I realized that the car I had unthinkingly leaned on— I must have been tired—was similar to the ancient old car which had belonged to young Galtimer at the prefecture, an old Citroën from the late sixties, a sleek car at the time but conspicuous. The one I leaned on had the extra vanity of a wavy silver line, not unlike the flash of a lightning bolt as it might occur in memory, painted down the ventral toward the dorsal, a stroke of conspicuous vanity highly atypical of our people. Perhaps Galtimer had sold his car to an Algerian family who'd wanted to smarten it up beyond what Galtimer's lackluster habits would have allowed.

"Like the wheels, Raoul?" asked Moses, sneaking up behind me, which I'd soon find out was his habit. "Come on. We got to get to where we're going." He smiled. "You know, like that's the tao of walking."

I smiled back at this ambitionless nonsense but I was thinking about foxhunting, and also, with unease, noting the tighter chill in the air. Raoul Tavelle didn't have much with him in the way of jackets or warmth: he was not a man who planned for much.

THAT NIGHT, we accomplished what for me was a rather extensive hike, one I'd not have managed had it not been for Moses' encouragement. He kept telling me to keep the faith, gramps, we'd get there soon enough. Moses called it the manse. "Just a squat up in the hills but really well-concealed for a squat." A word whose sound had struck me first as funny then as inevitable. A *squat*. My newest abode a manse but also a squat.

Moses guided me to the manse-squat, whatever it was, like some kind of delivering angel, his two dogs scuffling ahead or behind, always on an invisible tether, one Moses evidently trusted. En route, he removed his leather vest. I had to pause just for a bit, at the last streetlamp on the border of town, waving a hand in the manner of an old man, the old man I've become, the *don't-mind-me* of oldness, a gesture I've not had to use that much, since, barring my congress with Honsecker's widow in Buenos Aires and my exchange with the Paris lawyers, it has been years since I've had any real connection with others, hardly any. Moses waited while my pacemaker recalibrated itself. "Got to make the ticker tick," I said, though I don't think he understood. He stood waiting, betraying the over-eagerness of his youth, the very tips of his hair seeming to seek sockets—and I say that though Moses was hardly an impatient boy. There was something solid to his eagerness, or at least to its predictability. I found it kindly the way his own bare chest, skinny enough, also exerted its own reciprocal heaves after the effort we'd just made. He was scrawny and underfed and I was just old, an old don't-mind-me reprobate, and we came around the circle of age to meet each other. Not a bad escort, I thought, and perhaps the best way for me to meet Arianne. On second look, I noted that what I had taken to be shadows scrawled over his torso were instead defacings. He was a painted man, covered with multiple tattoos, writings and diagrams, thorn-ringed bands, esoterica which I couldn't make out under the lamp, barbed wire and circles crawling up his arms. All of these screamed with the rashness of youth: *mind me! mind me!* From them, I stayed at a modest remove; which is to say that I kept my eyes focused on the gentleness of his face, away from his torso and its billboard, away from all it proclaimed about the manner in which youth believes that the sole eternal, the ultimate and irredeemable truth, will always be a message of the flesh, embedded in flesh, scrawled over flesh. What can you say to such a youthful delusion? Nothing, I knew to say nothing. But he saw me looking. "You like it?" he asked. "I did some of them myself, believe it or not. It's like, people have done stuff to me so often I just decided to take the means of production into my own hands. Needles, the paraphernalia. Sort of like being my own pornographer, you know?"

I nodded, noncommittal, and he tapped my shoulder.

"Don't be polite, man. Say what you think. Why spend time if people don't get to know each other?"

Why indeed, I thought, his words almost as esoteric as his tattoos.

IT WOULD TAKE US more than an hour of hiking, slowed by just a few more don't-mind-me moments, hiking while the houses and their heavy edges started to thin out, my indecorous sweat making me lose all fear of being chilled higher up. Not to mention the more private fear I had: spiders we might encounter once we got wherever we were going.

Halfway up the mountain, under the new moon, Moses was explaining how the wastrels had come to occupy the manse. Rich people, he said, buy these country places and then leave them empty. Every now and then an old man, a laborer, comes to place a stone in the fence. The laborer must be hired by a rich owner to do this. A week later the same worker comes and removes the same stone. "He's supposed to be restoring it but never even looks inside."

All the wastrels were anarchists, this was something Moses wanted me to understand. He jumped topics, told me their place was really something. Basically in the morning I would look out and think I was in the garden of fucking Eden. If the state were really a moral institution, Moses could raise his three kids in the manse. But Mercury had been retrograde each time his case had come up, screwed up everything, and beyond that, the state needed to know all the *details* of your situation before it let you do anything.

"I understand," I said with some truth.

"I got a custody meeting next week," he said. "Now my drug problem's fixed. All those mothers, none of them are any more fit than me. I mean it." He was getting a bit riled up. "Those ladies are way less, man. I mean they shoot! Legs and arms scratched to high heaven. You're looking at some kind of fucked-up shooting range. Sorry. But those ladies got sugar daddies keeping them in real houses. See, the state wants to be right there inside your veins. That's what I'm saying. And then my kids are growing up without a real papa figure around." He shook his head. "You're judging me. I can tell, Raoul. You don't know the facts and you're judging me."

"I'm not." This was my first real lie to Moses, as I'd do anything to keep our conversation going, especially since we walked more slowly when he got excited talking, good for my don't-mind-me dignity.

"Sorry," he said. "It's under my skin."

"Don't worry," I said, imitating his locution.

"Until like two, three weeks ago, I thought those kids would get a better gig living without me. But now I'm clean." He opened his mouth to show off what in the half-dark appeared a rather mottled tongue. As if I were a doctor come to examine it. A ring on the edge of that broad wet carpet of a tongue glinted obscenely at me. "A decent life. That's what I'm all about. Now I got half a chance the state will let me see them. Maybe even house them. But see, I always thought it was better for me to live honestly." He tweaked his hair. "So I get a few stares here and there." Now he seemed to be flicking away the catcalls of an imaginary horde. "I've lived according to my lights."

"That's important," I said. "Or it's all we have."

"True," he said, as if I'd spoken a great profundity. He half-punched my shoulder. We'd come through some tunnel in the conversation. In strange rhythm he yelped out: "Old Raoul has the answers!"

"Not really," I demurred.

He was not satisfied. He wanted to justify more. "It's better than a lot of other things. Like I've never been hog-tied to some boss I wouldn't want to be seen in daylight with. Know what I mean?"

"I'm sure your meeting will go well," I said, but he seemed to need more from me. "You're probably a good father," I added.

For this he shone back at me, a nimble creature, a young uncertain lion's face. "You think?" He pondered. Then seemed to come back to himself. "Damn, man, that's scary. I don't know how you get people to tell you shit. You got talent. You were probably the kind who could always pull stories out of people, right?"

I shrugged. *I'm no one, I'm nothing.* "I was thinking the same thing about you."

"I mean it's a compliment, man. Don't get hang-faced. I had no idea. You don't look like—no one knows the shit I just told you. Seriously. And here we just met. That's all I'm saying. Not your face but the rest of you." I didn't know what he meant. His words had a vaporous quality, vanishing before me. "You could've been like, I don't know, some kind of psychiatrist. You ever considered that as a gig? Which kind gives out pills? But all those guys are big-time voodoo, man. Big time."

■ ■ ■

WE CAME UP to the manse but its perch on the hill had already made it seem to fall toward us. It was a house looking out into a valley. You could imagine prehistory had ignored its setting. The lip of the hill was extreme, poked out in a way I couldn't trust, though Moses beckoned me to come stand on the precipice.

"Hey! See how the other half lives!"

"I'll hold off just for now," I said. Somewhere beyond this extremity there trickled what sounded like a thin waterfall, and the valley gave way to sharp mountains, falling off in the distance. As far as I could make out, there were hectares of unforested trees, no sign of habitation anywhere.

Once we entered the ramshackle house, a couple of his friends raised lazy hands from where they'd bedded down, one of them letting out a sleepy moan. A few distant stars glimmered through a corner of the ceiling, while the floor itself was an uncertain medley made up of planks. At first I saw a piled rug, in spots where sections of planking had not fallen through to the earth, but this turned out to be a tribe of dogs. The two mutts who'd trudged all the way up with us had already found their niche amid the other strays, stirring, sneezing. There were dogs upon dogs, dogs hunting in place, stretched or curling, dogs rolling onto their sides, sniffing nightmares. In the half-light the dogs made up a living floor and wall.

"So you're happy, right?" Moses whispered to me. "We're here at least until Jacquot pulls off his scheme." I hadn't heard about this, and even in half-light, the boy must have sensed me recoiling. "Nothing big," said Moses. "You don't have to be involved. Just a little art project. It's about big issues. You'll meet Jacquot. I'm going to help him. So—you like the place?"

"There probably aren't spiders here," I said, struggling for diplomacy.

"No spiders," Moses laughed. "Is that a condition or what?"

"I mean your home is well inhabited."

"I like that!" he said, laughing under his breath. He tapped me on my shoulder, a comradely tap, this time a little too hard. "You're right—no spiders."

The other consolation was that the squat-manse was warm. If it was also true that it was brackish, reeking of mysterious things. Wood shavings, malty bodies and urine, damp dog above all. My nose could handle such stench, knowing how to embrace it, analyze it, and then ignore it, while it was always impossible to ignore the cold. Here there was only the one stone window and any fresh breeze that entered, any thin strand, immediately got soaked up into the heavy atmosphere, into the soot from candles dripping huge froggy pools amid spots of moon. We had to tramp over the candles and dogs to get to the corner which belonged to Moses.

Once we settled on his two pads, laid over with sleeping bags that stank of scorched oregano, he continued whispering to me. The squat-manse was the best place the wastrels had ever found. For the last three months it had been their house. No one had disturbed them. Only a neat-featured man with his hair cleanly pulled back, whom Moses called a real musician, appeared fully awake.

"Christian used to play for the circus," Moses said, "until the lady boss cheated him. That's little Max sitting next to him," he said of a cigar-shaped young man sitting with his head back against the wall next to Christian, short legs sticking straight ahead. Max nodded. "Meet the new wastrel," said Moses in his general direction, to which Max let out a small grunt. "So you didn't say what kind of music you like. You into classical stuff or people like Zappa?"

"All kinds," I said, aiming for blandness, feeling a bit shamed by all I'd unloaded earlier. What was I doing in this youth kennel? Christian, sitting by the entrance, had started to work away, for our benefit, I supposed. His eyes closed, Christian struck some repeated melody on a guitar, though its strings sounded as if they'd been winnowed down to three.

The guitar must have lacked certain frets as well, so the sound that came out was more akin to a broken cello, a hunting whistle, a cowbell. The music scattered me. Inside that reverberant space, Christian gave voice to the courtly feeling a troubador might have shown. *Rosemarie,* sang Christian, *rosemarie rosemarie.*

It had been a while since I had heard anything played with such passion. It almost sounded for a moment like my favorite, Debussy's long orchestral piece about the sea. I told Moses this.

"See this color inside the manse?" Moses asked, tripping from topic to topic. "That's my favorite. It's better than anything in a museum. Once the moon comes out, everything here turns into my own blue. Moses blue."

That night, Christian's three-stringed guitar playing the same tune again and again increasingly reminded me of hunt-whistles. It could have been the guitar or the smell of damp dog that made me recall fox-hunting—fox-hunting my savior in that cantankerous age between twelve and sixteen, an age when whether or not you've had a hump recently removed from your face, whether or not your face is a sneer of contempt or idiocy, you first tighten, unfolding only to tighten more, only starting to taste the panic of power.

FOURTEEN

"Listen, let's talk about risk, man," Moses was saying. The first morning of my stay at the manse had burst open and giant mercenary shadows crossed the valley. To me, the view from the manse's lookout had the feeling of an inverted Eden, the negative photograph of Eden long before Adam, a tantalizing promise ready to be taken away, the clouds yellow and turgid as they passed over us. "You don't have anything to fear with us."

What I really wanted to ask was *do you people never wash or eat?* but he had been more than hospitable to me for the past eighteen hours or so. It would have been ungracious to complain. Christian had long since left, leaving his three-string guitar behind. It is Sunday, I thought, trying to hold on to that fact. *It is Sunday and I am looking out over a valley. I have not washed.*

The scent of the manse, the dog-body perfume, had probably made us more informal with each other than the brevity of our time together would ordinarily warrant. Though, according to Moses, it had been hours earlier when all the dogs had departed with Jacquot, whoever Jacquot was.

∙ ∙ ∙

MOSES HAD found me sitting on a rock outside. "Ah Jacquot, man. He's like the pied piper of Finier. You should see him. All the strays know him." Yawning, stretching in his full boy grace. "They like me, but Jacquot? The guy is purity. Lives off shrubs and roots. Never animals. They follow him. Me, I go for the real thing, man. For blood. Kidneys I eat only if they have the right taste, you know. Speaking of, you want to go see my pigs?"

I tried to stand, my bones made of angles and aches, as if they needed to be ironed out from the night's rigors. To hide my inability to stand straight right away, I fixed my gaze on the tattoo radiating out from Moses' heart, a giant circle like an old-fashioned mirror, its frame made of snakes and roses.

"You like that one?" he said, poking it. "Got it five years ago. The first needle." I didn't say anything. "Don't go have a senior moment on me," said Moses, and then repented. "I didn't mean that. You're not bad for an old mec. We're here to share some life experience together. Hey," he said, trying to restore his hospitality. He tossed a book at me. "You might want to read this."

THE BOOK OF SECRETS. The back of its violet cover was waterstained: *It should be certain that the jews had of themselves a particularly favorable opinion, that they found themselves more noble and cultured than others, according to Freud.* And the author had added: *these are exactly the same thoughts of the people of ancient Egypt!*

Moses took it back, reading the back cover to me. "Basically, there's this forbidden history of humanity. Take the oldest document in the world, the book of Enoch." He proceeded to go on about Enoch, like all the guys in the Bible, born of an unknown father, raised like them in heaven, how the book of Enoch dedicates 105 chapters to angels who come down from the sky to mate with the people of the earth. "See, my question, like this guy's, was who were these angels? There you have the biggest secret. It's our unknown history. Unknown because it was and still is forbidden," he said, still half-reading. "But that's not the only mystery clarified here. The author shows the world didn't start at Sumer. And not in Delhi. Not in Egypt but in America, in Florida. That's where the jews started. *In this prodigious Florida that we must identify as the Hyperborée of the distant Western ancestors. This book shows some shocking discoveries, some seminal revelations, some dangerous truths to know and say.*" The oiliness of his reading voice made it hard for me not to smile. "It's true, man. *But it is time, in the author's estimation, to say such things.* He thinks they should start another Zion in Florida, bring about the end of days." He let out a little laugh. "What do you think?"

I told him he had sensible ideas but I was not much for talking in the morning. Nothing stopped him, though. He wanted us to head back into the town of Finier. I wasn't sure I was ready to see more refugees. Or risk running into Izzy. But Moses wanted us to see the conference and festival Arianne Fauret had arranged, and I tried to remind myself of my purpose in this third return. "They're supposed to install a resistance statue in Bomont in a couple of days. You know, war stuff? That's what Jacquot wants to get involved in. He wants to use that whole refugee event to make a general statement about war. What do you think?"

I didn't like the sound of any of it, and cleared my throat, which seemed to make Moses recant. "We don't have to get that involved with that, you and me. I'm just into, you know, hanging. If you want, this afternoon we can check out the concert in Finier. But first let's go check the pigs."

BY THE TIME we'd reached his pigs, I was well fed. Along the way, through gates and on patio walls, we'd been gifted with small covered dishes of food, most on silver trays weighted down by rocks, all of them set out for Moses. A terrine of foie gras. At one house, a smidgen of quail pâté and beautifully veined cheese. At another, a dish of thick hundred-day cassoulet with sad fatty duck legs floating in it. A seeded baguette left at the bakery's back door, cutlery rolled up in cloth napkins. A platter with a few curled pieces of English roast beef up on a garden wall.

"Excuse me," I said at the first house, trying to hide my swinging pendulum. I tried to accomplish the colloquy within my coatsleeve, a hard task, but pleased that my pendulum seemed determined to feed me, swinging confidently each time toward YES.

At the second house, Moses asked what voodoo ritual I was doing inside my sleeve with that silver thingamabob. This made me laugh; it was the first time we'd laughed together. "Hey, can I see it?" he asked. Ordinarily I let no one finger my pendulum, but I permitted the boy to hold it in his hand, where he regarded it with the respect he might have given a damaged hummingbird.

"It tells me what to eat," I explained. "Sometimes it also tells me what to do."

He said he was into the idea and asked if I could swing it for him. "I can't," I said. "You have to choose your own personal direction for YES and NO. Then you have to put your imprint on the pendulum." Honsecker had been quite clear about this part, in our first meeting after what everyone else called the liberation.

Moses put his hands up as if to block an invader. "Cool. Hey. Isn't this a good haul for a Sunday?" At the next houses, I saw a few of those who'd set out our platters, girls with the aura of being rebellious vegetarian daughters of the bourgeoisie. Girls who, when I saw them at a window or in the garden, all seemed to have onyx hair, straight and serious across the brow or pulled back severely, *poetry lovers* as we used to call them in my student days. Abstracted girls wearing granny skirts and multicolored knit vests, or farmer's overalls, suggesting rural girls whose sophistication could trump any urbanite's, especially since their unfussiness became most forceful when it came to showing the slim shine of their pillarlike arms.

"They know me. I eat in the mornings. My posse takes care of me then and sometimes later." Moses used the English word and paused for effect. *Posse.* A word from the English books about cowboys I had read while still in primary school. "These girls usually believe what I do, but think they need a house with walls. Some of my older posse, none you met so far, those ladies gave me children. Sons and daughters." He stared back. "Don't give me that look. Tell your pendulum. We're splitting the difference."

I shook my head, his words again evaporating before I could understand them. He was back on the subject he couldn't fend off.

"The kids are here and there. I tried to be a real dad. Tried to do everything according to the law." For my comprehension, he made a little mincing tightrope dance of exactitude. "But when I wanted to take legal control of my three kids, I had to live in a house with a certain kind of toilet. I'm not kidding, man, when you shit," and here too, for my benefit, he performed a small incompetent mime, in bad taste and employing oral accompaniment, "whatever you do, the state wants to be there inside with you. In your orifices. It's crazy. I couldn't take it. I gave each kid back to the mothers. Now I want at least part custody. We'll see."

He wanted a response, it seemed, so I searched a bit. "How does one achieve custody?"

"I'm trying, man." He squirmed. "Whatever I can. You'd do the same. I love those kids. They wake you in the morning with that crazy papa-papa stuff. Crawling all over you. And it's like they haven't been kicking you in the head all night. They *want* you. I say that shit's better than anything you'd find in a shooting gallery. Hey, why're you giving me that look?"

"I envy you," I said, this time not fully lying.

MOSES' PIGS, there were three leaders and dozens of followers, did look clean and happy. They lived in a large and fenced-off portion of a friend's farmyard, just beyond town. This was where two men shared land, a Frenchman and a Moroccan, and according to Moses, it was all cool, organic, because the guys understood the soil; both came from generations of farmers.

In honor of the old Roman virtues, his friends had named the leading pigs Gravity, Piety, Simplicity. "But me, I raised them," said Moses. Tomorrow he would castrate the young ones. Starting at age three months or so, if you wanted tasty meat, you had to castrate. Then Moses would work to make blood sausages and head-cheese, sweetbreads or pâtés, cured ham, it didn't matter.

"Spirit beings come to me," he said. "I remember the first time I had to watch a man butchering a goat. That night the goat came back to butcher *me*. I learned. See, the man who'd been butchering the goat had made two slices, because he messed up the first time. The second time worked. But what the goat said to me at night, what it showed me so I could spare others, was that you got to get it right the first time. The first slice, the goat feels like it's going to sleep, losing a little blood along the way. But the second slice, that's when it gets all that fear going in. Clean cut, that's what it's about. You got to get it right the first time."

HE GOT ENTHUSED over the idea of taking the pigs to a mounting station. You had to have them make love piggie-style. Last time he'd done this his thumb had gotten injured. But it was okay, because he lived from the ideal of auto-consumption, he said, solemnly, and these things happen. Which made me think, ridiculously, that he'd taken a bite out of his thumb, somewhere between the mounting station and castration. But the accident had happened when the guillotine had been too slow.

"Jacquot wants me to help with his plot," he told me. And again, seeing me cringe: "Just an art project. Don't worry, grandpa Raoul. You see, we can't do everything he wants. Me, I got to tend pigs." He spoke like this. His speech was speckled with *me, me, me*, and also *I am* and sometimes *you see*. As though the self were also a stray dog, a scrabbling entity which had to be constantly retethered down to some central home idea. There was the speechifying self, the one doing the talking, but sometimes you, as his audience, had to be tethered down too, with the endless *you see*.

"No, you see, I chose auto-consumption because it means living off your own land. Depending on no one, hurting no one else. You barter for goods only with others who live as we do. Auto-consumption. That's the wave of the future."

"Really it's the wave of the past."

"Both," he said, "both," waving his battered hand but genial enough. "Me, I think we're after the same things."

I felt pleased, more in the present tense than I had been for years. He was urgent, this boy, speaking to me, and the quality made me feel urgent but in a rewarding way, as if I too leaned toward life, rather than having spent a goodly portion of it avoiding death by imprisonment. He wanted me to know why his friend had named the pigs after the virtues. The idea for Gravity is that things have consequence. "That a man's authority be respected. Piety is you're supposed to see things clearly."

"And what's Simplicity?"

He looked at me as though the question itself could have registered me as insane. And then said he heard the dogs—could I see Jacquot heading down toward us? There was after all someone coming, surrounded by a pack of dogs, making the pigs squeal and burrow toward the muddy field's center. But Moses wanted to know: couldn't I see the way animals just loved Jacquot?

FIFTEEN

Justice: I had to admit that despite all my scorn about its workings, coming from Paris to Finier had been about justice. I'd wanted to come even with Arianne Fauret, have her admit a truth about our past, about her past in particular. She'd chosen me as her plaything, first making me her schoolyard victim and then her promotable pawn, someone with a fate under her control. One could say I'd chosen her not as my moral hero but as my judge. Don't all of us choose one person who will play out for us, in life, the judge?

IN THE INTERREGNUM between the time I returned to Finier after my studies and the night that she and Paul promoted me in Bomont, the richness of *what might have been* between Arianne and me had begun to assume its deepest flavor. This was something I lamented later. What we almost achieved would become so rotten. In retrospect, it seems the events of that signal year—the onset of war, the refugees and camps, the new dictates—had turned us in the wrong direction. With Izzy still in Paris, in this interregnum (and I'm not sure how it commenced, one of life's happier little instances), Arianne and I had struck up the habit of going daily to the market, a bit of harmony stolen from the erratic workings of the prefecture. I helped her with the hotel's daily purchases, escarole and beets, carrots with bits of Bistronne earth still clinging to their tops, bright leeks, spheres of goat cheese and also apples for our Finier cider, not just for the hotel but for her moribund mother-in-law, for me as part of the Arianne family.

In the choice of items, she and I spoke not about cheese and apples but of scent, rigidity, ripeness, touch. And she would also ask about my duties at the prefecture—keeping abreast not so she could manipulate me, as I later came to believe, but rather, I foolishly thought, because she maintained an interest in me. I did not think of any extracurricular activities, but merely let the closeness between us develop, just as if one might drop a card on the floor of one's house and allow it to lie there for weeks, a decorative touch. I studied turnips with her, carried her bags, and if occasionally our shoulders brushed against each other, if I momentarily inhaled her skin's boiled-milk scent, she did nothing to disallow these intimacies, nor did she disabuse me of the special nonchalance we made our habit.

All this time, Paul was busy, Paul was traveling to Algiers on a special mission, Paul was required to travel without keeping his wife too informed.

"He plays the trumpet so beautifully." She always found a way to extol yet another of Paul's virtues, though I believed she barely knew her husband. "But when he's here, he plays with one amateur jazz group after another. Each one keeps breaking up. Something doesn't happen—Paul exists in his own world. One day his music group sees this, hears it, they break up. People like being around him but somehow he fails to—"

"Connect?" I said helpfully, having learned a few tricks from Izzy just those few summers earlier. I had no taste for jazz then, as I would later, when it bore greater relevance to my own life's pattern. At that time, I heard it as a heartless and infinitely adaptable cacophony zigzagging across piles of ideas. But I knew its basic principles from my student years in Paris, having heard enough people raving about the latest at the Club Marche or the Club Amerique. "His melody is there—" I ventured.

"Yes."

"But there's no interaction with others' harmony." I was quoting someone who'd once reviewed a show at the Marche. "It's a parallel world."

"You know so much, Emile," she said. "I don't know why you let me babble on to you."

This was the Arianne I might have held onto. But our foundation was flawed. First off, none of my knowledge was earned; it was aped, based on what I'd learned from Izzy, on my student eavesdroppings, on certain insights I'd gained from the reading of cheap novels. I might as well have spent my life in a cave hooked up with a radio transistor. Nonetheless, she and I forged an intimacy. Once, for instance, she told me that Paul liked her for her discernment, and that she often withheld her opinions of a party after they took their leave so as to make him press her. How great a confession this was to me, how included I felt in her private arena.

At the time, I thought it lucky that Izzy had decided to abandon his legal clerk work in Finier. Only now, I realize, he must have been responding to the new regional strictures prohibiting foreigners in certain professions. He'd returned to Paris to pursue acting, the avocation he'd dabbled in all through his student years, and was now apprenticed to a master pantomime artist while working nights as a comedian in cabarets. Had he stayed in Finier with Paul gone, I'm sure he might've pressed his suit with Arianne, and could well have been successful, as his student years had exorcised any lingering adolescent gawkiness, making him into a powerful figure, cryptic and sinuous, a magnet for female attention. He still surfaced, occasionally, as a topic in Arianne's conversation, but I sensed she saw him mainly as a placeholder for our shared summer. The competitive grit left my heart and I felt fond of Izzy all over again. With him gone, I could open the door to which he'd escorted me.

Meanwhile, during that first period which people came to call the phony war, no one knew how quickly our collapse would occur. This uncertainty rippled down to us in the provinces in small ways: we had to fill out forms in triplicate. Also, a certain unpleasantness began: I had to endure discussions with peasants who showed up in a salty rabble to the prefecture, protesting quotas we'd had to impose, requisitions we tried to keep as small as we could. It was not our doing, of course, but rather our government's urgent need: we were obliged to send north to our patriots a quota of Bistronne onions and chickens, cheese and wine and pâté, our millers' flour.

I took my mentor's advice and tended to delegate these meetings with the peasants to an underling, as no good ever came from my meeting with the rabble. I failed to placate those peasants; they failed to hear me. Some, in fact, had been my old schoolmates, but I hated when any of them brought up our past acquaintance, preferring that they acted as if we had never met, as if they'd never heard me called Poulquet the Ugly or Poulquet the Hump. Whether or not they visibly recognized me, it grated me to listen to them—that it was unfair for us to be giving up the fruit of our Bistronne land for the greedy north. Nor did I enjoy sharing my idea with them—that this surrender of goods was a necessary and small sacrifice for our France. This was a period during which, if people would just quiet down, we could almost forget the threats our leaders attempted to placate.

Many of the men who habituated my favorite café, most of them peasants who came to town to sell their goods, made a point of never mentioning the Germans and their approach. I was grateful for this dignified prudence, especially when we in the provinces were still kept (but for the onslaught of refugees, and the question of how to handle them) in the dark. I especially wished not to confront men who, whatever they'd been as schoolboys, now had the irreproachability of our Bistronne sun and earth tracked into their hands, while my own stayed as pale and unworked as during my lonely youth.

In so many ways, during this time, Arianne was my helpmeet. When she wanted to listen, she listened forcibly, determined to root out problems. At the core she was bored by other people (I saw this in her interactions with the hotel staff) unless they could reflect what a good problem-solver she was, and hence, what a good person. She could annex any bit of trivia, and especially enjoyed giving advice on the subject of the peasants. At which point she could not keep herself from repeating any advice she had offered several times over, perseverating as if the listener hadn't heard the first time. I was a sitting duck for this advice, loving her attention, her determination to identify herself as a good person rooting out unfairness. She was smart about the problems that beset a bureaucrat, though I admit that often the problems she solved best were those I'd invented a minute before.

After marketing was done, we'd stow our gatherings at the river, under the willow tree I favored. With our chores finished, she became even more mine, in our little private bower within shouting distance of the hotel. Whatever we did there, whether sharing a baguette or sipping from a jeweled flask she'd given me, whether we spoke of her or delved into Emile's life to solve problems, I had never been so close to anyone. Not to Izzy, not to Charlot, not to myself. Many times I had to hold back the urge to reach out and take hold of her hand, to smooth her hair. Equally often, however, her very skin disgusted me; shiny and innocent, unbroken, a landing spot for flies, filled with half-truths, and perhaps this halfness was part of her magic.

Solving others' problems must have been a way Arianne could excuse herself from the hotel, for which she bore too great a sense of responsibility, given that its fortunes were so faded, its heyday long past. A great-great-grandfather Papa Fauret was rumored to haunt the hotel's halls, able to shatter a window into a crystallized spiderweb, turn on steam irons and clatter laundry chutes. I told her that her exaggerated responsibility toward the hotel made it seem she had sworn an allegiance to old Papa. What I did not tell her was that I felt she had begun to live a tragedy. In my view, Paul had seduced her and immediately abandoned her with his need to travel so extensively, no matter how highly she thought of his work. Only now do I see that the new war-related burdens which I faced at work and her abandonment were linked, but at the time, I thought he'd betrayed her and that she therefore did whatever she could to ensure her place in his family, ending up overconcerned with details such as the hotel's plumbing. She went so far as to have a woman weave a showpiece heirloom quilt for the hotel, crassly delineating the Fauret family line and ensuring her own name skirted the lower-right border in shiny gilt thread.

I never shared with Arianne my view of her tragedy, as I had no wish to upset the terms of our exchange: I made up problems and she listened, an overactive saint. At the same time, it did not escape my notice that her listening was inaccurate, tweaking me into someone else's form. She listened in boxes. Was it Paul she wished to make of me? Or perhaps, more likely, one of her childhood Redons, the men who seemed to have such depths of loyalty and bravery.

Like you, I wanted to tell her, a catacomb truth, a place where we could clutch each other, *I am not made of heroic stuff*. Or, sometimes: *we're better than heroes*. Yet as I spoke to her, despite the peasants and my evasions, with the lure of Paul's image pulling me on, I could not help portraying myself as heroic, riddled with lesser minds all around. When the national emergency seized the rest of the nation, when fifteen thousand were put in internment camps, when our Bistronne was still left relatively untouched, I took on the habit of inflating small events in my department. It was easy to grant valor to the smallest of bureaucratic transfers and communiqués, to events related to the threat of invasion we stared down and those from another galaxy altogether, such as my hosting of the chairman of the Paris Polo Club, who came on a day trip to size up the height of our bistronnaise horses.

Once she surprised me, seized me by my shoulders as I prattled on about some inconsequentiality, a trifling misunderstanding between my department and another, a small affair in which I'd been required to write a damning report to Bordeaux implying that a certain bureaucratic strategy for listing citizens was itself potentially of foreign derivation. She reproached me: *Don't you ever admit to feeling anything?*

I just shrugged, a stupid smile on my face, because I didn't want to sacrifice the balance between us, feeling perhaps that I'd misunderstood how she listened to me. Perhaps I was not her friend but merely her little placeholder, a helpful little eunuch holding the vegetable basket. *Don't look so long in the face, Emile*, she chided me.

It did not escape me that any time we approached anything that had to do with discussing our relationship, she banished the discussion by throwing her arms around me in an outburst of girlishness, saying *You know I love you Emile!*

I took this as both truth and insult. A truth, because masked under that girlish front was the fact that she needed me. Every day I was simply there, avoiding the hubbub of males, from teenagers to men already past their prime, required to queue up outside our assembly centers to await conscription. Instead of being part of that mass, by virtue of my position, I was a peaceable enough young man, hands folded, not unhandsome from certain angles, seated at noon, awaiting her by the fountain in the small triangle outside the hotel. I was an available fact. Also a daily requirement, if she were honest. Yet the dispassion with which she said she loved me insulted the truth: she actually *did* love me. One day she might wake up and realize that the person who had remained her steadfast confidant was none other than Emile Poulquet.

One particular day, the sun harsh upon Finier, dazzling as her smile, she and I wended our usual way to the river. I remember feeling I'd been given the keys to an earthly paradise. The dazzle invited me and clobbered me. She was so *positive*. She had moved beyond her obsession with the hotel and was now quite spirited about a pamphlet-and-poster consortium she had organized, ostensibly meant to get youth to rally behind their country by improving their wilderness skills, another link I did not quite understand. It was 1939 and she was good at drawing people to her causes. I found her most persuasive when speaking of the storm awaiting us if we did not act conscionably toward our fellow patriots—Spaniards, Belgians, foreigners—who had come over the mountains, whom we had already needed to intern in other regions' camps. I could almost drop everything to follow her. In her was a demonic will, and she'd learned well how to channel this: her radiance could draw people close yet averted reproach, making her an impassable fortress. Already she'd begun to establish her good reputation in town. You could see it on so many storefronts, bright multicolored posters advertising less her cause and more herself: a woman of principle.

But we didn't talk of any of that on this day. Instead, she was gleeful Arianne. "Look at those gardens!" she exclaimed, as we walked toward the river. "You know, Emile, I envy people who have that kind of energy and talent."

Her positivity rendered anything one would bring up about the past irrelevant. There were times it rose in my craw: how easily, with a single frank apology, she could lay to rest the childhood dragons which had ruled my life, all that had left me feeling, no matter my career, a shamed fumbler operating in the margins of respectability, missing hints, trying to create whatever adulthood I could by working toward honors at the prefecture.

However, if ever I broached the subject of the schoolgirl she had been, before the hotel summer when she'd moulted before my eyes, her tone turned clinical. At such moments, she was superb at treating me like a specimen, *handling* me. Once again Arianne was so insufferably in control. It was worth more to hold things within until I felt they'd sweat out my pores. Far better than being entered into one of her categories. Her mind worked with such strict boxes, neatly stacked in a row, that I resisted being labeled by her one more time.

At times I chatted with Odile, who had a certain friendly conversation with Arianne—the two of them favored the same linen shop, apparently—and I'd tell her how Arianne was not all that she seemed, that her sunny do-gooder aspect kept her dark side well covered.

Odile would look down at her desk, at a sheaf of papers. With a certain audacity, that trait of hers which would prove so useful in later years, she'd say: "Ah, Mister Poulquet, she's weaker than you think. You give Madame Fauret too much power."

"How can one give power? People *take* power. Tell me I'm wrong," I'd say, though she'd demur.

Odile was eventually persuaded to confess. "Madame Fauret has told me how she thinks *you* have a mania for controlling everything."

"Me?" I laughed this off. "She's just seeing her mirror."

"YOU'RE SMOOTH, Emile, did you know that?" Arianne asked me one riverside afternoon. "While, I don't know, I hate myself sometimes." A rare show of self-questioning, a softer voice. She had just fired the hotel steward, a man who'd seemed ancient to us, all shuffling mannerisms and nose-hairs, having held his position some forty years.

She'd fired him merely because he'd looked down that nose at her every morning. "I don't know why I behave as I do. I can't tell Paul these things, he's too good—" allowing a frequently repeated unspoken argument between us

> *Paul is not that good.*
> But he is.
> *You don't know him.*
> Why can't I believe someone's good, Emile?
> *Your life is your own.*
> You don't believe in goodness, Emile.
> *I've got my own version and it works. If you were honest—*
> Anyway, he and I are married.
> *That's your epitaph?*
> Yes.
> *Haven't you heard of annulments?*
> I'd never find anyone better than Paul.
> *Doesn't that go against everything you say about optimism?*
> I never said I'd be consistent. He's a good man, Emile.

to transpire in its silent way before she corrected only the last ripple of connotation. "Not that you're bad, Emile, you're just easy to talk to."

I knew the real answer. *You love me*, I wanted to tell her. Though this couldn't be reciprocal. No one can love a perfect being; there's no room for love to grip. And it may seem strange that I considered Arianne perfect, as I delight in pointing out her flaws and inconsistencies, but even her past cruelty was perfectly contained by her beauty. All her flaws and illogic, catalogued by me privately, made her untouchable—that repulsive, alluring skin—and also my belonging.

Just one more afternoon with Arianne. Yet it was as special as all the other days we spent together, 152 days if my private tally is correct. In that interregnum, before my promotion that night in Bomont, before Paul had returned, Arianne and I had a certain understanding. Who else had been her victim? No one. She had unmasked herself with greatest specificity to me. Because love lives in what is specific, with me, therefore, she had been the most intimate.

The days on which business at the prefecture or hotel intruded and we did not see each other, I felt watery, adrift. Her mood had begun to shape my own. So that when we met, such was our dance, as she burst from the hotel doors, I knew exactly what kind of engagement we would have. Admittedly, she was not the world's most subtle creature. If happy, she might fling her arms around me right away, shocking the staid concierge and exclaiming her awful *you know I love you, Emile!* As loathsome as I found it, this was rather daring, given her position in the family Fauret. Already she risked something for me.

What was strangest was that after I became prefect—after she performed the kindest thing she had ever done for me, making sure that I achieved my ambition, after she'd used every bit of sway with Paul's family to do what I thought was a favor for me—after that, we were no longer friends. We gave up our noontime marketing just as if it had been mere youthful folly. Weeks went by in which I didn't see her. When I did, it was a chance occurrence. All manner of refugees, including jews from outside Finier and the foreign communists, had started to jostle us in our very marketplace, words rumbling in a town which had started to seem too small. I stood outside the hubbub, speaking with our postmaster about overseeing a shipment of children's wooden clogs and puppets, meant for use by the Red Cross up north. At that moment, Arianne passed by, wearing a tight felt hat with a veil before it, holding Paul's elbow. It is true that almost every gesture of hers spelled exclusion of Emile. Only her furtiveness, peeking through the veil, offered clear evidence that she too suffered from the pain of a ghost limb.

ON MY THIRD return to Finier, while settling in with Moses and his tribe, I wanted to be sure my intentions toward Arianne were firm. I would thank her for her court appearance, certainly, but after that, I would press for her admission. First, that she'd been wrong to behave as she had throughout our shared lives. That she had sought Emile only to discard him as if he, I, were a rag doll without soul. Once I confronted her, she would release me from a certain spell, and I wouldn't call it *guilt* exactly; rather, it was that pesky cousin to guilt I'd first started to feel while in that café as the survivors had streamed in: a desire for vindication.

Once she acknowledged that her actions had been wrong, that she'd controlled me from the day my hump was removed, there would be some reparation. I would give her my last will and testament. Barring her death before mine, which I didn't envision as likely (Arianne was too mean-spirited to die merely in her eighties), she would have to execute my will, deal with my holdings.

Nowadays experts love to speak of closure and apology, as if you can just slam shut a door on history. Though I'd laughed at these experts, I thought I could come clean by denying her whatever it is that they call closure. Instead she'd have the eternity of me, the testament of Emile Poulquet, appended to the correct history I'd write regarding her life with Paul. She would be bequeathed my papers, now locked in a claptrap storage facility in Clamart, along with my ashes in an urn. It would take her forever. She would have to deal with the weight of Emile Poulquet until her last breath, forced to go through every tiny decision, waiting for a strong outbound wind to release my last bits of self over the river Xerxes.

SIXTEEN

But Arianne was unreachable. This at least was what Moses' friend told us, Jacquot walking with us from the pigs, away from gravity and piety and simplicity. Jacquot in his high boots and with his army of dogs contentedly sniffing alongside him. Jacquot had a smoker's cough and a greasy leather look, an all-over happiness that he knew way more about the big story than either of us did.

"You'll see," he promised, shivering in the morning's chill.

He smoked too nervously and this was a giveaway but not a huge one. Being such a tall pole of a fellow with such pulsing blue veins made his story more believable, that he had been an aristocrat's son somewhere *it doesn't matter where*. He did look as if he'd been bred to be a greyhound, if one now preferring to live in a mutt's kennel.

JACQUOT EXPLAINED in his rush of words that he had kind of hooked up with Moses early on when Moses had first showed up in Finier. He said that even if Moses thought Jacquot was too much a partyer, Jacquot knew Moses secretly wanted to party as much as Jacquot did and that Moses wanted to have as good a time as Jacquot knew how to give. And that Moses would confess it to no one but he'd even helped Jacquot make the stuff that Jacquot sold which you had to be careful about making and selling because neighbors would see you throwing out vast numbers of bottles of household detergents and they'd also smell the chemical fires you had to burn to make the stuff. They could see the burnt aluminum squares and then if they decided in their puny little heads to report you to the authorities there was a lifetime you had to spend in the pen. Which was so stupid because there you were just trying to live a simple life and bring fulfillment and variety so people could live with more enjoyment if that was what people chose, just like making a movie for someone, so why should that be called evil? Then you have people like Moses who are so-called friends but who are too chickenshit to ever help Jacquot cook the stuff up again and then there are also all the sorry excuses Moses makes like that he prefers to live cleanly but anyone seven kilometers away could know that was total bullshit since Moses leaves trash in wastecans like the rest of the pigs. And also because of Moses' pretty-boy looks he gets fed by the rich daughters of the bourgeoisie so what's he talking about? And there was also a hell of a lump of good money to be made in the stuff that Jacquot sold. Mainly because he didn't fleece anyone with his price. He believed in fairness, was anyway just another prole mec doing hackwork to make ends meet here and there.

"Whatever," was how Moses had answered this stream.

JACQUOT HAD COME to find us at Moses' pigs. He had known Moses would take me to see the pigs first. Jacquot had heard about me from Christian and had also seen me sleeping. He had therefore wanted to meet *in a formal way* the new guest of the wastrels.

"How do you do, sir?" he said, taking a breath, mocking courtesy, withdrawing his hand before I could reach it. He said people were going crazy in town and guessed we'd be interested in knowing that. He talked forty words a minute, smoking a cigarette every few sets of forty. So it seemed. He said he could walk with us part of the way toward town. But he'd have to split before town so he could meet his two girlfriends.

"I always prefer to have two girlfriends," he said, "Cerb-X and Delhi. Share the love." He spelled out their names for us with the hostile precision that lived in his face, probably the very quality he'd lived his life to escape: I knew all about the outlaw life and the immunization it could offer against one's own self-disgust. "See, things and girls go better in pairs," Jacquot explained with an overhearty bravado, speaking of sharing the love. Sharing two sets of ears was more what it sounded like to me.

Jacquot was going to make Cerb-X and Delhi part of the wastrels if Moses could promise to stay trustworthy in their presence because Jacquot wasn't into all that polyamory shit, and he hoped I wasn't, but maybe Jacquot could later sort of be into polyamory so long as there was generally respect in the tribe. The most important thing right now was the plot, the big art project. The art scheme. He tried to get Moses to agree with this. I didn't like this idea at all, wanted no part of any scheme, but as the guy started to speak, sounding useless enough, clearly a self-immunizer, I decided his plot sounded halfway benign, for the time being at least. I had the feeling I should stick by Moses, part of the survivor's logic and instinct which has kept me going as long as I have, and when I privately swung my pendulum, turning a bit from the two boys, it offered a rather weak-willed YES, but a YES nonetheless. At least somewhere between MAYBE and YES.

"Yeah," said Moses. "I'm with you, Jacqui." Though to his credit the boy did shoot me a look of weak apology.

All right, so Jacquot was saying maybe tonight he'd bring the girls up to the squat and that could be their inauguration. Since two people had left last week maybe that would make the squat not too crowded with this new old guy included (tossing his head at me), something like fifteen of us loosely creating the new tribe which was okay with Jacquot if it was okay with Moses since after all it had been the two of them originally who had found the place and brought people together under the same ideals of wastreldom.

"Whatever," Moses had said again, appearing diminished by the company of fast-talking Jacquot.

Jacquot's thought was that the wastrels should consider a way to use the current disruption to their benefit. I didn't know what that might mean. The current disruption? Did he mean the reunion of refugees? Jacquot scared me. I did consider—with great fatigue, I'll admit—spending the night somewhere else. But the pendulum had spoken: I listened to it with respect, and to Jacquot as politely as I could.

AT THE END of his little discourse, just before he had to go hook up, as he said, with his friends, Jacquot returned to explain the disruption. As just about everything in my life has seemed to edge forward or backward from her, what Jacquot called the screw-up had to do with Arianne, whom Jacquot called *the old lady who'd been screwing with the wastrels for a while*. At first, he said, she'd hired Jacquot last year, or her foundation had. She and the Polish guy in charge of her foundation had wanted Jacquot and his clique to be in charge of getting the youth out for her annual Days of Remembrance, when the resistance was remembered, the Days which were different from this one-time refugee deal. Arianne had wanted people to remember the resistance and the role her bigwig family the Faurets had played annually. She'd asked the youth to sing songs which she'd teach them through Christian, the guy with the guitar up in the manse. And she'd asked them all to march through the woods like a bunch of clowns for hire. All to be well documented.

While I had heard of Arianne's general renown—RESISTANCE WIDOW PLACES RURAL SOUTHERN VILLAGE ON MAP OF WARTIME REMEMBRANCE—RESISTANCE WIDOW CREATES FOUNDATION TO RESTITUTE MEMORY—RESISTANCE WIDOW ORGANIZES TOURS OF WARTIME SIGNIFICANCE—RESISTANCE WIDOW HELPS CONSOLI-DATE TOWN'S HOLDINGS—these developments, over the last few years, reminded me less of opposition France and more of Vichy France, as if Arianne had decided to borrow from the tactics of the old marshal who'd led us bureaucrats, the marshal to whom we civil servants had sworn our personal loyalty, whose aristocratic face had stared down at us from every office and school during the war, a man who'd cherished the youth scouting movement, whose mien had shone upon everyone, a grandfather whose eyes made you wish to be worthy. Perhaps Arianne was trying to figure herself as some kind of marshal of memory, starting a new national revolution, her foundation going to the extreme of hiring someone like Jacquot to get out the youth. The Faurets must be desperate, I thought, desperate to reconstitute *their* history.

None of her plans had come through for the Days, Jacquot was saying, and perhaps this was what gave him a certain vindictive triumph as he spoke. He said Arianne was getting blamed for the death of a farmer. Because, according to Jacquot and his récit, some farmer had refused her, for months. "And she's hot for an old lady," he hacked, his smoker's laugh rattling the quiet of the morning, the road flanked by its forest, a forest which could soften and hide so many things but not this ugly excrescence of youth, this tall smoking bloodhound of a youth with his pretense of knowing Arianne. He knew her no better than he knew a stray stone.

I wanted to punch him but held back, as not only have I made it a private code of honor never to act in bad temper, but my hitting arm was not up to snuff. As much as I could ridicule Arianne in the theater of my own mind—the extremity of her gestures, her love of making the Faurets stand in for so many other things, *the Faurets* meaning *the resistance* and *right thinkers* and *noble history that should be remembered*—I also wanted to protect her from becoming a debased currency, her name slung about on the cleft tongue of this fellow Jacquot.

I didn't understand what he meant—*a farmer had refused her*—and said as much, which gave Jacquot more than I wanted, a great puffery of pride. But he explained it all. There had been a different kind of refusal than what he'd insinuated. Some farmer in a duck-billed cap had said he wouldn't let Arianne and her group of refugees use his field, where a camp used to be. She and her refugee society had wanted to use the farmer's field as a pathway to a cemetery and museum in honor of those who'd lived or died in the camp. The field and the neighboring museum would become a French monument, opened for free on *annual patrimony days*, a place to which tourists could come in order to learn the truth of history.

"So they can come learn *her* version of history," I inserted, unable to stop myself.

"Right," said Jacquot, another sarcastic citizen of our times. "Her version, someone else's version. Big difference. All I care is we get paid. She used to be decent with that. She pays, we get out the youth!" and he sprang up as if in some imaginary tournament, dunking a ball into an unseen hoop.

"There is a difference," I said, still on the previous point, but Jacquot ignored me, headlong into his hushed explanation. Whether more for his benefit or ours, I couldn't say; the boy had a flair for the dramatic. Apparently, the duck-billed farmer had refused Arianne, preventing the refugees their memorial museum by forbidding them right of access to the former site of the camp.

"Private property," I murmured, wanting to close the conversation.

Jacquot ignored me. Because it was the farmer's land, named after his family, in his family forever. It used to be a forest, but during the war the government had made him give it up, turning it into the road to the internment camp, using the trees to make charcoal for supply trucks. And this was just one of our camps from which people got carted off on trains to death camps in Poland.

"These stories," said Moses. "Camps in the Bistronne?" he was incredulous. "That was Germany. Jacquot's making this up, don't you think, Mister Raoul?"

I shook my head no, what Jacquot was saying was pretty much the case.

Moses was scratching the source of one of his long woolly braids, as if in wonderment. Jacquot went on, five hundred volts of self-justification making him speed up: what bothered Arianne the most about the farmer's refusal, and why she'd gone public with being bothered, and why she'd made this such a big-deal event, inviting the foreign press to the reunion, promising some great revelation, having recruited so many types to Finier, filmmakers and journalists coming in from all over like pigeon-droppings landing on her hotel, supposedly a bigger deal than when Mengele's remains were getting dug up in Brazil or whatever, was that the guy, the farmer, his last refusal had been about the statue.

"The statue," crowed Jacquot, "doesn't that just about kill you?"

Arianne had wanted to erect a great iron statue to her late husband, Paul, he said. Another hero-of-the-resistance statue, iron with bronze detail. It had already been cast by a famous sculptor, the young Pole who was actually her lover. Jacquot knew all about it, how the young Pole had spent a lot of time stealing money from Arianne's foundation, and how she was letting him do this because she was blinded by love, thought his artistic fingers would make the next new thing, a great discovery.

Arianne and her Pole liked to ride gelded horses together in the hills, and even, one day, Jacquot said, speech speckled with *shut up Moses*, he had sort of gone vaulting with the two of them, with Arianne and her Pole and their thoroughbred geldings.

"Whatever," Moses said again, with greater incrimination, playing *whatever* as musically as Christian had played his three-string guitar.

But Jacquot went on. In his view, the sculptor had done a great justice, he could say that much, to the image of old Paul. Jacquot had known Paul when he was older and kind of going crazy. But shut up Moses, he did know them, and so he thought the sculptor had done a damn good job. Yes, Arianne had said publicly, the statue was of Paul, but it was really just a stand-in for all the brave heroes who'd died fighting with the resistance in the war. "Hey, I'm talking, Moses," said Jacquot.

Moses had made no gesture at interruption, but Jacquot's words seemed intended as an insult directed privately at Moses and his most tender joints.

Last night, Jacquot went on, he had taken his two girlfriends and had gone to see the big sculpture of Paul lying butt-naked in the giant quonset hut where the mercantile factory had boomed and busted. Jacquot and the girls had just axed themselves into the shed (Moses could ask Delhi and Cerb-X if he doubted this). And they had seen it: the sculptor had cast Paul massively, with bronze fists, massive biceps, an orange fake-jewel sparkle in the eye. A larger-than-life Paul with all the bulging muscles of all those guys who fought in the resistance.

"Cool," was all that Moses said to this. Placatingly.

The sculptor's work was waiting to be installed, in temporary internment in the quonset hut right off the road near the farmer's field, fifty yards from where the entrance to the actual internment camp had been. "We've got to use it somehow," said Jacquot. "Not sure yet." He turned on me. "We thought we could get you to do something for us."

"With the camp?" I almost screeched.

"The statue," he corrected me, "old man."

DESPITE THE PENDULUM having swung its weak YES, I did not like at all the sound of this art project—far too many angles were involved. As a successful fugitive, I had something of an instinct for unsuccessful projects, and by this token you could say Jacquot's whole gig, as he called it, was a giant elephant balancing on a sou. It could interfere with my own plans to remain incognito until I got to see Arianne. Before I had time to respond, we'd come to where Jacquot's ladies awaited him on a swingset in an abandoned playground. Or rather, their dogs pelted toward us first, one black, one mottled white, friendly once they sniffed Moses.

"Don't worry, Raoul," said Moses, laughing at my balking.

Raoul, I reminded myself. Raoul Tavelle.

In the playground, the two young ladies dismounted from their swings. They had the look of those who'd spent weeks living in desert and forest. Sunburnt, lips cracking. *Lula!* cried one of them to her dog. Both young ladies, in point of fact, had dog collars around their necks, but one held herself like a blueblood, a tall broad personage of Russian stock, I thought, wearing clothes that hung off her, a man's undershirt, low leather dungarees, hair spiked like a coxcomb with an actual chicken's bone holding it upward. How dirty was she? Her bearing was that of a savage tribal queen descending from the clouds to address earthly peons. This was the decadence I'd learned of as a schoolchild in history class, the sinister decline of values and traditions threatening France, and it was now walking toward us.

"Hold it right there," said Jacquot. The girls froze while Jacquot held his hand to his ear as if receiving a transmission. "Can you hear it?" He waved then at all the surrounding world. "These linden trees, man, they were just cut. Can you feel them? Shrieking?"

Moses shook his head. "I don't," adding quickly, "but that doesn't mean it's not there." He looked half-awed and I immediately wanted to disabuse the boy of any illusions regarding countercultural sovereigns like this Jacquot.

"Those trees were just cut," boomed Jacquot. "People don't care. This all goes and runs off into the rivers. Then into bad karma. Then the atmosphere."

"It's bad," I agreed, wanting to lubricate the machinery, give Jacquot enough attention so that he could cease speaking, but it just made the queenly girl tilt her head in my general direction.

"I have a message for people," said Jacquot, grandstanding perhaps for the girls' benefit. Perhaps this was the contemporary equivalent of courtly poetry. "People got to get together. People should learn to listen to each other better."

"I know someone for you," said Moses. "Maybe you should talk with him sometime."

"Yeah," said Jacquot with his own breed of vagueness. Then he too unfroze, as if coming out of his spell.

"Jacquot," said the savage queen girl. Essentially, she rushed him. She took his arm and didn't acknowledge either Moses or me when Jacquot introduced her. Instead, she just leaned in, delivering a rant about the barn where they had tried to stow their stuff. There'd been some guy who'd bothered the girls, who'd *upset them*, but whatever the trouble, her talk was hypnotic, capable of stilling Jacquot if for just a moment.

The one Jacquot had called Delhi had walked carefully after her friend, Delhi a small girl in tighter clothes, walking as if bowlegged on a tightrope, clearly warm-blooded on this cooler morning, holding a beer bottle against her flat exposed navel. She called to her piebald dog *bad Lula!* and then looked straight into me. I don't know if I'd ever paid such attention to a lady's navel. Beyond that little curlicue at the center of her being, she had sweet features but a dirty face that made her almost as harsh as Cerb-X, who now interrupted her flow of speech to nod and smile knowingly at Delhi, their girl beauty flashing a secret between them. The message being: they had a knowledge beyond what any of us could grasp.

"Just one of his moods," Cerb-X explained to Delhi at one point in reference to Jacquot. "Not to take seriously."

"So let me understand," Jacquot was saying in a voice far more amiable than I had heard from him yet. "You don't have a place to put our stuff."

Another condescending nod, a close-lipped smile. As if the young ladies had already been informed of all our destinies. As if they were biding time while destruction played itself out, with only a few scattered pleasures to look forward to along the way. I was wondering about their parents: what did the parents who had given birth to two such tribal queens think? What could anyone see when looking upon Cerb-X and Delhi?

Young ladies who presented themselves as being far closer than anyone else living to the truth of sand and sex, close to dirt and beauty and aggression. Something way beyond sex. They profaned this era, seeming to announce that they were of an earlier era and perhaps of a later one, one in which we crawled over the surface of the earth, killing, finding shelter, feasting or starving, tribes warlike or peaceful, with spirit beliefs or without spirit beliefs, always leaving behind a litter of bones.

Both young ladies also knew one couldn't take one's eyes off them. Self-consciously nubile, I thought, girls clearly feasting on this knowledge.

"What do you do?" I asked Delhi, wanting to stop the hypnosis which Cerb-X exercised over me.

"We make art?" she answered, bored but polite. "We just came from nine weeks in the forest. Now we're going to make art about the war and memory?"

"We got stiffed," Cerb-X explained. "Jacquot's Arianne lady didn't pay us for what we did. In getting out the youth. We got kids here from all the way up in Toulouse."

"Rounding up the youth!" said Jacquot. "We were good," strangely gleeful, his fist against the sky again, everyone around me prone to making this abhorrent power salute.

"They said we'd gathered up only vagrants, people coming off the bus at the Bar Central. But you know, they didn't specify in advance. So that's their fault. Right? Like they didn't say what kind of people they wanted us to round up. Then they think it's fair if they don't pay us." Cerb-X almost spat. "It wasn't the world's easiest job, you know?" actually going so far as to *grab my cuff*, my soiled cuff. "I felt like a whore," she laughed. "Whore for history." For some reason, she was trying to persuade *me*, and I thought it was that I was a stand-in for all old people. Old Emile Poulquet, old Raoul Tavelle. Whoever I was, Cerb-X scared me, so sharp in cutting off her words. "It's bull if you ask me. People like Arianne Fauret." Hot with girl-beauty and emphasis. "Bullshit how people like her control everything. There's like no toilet in town that doesn't have her family's name plastered all over. Fauret bullshit this and that. The Faurets just swallow up everything."

"You're right," I muttered, despite myself.

"They think they're so fucking pure. It's disgusting. They think we're just a bunch of I don't know." She hadn't let go of my cuff. "And we're sick of being fed that *bullshit* that rich people's history is everyone's history. The books and schools and everyone, you know? They don't own all the rights. Now's a different time."

Jacquot appeared struck by admiration, as if this speech had been the equivalent of an aria. "We're taking back the land."

"Excuse me," I said, which brought Cerb-X to focus more intently upon me, though her look was, it didn't escape my notice, a bit rich in amusement. She let go of my cuff. A certain queasiness told me she would imitate me later. "What," I said anyway, "or who is it you're *for* exactly?"

It was a ridiculous question but had to be asked. I could not take my pendulum out of my pocket to size up the new girl-equipped situation, so I made do with the means available. The girls' presence had, as they say, thrown me for a loop. I wanted to size up my prospects. These types might turn out to be a bit more of the rabblerouser persuasion than what my pendulum or I could handle.

"We're about victims. We help anyone who was a victim," said Cerb-X. "Or is. But at the same time we like to get rid of victim consciousness, you know? No master, no slave."

"Any time, any place," added Jacquot, helpfully.

"—the refugees?" I said, managing to squeak.

"I'm saying we're sick of fucking history landowning rich fuckers thinking they control everything. Fuck the matter with someone who doesn't pay?" She almost slapped the back of her hand against my shoulder. "Like we're beneath her? It's just money. I mean isn't that what it's about in the end of the day? Coinage? A bunch of metal and paper?" It seemed like a bunch of non sequiturs, but clearly the others were in agreement. *Yeah*, they muttered. Even Moses was gripped.

"I see," I said, dour as a census-taker. I will admit that just being included within their tribe, however provisionally, did give me a weird thrill. How to explain it? I'd been in many milieus as a refugee myself, sidelining along history, but what contemporary group had so forcibly opened up and ingested me into its midst, treating my ear as the gentle protection into which complaints might be entrusted? None. It was almost like old times at the prefecture, though my membership among the wastrels had been subscribed solely by virtue of my association with Moses, however tenuous that was. Meanwhile, Cerb-X was looking at me, awaiting some vital response, chin thrust forward like a bulldog's.

"I couldn't agree more," I found myself saying. This happened to be true; I did think Arianne controlled too much.

"See?" said Jacquot. "Moses got himself a cool friend."

"It's not fair. So we're protesting," Delhi continued, picking up the stream. "Not against the refugees, you know. Against Arianne having organized this big thing. It's all ego. So we're like protesting for the refugees but against war. We want to make a big piece out of skeletons. We're using this roadkill we saved up. I have a friend who's a taxidermist in town. He'll preserve our stuff. Anyway, he owes me a favor."

"We'll set it up right after they have their concert," said Cerb-X. "It's for victims. Any undergod."

"You mean underdog," I corrected automatically.

"Right. Un-der-dog. Excuse me." Already the imitation came my way, the phrase drawn out in old-man accents. Perhaps the girl was one of those who thought any person over age forty was a joke, one to be regarded and dispensed with. "First we have to pull off the heist."

"The heist?" asked Jacquot.

"We want to steal the statue."

"The Paul statues," Delhi explained. "Her *hubby*," but the word was poorly suited to her. "That'll get her goat."

"The plan was not to *steal* the statue, ladies," said Jacquot. "To use it, yes."

"But we don't like big iron art." Cerb-X had on the smile of someone recently pleasured. "This'll be against the organizers. You know, against organization!" and her fist at the sky imitated Jacquot's. In general, the girl seemed to be a collection of tics and habits drawn from a motley group of acquaintances, as if she were a loosely rolling juggernaut of gesture, conquering others' random aspects.

"It stinks of war," said Delhi, suddenly bending down to kiss her dog, Lula.

"We're for peace," said Cerb-X with greater aggression.

JACQUOT ENLIGHTENED THEM with what he had just told us: that Arianne was being held for questioning, that she was a prime suspect in a farmer's murder. "Does that change your plans?"

"You're not telling us everything. Which guy?" said Cerb-X.

"You remember the guy we gleaned from?"

They smiled. "He was cute," said Cerb-X. "In an old-man way. Sorry," she winked at me. The girl was a slippery beast, hard to contain. I had more sympathy for her friend Delhi, more tranquil and watchful, her voice somewhat melodious, her whole being something I could catalogue as female. In fact, Delhi was someone I could imagine having worked for me in the prefecture all those years ago, though there was something Asiatic in her features and we couldn't have worked with anyone from Indochina back then. Some Bretons, however, have a certain tilt to the eyes; I could imagine this Delhi girl as a bretonnaise secretary, wearing one of those neat skirt-and-jacket ensembles ladies once wore.

"You're saying now's not the time to organize," said Delhi.

"We don't need trouble," Jacquot added, but checked Cerb-X.

Cerb-X clearly thought he was wrong. "All the better," said Cerb-X. "Just feel the need," slipping her wrist into Jacquot's grip, her other hand grasping his shoulder, the girl a picture of urgency, making an unstudied bliss steal across the bloodhound's face. "Seriously. I'm not saying massive. Massive's too much. But I'm saying this Arianne bullshit woman's all about war. I'm sure she screwed over other people if she screwed us over so royally. Bullshit Arianne savior of the Bistronne!" she aped. "Fucking Marianne Joan of Arc bullshit."

"Actually," I found myself saying again, the silence around me rather too close. "I—" They watched me, expecting me to continue. Clearly it took some pluck to interrupt Cerb-X. "All I mean is you're right. She wasn't a saint during the war."

Moses smiled. "You knew her?" he asked. "Cool. Tell me later?" But before I could answer, Cerb-X was back on her case.

"See! Eyewitness!" said Cerb-X. "I told you she had a screw loose. Bullshit not paying us. Art's the only way to screw back."

Jacquot shook his head. Indulgently, as if the father of headstrong daughters. "But we can't use *all* the skeletons. You'll save some."

"That's her decision," said Delhi, nodding again at Cerb-X. "Want some beer?" she asked me.

SEVENTEEN

"So now," said Jacquot. "You listening?"

Cerb-X and Delhi had headed down the road, Delhi's saddle-sore gait not without a certain pathos. Presumably the girls were picking up their stuff or going off to organize the skeletons; I couldn't keep their trajectory fixed. Jacquot snapped his fingers in front of my face.

"We don't know if they're going to hold that concert," he said. "Now Arianne's being held or whatever. So don't listen to those girls. Actually, it isn't a good time for us to go too public." He looked queasy, as if he wanted to shout after them, but they'd gone.

"Go easy," said Moses, trying to calm him.

But the girls had made Jacquot more jittery, making him speed on with his tale, his conjecture that even as we stood there Arianne Fauret was being held near Bomont, in a cell, where he presumed she was being questioned by the police.

He didn't have all the details. Basically the word on everyone's lips was the same: everyone believed that Arianne had arranged for the farmer to be killed. I was fingering my pendulum, half-listening.

"If she didn't do it herself, there must have been someone hired," he was saying. "She's murderous. Man, the guy died right near where an effing inspector was having *coffee*. Crazy. Just to build her museum?" He waited an emphatic moment. "You knew the woman," he said: an insult.

I just shook my head, more alert, aware mainly that I'd introduced an inconsistency. Moses defended me. "Don't apeshit, Jacqui."

"Actually, Cerb-X has a point. Maybe this is our chance."

"I'm not getting you, man," said Moses, retreating. "You're losing me."

"We got to focus, crazyhead. At the Fauret woman's trial. She's some kind of Marie Antoinette, right? We invite enough people. Take advantage. We might be able to claim some houses. She probably has squats all over, places we don't even know about."

"That *is* crazy."

"No, man. Got to see openings where they come. Declare our rights. It's people like her."

"People like what?" Moses pretended to be deeply involved with the end of one of his snarly braids.

"Cerb-X is right—the Ariannes disowned us. We got to join together, I'm not kidding, *reinhabit*. In the big scheme. You don't get the facts?"

"What facts," Moses said, eyes dull.

Jacquot returned to his theme. The farmer had been kind to the wastrels. Only the previous year, he'd let them reap the gleanings of his wheat and vegetable fields, saying he'd felt instructed to be kind to the wastrels by something he'd heard the village priest quote from the book of Ruth.

For an old man in Bomont, Bruno Somport had not been a bad guy.

EIGHTEEN

Bruno Somport.
I could not ignore it. Somport. Somport.
It was indisputable. I thought of the chimney-sweeping receipt in the dead man's pocket. And the American in his rental car. Could there be another B. Somport? Could the dead man himself have been a chimney-sweep? It didn't seem likely. The bicyclist had flown through the air, landing with his farmer's hands outstretched.

Bruno Somport. But all I really thought was how once again they all put the choice to me. Once again everyone badgered me. The world kept wanting to drag me from being a fugitive to acting as witness to playing judge.

And Arianne. At least certain things about her had stayed the same. She had gone public with her anger, had made it known that she wanted to organize the refugees against the farmer, had invited international journalists so she could get her way and raise great pressure against the farmer.

Yet her instinct for revenge had done her in. She had invited the American filmmaker, a man clumsy on the road. I knew who had killed Bruno Somport on the road near Bomont, and I knew without a doubt that it wasn't Arianne.

Was I supposed to all of a sudden jump forth like a musketeer? Come forth in a cape to save Arianne? Come finger the bad guy, point him out as he fumbled around with his American camera?

PART TWO

NINETEEN

It was the midpoint of August when, even without the refugees' reunion, there still would have been plenty of tourists, most bearing cameras like breastplates along with shiny, pointed walking spears, so many entering Finier like a conquering Valkyrie horde. Mid-August made it clear that all of them—the regulation-issue tourists, the backpackers and divorcées on their well-laden bicycle tours—were having their last gasp. All the bared adolescent male torsos heading for the underground riverboat ride were a little more emphatic, buttondown shirts tied in that insouciant, female way around their waists. I'd seen the lot of them the previous day outside the café, near one of the new photo stores, on the outskirts of the refugees, tourists a bit modified from the crew I'd known years earlier. Still eating the same sheep's-milk ice cream they always had but with an end-of-summer desperation, showing the knowledge they'd soon be kicked out, that their vacation in Finier would snap shut with the certainty of a suitcase latch.

■ ■ ■

I HAD ONLY SPENT a day and a half with Moses in his squat. I had been up at the manse, I had visited his pigs, had met Jacquot and his two lady friends. But after Jacquot's news, having learned that Arianne was being kept captive because of some bad American driver, I had requested Moses' forebearance, suggesting to him that I'd like to go my own way. "So soon?" Moses had said. He seemed reluctant to release me. Admittedly, this touched me, how these people formed connections so easily. "Don't worry," he said. "I'll find you. Just stay in Finier. Hey, it's small. Worse comes to worse, we'll hook up at that bar we stopped at, you know? Just hang. Where you said the music was so loud you felt it in your heart?"

One fact was that despite the morning's bounty, the overrich foods of Moses' posse, the generosity of his girl bourgeoisie, my stomach boiled with hunger. Another truth was that I felt the need to warn the American driver, inform him regarding the fate he was escaping. A certain compulsion to help him remained, though this was unusual and made no sense, given my limited resources. In retrospect, I suppose it had largely to do with the moment after the accident, when I'd urged him to make a run for it: we'd struck an unspoken contract. There is, after all, to paraphrase the proverb, often great honor among fugitives.

It was not that I wished to incriminate Arianne. Far from it. I was just trying to continue the terms of my contract by staying impartial. I had chosen to play judge, and that meant I had to find and notify the American. No one has ever said I was not, in the main, a dutiful man.

Before I left Moses, he and I made plans to meet later in the day at the concert, if it should still be held. I was disinclined to head back into the fray, but had also learned this lesson as a prefect: one promises first, then sees what one can deliver. Whatever part of me was still legitimately bistronnaise made me a contrarian, and the contrarian wanted to know whether there still might be, despite everything, a concert in the early evening in the main square.

There, finally, I might be able to see Arianne. She could be released quickly: this was also my judge's hope. Enough information would be found, I was sure, as my lifelong torturer was powerful enough to be set free, to stay the blameless lady she'd always wanted to be—a positive, prevailing wind, the organizer, *Arianne*.

I reminded myself, as if in a quorum of Emiles, that I was in my right mind; that I had lost no clarity over the years; that (so far) I'd stared senility in the face; that, however tired or forgetful I might sometimes be, my mental state had survived all my aliases; hence my decisions were sound.

"You won't mind if I go off by myself for part of the day?" I said to Moses. I will not say it was solely my need for a backup place to stay the night that made me polite. I found myself loath to burn bridges, still feeling the boy would be the best road to Arianne, mainly because he had so far seemed to hear the spirit behind any request I'd made. Not to mention that there was something special to him, and I am old enough to know when an alliance deserves cultivation. The only certainty was that I felt required to investigate whatever dust was being raised around this question of the American's accident and the false accusation against Arianne. Brute that others believe me to be, I nonetheless didn't want her to suffer, not needlessly. Perhaps if her circumstances were stable, I might meet with her, let slip a few details which she could use in her defense, and, as if an afterthought, thank her graciously for her recent protection of Emile. At that point, I would hand her my will, she'd reckon with my version of events, appreciate my evenhanded understanding of history, and our score would be leveled—I would have imprinted myself upon her fate. After which my plans diffused, like the end of a road one already senses from a great distance. I might head up to the old family land and see if I could find the gold ingots Charlot had once hid for me, what I'd never been able to find in my previous hunts. It was true that our old house, while some mixed-blood tenants had occupied it before my janitorial time, had gone the way of arsonists and insurance fraud. While janitor, I had seen it, feathery splinters crumbling to dust. Now that I'd returned to Finier, I wasn't sure I wanted to subject myself to that particular melancholy, digging behind the site of the former pissoir.

But what then? I had an awful curiosity about the refugees, a desire to keep tabs on them. Yet how long would my guise keep me safe? And how long should I stay in Finier, up at the squat with Moses and his tribe and the dogs?

"Excuse me." I turned my back to Moses. Under the cover of coughing, I withdrew the silver pendulum. STAY UNDER THE PROTECTION OF MOSES? I asked, but my friend was persnickety and fussy as a newborn, swinging again toward a maddeningly indeterminate MAYBE.

"I need to take care of some business," was what I told the boy.

"No, man. Don't apologize. I'm easy," he said. Under all that hair he was a handsome boy. Despite or because of his name, he could have played Jesus in some country pageant. As I considered him, struck paralyzed in my tracks, I noted the resemblance he bore to rough-hewn Charlot, stablehand of my childhood, sharing his height and lion's features, but like the girl Delhi, Moses possessed a certain oriental fillip around the eyes and lips. Might one of his parents have been a maghrebin?

Moses then offered both advice and courtesy. It had been an eon since anyone had bothered to say anything quite so polite back to me, so gracious and well-mannered, even if his etiquette used words which were, for me, a bit off-key.

"Hey, do what feels good," he said. "Seriously. I'm not interested in policing you. Look forward to seeing you around. Later, yeah? We got stories to share, right? We'll connect? We'll hook up at that Finier bar." He studied me for a second. "Take care of yourself."

I hate to say that I must have blushed. He repeated himself. *Take care of yourself.* As if he cared. One can understand why I might have wished to give that wild-haired boy honors, kudos, let him taste some of what I had known in my life. Receptions with multitiered golden serving plates. If a committee had called upon me right then, I would have made him prime minister; or would have given up a whole succession of meals and safe beds to have hinted who I used to be. Not to make myself a bigger man, necessarily, but to hand the boy a gift. *Did you know that you're speaking with Emile Poulquet?* Not the Emile Poulquet? *Yes, Moses, you're as much a part of history as.* It's an honor, sir, I had no idea. *Please don't sir me.* But, sir. *You heard me, Moses. We're on a first-name basis here.*

Of course, few things rest within my power anymore: I couldn't even tell the boy who I was.

AS I TOOK LEAVE of him, folding Raoul Tavelle back into the ranks of the exhausted, bedraggled visitors, the touristic idea came to me that I might use the old Hotel Fauret. There, perhaps, I might find a way to get a decent meal and a wash, employing one of the guest rooms in a reasonable manner. I trusted that, given the general end-of-summer chaos, as well as the approach of the Reentry, when summer staff leaves, there might be something available to me on a higher floor. So long as the hotel had stayed the same, so long as it too would not betray me by having metamorphosed into something impossible for Emile Poulquet to recognize.

TWENTY

Loyal to a fault, stuck in an endless waiting, the Hotel Fauret hummed a song of itself at eleven in the morning that Sunday in August. The same eerie, tinny sconces still buzzed themselves to eternal life among the lobby's dim stone, the carpet still muffled footfall in its spongy gray weave, a carpet so nondescript it became higher-class, like the wealthy elderly widow we'd scrutinized as children, whose puffy blue legs, shod in scuffed sandals and a general pretense of poverty, practically glowed with eccentricity as she washed her clothes at the public well. We French have a way of hiding our wealth, and the hotel was as good at this game as the pathetic well-washing widow, the carpet one more way in which the hotel proclaimed that all riches, accrued legitimately or not, remained in its veins, never meretriciously emblazoned on its skin. There was nothing the hotel had to prove. Safe in its own context, it was blameless. At the café downstairs, there was still the unevenly hinged door, one rattling with phantom drafts, revealing to the lobby's passersby the café's semipermanent vacancy.

I found a spot for myself in that café, leaning against a wall. Beyond the bar, the grand dining room overlooking the river was being prepared for lunch. Nothing to do but stand with stomach rumbling, suppressing a giant cavernous belch as I watched the staff laying out a giant buffet. Such glisten and opulence to it that the whole thing might have been a waxwork. Once I had been one of the staff and might have helped myself to some of those delectables, but now I was required to watch a shade of my former self, in the form of the waiter, flit past, passing the door with a statesman's importance. Intent on fixing a knife, a plate, a tray of fruit.

Could I offer myself as a busboy?

Too old, Emile. I knew the dining room as well as I knew any room, a grand blonde teetering on stilts over the river Nodaire, a flag from each window asserting our occitan past. Rubbed raw but alive, a room in which Emile Poulquet belonged. But despite my prior claims, despite my gratitude for those tawny chairs during countless official lunches, I could not enter. No leftovers for Emile.

So it remained: how to get upstairs? From my perch, I could hear the concierge, an Englishwoman slaughtering French; fortunately, not at all the same concierge as during my time. This new lady was greeting people with a tirade of friendliness, her visitors equally adept at slaughtering French, this particular circus lending me confidence— only I truly owned the hotel, only I knew what it had once been.

The café, meanwhile, also boasted the same dim lamps, held by the same lung-shaped metal frames, all of it oddly medical, as if in a diagram. More than fifty years earlier, around the time of my advent to the prefecture, the whole place had been designed to suggest a wine cave, so that the wall was an exercise in rustica, its rocks protruding from the walls' rough plaster surface, its brackets holding up fruity, flowery plates, isolated in small pools of light. Not a mote of dust had changed in the larger swirling pattern, all of it a mirage of sameness, much as it had been during my hours with prefecture colleagues.

In that era, if I recall correctly, there had been certain Germans who'd favored this hotel for its baroque, ill fitting decor. They'd liked its five-course meals and the general Fauret aura of sophisticated rural living—these had been among the better visitors. At the time, I'd heard the rumor that the hotel had silently resisted its occupiers by passing off certain inferior wines of our local vintners, wines heading toward vinegar, as being so special that they needed no label, so superior and authentic that bits of cork adrift in the wine showed proof of an old occitan formula. But these particular Germans, as I remember, never complained, drinking up lies with visitors' grace, showing admirable speed when picking up the tab. *We prefer the word cooperation,* more than one had said to me.

    I knew not to linger long—not only that the café offered too uncontested a vale of memory, but hiding against a wall, biding time, catching my breath, was too conspicuous. It was time to find a room upstairs not yet visited by the maid service. Reminding myself to walk smoothly, unworriedly, an effect I could accomplish if I pulled up my gut a bit, I retraced my path out of the café, nodding cordially to the concierge, who fortunately had a phone to each of her long ears. I headed up stairs I'd once known so well. Only once did I have to hold onto the banister, waiting until my pacemaker slowed my heart to a more righteous speed.

TWENTY-ONE

From what I'd heard in the lobby, I'd surmised that to get to room 316, I'd need to pass through a great deal of bustle, the activity of arrival, yet that the first two floors would contain it, as the top floors always went ignored until the lower ones filled. Around here we know tourists will hike miles up our mountains to see one more fortress built by our ascetic Cathars, but they hate having to climb yet another flight of stairs in our birds'-nest bistronnaise hotels.

So it was true that the first two floors were a mess, given the Algerian maids in their crisp black and white uniforms, their rolling buckets and towels stacked to look quaint in wicker baskets, and, within the maids' path, giant obstacles to work, the guests of various nations who hung about, waiting for others to clear out or arrive, guests with suitcases like crippled friends appended to them, transparent or black valises holding the visitors' predictions of Finier's rigors. Sunscreen or water bottles, formal shoes or ties, whatever they had brought, *it will never be enough*, I wanted to tell them, *you will always be surprised by Finier.* From their loud commentary and varied visages, I further guessed that these were not refugees, not at all, but reporters. While the refugees in the café had seemed, it had to be said, *pleased* at having survived, as if they'd just been parachuted down into the present, these new guests in Finier kept up a complaining patter more suited to a foxhole's slow moment. They sucked cigarettes, awaiting the future's mortar and shells. In between plumy exhales they announced themselves to one another, or shouted with public shows of secrecy into their portable telephones certain phrases I could halfway make out. *Omigod you'll never guess who's here.* Some had flung themselves across historically mismatched sofas which by some grace still decorated each landing, the same sofas on which I as a boy of seventeen had jumped with Izzy. In general, flung, verbal, these reporters made it seem that slowness spelled doom, their very impatience no doubt a factor in the way I had been hunted down so unceremoniously in Buenos Aires and dragged to the carnival in Paris, dragged to someone else's idea of justice.

Slowness is bad unless you make a friend of it, I wanted to tell them. Which is what I am good at doing, carving up time. I passed through their melee, almost dawdling through those first two floors, aiming for the manner of a solemn widower, say, on his first jaunt without his beloved wife, a man overwhelmed by the morass of contemporaneity. This, I thought, was a strong guise among these fellows. Like a good actor, out-Heroding Herod, I found it easy to pull one over on these masked people. One can understand that I was familiar with the reporter type: in my travels, I have often, both metaphorically and not, shared beds with reporters. Despite a certain native repulsion which they excite in me, given the fact that our nation lauds them as heroes for risking their vitals in the service of truth, it is also true that they have offered a miserable cheer as trek companions. In various purgatories, their complaints against life-as-it-is are a reliable constant, and they always bear the most wonderful fetishes: the cigarettes and streamlined gear, the shiny valises, all of it an admirably energizing talisman against the world's dust and chaos.

As I made my way among them, the reporters joshed one another, like kids released onto a beach where the very sand was newsprint and bylines, joking with the chic of international accents, using English and French and other unknowable dialects. I heard one say *what the fuck, Martin* and another respond *I'm not pulling your leg*; I saw two reporters click from jocosity into a scary efficiency once the maids signaled they could enter their rooms. Sealed into my character, as if on my way to attend to a ghost in the attic, heedful but self-absorbed, I tramped among them, no one paying attention to me. If one can muster it, one can always depend on the dull cloak of dignity.

IN MY TIME, the third-floor skeleton key used to rest on a high wainscoting outlining the landing between floors three and four. Making sure no one was around, I ran my finger along that rim, despairing until the moment when my finger met its edge. Dusty, yes, furred with spiderweb, but the same key, the same notch and groove. Unless the locks had been changed, it would work. Back on the third floor, from behind, I heard something that sounded like the approach of an army of rats: probably the protest of pipes, or Papa Fauret rendering his phantom mischief. I did jump, dropped the key but then regained my cool, returning toward a room which in my time had been rarely rented out to guests except under duress, as it was off-putting, a small, triangular maid's room. I fiddled at the door, held the key close, opened into the room and finally found the true smell of the Hotel Fauret, the same rosemary soap. I locked the door and lay down on the bed of room 316, my first clean bed in at least a hundred days.

The bedcovers had been so perfectly turned down. Perhaps it was this detail (or the scent of rosemary) which precipitated the memory attack. All I felt capable of doing, to stave it off, was lying on my back like an overturned crustacean and leafing through the WELCOME TO THE BISTRONNE manual. Of course, I recognized the diversion as a flimsy ruse offered by one part of the psyche to another, a wilted flower, a tardy stratagem: because, already, something had begun to bite its way out of me.

■ ■ ■

BUT WELCOME TO THE BISTRONNE!—a laminated manual in three languages, left thoughtfully on the nightstand. According to the manual, the Bistronne was a well-kept secret, one of the most beautiful areas in France. A region capable of seducing anyone, about the size of the Creuse, lost between the Ariège and the Haute-Garonne. The Bistronne a region known for the epaulets sewn onto men's shirts, still worn during Easter, made of fringed cow-leather.

And in Finier, the boisterous manual continued, older houses are distinguished by an architectural peculiarity, particular only to two other sites in France: a commodious crawl space. So far as records show, this huge crawl space is repeated in the homes of a single village in the Dordogne and in a banlieu of Paris. All three sites—one region, one village, one suburb—bore the happy-go-lucky imprint of some visionary revivalist of the Napoleonic era, a man named Legère, alternately gratified by history and reviled, who had left his architectural signature. Some residents of Finier use Legère's extra space, halfway between wine cellar and basement, for storage.

What the manual failed to note is that most crawl spaces are not quite solid enough to deter ground infestation by potato bugs and termites. You face questions of water diversion, leaky pipes, flooding and rot; you must choose whether or not you'll employ the traditional gravel constructions called French drains by the rest of the world versus the relative modernity of electrical sump pumps versus mere surrender. Hence our crawl space is more of a contrarian's device, something that riddles the homeowner and landlord with questions of utilization, as there should be no apparent favoritism among tenants. The crawl space all too quickly can become contested territory, employing endless solicitors and lawyers, proliferating attestations and depositions on who gets *the right of passage* through such a space. Solicitors run amok. Sometimes a neighbor from a neighboring home, long ago subdivided, can still walk through another neighbor's space, at which point no amount of sacrificial goat or apology or pleas can get the resulting fracas to die down quietly.

Another truth is that you could conceivably live an entire life in such a space, never actually needing to crawl. One can walk, if forced into a somewhat neanderthal hunch, feeling the particular weight of a house, its clammy press, while the upstairs life becomes far less relevant than your own navigation. You often also find the most unusual ornamental detail, so different from the shoddy foundation work done in other regions. In our Bistronne, crawl spaces have often been built with an attention to ornamental floor tiles, to mosaics warped and riddled with age. Under your feet, for example, quite accidentally, you'll find a half-restored suffering Madonna, her face distorted by unclaimed root structures and the disintegration of bodies buried beneath, so that at times she will almost grimace, rather like a basement convert during the Protestant years. You easily start to feel as though you stand in the catacombs of the very Vatican. People are inventive, dedicating what is neither cellar nor basement to crates of papers, defunct bicycles, outgrown children's toys, and such irrelevancies as the gloves and shoes of deceased relatives, as it is hard for us to give away a dead person's clothes when that dead person once held your hand on a walk. In many of these homes, families do prefer the crawl space over the common mouldering space of the public cemetery, a relatively recent invention, as our bodies used to be buried in private plots and potters' fields. Hence, one never knows what story lies underneath the serenity of the Madonna.

Perhaps, after 1900, the manual resumed, if not after the revolution itself, landlords no longer had as many extra rooms to be called maids' rooms, and though hierarchical designations remained important, there were fewer to sort out. Thus, greater room was made for the crawl space, a space of choice and memory, opposing in its yawning, wide-open nature the principle of specificity which dominates both our modern and traditionally provincial French homes: grapes drying in the larder, jellies piled in the pantry, hams and saucissons wintering in the attic's dry cold.

Wintering, I read again, a word I'd never seen before but which certainly made sense, *wintering*; and though this was not like me, tears filled my eyes, making the words start to twirl like Spanish dancers. *In addition to the crawl space, the Bistronne is also known for a unique goat cheese which one makes by stirring into the starter milk a sheep-milk rind from the previous year, that particular sheep cheese having been started by a cow-milk rind from the year before that.* Tears came on their own, no matter how much I stubbed my fingers on my tongue, toward the throat, trying to quench the weird sobbing. The cry emerged not because I was such a fan of crawl spaces, or that our stablehand Charlot used to make me bistronnaise cheese. The cry came not because of the way that Charlot made the bistronnaise in December so one could taste layers of history, goat leading to cow leading to sheep. I did not cry over all the years that had passed since I had sampled an authentic bistronnaise, nor because I had once worn a typical bistronnaise shirt with a fringed epaulet, sewn for me by the Polish nursemaid.

The Bistronne is further known for its winter pears, called pears of the Madonna, because of the visage that appears in candlelight. Hers is a suffering face, visible from the rounded lower belly surface of the pear. The Bistronne is lovely, in short, the manual concluded in a peremptory tone, *even were it not for the pears, or the fringed epaulets on our traditional shirts, or the miniature roses framing our picturesque hedges within the crumbling stone walls.* I did what I could to stop the ass-bray of a sob, but cried for all the reasons an ass would have: a longing for home.

IN THE BACK of the Bistronne manual, someone had slipped in advertisement cards. Here were ladies from the Bistronne pictured as lusty French maid types, wearing painted clogs, their faces occasionally blacked out.

There were also Women from North Africa! These showed a more wistful mien through filmy head scarves, standing bare-breasted against windows. I swallowed while dialing. Yet when I got the voice of a Woman from North Africa, I was surprised.

"Hello?" said a Woman from North Africa. "Say something please."

I heard her light accent and thought of the queues I used to see extending out from the office of the methodical Galtimer. All those scarved ladies wanting their permit visas, some hailing from North Africa, some from countries so far east they are barely on our continent. Ladies of the prior sort had been either chatty or patient, waiting in line on floors I had mopped well enough that, had they wanted, they might have been able to eat their proverbial dinner, however spice-scented, off the very marble. I often had wanted to tell them that I'd prepared the halls for them, but they never looked at me, and not because I was a janitor: I'd found their modesty both appealing and upsetting.

"Hello?" said a Woman from North Africa.

I hung up without saying anything, because I had other concerns. Not that I felt I would be discovered. Time had moved on, enough to deposit an English concierge at the front, a woman too clueless and busy to pick up 316's line. Enough time had transpired to shield me.

Yet in the last moment on the phone, I'd wanted to disclose myself to the Woman from North Africa. *This is Emile Poulquet and I was wondering if we might chat a little.* Emile who? *Emile Poulquet.* Poulquet, what a beautiful name. Where does your family come from? *Oh, the Poulquets, we're French, you know, we go way back.* French, that's wonderful. You know, sir, in my language, Poulquet means something quite fine. *You're kind, Madame.* I'm not being kind, I'm only stating the truth. *Perhaps you say this to all your callers.* No, sir, you sound special. Your voice touches me. *There's no need to sir me. Please call me Emile.* Emile? *That will do, thank you. And you, what should I call you?*

I squeezed my eyes shut, picking up the phone again, and tried to imagine her, the woman from North Africa, filmy scarf over her head, receiver tight to her ear, voice sympathetic to my plight. I thought I knew she wouldn't turn me in, and this was a dangerous thought: the fugitive can never trust. I had to slam down the phone again. Yet I wanted to be called any name pertaining to myself, even the name Arianne had begun to call me when I was eight, after the monstrous hump had been removed from my face: Poulquet the Ugly.

So I managed to pick up the phone again and dial. This time I just breathed into the line for the benefit of another woman from North Africa.

"Hello?" said the Woman from North Africa. This one had a voice one might term husky.

I breathed back.

"Hello, what sort of thing do you like?" she said, with nicely orchestrated tenderness. I had to admire the skill, one I certainly could have used more of at various moments in my career. "What do you like?" she repeated.

I would like to be able to speak. Freely, as if among friends.

"Look, if you're a breather, we have to arrange things first," she said, all softness fled, replaced with the grind of Mammon. "There's a different number to call." Which she now recited. "Give them your card number. Then call back and breathe all you like."

But I wasn't done.

"Either talk to my boss," she said.

I tried to mouth a name into the phone.

"Or I'm hanging up," she announced.

And yet when she picked up the phone again, I was still there, clinging to the static between us. "Emile Poulquet," I whispered.

"I'm hanging up," repeated the Woman. "Breathe all you want. Call when you're ready."

But I am ready, I mouthed to the phone. *I am readiness itself.*

I found that even the woman from North Africa's angry returning click was far friendlier than the bare beliefs to be found in room 316. Once the woman was gone for good, I stayed awhile listening to the receiver until the Telecom voice came on to inform me the line had been disconnected. In its officialdom, the Telecom voice soothed me, a voice far more knowable than that of the woman on the phone who had clicked from soft through a stop at matter-of-fact, slamming shut at angry.

THE LAST TIME I'd been in this hotel, before the era of the English concierge, I'd waited all night for someone, for Arianne. You can say this happened to be the night, as my doctor friend had hinted, on which I may have taken a turn for the worse. Actually, he thought it was the night on which I might have lost a bit of my senses, soon after Arianne had come to visit me at the prefecture.

She'd come only months after I'd been promoted to being prefect, but long after I'd grown used to our failure to sustain the closeness of our interregnum. I had been distracted all morning, as it was a time when our office was being pressed with three demands: first, we'd been asked to draw up lists in order to fulfill our region's quotas not of onions but of labor service to be sent to Germany. Before the central office had given us time to process the request, we had to help complete the paperwork for the regional police overseeing the first arrests of foreign jews. What we called the occupation was now fully upon us, and the worst pressures rested on those who had to carry out the job of keeping our fine balance: satisfying the occupiers with numbers but retaining our France. Everything was made up of which threats one could keep at bay, and what industry one could demonstrate to preempt any bullying. In Paris, with the stocks of metals beginning to run out, Germans had begun to melt down our bronze statues, promising, however, that they would keep safe our prized Victor Hugo. To the end of increasing our own native reserves, our Bistronne had been chosen to institute what were called rural centers for the revival of the peasantry, amounting to training centers for which we had to find qualified instructors who could teach girls and boys such lost folkloric arts as the spinning wheel and shoemaking. My head spun with the execution of these details, and without Odile, I would not have been as successful as I was. Not to mention that every last French-born jew had to be listed and documented, without any more exceptions. As one can imagine, such tasks presented arduous obstacles, and the fulfillment of these imperatives often kept me up late at night, considering superior methods. At the same time, the tone of Arianne's red and black posters had changed; they'd started to appear overnight on storefronts.

After she'd met me in Bomont with Paul, after she'd operated those old Fauret strings, strong enough to withstand the advent of our Vichy government, she'd ensured my promotion. Then, as if I were a rag doll which one picks up and drops, she'd ignored me (but for her ghost-limb glance). Was it that she'd discovered my political bent was not hers? Or something deeper? She'd given me no more than the most basic formulas of politeness when I saw her on the street. With one stroke we'd lost the cozy intimacy of our interregnum, our marketing, all that she had admitted, all that might have arisen. At least a friendship. I hadn't expected anything more—had I?—than friendship.

A man could be upset by this dwindling.

A man could fume inwardly, finding both the name Fauret and

her posters upsetting. A man could find himself in his off-hours, during his dalliance with a certain elegant jewish lady who owned a notions store in Finier, annoyed at the way Arianne Fauret continued to monopolize his mind, the way Arianne Fauret continued to dance through moments of the most intimate congress.

So it was with some surprise that, however many months had passed after our cozy interregnum, an annoyed man would find Arianne on his desk, mistakenly let in to his office. A violation of what a man might have considered the one space in which he ruled. Not just that, Arianne had closed the door practically in Odile's face, and then impishly sat herself on my desk, the seam between her bare legs twisting in front of me.

As if we had magically found ourselves back in the era of my seventeenth summer, as if she were still my manager at the hotel. Later she'd behave as if this had never happened, as if she'd never sat upon my desk, leaning toward me, *spilling* toward me, wearing a crinkled yellow dress spread with roses so full they looked as if they could burst and shed petals all over, a dress I'd seen her wear with Paul. She'd chosen the right delicate armor in which to sally forth, sitting so near I could have taken a bite out of her.

Paul would like to know when goods are being requisitioned, she'd said, without introduction.

Of course, I knew Paul had become a great ally to the communists—this was no occult knowledge—and that he'd converted to his function fairly recently. I'd heard my Bordeaux colleagues sniff a bit nervously when they mentioned the communists, and I'd also heard mention of the role Paul played among them, his particular group dubbed the Famous Four.

But as she explained Paul's activities, I slowly came to understand the depth of his months-long disappearance. To hide my ignorance, feeling doltish, I forced myself to pay attention to the words she invoked, ones she'd never used quite so frequently, not just *patriotism* and *our France*, but also *loading stations* and *labor dispatches* and *munitions*. All this sounded to me as if she were reading from a slightly waterstained version of a politician's speech. "Can't you help?" Arianne finished. "There's nothing that would incriminate you. Paul has a front business you can use—"

I refused immediately. Wouldn't Arianne have known I wouldn't wish to help Paul? Or was hers a latterday version of the same childhood cruelty? Now I fully understood the reason they'd wished me to be promoted.

Outside I could hear Odile filing papers, intermittently resorting to that spendthrift habit of hers which I could not get her to change, tearing up carbon sheets rather than reusing them. My secretary had made the mistake of letting in a Fauret unannounced, and I would let her know this posthaste.

"What would it take for you to help us?" Arianne was asking, burning that *us* into me. Clearly she'd been fired up by her hero-man, enough to come back to Emile.

What I couldn't understand was who held the power. She'd had me hired. Couldn't she finagle things *without* help from Emile? I wanted to say this, but then again, I didn't want to remind her of any of her advantage.

"You should speak with Odile," I said, counter-feinting. "She's the true motor of our prefecture. After all, she's the one who gives me papers to sign."

"Can't you help?" repeated Arianne, smiling, the slit in her dress parting as if unintentionally. "What could we do?"

She was reminding me of her naps that hotel summer, and how I too had peeked in upon her. Before me was a new Arianne, one never before explicitly directed at me. With a finger she outlined the air near my collar.

"So formal," she giggled. "It's always hard to know what you're thinking, Emile. Or what you really care about," in a decadent whisper, pure throat. Then prepared to issue her hex again. "You've only cared about one woman." Then waited. "Am I wrong? You never loved anyone else the way you—"

I couldn't say yes, nor could I shrug it off.

She said a few more things before she made as if to get off the desk. "Tell me where."

I understood though I didn't want to. I didn't want her to leave. Shocking myself, cursed by her again into an unwilling submission. "The triangle room."

She blushed as if on cue, knowing the room I meant—rarely rented out, especially not in the early summer. Visitors soon found out the room was odd-shaped, hotel staff knew it had once housed a suicide, and between those two poles, 316 stayed empty.

"I'll arrange it," she said. "Saturday at six, Paul's gone, it'll be easy. Finally," she said, as if still the Arianne I'd known during the interregnum, "we'll have some time."

Is it wrong that a man would be happy that she had prostrated herself? That she had offered a chance to straighten the balances? *She's seen the truth of her cruelty*, I exulted, *she's trying to make up for it. She admits to both of us that she's always been drawn to me.*

Rooted in my chair, holding my ledger on my lap, I was also happy my bureaucratic tone hadn't wavered, having watched that seam between her twisting calves slide up and down, a line calculated to lengthen and contract. She'd offered her proposition like a diamond, losing none of her dignity. And we'd come to an agreement, a beautiful treaty.

She'd insisted she was sincere. At the end, she'd implied that it would be helpful if, further, I could abstain from a little habit of putting Paul's men on the deportation lists. Did I need to know whom should be exempted? If I knew, all the better. If not, she could forward a list to me. She said all this as if it were a wee little favor, and that her real intent had been to arrange our meeting. It would be good, she added, if I told no one about it, giggling again as she said *especially not my jealous husband.* In her session on my desk, before she let herself out, many topics had been covered, quite deftly.

I HAD THAT DAY at the prefecture, not having seen Izzy for quite some time, the strange sense that he stood right by me. I wondered whether I had finally beaten him to something. Or had I been beaten without knowing it?

Her legs twisting, the milky scent of Arianne, all of it unforgettable despite the grand-lady behavior of the years to follow. Because it led into one of those memories I have no hope of erasing: the Saturday night on which I ended up waiting for Arianne, in room 316, from six at night to six in the morning, twelve hours stretching with the humiliation of centuries, the great loneliness of the Hotel Fauret.

People wait for love and then lovers wait, loving the waiting, lack a part of their love. Yet I failed to understand why she made me wait when she'd wanted a favor. First she'd shamed me into admitting what I'd only call lust, and then failed to appear. Had she gotten Paul to break into my office while she knew I was otherwise occupied? Why did she so love to mortify Emile?

A few days later, I saw her on the street. Having verified to my satisfaction that my office had not been burgled, I tried to speak about her failure to show, but she merely pursed her lipless lips and gave me her blue stare. Clearly, my use for her had passed. Or her repugnance about Emile, Emile of the childhood hump, had prevented her from following through on whatever she'd invited. Or else she wanted me to think my memory of her visit was just a phantasm of my deepest desire.

NOW I GOT UP and checked that I had locked the door twice and this small rite calmed me. I lay my head back down on the larval sock that has become the pillow in most of our hotels. Even in the finer hotels. A pillow moist, unpunchable and unfixable, at odds with the rest of the decor, unfitting with the yellow braids on the wallpaper and the mauve ruffle curtains. I tried to punch the pillow into better shape but it resisted my efforts, and punching, I saw another irony: Arianne as usual had ruled my thoughts. The pillow refused me, retaining its own life apart from Emile and, while I had entered Finier, a different story had politely stayed at the border mountains, letting Arianne rule, much as the clouds of Chernobyl had done years earlier in honor of the sanctity of our Bistronne. My story had not stayed away from me forever; I'd felt its shadow upon me as I'd entered the town, as I'd walked up the staircase of the Hotel Fauret, and though I'd let myself think the shadow was Arianne's, I had to admit now that it was not about Arianne at all, but rather the one I'd locked up in a box called *the jewish lady of the notions store*. It was as if the jewess had decided to return and escort me, alongside as I'd fumbled for the key, practically shoving through the door, now a ghost scaling my bed, sliding next to me, hips sawing against mine, breath flooding my hearing, a sticky ghastly self doing what it could to suffocate me in room number 316.

I'd thought here I might have found a middling place, both intolerable and clarifying, inside the belly of the beast. But instead, the room reminded me how much I hadn't stopped, from the base of my gut, that certain feeling for a lady independent of Arianne, a lady exiled far from Arianne's desire to humiliate me in any room, let alone in 316. The paleness in the room knotted my belly: had Arianne always held in ransom my ability to care?

TWENTY-TWO

That first year I'd worked at the prefecture, I'd been a young man filled with barely suppressed self-loathing, a beast satisfied temporarily by any acclaim I received, whether for eloquence or diligence, until the loathing would start its raucous song up all over again.

One morning, however, a gift of grace, I'd risen to a different tenor, sensing life passing me by. I'd felt drawn to entering Natalie's notions store, where I'd never been, though I'd long envied householders who penetrated that zone of hanging tapestries and ribbons. Immediately I'd found the curly-haired lady behind the counter someone I wished to know, to speak with—at least to hire—managing to tell her I wished for a consultation on my apartments. A few days later, as I meditated on whether to leave a centrist or right-wing paper out on my table, the notions-store lady came over.

With her first glance around, she seemed to take in more about me than anyone else had ever bothered to glimpse. Taking a pencil out from behind her ear, she told me that what I lacked was a human touch. Soon after, the two of us began to spend entire weekends decorating. At a certain point, she stopped submitting invoices. Around me the human touch did appear: a golden fan splayed on a chair, red swag circled my bed, a faux-emerald chandelier hung over all our polite conversations.

However, once we consummated the forces amassed between us—wasn't this consummation inevitable, if seen solely from the viewpoint of the caveman we all bear within?—I found myself horrified to glimpse the real animal lurking within Natalie's civilized front. At some point, she'd asked me to pin her down, and other details with which I will not sully this account: suffice it to say that Natalie was as much Salomé as any Parisian whore, perhaps born with the perversity jewesses have long been known to bear, something like a primal script in hebrew letters glowing cryptically within their very marrow, which must instruct their behavior.

I quite naturally avoided Natalie after this event, for about a month. Perhaps she was a glutton for humiliation; I don't venture to know; she sought me out again one dawn. Though ostensibly we renewed our connection—if now an even more clandestine pair, given the tightening strictures around us—we'd lost much of the intimacy of our early days spent decorating, prior to the consummation. As for the first moment I'd realized she was a jewess, it had occurred shortly before that unfortunate first moment of congress, when we'd gone to her mother's apartments, adjoining hers, and I'd noted the brocades, the dusty rolled-up carpets as if freshly stolen from an oriental marketplace. We'd dined on boiled potatoes and some stewed meat not at all well-married to my tongue: the entire milieu made me understand why Natalie had tended to take on a furtive air whenever certain topics arose. Part of my noblesse oblige toward her, however, consisted in my never revealing any knowledge of her origins. I merely inscribed her, privately, soon after, on our prefecture's list of *interesting or useful jews not to be deported.*

However, and despite the measures which our government was required to institute as a means of buying peace, to Natalie's credit, she never once toadied up to me as others did. Never once did she ask me to use my position at the prefecture to bring her and her mother any ease, not even when the two women began having a dispute with an upstairs neighbor who must have scented their foreignness. By coincidence, Natalie was employed as a sewing teacher at one of our training centers for rural peasantry, but this was not due to any pull I'd exerted.

After she and I resumed our liaison (and after its consummation, I called it solely a liaison), one midnight Paul Fauret had come knocking upon my door. I opened up to the fellow in a fit of edgy intolerance. Did he think I'd be glad to see him? Directly, in the hall's semidark, he asked for certain wartime favors. And unlike his wife, who'd paid me a tyrant's visit at the prefecture during my month away from Natalie, Paul spoke without vapors: he wanted help, he and his renegades. He needed lists, names of those who were going to be deported. Of course their stock was rising, these lists: I knew they were gold, yet I lacked full control of them. We were required to maintain one copy for our files, sending the second to the police station, the third to Bordeaux. Our procedure around the lists was tight, involving locked boxes, doublechecking, carbon copies, guards as they were transported.

"No one saw me come," Paul said in his chiseled manner, letting himself into my kitchen, sitting on one of Natalie's stools. "Of course, someone will guess there's been a heist. Potential victims will disappear, unaccounted for. But *you* won't have to answer for anything." I both hated him and felt the heaviest of obligations, as if he had just handed me a recipe for becoming a hero. Years ago, Arianne had injected me with a strain of Paul-respect, and despite everything, I couldn't rid myself of the disease.

Yet that he thought I should be so willing to hand something over (when everyone and his mother implored me for those lists) was a gradation of human foolishness beyond my capacity to understand. Surely Paul must have known that if I gave over the lists, I would be detected. He therefore asked me to put my entire future on the line, at a time when the avalanche of pleas and excuses we had to deal with surpassed anything Odile and I had ever faced.

What surprised me was not that Paul had come to tinker with the lists. This was like a Fauret: sensing a precinct of power and wishing to jump right in. It was only unusual for Paul to believe his command would compel old Emile into handing them over. Also, he'd come at such an undignified hour, an additional insult. I made note of this. "You keep unusual hours—it must be hard to be such a wanted man."

To this, he offered me an insipid smile, waving my comment away just as if we were old friends, in a state of peacetime ease, lacking lists and *gatherings*, rations and headlines, ribbons and requisitions, posters of our twinkle-eyed marshal. Neither of us mentioned his wife, which made me guess he knew nothing of her escapades and her desire to continue entangling me, even as a woman married with what one might presume was some modicum of happiness.

Naturally, I told him that whatever he wanted was impossible. Simply too much procedure was invested in—

He did not move. It was terrifying to have that face fixed in such a glare. Evidently it took tremendous effort on his part to control the rage under his sheen.

"Emile," he interrupted, clearing his throat. "You forget who promoted you?" As if I could have been deluded about the conditionality of all favors I'd ever been shown by the family Fauret. However, at least a remnant of my pride, after Arianne's visit and the night which had followed it, stayed intact.

"Impossible," I repeated, and can still feel the diffidence in my jaw, the sanctity of officialdom's stiff smile. "You hired me—you helped me be hired—to do a job. My orders come from above. You wouldn't want to jeopardize that, would you?"

"Jeopardize which?" he said. "The orders? Or you?" He'd risen, his frame shrinking my kitchen. And asked about my *acquaintance from the notions store*. "You care for her deeply, don't you?"

"She's helped furnish my apartment," I answered. *Acquaintance from the notions store?* I was not in favor of his insinuating anything about Natalie. "She has great talent."

"Nice job," he'd said, imprinting his words deep into my memory before easing himself out, a tall bloodless line. My hands were so filled with fury that it took a while before I could grasp the knob to close the door after him.

. . .

A WEEK AFTER Paul's visit, in my office on a Monday, going over routine matters, Odile alerted me to an anomaly: two names typewritten into a deportation list from the previous Friday, the typewriting clearly not issuing from our machines at the prefecture, nor possessing the familiar rounded clefs of the police chief's office in charge of round-ups.

Two names which Odile hadn't sanctioned, she was vigorous in pointing out. No, she lacked a carbon copy of the emendation; she had proof; the names on the official record which boomeranged back to our office for recordkeeping had been typed in somewhere between our office and the police station, or between the police and the train station. "Please, Odile, get to the heart of it," I said, barely looking up from my blotter.

Someone had undoubtedly lowered the standards of one of our dignified gendarmerie, offering them a bribe, Odile said, waving the paper before me:

MADEMOISELLE NATALIE SOULA, 28 Y.O.
MADAME RUTI SOLOVA, 52 Y.O.

Clearly, Odile had sensed what had been going on between me and the woman from the notions store. In my secretary's kindness, or as a last-ditch desire to win me over, she'd felt compelled to confront me with what she kept calling the *anomaly*.

I'd tried to focus upon the names, the letters wavering. Natalie, Natalie and her mother. I'd instead burst out in a laughter, one I couldn't control, trying to restation myself by looking upon Odile and her pearl-drop earrings, a reminder of our office and its functioning, a promise that nothing could slide by Odile. The words I'd used only weeks ago in secretly tagging Natalie and her mother—*useful, interesting jews not to be enrolled on the lists*—came back as I watched Odile's mouth working up and down. *Natalie, anomaly, useful, interesting.* I was already imagining myself, in the worst-case scenario, at the internment camp. I'd be tall as Paul Faurct, able to find her immediately. *Natalie, I've come for you,* I'd say, *my apologies about this little fiasco.* I'd use my position, talk curtly with the man at the gate. All others would fade away as Natalie would come to take my arm. *Darling,* she'd say.

Odile interrupted me. "Sir, you seem a bit—" she said, but there was no good cause for her to make comment, as I sat at my desk, hand on my familiar blotter, Emile Poulquet's usual posture. To me it was Odile who looked deranged, color high in her face, pose scoliotic, fixed by my door. "You realize what this means, don't you sir?" she said, her tone terrible, arrows of accusation in it.

"Of course," I said. "Or what do you mean?"

"The lists, sir," she said, her spinster's hand stopping short of slapping the papers. "It is now a *transition* camp, Mister Poulquet."

I hadn't visited this particular camp since ground had been broken at the outset of the occupation. I could imagine myself, though, leaving it, arm in arm with Natalie and her mother, nodding at the gatekeeper, entering a chauffeured car in which I would apologize to the two ladies for any inconvenience they might have suffered, leading seamlessly into a marriage proposal and a ceremony in which Odile could play flower-bearer. But Odile had stamped out of my office, shaking her head. I found my brain had gone numb as an ice drift. Call it conscience which finally trumped my paralysis. Late morning after hearing the news, I managed to steer myself to Natalie's apartment, though my head still floated somewhere else, legs operating as if motorized, bearing the greatly unearned belief that I might find Natalie asleep in a closet, dreaming in the red satin robe she favored.

In this abrupt way I found exactly how afterness begins: in the empty apartment with its disappointing smells and inescapable domestic traces. *She'd not left, she'd been taken.* I found irrefutable proof—my Natalie would never have left her apartment in such shoddy state. Potted cheese on the table sprouted furry spores, milk in the tin pot filmed over with a waxy skin. I put a hardened bread crust in my mouth, and just as quickly spat it out. For a second I read on her silk duvet the message *don't move*. If I just sat on the bed, could sheer magnetism compel Natalie back? The more I stayed, all human power would drain from me, I'd be left a weak and shorn Samson. If there were decisions to be made, I could only make them from the seat of my power, the prefecture where I belonged, my prefecture with its gargling telephone and filing cabinets, where the map of all actions would be clear.

As I roused myself from her bed I found not just the signs of a hurried departure but also the handiwork of Paul Fauret, all I'd missed upon my hasty entrance. But how emphatic he was, Paul, with his red signatures. The little resistance bows tied around every leg of furniture, every tassel, every curtain-string. He'd left a message, obvious enough, as if I were a dullard. He wanted me to give him the lists and in exchange he'd return Natalie. Once again the Faurets were sticking it to me.

For a second, I also thought I saw on Natalie's little gilt bedside table the carbon copy of the deportation order, bearing the very same typewriting which had whisked Natalie and her mother off.

When I looked again, however, there were no red ribbons, no carbon copy, just an apartment, a bed and table. Shaking my head, I tried to descend the same stairs I had just taken up, making my way down the stairs, legs unbending stilts, breath staying far behind. At this point my intentions were that I would stop at the prefecture, corral some official forms regarding *Exceptions to Deportation* in relation to *Interesting and Unusual Citizens* who might require *Administrative Procedures for the Release of Misapprehended Citizens*. I thought I would head immediately to the camp at which she must be interned. It was already clear Natalie must have suffered what I'd feared, and for exactly the reasons I should have foreseen. She was being used as a prop by Paul and his friends.

But as I descended from Natalie's apartment, I made a decision which must have made true afterness begin. The invalid neighbor who'd always eyed my comings and goings wanted to present a roadblock. "Now you'll have tea, young man?" she asked, indefatigable. Why did I do it? I entered Natalie's neighbor's kitchen with a sense that I had surrendered to something greater than hospitality. It had seemed necessary to settle my nerves. I saw right away the mistake I'd made in accepting. It was evident that the neighbor—her name was Madame Parrouge, she volunteered—had fallen to her particular domicile from some position in society. Chandeliers like glass spiders sat on bombazine chairs grayed with dust, photographs of withered men stared us down, all gripping riding whips on even more withered estates. Distracted, for a second I felt sorry for the woman, so stuck in her past. My mind was spinning upon itself and I tried to anchor it by scrutinizing one of the photos, in which a man with prominent moustaches stood before a colonnade. "Ah, my husband," she said. "Dead in the Legion," and I didn't know whether this might be a polite-society way of referring to some exotic disease or whether he'd actually served.

"Poor fellow," I echoed, unhearing.

"You never met *Mademoiselle* Soula's son, did you?" asked the dowager, setting down two teacups. "This is tilleul de passion," she said. "A special infusion from my friend who lives—"

"A son?" My ears prickled with what later gets called destiny. I should have known the betrayal would consist of something as simple as this. A *son*. Natalie had a son. By Francis of Provence, the single former suitor she had mentioned once?

"Try some," said Madame Parrouge. She minkishly pursed her lips, raising the cup to them. She had smeared her mouth with an orange crayon, not at all literal about exact contours, making us all the more lurid and obscene, like two clowns, our circus roles suddenly changed to speaking parts.

"A son?" I said, awkward. "Sorry. I need to—"

"She never told you," she said. "I figured. That kind of woman—"

The statement trailed off into innuendo, as palpable in that apartment as the smell of mothballs, the mucked chandeliers, the passion tea. "You think you were the only one to visit?" she finished.

Without full intention, I slammed down my teacup and was already at the door, unsure whether to thank the woman or curse her.

As I took the stairs down, Madame Parrouge came out to grip the balustrade. "Besides," she said to me, robe parting enough so her nightdress with its sweetheart collar could reveal her tired poitrine, and then must have thought better of whatever final coup she'd wished to add.

• • •

I SPIRITED MYSELF toward Arianne's house rather than to the prefecture. Later I could not remember which route I had taken, as I could not know where Natalie's betrayal lived, when it had first entered, when it had begun to unravel the life I'd thought we'd been planning to live. Had it been her israelite legacy intruding? She'd had a son, or perhaps something even more unguessable?

She had betrayed me, I started to think. *Yes, the upcurve of her breast*, another phrase echoing in my head. *The upcurve.* As she lay on her back. An intelligent curve, weren't jewesses known for this? Something a little too ripe, like the clamor of their music, like that her mother's ancient phonograph had once played for us.

SURELY THERE'D BEEN something all too debauched in the sorties which Natalie and I had known, far more than those I'd shared in my student days with the gartered women of Montmartre. As this idea repeated itself insanely, *all too debauched*, I had already arrived at the Faurets' and gazed up at it. In only a few weeks, Paul and his beloved would move closer to town, to apartments in the annex to the hotel, but for now, their house was a stronghold, still a repository of Fauret history, perched above town so as to better look down on it and the river, a house eye to eye with the old chateau that had put Finier on the map, the chateau where the Cathars had starved themselves. The Fauret residence: those impenetrably white dormer windows, firmly closed. There was nothing to be done for it. I would simply have to storm in, grab Paul Fauret by the collar if he was haunting the house, force him to reveal where he'd secreted Natalie and her mother, yet admit no exchange of information. After all, perhaps Paul's Famous Four had merely stowed the ladies in the Faurets' crawl space until I consented to sign over a few lists. Perhaps the typewritten names had been merely to taunt me. I would go in and—

It was as I was standing there, trying to figure out how to burst in, that I saw Arianne Fauret, in what must have been her nightdress, which was more of a white slip, revealing what now seemed very much a little-girl's body, all skinny arms and jutting hipbones. She was in her slanted backyard, humming through a clothespin as she hung up her underclothes, Paul's underclothes, naïve bits of their domesticity, white clothes hanging in a backyard behind which our Xerxes river ran. Birds perched, squabbling on an ancient apple tree; the river trickled its din; and she clearly enjoyed herself in what must have been her own private film-reel of Arianne in household bliss. How could I break in, beseech a Fauret? How could I speak punitively or beg any favor? Perhaps it is hard to understand, but I could not. The circumstances of my life forced me to turn away: I was *their* victim.

Years later, in the Plaza Mayor, I tried to explain to old Honsecker my dalliance with the woman whom I had to start calling *the little jewess*. Yet when I came to the point where I failed to tell Arianne what her husband had probably done, wreaking vengeance on Emile, even Honsecker failed to understand why I had not stormed Arianne's gate in pursuit of Natalie. "Your Arianne was doing laundry, my friend?" he kept saying, until, incredulous, he finally sounded a judgment. "That's human perversity for you!"

What I did not tell Honsecker was that Odile questioned me for three days about the *anomaly*, each time a shade less persistently. Each time I waved her away. "It's been taken care of," I said briskly. Many truths coursed through me. I'd waited too long, I hadn't waited enough. Mainly I was not ready to see Natalie yet.

Be strong, I thought-telegraphed to Natalie the next day, which I believe must have been Thursday, allowing myself to think *my pet*, seeing her face amid a blur of others. *Be strong, pale lily, pale blur.* I renounced my disgust at our consummation, I saw her all the more as my bride. Friday at lunch I remember writing a letter to the chief authority in Paris, an official justification on behalf of Natalie Soula, then immediately using the letter as kindling. I wrote another that evening and decided not to post it.

FINALLY, Saturday, midday, I recovered enough to go find her, my throat hot and dry despite the half-hearted summer fog laid in at the base of our mountains. I took the train to Bomont. At the station, I hired a cab to take me to the mouth of hell, where I had to repeat myself many times to the driver, a sad basset of a man loath to drive anyone to the camp. Let me shorten the story by saying that at the camp, an officer with crossed eyes, pleased with himself, mistook me as being someone who'd come to check up on the correct application of our region's funds, rather than someone seeking a lost mate. He'd bustled along, addled, boasting about all the hygienic measures employed in the Bomont camp, which he termed *only a temporary inconvenience for us*. He went on about this summer, how pollen abounded, unusual and hence people were coming down with catarrh: everyone had a complaint. As the camp was a temporary inconvenience—

I had stopped the man's chatter and had asked *for whom* it was an inconvenience. For the government or its citizens?

"Ah," said the official, confused about my sympathies.

Nor do I like mentioning my hallucination of seeing her, many times over, replicated among the lone figures huddled in long wintercoats on a platform where the sky made up the walls and the ceiling, where they had slept all the previous nights like rats, nor will I mention that a few actual rachels with dark eyes sidled up to me and whispered inducements of a kind that made me certain I had entered a nightmarish funhouse. At one point, I recall the official interrupting whatever I had said to him by saying *I cannot understand what kind of mistake you might mean, sir.* I said that Natalie Soula was a useful jew. The man said *She is no marquise, is she, a countess?* I told him she was an economically useful refugee, in the process of receiving a certificate of aryanization. *There is a black market in those certificates, sir*, the man said then, in genteel tones, his eyes crossing maniacally. I told him that this certificate happened to be legitimate, that she would receive, and I made a point of not using the German word we'd all had to learn, *an exit pass*. I found the story as I spoke: she was to receive an exit pass as her trade had been given priority. *She's a cobbler?* he leered. I said she was a furrier, one of the wartime professions deemed more necessary than others. I also recall how I kept saying her name as though this alone could open a door and allow Natalie to burst forth.

∎ ∎ ∎

NATALIE HAD BEEN indicted because of her association with me. We'd begun before Easter and now it was August. Riding the train home, I was annoyed by the prattle of my fellow bistronnaise citizens in the compartment, two elderly women gossipping about the poor prospects of a certain friend's daughter, making me wish that like them I could dwell in the simplicity of certain answers, as if all of life could be a call and response between one's need and an appropriate label for that need, just as our village used to promise. Trying to contemplate a good course of action, I could not think of anything but my simpleton's chronology: Natalie and I had begun before Easter, now it was August. Once I returned to my well-outfitted home, sitting on a gabardine chair, I tried to focus on a steely revenge, which was far easier than thinking about other fates. Anyway, who didn't know about Paul's resistance activities? I'd played dumb with Paul, but who could have occupied my position without knowing about the famous four, the maquis in our region so intent on self-publicizing? For a few days I dwelled on my hatred of that spiky word: maquis, a low-lying island shrub, a revolting word from any angle. The day lapsed into a week and I'd barely moved from my chair, failing to go to the prefecture. I sent word to Odile that due to the odd weather I'd fallen ill from pleurisy.

Like an itch inside the veins, my instinct told me my own survival had come into question. Would the maquis come for me? Would, for instance, Odile betray me? I might have made a mistake in going so public with my concerns, having revealed too much heat vis-à-vis Natalie not just to Odile but also to the officer at the camp. Perhaps I'd put all our fates in the balance by being so obvious. I'd placed a call to an old school acquaintance. Also to Honsecker. And all this self-revelation had amounted to nothing; no one had divulged anything to me about the final destination of the trains leading away from France. Was I supposed to go to Poland, the hinted-at destination?

It was after this fruitless time that I sent a misbegotten telegram, trying to reach Natalie's particular cadre, which the civil telegraph clerk assured me could be stopped, if I slid over a bit of extra wheel-greasing. Signing the telegram form, I changed my name to Pulkheim, hoping Natalie would understand. I believed the official imprimatur of the prefecture would help, and trusted that with her canniness, her ability to manage, she would be able to use the *official prefecture business* I mentioned in the telegram as a passport, and could thus arrive whole at a particular bench we favored, on the outskirts of town, a person still intact.

Whereas I was not so sure about myself.

The first day I waited from afternoon into evening for her. The next day I lingered at the base of the hill leading up to the bench. Sometimes I brought myself to stroll by her apartment; sometimes I walked by her shop. The worst of all this for me, as those first days turned into the first weeks, was how often I brought myself to sit at that bench. I still had the hallucination: every approaching form became Natalie, every receding one damnation. YOU ARE TO COME IMMEDIATELY TO PRESIDE OVER THE BENCH MATTER, my telegram had said.

Once I came to understand Natalie's own culpability—she must have lost her will somewhere—I cauterized myself, wondered whether or not I'd ever actually cared for Natalie. Had she known me at all? Had I really been so taken with her? For privacy she'd given me heavy drapes, yet the drapes between us were the heaviest: I had never known her. Everyone wanted me to be cut, tiny pieces of Emile Poulquet fed to river trout. If anyone at all was looking out for me, she should have been able to come back. And so when the vision began, I called it nothing.

That week, an official foreclosure notice had been posted on her store's door. I peeked through the dusty window. Despite my decision not to care, peeking through the dusty window of her store, I noted that the miniature Persian carpet which had once hung beneath the SOULA & CO. stencil now made dinner for moths, a latticework of holes peckering the faded perimeter. Through the holes, I must have hallucinated someone moving inside her store. I had the supernatural sense that she could pop back in, that she could push up as if up through a hole in the floor, that if she really were being held in Poland, she could just tunnel her way back.

The jeweler whose store neighbored hers hopped out to comment upon my newfound habits, peeking through all that rug and damask and lace. *You're looking for something you won't find*, the jeweler said to me, looking out over his magnifying glasses. Though he sniggered, pulled at his beard, I sensed his was an anxious laugh, all of us suspended over an abyss. No one can ever explain absence. *We're sad about Mademoiselle*, he then confided. *She had a nice way about her. I didn't know her that well, but she was refined. She always gave small gifts at the right holidays. Not all her people are like her, of course. But the police had no need to treat her the way they did, did they?* I heard in this that not only had he seen her be carted away, he was suggesting that he knew her better than he wanted to let on. What sort of gifts had Natalie given the jeweler? When I tried to pursue this line of questioning, however, he wouldn't tell me more, closing up in our bistronnaise manner, unpryable, as if he'd only then remembered who I was, my position as prefect and dispenser of favors. From then on, if I saw him in his own window, I did my best to ignore him.

OF COURSE, across town, other vacancies had occurred, and they were unfortunate. The florist, a blond mare of a woman who favored thick-stemmed flowers, had her shop closed. The pastry shop had a new owner who made buns a bit too flat and dense. No more clunking fifty-minute piano lessons filtered into the alley near my apartment. Though I had little time to mark these effects, busy as I was at work and in my after-hours, they gave me and others in town an odd feeling we did not remark upon, as if one were constantly awaking from a dream only to find one's bedroom furniture rearranged, a few unnameable pieces missing.

One day in front of Soula & Co., as if to ensure that I'd know I was being watched by Paul and his cronies, I found a child's red hair ribbon, dirty, swept into a small refuse pile near the corner in front of the store's door. This bit of red was so slight—such a small flag of triumph, the most subtle *I-told-you-so*—but this was how these people worked; it might as well have been a red show-off banner screaming Paul, tied on the satisfyingly heavy handle I'd loved.

Before I ripped that child's ribbon to shreds, before the shadowed eyes of the jeweler inside his store, I made the vow: I would heighten my revenge on Paul out of the memory of whatever I'd almost called love, purging Arianne out of my system as well. Against the Faurets and in Natalie's honor, but mostly against the past, which had once again swallowed much hope for my future.

As fall began, I returned to work. Odile had kept our functions going so smoothly that no one truly noted my absence. Whenever Odile inquired how I was, I shut her up, telling her my cold was better now, thank you. When weeks and months went by without Natalie's return, when there were only days of compiling lists, summary tables for the Vichy office, all that painstaking demographic work to anticipate, Paul Fauret offered a useful focus, certain as I was that the disappearance of Natalie had been the handiwork of Paul and his cronies. I would not bend to the will of a Fauret: those people wouldn't get their Emile Poulquet over the barrel one more time.

Our tasks continued; and still I frequented the bench, sometimes leaving work early to do so. Yet I did not slack at my job. To the contrary. Upon my return, I found greater focus in my actions. Where before I had been cautious with my signature, asking Odile to perform double-checks on certain citizens whose blood could be called Gallic if one smeared their origins a bit, now I took all central-office imperatives and quotas to heart, becoming quite forward-thinking, adopting the protocol we'd received from the occupying power. I started to authorize the deportation of those possessing even just an eighth of jewish blood in their veins. And how many families there were! In this manner, our numbers grew, our totals swelled. Soon enough, we heard compliments of our office from Bordeaux.

Odile was surprised at my fervor but, in her calibrated way, went along with it, enough so that for our thoroughness, we eventually received by special courier a gift, a favorable citation from the marshal's office in Vichy itself. Odile immediately mounted the double-headed axe they'd sent, the francisque a sign of great approbation, right behind my head.

We were on a spree, we could have done our work forever, though nothing lessened my blankness each day as I hovered near that bench, pretending to study magazines, newspapers, briefings, my mind gone blank as the face of our war, whose human aspect we knew mostly as a few Germans drinking our hotel's wine.

This was the season when, ironically enough, I seemed to have garnered a new nickname: *Poulquet the Ruthless*. I saw this once plastered on the headline of one of Paul Fauret's underground news-sheets but I didn't care. Let them call me any name they wanted. They would still be who they were; I would still have to apply myself to the job I'd set for myself, however unnameable it also was. A breach had opened. And into the breach I kept signing away more and more names, a frenzy of names, jews to be deported, though I never completely gave up my bench habit, secretly waiting for the return of Natalie.

Yet on one of our crisp Finier days, not long after the Italian leader had fallen, on a day when most of our populace had lined up in the square to exchange a kilo of bistronnaise butter for two kilos of imported sugar, I made the decision consciously: no longer could I afford even my numbness about Natalie. I'd have to stop questioning whether or not I'd cared for her and just let the facts lie. Another Emile had been involved with her, another Emile who used to love all her questions. Exactly at which hours did I best enjoy the view out over the river? she'd once asked. *The view was the view. The river would go on tumbling whether I looked at it or not.* She'd asked whether at five o'clock I'd favored the western or southern exposure? *Such trivia. Exposure matters as much as a rat-trap.* Did I prefer the small austere library, she'd wanted to know, or did I prefer the living room with its views of stucco roofs and the mountains beyond? *I preferred her.* The way her dark hair had been curly enough to have hidden plump grapes, curly enough that she could have been the vintners' Marianne. Once I'd tested this theory by putting a grape under a curl until she laughed. Her eyes were so dark that rather than twinkling—twinkling which is a shine content to keep you at a distance—they drew you in, you entered their luster, you were drawn close enough to be cut.

TWENTY-THREE

In room 316 at the hotel, having failed miserably at napping, I bathed and shaved, happy at least to use the new razor, tweezers, soap and cologne left in the bathroom for hotel guests. In these mundane activities, I put a new man on. If only I could find cleaner clothes. Instead I trimmed nose-hair, used the steam iron, sewed back the button on my sweater, shined my boots and sprayed myself almost senseless with complimentary cologne. I went downstairs nearly immaculate, a fragrant man, clutching the hotel's small courtesy notepad.

I paused at the foot of the stairs, hand on the banister, the other holding the notepad before me, wondering how best to grab an apple from the table nearest the dining-room door. A man with a silver ponytail and a giant turquoise belt buckle broke my contemplation, stepping toward me, using that broad English of the Americans. "You're Liston?"

"Ah." I was used to thinking on my feet. "That's a crime?"

"Come on," he said, beckoning impatiently. "We're figuring out tables. The first press banquet. You're about the last to show. Hotel's crazy, no one gets served if we're not all here. Lots of rules in this place."

"Ah." I understood more. "Sorry. Lis*taing*. Agence Presse."

"Wonderful," he said, handing me a table-card. "I'm Martin. The *Times*. It's unorthodox but they've appointed me. Things are a little wacky. We're going to have an official tell us what's going on. Better correct your card. Take the one by the window," and pointed me in. I could not tell yet whether this was luck or not, to be ushered in with the reporters. This was not the first time I'd had this effect on nervous people: they often took me to be some kind of official. Such misrecognition had been true after my operation, long before I became a real bureaucrat. Perhaps the sneer left on me by the botched job made me appear endorsed by authority.

So I entered, relieved that the other reporters paid little attention to me, milling at the hors d'oeuvres table as if starved for days, exchanging greetings, exhaling. There was the tinkle of wineglasses being slammed, a sense of reprieve. There was the hotel's ancient one-eyed chihuahua sitting in the corner on a brocade pillow, eyeing all of us. I knew the scene well enough. Right after I'd found Liston's chair, hoping it wouldn't excite all that much notice if I was seated alone at the table, not sure what I'd do if the real Liston popped up, the silver-haired ponytail man, Martin, came to hold forth from the center of the room, banging his fork on a glass to quiet the babble.

There was some problem with Arianne showing up to start the reunion, he said, to which a muted protest started in a corner of the room. Instead, the members of the media, here assembled to witness this first reunion, had instead received some kind of public relations visit from Tomas Kosinski, who headed Arianne Fauret's foundation—

—and Martin gave the floor over to a familiar-looking young man with close-set eyes, curly blond hair, his cheeks a rosy-blotched cherub's over the sharp chin of a violinist. This fellow Kosinski spoke a careful French, telling them how honored he was that we'd all come from such great distances, his needle-thin fingers clasping and unclasping before his chest with studied emotion. He claimed that representing Arianne Fauret's Society for the Restitution of Memory made him undyingly happy. Because of a little *problem*, he was saying,

Arianne could not be with them today but that shouldn't impede their happiness. He kept saying *honor* and *happy*, though he looked far more furtive than happy. Things would surely resume in two weeks per the plan, he said, if not before. "But don't leave," said Kosinski. "You'll enjoy lunch. Stay with us." The concert was to go on as planned. He seemed to be making a joke when he said he'd like to trespass *conventional* journalistic protocol by asking the reporters to call in to their bureau chiefs and offer the pretext of a sudden family emergency. "It could be like a sudden plague," he said. No one laughed.

One woman by the fruit table raised her hand to ask what *exactly* had happened.

"Unexpected things in life, no?" said Kosinski, aping Gallic charm. He stifled a cough. "But after lunch, please, explore the town. You'll be happier for it. Most survivors are staying at the Perigord," he told the reporters, "not a Fauret hotel," pausing again for the laugh that didn't come. A young man, he must have made prior public addresses solely to clannish members of the Fauret mythology. "But the first official meeting is the concert. We'll know more what has happened by then."

THE REPORTERS took in Kosinski's message. Some surprised me, already deciding to head right out, in the middle of their meal, astonishing the waiters who were bringing in the amuse-bouche, prune and bacon roulade. Unthinkable rudeness, the waiters' faces transmitted, turning sour for the benefit of the more couth. If you were French—which my travels had taught me meant if you'd had your childhood beaten out of you, if you'd been taught and cautioned with an ever-present *no!* to be a little adult long before any sign of adulthood, thereby if early on you were accustomed to feeling criminal whenever any urge beset you and hence a need to be sophisticated when justifying all your base urges, thereby if you were a romantic (as we French are often called) in carrying from childhood on the simultaneity of crime and romance, an impulse toward duplicity part of your psyche you would have known *not* to affront this kind of waiter.

But these foreigners, they could not know such things: how a sour waiter's face could lessen one's standing in the world, give rise to a shame nothing would heal. Because the foreigners thought they lived beyond our breed of shame. I overheard them, the more loose of lip: they stood eating their appetizers, prune-toothed, wanting to fax arrangements for trains, hotels, flights.

"I understand," said Kosinski, attempting to sound soothing. Had he just offered the highly unethical inducement of a free stay at the hotel? I sensed it: there was a large gray area between the publicity sham the Faurets had cooked up and what the reporters would consider a legitimate news story. About eighty percent of Kosinski looked relieved that so many reporters were making plans to leave. Was this the Pole whom Jacquot had mentioned Arianne loved so much? He glanced hurriedly out the windows of the hotel and then, having dispatched his duties, fled the dining room.

"One-tenth are staying." Martin came to sit next to me in the middle of his own reporting to the big Irishman at the next table. "What do you make of that? Or what is that Fauret lady going to make of it?"

"Dunno." The Irishman shrugged. "I cancelled a hell of a lot to be here. Their pub machine sure made this seem like some friggin historic event." He chewed off the end of an unlit cigarette. I had surreptitiously swung the pendulum over the roulade, and it had given me an enthusiastic YES, but now, wiping bacon grease off my mouth, I couldn't openly swing it over the next course that had been brought to our tables, some kind of pastry. "But there's a story here, don't you think, Marty?" the Irishman continued. "Might try a human-interest angle. For the Trib. That Kosinski fellow's the only one I've had contacts with. The lady's a real Mata Hari, what do you say?"

TAKING ADVANTAGE of the commotion, one offering the dual advantages of both lunch and disguise, I was not unhappy. Not unhappy to be seated at a table sipping wine between Martin the *Times* man and a tall Spaniard who plopped down next to me, speaking neither French nor English very well, other than occasionally interjecting what sounded to me like "my beautiful body!" The Spaniard was jolly enough, not a suspicious sort, well-trained to laugh at various conversational junctures, but I didn't wish to speak the simple Spanish I'd recently had to learn, as any Argentinean trace in my accent might've raised questions. Anyway, a South African woman in flossy braids across from me, perhaps a mixed national, was a good enough opinionated sort to keep everyone's conversation going without interference from old Liston or Listaing or whoever they thought I was.

I was doing what I could to dispatch the pastry (I'd asked the pendulum's forebearance for its exclusion from this decision) right when Martin turned an entire foie gras tureen onto his plate. A shocked waiter came to redeposit the mound back into the pot.

"Here we share," the waiter scolded Martin. Had Martin been a man with more avoirdupois, he would not have been able to weather the scorn which wanted to come his way but which, failing to find its target, located itself in pedantry. "In France, this is not an individual portion."

"That's okay," said Martin, barely looking up. "First meal I've had in weeks." He was already attacking the pastry on his plate with unabashed vigor, and I felt a certain comradeliness toward his efforts. Making a point of ignoring the fuming waiter, who reciprocated by stomping off, Martin looked over at me. "You know, Liston, I must have seen some of your pieces. Didn't you do that series on the corruption scandals? Must have required a huge effort."

"Oh," waving my hand, "that was nothing."

The woman who'd asked Kosinski the question about the delay came to our table and asked if she might scoot in next to the Spaniard at an unclaimed chair. "Barbie Rotesc," she said with an awful nasal twang. "You don't mind?" Trailing behind her, genially holding his plate before him like an oversize altar boy, was the Irishman.

Martin rose out of his chair. "Not *the* Barbie Rotesc from India?"

The Spaniard imitated his gallantry just before everyone sat back down. The group allowed a vortical pull to swallow them up, a gossip familiar to me from all the time I'd spent in the terrific, clouding company of reporters. I loved hiding among reporters. Whenever I'd been among them, they paid the least attention to me, and in the very worst situations, their gossip shrouded me wonderfully. Of course, I knew the themes of their conversation, if not the local variations. In towns across the world, right now, there are reporters boasting and complaining about where they've been posted, who was promoted over whom, who stole another's story, what threats they've stared down. When discussing issues, they often sounded to me like parrots who'd once been the favored pets of a leftist politician. Usually they lingered on their more favored topics, how hard it was to balance one side's viewpoints against another side's vehemence, and how one must put up with all the acid complaints one received about bias, when surely on one day one side was morally superior while the next day the other side deserved to be cited as moral champion. Here, the only local variation they inserted was their conjecture about the delayed entrance of Arianne Fauret, the damned lady who'd announced this reunion. She's a grande dame all right, Barbie Rotesc had said, and hence, maybe, her conjecture continued, this was just a French way of ensuring a grand entrance. Hadn't the Fauret woman anyway compromised journalistic integrity by having invited them all to her family's hotel? An odd move, Martin agreed.

Barbie had the biggest need to confess, admitting to many things soon after her arrival at the table, as if we wanted full disclosure. She was unmarried, we learned, tired of having been the bureau chief in hot dusty countries where no one gave a damn about what stories she spun. She knew it was tactless but confessed that her dream was no longer to save mankind but rather to see her byline flying high over some big-city paper, much like Martin's. "BARBARA ROTESC," she sighed, "call me crass." She'd had a failed novel about her dusty country, and it had made her resentful about others' successes, she admitted. One could tell she was the kind of helmet-headed woman who would check lovemaking off on her to-do list. In other cities around the world, I had met reporters like Barbie Rotesc, women and also men akin to the meat which one buys plastic-wrapped in supermarkets. But I was only half-looking at her, more interested in the main course—though I knew this meal would only make me more hungry later on, such is the condition of a fugitive's stomach. Yet I must admit how much I enjoyed being served by a new crew of Hotel

Fauret waiters. For more than thirty years, no Fauret waiter had ever shown me such relative politeness.

For the first time, however, I began to feel uncomfortable being part of a group of reporters. They were outsiders and because it was Finier where we were stationed, I hated being forced to the corner of their ignorance, a group of flies buzzing without purpose.

Until Martin, having left the table for a brief bit, returned in a tizzy. He'd been told that Arianne was being held in custody, and that no one knew in which town or police station she was being held. "Everything's hush-hush," said Martin, employing that all-purpose, self-shielding phrase I'd heard employed by countless reporters in every possible locale. "We don't have anyone to ask. Not really. I spoke with one of the returning guys, a real character. Guy named Natz from Brooklyn. A painter and his wife Anya. She said Natz had it up to here with the survivors acting like this was some huge party, everyone real tight-lipped about anything meaningful."

Barbie was annoyed, competitive instincts seeming to flare. "What about the reunion?"

"The wife said most of the reunion people are heading back to that hall they rented."

"They still here?"

Martin sucked in his cheeks, protecting his sources.

"They know anything?" Barbie Rotesc asked.

His gaze narrowed. "They weren't that direct. Natz said it's hard to be back. Anya says there's a group of refugees that can't stomach being around everything the Fauret woman planned for them. Films and fables. One group wants to secede. That's all I know. Or all they're telling." Barbie took this in unhappily, applying herself to her plate with finicky gusto.

In between courses, needing a bit of silence myself, I returned through the lobby to pick up the complimentary newspaper which Martin had mentioned, but mainly to get a sense of the greater goings-on. The English concierge looked surprisingly deft, still holding a phone to each long lobe. Overworked, clearly someone who wouldn't pay attention too much to any single man's comings and goings, barely taking in the tonic of the reporters clamoring around her, the mass of them making urgent demands. No silence to be had for Emile Poulquet amid that din. The reporters were addressing the concierge by her first name, *Delia*, as if she were a long-lost cousin. *We need cars, Delia*, they told her, entreating her with that plaintive entitlement I knew well. *Delia, just a train schedule if you don't mind, Delia?* As if using someone's correct name could summon that person's entire history of acquiescing to others' desires, as if using a name was all it took to make people bend to one's will. *Delia, we just need to get back up.* Up was Paris and Finier was down, which had been our great advantage at various moments in history. Mostly, the reporters wanted to scatter, billiard balls cracking away from one another.

PAPER IN HAND, I returned to the dining room. My table of reporters had dug in, determined to hold the fort. "A maverick move," said Martin, self-congratulating. Only two other tables stayed. This quasi-stability would appease at least an ounce of the waiters' disdain. Martin stated loudly, within earshot of Barbie, that he was more than game to take up Arianne Fauret's offer of staying on in Finier. He sensed a giant rat burrowing in a haystack.

"Story's a story," Martin said to Barbie, more directly.

"I'll stay so long as Essvee stays," she said.

Martin had this idea: they should dispatch a kid to room 218 just to find out whether the reporter Essvee, who hadn't shown up for lunch, did indeed plan to stay. This began a certain melody around the idea of the man upstairs. Barbie started it but Martin picked up the chorus, saying Essvee practically *made* the news, *made* history— that if anyone would know the skinny, Essvee would. He'd have the scoop on what was going on with Arianne Fauret and this whole reunion. The Irishman jumped into it, as did some other national hovering over the table. I was keen on getting on to the next course but paid half-attention to them, the group sliding into a sloppy boast-festival concerning the great journalist. They pegged him as lady-charmer Essvee, honorable guy-buddy Essvee, biker Essvee. (My stomach rumbled, unavoidable and loud.) Former government operative Essvee, multinational Essvee. I tried to control my stomach by registering some of what they said. How they loved the weirdness of it, that he was sidelined upstairs in room 218 in a nowhere French town (a slur on Finier which I took as a personal affront).

Essvee was their prey: that's the heart of what I understood. Just because of some terrible cast on his leg. They didn't know what made Essvee always get the story, despite or because of that bike he took with him everywhere, the bike he called Mojo. I realized their Essvee was probably the same motorcyclist who'd so bothered the inspector in the Bomont station café. Now this fellow's Mojo was smashed up behind this rickety Hotel Fauret (again I took umbrage) and any one of them could testify to the bike's potency, its ubiquity. They threw around the names of places Mojo had been parked and though my stomach continued to rumble quite awfully, the pendulum having failed to sanction the pastry, I tried to pay attention to their phrases—Christian Aid in Rwanda, Sarajevo, flying a Red Cross flag. Mojo roaring through Los Angeles with a flag whose colors could flip to red or blue depending on neighborhood.

"Details, baby," Martin said.

Barbie's theory was that Essvee's Mojo could get him behind the worst security lines. Years ago, unheralded but now way more than rumor, that bike was somewhere I couldn't understand—Aiyeaud'eau?—and that was right at the beginning of the troubles.

Martin interrupted the Essvee worship session, speaking across me to a dark-haired woman who'd slunk into the room and now pored over the contents of a folder at the next table. Something about her made my ears prickle, my belly tighten: such midnight jungle animal senses are one of the fugitive's few gifts.

Had she found out anything new at the prefecture? he asked her. "Simone's on a special investigation, guys," he explained, lording it over the others. "Our stringer. A photojournalist. Actually from France." She ducked her head, smiling. "Our only local." I heard what *local* meant: in this case, a condescension, meaning *diminutive, small, blinded but attractive, useful*, possibly *a bedmate*. Simone muttered something about a special investigation into the death of a farmer on the road, the old bicyclist felled by a hit-and-run. As she was collecting both photos and information on the story, she said, people could let her know any leads. Once she finished her little speech, she sneaked by me to take a quick photograph of all of us. "A souvenir," she murmured.

"You have a special connection?" the Irishman asked Simone.

"What?" asked Barbie. Her screech an awful sound in the universe, but she seemed pleased enough with herself, withdrawing her notepad.

"I'm saying a connection to the farmer," said the Irishman. He couldn't restrain himself, folding and unfolding his arms. "You knew him." He leaned in toward Simone.

"You could say so much," the photographer said. Her English wasn't half-bad, right as she snapped another photo of our table. I tried not to turn away too suddenly. "Sorry. I am interesting in this topic particularly."

"You like photos of reporters?" Martin mock-preened. "Crazy."

"My beautiful body!" was the Spaniard's interjection, as far as I could understand.

"Actually," said Simone. "I'm interesting in this Essvee of yours."

They didn't need much goading; the subject of Essvee reignited them into calling him by many holy names. "Because Essvee has his aspects," said Martin. There was truthteller Essvee, morning push-up fiend Essvee, Essvee who couldn't shake certain military brat's traits. He was Esvic in Bosnia, Tsvi in Israel, Achi in the Jordanian son's palace: wherever he was, he acted as if his very skin were bulletproof.

I felt foggy from the sips of wine I'd taken, and though my hunger made me focus on the food, I pinched my thigh to listen to their words, the lingua franca of the reporters' English a bit hard to take, fired off so quickly. They were saying Essvee could be wearing a bright red flannel shirt and fix in his sights some village kid with an S47 slung across his chest. Ten minutes later you'd see the kid wearing Essvee's baseball cap, cozied up next to Essvee, the two hunched over and secretive. (As we were between courses, a waiter came to refill the bread basket before me; I considered using the pendulum again but decided a bit of bread wouldn't kill me, that this hardly could be the kind of bread potentially poisoned, through mishandling, by ergot. Bread could only help my case.) Essvee would've chosen the one articulate kid in the village, they were saying, the kid who knew everything, who could disclose tribal loyalties, old clashes, morganatic claims. (The bread was so exquisite, I considered how to secret a loaf away on my person for later consumption.) They were speaking of the kid, Essvee's informant, I supposed, who could disclose and not ask you to take him back to America. The kid who wouldn't ask you to hire his eldest sister as a maid in Dubai or Kuwait or London. (All this sounded like nonsense to me, but I knew reporters had to have their talk. Who was I to begrudge them? I began on my second slice, spreading the crust thick with a butter made from the milk of our cows, a patriotic, saltless butter made in a manner true to our republic's depths, a butter thick with truth.) They were still going on about Essvee's informant, the kid who would happily stay stuck in the past, happy to let you *leave* with the information, happy to stay a smiling face in your photo album. Okay, maybe there'd come his way an occasional letter about the spoiled harvest and the new Gulf refinery down the road. Maybe a letter about his mother's health and his uncle's dream of being a taxi driver in New York. *My uncle drive good, my auntie cook good too. I have third cousin in New Orleans.* (With the third slice, I sopped up bacon grease left on my appetizer plate, a real impropriety to go backward in courses, though no one noticed.) But no *overt* importuning of funds, no families being sponsored to come to America.

"You got to understand. Essvee masterminds a hell of a lot of what we call contemporary history," Barbie was saying, showing off some intimate, bitter knowledge. Next to her was an ignored tureen of coq au vin, a steaming new arrival on the table, fragrant and tempting, but I wasn't about to interrupt them and ask for it to be passed. Nor could I very well reach over the table and grab it.

They couldn't keep themselves from their love. "The guy's zeitgeist. He belongs in a western," said Martin. "Mountains in the background. The one left at the bar, shouldering up to the bad guy, right as the credits roll."

■ ■ ■

THOUGH USUALLY I could have stayed among reporters for hours, an unease beyond the ignored chicken had begun to swirl my innards, making it hard to listen, making me think I should find a pretext to leave. Mainly, the photographer troubled me. I had no way of knowing the purpose of her photos.

Both times I hadn't been able to turn away speedily enough. She'd probably caught me with my mouth full, chewing Finier bread. Something of her, however, made her appear incapable of deceit. A sullen disappointed face, a good enough French face, familiar, heart-shaped as I gazed upon it. Come to think of it, the first woman I'd seen who really had a face practically stolen from Natalie. Or perhaps I was starting to see things: I'd also thought the refugee in the canadienne had looked like Natalie, hadn't I?

I believed, though, that the photographer may have turned on me something approaching the Look, falling just short of it, before she shot another picture.

Not wholly lost in hero worship, Martin turned on me. "You ever read any stuff of Essvee's out here?"

I dabbed my napkin on my mouth. "We do more than read your Essvee in France," I lied, using my best pokerface. "We memorize him. We treat him like the Bible." And this was said in full throat and so the journalists were satisfied.

But I'd lost whatever birthright appetite I might have had for anyone's versions of the hero, and this may have been due to the fact that in the background a certain range of tones and insinuations had begun to form a recognizable pattern. One of the waiters looked impatiently at our table before flouncing across the room where he turned up the volume on a small television, the awful box tragically imported into the ancient restaurant, propped just above the waterglass station and rattling the fine china. The waiter flopped himself down in a chair before it, watching that box with a degree of interest which should have been enough to alarm even a deaf man.

■ ■ ■

ONCE AGAIN, there were the two living saints, caught, as frozen in their moment of time as I am in mine: the mother-and-daughter lawyers talking about my case. The journalists perked up. "Ask the waiter to turn it up a little more," said Martin. I steeled myself to stay, guessing that at worst, the reporters would try to outdo the expert lawyers with their own versions of expertise.

"They had Polka in Paris. He was due to stand trial," Barbie said, snapping her chewing gum as if it could replace a main course.

"That's crazy," I mumbled again, so as not to seem too out of it. This will be my one contribution to this topic, I decided. The journalists didn't really need anyone to listen to them speak, but perhaps it was important for me to participate in their talk.

"Not Polka, Barbie, *Poulquet*."

"He escaped?"

"Maybe *that's* why lunch was so late."

"Be serious, man."

"You don't mean Papillon, do you?" I could not help interjecting again.

"The guy from Alcatraz?"

"It means butterfly, Papillon."

"They made a movie about him, right? De Niro, right? Swimming. I love that stuff."

"No. *Poulquet.* The sub-chief of the prefecture."

"What does that mean?"

"Prefect. Not sub-chief."

Though sometimes their words ran together and became hard to discern, or perhaps my sips of our Finier wine had made it harder to listen. "I'd check your notes. A City Hall manager I remember Bob once telling me Poulquet sentenced Finier during the war sentenced that's OTT what? Over the top Polka signed papers deported thousands now escaped his trial yeah that's old news," was what I understood.

"We should have been posted to Paris. Not Finier," I said. I was beginning to enjoy my new guise.

"What *is* this place?"

"I said Nowheresville."

"You got to ignore what the bureau chiefs say it's BS Paris is always where news breaks no real fugitive would stay in Paris anyway it wasn't that Polka sentenced *all* the people he sentenced *jews* of Finier."

"Did you know that in Polish or Yiddish *poulka* means chicken leg?"

"Show-off."

"So Poulquet means chicken leg?"

"Barbecue? Like briquet?"

It was repeated again. Poulquet means chicken leg in Yiddish. The great joke. I had heard it once before. Hahaha. Poulquet means drumstick. Honsecker had told it to me and then it had been repeated on many tipsy occasions by Honsecker's widow in Buenos Aires. At this, and not out of any sudden access of good taste, Barbie snapped her gum again, excusing herself, leaving at the table just Martin, the Irishman, the Spaniard, the multinational and the hovering joke about me.

Poulquet the chicken leg. In that jewish language that was also half-German. I did not have any special love for the Nazis' hatred of jews, though people liked to paint me as being one with the Nazis, when that particular word—*Nazi*—has nothing to do with anything French. And *chicken leg*—as though I should find that funny. As though I happened to be more cowardly than anyone else.

"I thought all those old Vichy guys just ended up returning to their villages," said Martin. "Quietly."

"But Poulquet was bad. I mean *bad*. He assigned one of the hugest numbers to be deported. Especially given how small his region was. They called him Poulquet the Ruthless. Also the Butcher of the South."

"How—" and Martin paused with a comic's timing. He looked a little drunk. "Heinous!" He searched for another cliché. "Dastardly acts!" The others smirking.

"Crimes against humanity. The banality of it."

"Have it your way," said Martin, shrugging. Luckily, I was listening more carefully to this part, eyes on the coq au vin, because Martin now turned to me. "What do you say, Liston? You must have known people of that generation," hedging my apparent age gracefully, not wishing to insult me. "You must have had some experience with that legacy."

"Banality," I agreed, in careful English. "Absolutely. You are a hundred percent correct. I stand with the banality people." This seemed to satisfy them more than it should have; they finally began serving themselves from the coq au vin, and Martin made sure I got the drumstick.

The main thing that unnerved me in all this later parley, however, was the sullenness of the photographer, along with her penchant for taking photos. She rose from her table, starting to leave the room, just as I should have. But the truth was I wanted to finish off the meal, drink the last of the wine despite my upset stomach, just drink and roll gently toward the cheese course, as any other compatriot might have, any older man of leisure. But I was forced to listen to these people joking about my name. These people who pretended to unwrap themselves to one another. All their urgencies and worshipful words, making a trellis for themselves, something solid upon which to lean and climb. While Emile Poulquet sat among them, vulnerable, only his chin resolute, the rest of him fading into ether. My disguise had become difficult, more than I expected, more cumbrous than finding a pretext to leave before dessert emerged.

So I did leave finally, sadly before the tarte aux pommes but not a moment too soon: however clean and fragrant I was, a certain kind of pretense was no longer the private laughing matter it had once been. The pendulum had begun to play tricks with my mind, and whether or not it had stopped channeling the impersonal force which has so helped me all these years, I could not say.

To catch my breath on the way out, as well as to avoid seeming suspect, I sat on a couch in the lobby amid the clot of departing reporters, the types eager for the latest story. Some stayed glued to another television, another small idiot box positioned over the bar. I envied them, wishing I could belong to them for just a moment. Reporters believing in the future, existing in the breaking moment or the moment after, never weighed down by the past. I wished to imitate them (however impossible that was); I wished to pay attention only to what I'd heard Martin calling *the facts on the ground.*

The spokesman Kosinski had said two weeks, and I had the feeling Arianne might surface sooner than that. I could stick around in Finier, I decided, fingering my pendulum. Lucky me: as far as I could tell, no bounty had been placed on my head. I had skipped my hearing, but didn't this happen every day? Tax evaders, petty thieves, countless Frenchmen on a daily basis skipped their hearings. These were the *facts on the ground*, right? I asked the pendulum, unable to swing freely in public.

Into the lobby came Barbie Rotesc in full plumage, luggage on pragmatic wheels, ready to leave but announcing she was open to persuasion. She thought Essvee might have made plans to get back to Paris: her hunch was that Essvee was on the Polka case, she broadcast loudly, but that wasn't why. She herself had her own ideas about which parts of Paris the fugitive would prefer. "Polka is perverse," she said, not without her own degree of perversity. She patted her sensible hair, snapped gum, weighed words. "My guess is he would go to the most jewish section of Paris."

"Brilliant," I said, softly. "You don't mind if we follow you?"

"Get your own leads," she said, beaming. "Just kidding."

Martin had come out into the lobby, wearing a napkin buffoonishly tucked into his collar, a small dessert spoon in his hand. "You're leaving?" he said to Barbie.

"Someone's got to hunt," she said, as if about to plant a flag on a remote planet.

"You couldn't be righter," said Martin. "Maybe let's have a last glass of wine. To celebrate?"

"Celebrate?" but the lines in her face loosened. "Okay."

"We could go to the concert," he said. "If you want."

"That's still happening? I just gave up my room."

"I won't try to get you to stay," he said.

"Good, because you wouldn't succeed," she said, taking his arm.

AMID THEIR WHIRL, half-sated, wine-softened, I tried to absorb molecules of commotion, gather momentum into myself so I could rise. I waited just an extra second, wanting to believe I was as much a part of the hotel as the vampire moths who used to flutter around the hotel lamps. Finally I got up enough impetus to rise and pass into the day. Out the hotel, heading out of town, I passed the last bunch of stores and, farther out, mixed in briefly with the dogwalkers and the children on small bicycles zippering along the river.

My mood was bruised but reflective, turned on itself, contemplating various unjust specificities, such as the lost history contained in the fact that no citizen of Finier knew what whimsy must have named their rivers, long after the Roman invasion—Nodaire and Xerxes. My walk was also a whim, or a perversity, in Barbie's word, a risk to ambulate so freely around Finier, but certain risks become not just necessary, they are also sufficient: one could die from such risks and almost feel fulfilled.

TWENTY-FOUR

I still hadn't seen the American. When I heard musicians tuning up near the old prefecture, I turned back from the river, and as I neared the square I saw a smattering of culture types, free-thinking older women in overbright flowing clothes, determined to claim metal chairs in the front row close to the musicians. Gathering at the periphery, some of the shabbier touristic breed had found their excuse to dress up, apparently at least an hour before the event, a few clasping rolled-up calendars, many still eating ice cream: they looked to me like vacant-eyed but well-meaning cows. In truth, I couldn't tell anymore who were regular tourists and who were refugees; it was like old times at the prefecture, when I had often played the game of trying to guess which country had birthed a particular refugee.

To my eye, most of these people now visiting Finier were difficult apparitions, though often I had enjoyed hours contemplating the mass of humanity, the flow of pedestrians, the many guises faces could assume. On this day, however, I found it hard to look upon them, their birth faces distorted by years of risk and calibration: how blind they were to the masks they wore, self-protection and precious self-regard. You could see it in every scowl and fearful smile. For my part, I tried not to be terrified of their mass, tried to make myself focus on the small grace-notes of a random man, a passing woman. Not only was I starting to see each person as a potential recognizer of me, but I believed I could see everyone's thoughts: how each person starred in a private movie, a movie poignant or magnificent unfolding in their idea of Finier the picturesque.

For the moment, the pendulum suggested, with only the quietest of swings, that I should continue to hold down my own private fort, sit among them, finally get to the last buttered slice of bread I'd stuck surreptitiously into my pocket during lunch. Yes, it may sound odd but this frugal storage is a habit understood by any survivor of wartime rations, even a prefect who'd possessed a superior link to supplies. I thought that perhaps in this motley group I too could pass as a tourist. Eventually the American would show up at the concert, and if I were to find the American now, what should I tell him? Was I supposed to tell him I couldn't protect him any further, that *the facts on the ground*—a useful phrase, after all—were the following: he had run over the old farmer, there were reporters tracking down that story, to wit, the sullen Simone in the hotel's restaurant, and further, he was starting to get in my way, because if Arianne was being held for questioning *about a crime he had committed, unwittingly or not*, it was interfering with my own purpose? I had come to reckon with Arianne and this meant I needed to meet with her, freely, and better sooner than later.

Although I doubted the merits of saying all that to anyone. Nor could I exactly testify *against* the American. Nor did I want to testify on Arianne's behalf. All that was given me in that moment was to be a confused fugitive.

Admittedly, I alone was to blame. It is probably criminal to return to a scene where memory claims too total a conquest. I also was failing to shun large groups of people, Honsecker's rule number three for the survival of a fugitive. In relation to this latter habit: I have always enjoyed sidling close to the periphery of groups and, having had such a tendency persist into my late age, it must have become one of those habits impossible to change. I sat on the cold stone, facing the church, forced by my perversity to be among others.

Under the blue-and-white-striped canopy on the central stage, a tall pianist was trying to get the other musicians to quit their picnic and begin a rehearsal. I could hear her saying *quick, just a tune-up!* In her long clinging dress, she resembled an upset yellow fish. Something alluring to that. In order to watch her better, I had to move and sit among the spinsters in their metal folding chairs.

Once the musicians had gathered, they raised their heads to an inaudible intake and then commenced rehearsing the opening of some chamber piece, probably chosen to commemorate the reunion of the refugees. It had the crash and thud of arbitrary modernity, as if a demolition crew had taken a liking to cello, violin, clarinet, piano. What I especially enjoyed were the movements of the male page-turner behind the pianist, how his back rounded toward her music as if leaning toward water. I understood his position and felt that he, perhaps, might understand mine. Though the piano had nothing of water to it, fully pizzicato, forced to ascend in fifths and descend in a lush, fake, casual manner. Again it went up the gangplank of fifths and then into a dying man's chromatic plink. The page-turner sat poised, then turned. The violinist had a flattened face, and between movements, she exchanged with the yellow-dress pianist a sideways pleased glance, like Amazons heading into battle, heads lifting at some inaudible concord. If this music had a season, it was winter, not at all about August or reunions. The page-turner got anxious about this concord, one which excluded him, and turned the page again. Watching the pianist, I could not stop thinking of Arianne, the minx, who shared something of the pianist's enchanting belligerence. Again the pianist went up her fretful fifths, the grand piano a beautiful sight in the middle of my square. Looking at her, one wanted to save her from an absurd repetition compulsion. *Must touch those keys*—stop it—*must touch it.* This was the dramatic style of her playing, irony ascending after a brief lull of sincerity, as if she had decided to pull hot taffy from the keyboard. Clearly someone had once told her the small of her back was expressive. Clearly she felt compelled to throw back her head at the end of an arpeggio, as if to say—*take that, you scoundrel! and that!*

She would have all the ears of the world bow to her, like heads of cauliflower. I recognized the type: she truly did have something of Arianne's high-strung nature. Everything about her said *I am world-class but stuck in nowhere*. She probably threw away cards she had received from old beaus. Watching her, I started to feel angry. She must have been the one to choose the piece, one I started to think I'd heard during my time in Buenos Aires. It was by the composer Krenek, wasn't it, another war survivor, a guilt-provoking piece by the man who after the war had gone to a place I believe is called Palm Tree, America. I saw the pianist wipe her hands before a difficult section and start in as though eager to grab the music away from anyone else. I thought of Arianne, locked in a cell, how her hands must twitch, wanting to control anyone.

Other types had snuck into the square to enjoy the pre-concert concert, and bore on their faces the curious solidarity of those stealing together. Krenek in Palm Tree had decided to impose something cranky on the world, a complaint, and it made the pianist's hand arabesque in the air after all his big chords. I was trying to remember whether Krenek was a jew after all, while the pianist was saying to her audience, to me, to all the tourists and stray journalists and organizers—*I know how bad life can be*. When the clarinetist stopped playing, his music having evoked something of a watery, subterranean space, he couldn't hide his disappointment at his role having ended, abruptly. The page-turner waited, then turned. What was Arianne thinking at this exact moment? The violin's line concerned the friction of bodies. But the piano in this piece was eternal trickery. When an absurd optimism entered the melody, to signal it, the pianist jerked her derrière back and forth on the seat.

I was so distracted by her performance that I had not noted the entrance of the American. He stood in the corner of the square farthest from me, conferring with the Polish Kosinski, the fidgety cherub who headed Arianne's foundation. The American had on his camera and a spotlight and was interviewing Kosinski.

I could not hold back anymore. I got up and, excusing myself, stepped on the toes of two culture lovers, eventually making my way along the line of chairs to where velvet ropes separated me from Kosinski.

The Pole saw me before the American filmmaker did.

"Ah," I said, politely lifting my finger. I had to let the American driver know, privately, the case against him. This was my great courtesy. I'd give him the chance to know the facts impartially. I would be a benevolent judge.

BUT WHEN THE American turned and saw me, his face stopped its charade of interest and nodding sympathy, its wise benevolence behind the camera. He wrinkled his brow at me and shook his head fiercely, once, twice, before returning to his filming.

"Who's that?" I heard Kosinski ask behind me.

"Some old man," the American said, using the rude word for this. "Don't know." He resumed with an expert's tone. "Sorry. Let's head over here. So the hope for this year's festival is—?"

TWENTY-FIVE

There are degrees of rudeness which one must accept as a refugee. I have graphed them, for my own edification, so that I will not have to feel myself so much at the mercy of others.

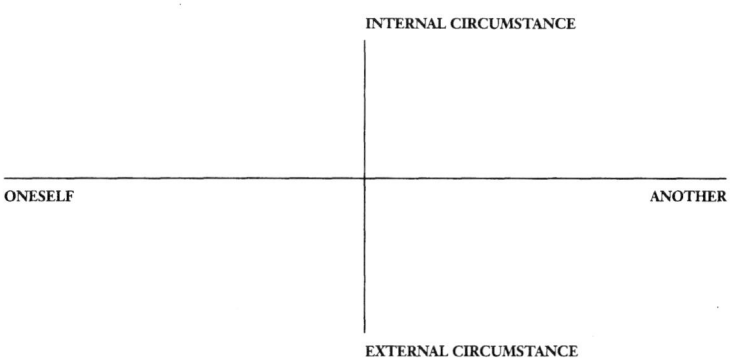

What I chart by this is awareness. It is sometimes possible for an insult to occur because a person is unaware of one's sensitivity or presence. It was this type of insult, an external circumstance (my proximity to him) coupled with the American's complete unawareness of Emile Poulquet's inner life (hence, my experience of his brute otherness) which pinpointed this insult on the right-hand, lowermost point of the lower right quadrant. Hence it could not hurt me as much as an insult which might have fully taken me into account, motivated by an internal circumstance on the part of the American, say, closer to the baseline.

The cross formed by this graph is not intentional, though it speaks to the sacrifices I endure, big and small, on a daily basis, forced to conjure up graphs to mitigate the battering of existence. At times, I find it best to conceive of myself not as a fleeing spot across a map, as we might tend to imagine the movements of a fugitive, but rather to imagine instead that the insulting party is the fugitive, and that he or she is fleeing me, while I am the mountain, well-stationed, stolidly bearing the assault of rain and sun, fickle clouds.

Dispirited nonetheless, trying to stay clear-minded about how best to find the lady I'd come to reckon with, I decided to head back uphill to the manse, thinking that perhaps at this moment I could use the highly unhypocritical Moses. He would be a refresher course in various ways: it was not just the boy's unstudied nature which might be uplifting, but his knowledge of the town's nooks and crannies had seemed profound enough that I thought he, above all others, using unconventional means, might be able to lead me to Arianne.

I was taking a breather halfway up the hill, on the narrow walkway, leaning against the stone fence. As I stretched my back a bit, closing my eyes, I bumped into Cerb-X and Delhi. To tell it straight, Delhi's little piebald mutt ran between my legs and I nearly tripped.

"Sorry," said Delhi, "we were trying to surprise you."

"A joke," Cerb-X said.

"But it's good we ran into you," Delhi explained. A man could get lost in the radiance of that girl's face. "Jacquot forgot us. We need someone to help."

"What are you up to?" I asked, aiming to ape their casual slang, though I was aware my pacemaker had gone into overdrive. I almost heard a warning, faltering *tick-tick-tick*, though that was probably my imagination.

"We're getting the statue, what do you think?" said Cerb-X, the queen. Her face was full, all sexual meat. She looked at me from under bleary lids. "Come help." There was little denying her. "What else are you waiting for?"

"Just hold on," I said, unfond of the way certain ladies could exercise control over me. I told myself I would walk with the two of them, however briefly: that they might be an unlikely gift from the same source that powered my pendulum, that they might lead me to Arianne, that all this was fully my choice.

AT A QUONSET HUT on the rim of town, Cerb-X leaned over, hands on her knees. "Step on my back," she said.

"I can't do that," I said. I had principles and was always glad whenever one surfaced intact. "Not to a lady."

"What good are men of your generation?" she asked, and stared into me. "That was a joke, guy."

Instead, Delhi gave me the dog's grimy leash to hold for a moment, while her face took on an acrobat's fixity. She then stepped on Cerb-X's back, managing to tug her small frame into a window left half-open. We heard her jump down inside. What followed was an awe-inspiring silence.

"You're all right?" I called.

"Into my friend?" said Cerb-X. "Sort of?" She sized me up. "That's what I think."

"Merely a human being."

"Human," Cerb-X grunted, unconvinced.

We went around the front where Delhi, her face more smeared than usual, hands raw from the fall, had unlocked the door and waved us in. "It's amazing," she breathed. "Intense to see it in the daylight."

It was true. Paul's profile, such as it was, sculpted by Kosinski, looked *intense* as Delhi had said, straight up toward the skylight. The head was secured on a truck's flatbed, eyes glinting and neck muscles bright with bronze strength, while the rest of Paul, his bulging body, lay on the ground strapped around with hauling ropes.

"It *is* him," I marveled.

"I *said* you knew the guy," said Delhi. She punched Cerb-X's arm. "Didn't I say that?"

"How were you planning on moving him?" I asked, and then realized the idiocy of the question.

"Thought *you* could drive that hulker for us," said Cerb-X, following my gaze to the head on the truck. She shrugged. "You wanted to be useful, right?" I found myself nodding, but did Emile Poulquet wish to be useful? "We don't know that kind of engine," Cerb-X was saying.

"My apologies." I sucked up my gut. "I can't do it." I started toward the door. I needed to catch my bearings, to find Moses, to get to Arianne. I had not bargained on these two creatures who wanted, of all things, to perform some sort of publicity-grabbing stunt, the heist of Paul. "This is the last thing I need," I stammered over my shoulder.

"You think we know how to drive? Come on, Papa Raoul." Cerb-X had run in front of me and now blocked my exit.

"Please," said Delhi, kneeling before me, taking my hand in her own soft one, Cerb-X kneeling next to her, and I smelled their exotic girl-sweat perfume, pillow breath, arm-hair, old leather, whatever it was. "It's for a good cause."

"Pretty please," Cerb-X echoed in her ironic monotone.

"I can't," I said. "You think I'm a joke."

Both their faces looked up at me, glowing under all that dirt. "We don't," said Cerb-X with the first softness I'd heard from that big girl's mouth. Cerb-X handed me the key. "Delhi will ride next to you. She'll direct. I'm taking Lula."

"Lula?" I asked, thoroughly confused.

"Delhi's dog."

"But where are *you* going?" I asked.

She jerked her finger over her shoulder, in command position. "I'll walk ahead. I got to prepare the site. We're calling it Attar of Roses, Attar of War."

I found myself up in that high seat. "Do you—?" The closest I'd ever come to driving a vehicle like this was when I'd once helped Charlot with his tractor.

"Do I what?"

"Have a hat I can wear?" What had happened to mine? I must have left it, incriminating evidence in that terrible room 316 at the hotel, or worse, at the table with the reporters.

Delhi had taken a shawl out of her backpack. "Put this over your head. You'll look like my mother. You can be like, I don't know, the ghoul of our art piece."

Approximating what I'd seen others do in similar rigs, after a few false starts, I unhitched the emergency brake and engaged what I assumed was the clutch. With a bit of ruckus back and forth, we managed to pull out of the door which Cerb-X had pulled up. I'll admit this was exhilarating. For a second, I felt like continuing on in that truck, hitched up to the trailer bearing the giant head of Paul, with the lovely bare-bellied Delhi beside me. I would head somewhere far from Finier, toward the sea.

But Jacquot and Moses—first I'd seen of them since the morning, since before I'd returned into the bowels of the Hotel Fauret—were running toward us, down the gravel driveway, Jacquot first.

"Hey!" he called. "Old man! Stop!" The cavalry of dogs around them hurled toward us, barking. "Shit!"

"How does it stop?" I asked Delhi, the girl tucked next to me, shrieking as if on a wild festival ride. It took all my strength to steer.

"Get him off!" Jacquot screamed at Moses.

"Hey man," said Moses, quietly, to my left. I took my foot off what might have been the clutch, looked down and pulled what must have been the emergency brake. The motor died, everything ground to a halt. Cerb-X, up ahead on the road, fingers looped through her belt, laughed at us.

Jacquot was already brutely shoving me out of the truck. "This is my job," he said. "You know you look like an old lady."

"I didn't *ask* for this," I said, fully mortified, handing Delhi her shawl.

"Right, you didn't ask," he said, mimicking my tone, better than Cerb-X had, Jacquot being a perfect bully. "Del, get her?" he said, twitching his head in the general direction of Cerb-X. "You could've gotten us in trouble," he told me.

I stood below the big contraption with Moses. One of the three dogs around him nuzzled me from behind and if I could have, I would have fallen through a hole in the ground. "What's going on?" asked Moses, mildly. "How'd you get roped in?" he asked.

I found myself speaking in my prefect voice for the first time in ages, fluted and proper, the tone of a gentlemen's understanding, as I rid my coat of some imaginary dust. "Thank you. You know, I didn't want any part of this."

We watched Cerb-X lope back, dragging the dog, its tongue flapping happily. She pulled herself and the mutt into the open truck next to Delhi.

"See you fools later," said Jacquot, waving at us.

"Where *you* going?" asked Moses.

"The square, that's the plan." Jacquot was leaning out the window. "Sit tight, Mosey, hang with our father-figure-in-residence. We got to mount our protest."

"But what about the skeletons?" asked Moses.

"Our roadkill. Skeletons go nowhere!" Jacquot declaimed. He gestured to the truck, the throbbing motor, the statue staring up at the bright sky. "Who needs skeletons?"

He roared off, his two girls and the dog riding shotgun, Paul's giant head rattling on the flatbed behind him. Paul almost didn't make it around the corner, I thought, but the sculpture had been well-strapped.

"They're going to town?" I asked, considering the concertgoers. I couldn't quite imagine it: the yellow-fish pianist, the stage, the narrow space for the truck to enter, all those colorful culture ladies. "To the square?"

"Something like that," said Moses gently. "Or who knows? I'm not really in on this one."

"Better," I said, rubbing my chafed hands. We probably both felt a little left out. But I shouldn't have; it was better for me to hide away from the stunt. I saw Moses wearing a new black shirt with a proper collar, though it said across its chest EXCELSIOR. "I like the clothes," I said. "Ever upward."

"For my interview," he said. "I told you about it, right?" He didn't need an answer, perhaps already knowing how hard it had become for me to fully listen to others, if I ever had been able to. "You hungry?"

"Tired, rather."

"Rather," he said, imitating me without Jacquot's malice. "Sorry." Without discussing it, we were heading back up to the manse. Walking, I explained a little to him about Arianne without mentioning her name.

I need to find a woman here in town, I said. Essentially, someone stage-managed my life, I said, and she's doing it again, so I need to thank her for her help.

"Sounds more like you need to curse her," he said.

He was right, but which impulse had the upper hand, I couldn't say. "I've got to get her to stop protecting me, whatever reason she has," immediately realizing I had said too much, wanting to backtrack. "I want the cards to fall where they will. Not where *she* wants them to fall."

"And then what?" asked Moses.

What could I say? That I was going to get the last word, finally outdo her for once and for all? The thrill of driving the truck with Delhi next to me must have acted in a manner similar to the pills, disinhibiting me. "I'm going to give that lady my will. She'll be my executor."

He got excited by that. "You have a will? That's cool. Show me sometime?" But then stopped. "Don't tell me you're one of those guys believe in suicide. I met someone like that. A guy collecting pills. Kept them around his neck. Ready for the apocalypse."

"There are worse ways."

"I'm serious though. *That's* the worst. Your spirit wanders in a tunnel forever. You heard of hungry ghosts?"

"But I already am." I laughed at the rightness of the phrase. "I'm your original hungry ghost."

"No wife or kids, huh?" he asked, but didn't seem to need much of an answer. "Hey, I'll be your executor if you can't find her," and though he said it casually, he seemed to mean it.

We were going a different way, on an old goat-path flanking one of the city's medieval aquifers. Shops and homes had been built above one side of the rounded aquifer, so that we could see into homes where people shuttled around in sunlit, furnished rooms.

"I can probably help you," said Moses, after some thought.

"With suicide?" This was my attempt at humor.

"You're morbid, man. I'll help you find your old lady."

"She's not—" but then realized she was. "That was my hope," I said. "That you could help. But how come you're not joining the others?"

"I got stuff to prepare," he said. "That custody talk. I got to be in no scrapes. No public stuff. I got to be rested. Those officials really give you the once-over, know what I mean? Last time they refused me."

"You seem reliable," I said.

"Thanks for the vote of confidence," he said, clasping my hand suddenly in his young boy's hand. "Friend."

TWENTY-SIX

One truth is that during my few weeks as janitor, so great and difficult was Arianne's cattiness, so malevolent her skill, that only once, at Paul's funeral, did she perhaps let on that she recognized me. We had brushed near enough to each other a few times, but I was never sure *if* she recognized me, which perhaps she didn't—all of that made me need to leave Finier. I could not take being so ignored at the same time that my survival required it. In that period, she was just beginning to burnish the reputation of her husband. She must have foreseen that once Paul died, she'd eat out on his legacy for years. Don't think I lack compassion. I believe Paul's dottiness, down to his suicide, must have made her feel life had lashed her to a richly unfair burden: surely there were nights on which, similarly, she'd had to leash him to his bed.

I say this with some information on my side. One night that first week back, I'd gone out drinking with the janitors' and plumbers' union, quite pleased with the success of my new alias. Having successfully introduced myself as Roland Molton, a taciturn fellow who could be jolly if plied with libations, I therefore thought I might stay perched in Finier without problem. My guise had a dignified, criminal legibility. Just shy of midnight I'd been returning to my hole in the wall when, along the somewhat wider hatters' road, I saw Paul fleeing, running in his nightshirt. As I stepped into a doorway to let him by, Arianne passed in pursuit, hair tumbled down, wearing a filmy housedress, imploring her hero to be good and let her catch up.

I backed into the darkness, shocked at the raggedness of her voice. This was my first time seeing her for some time, and neither she nor Paul noticed me. Let me state that it was not alcohol I saw in his eyes. Toward the end of the war, I thought I'd witnessed the onset of his craziness, but what good had that done anyone? What good would it have done anyone if I had jumped out in my janitorial guise into the night, smeared her nose in her mistake, as it were, forced her to recognize me? What could I have said? *Arianne, my apologies for your choice of the wrong man.* Knowing her as I did, she would have laughed in my face.

IN THE FINAL DAYS of the war, while still prefect, I'd taken tabs on who and how many of his resistance fellows Paul was taking out to our forests. *Taking out*—that was my private euphemism.

After his terrible revenge toward me in taking away my jewess, after he'd ambushed one of our lists and had her name typed onto it, after his victorious use of a red ribbon outside her house, after all that had sprung up around the disappearance of the lady I call Natalie, I'd decided to let the fellow hang himself with his own rope.

I began to notate his forest visits in code. My guess was that Paul harbored slights, that he tallied wrongs that had little to do with Vichy or the occupation: perhaps he'd guessed his wife's secret feeling for me. I remember this as the period when broad women were just beginning to sell boxwood at the church-doors and when apple blossoms were appearing on our trees, heedless of our national predicament. Not to hunt mushrooms but rather to follow up on Paul's doings, I began to take epic walks, as angry at the fellow as I was curious. Some might think I should have intervened immediately, but whenever the Faurets had intruded on my life, they had assumed center-stage, while I'd been their observer and pawn, and I didn't trust my ability to retain the upper hand. In retrospect, given how history recounts our era, the true occupation, if you ask me, was not done by the occupying nation but by the resistance, which made everyone who followed other paths into merely peripheral narrators.

I will say that I never actually saw Paul do away with a single one of his colleagues. Rather, on more than one occasion, I saw him—forthright Paul, noble Paul, hero—head out to a shed in the forest, arriving in the company of another but always leaving alone. No one else ever stirred from his shed, and I stayed late, watching, wondering at the witness of my eyes. One might say that my conscience or its equivalent had scared me into a mute remoteness, stripping my legs of their ability to head downhill, blinding my eyes to any possibility of investigating that awful shed's contents. Much later in life, a bit too late, it occurred to me that within his shed there might have been no decaying bodies, none at all, but rather a tunnel leading through the mountains toward Spain, an exit hatch as if in a children's fable. But who knew anything in those days, and was it my job to keep Paul's ranks thriving? I was not the one to ensure his cadre stayed full of those protesting our mission, rejecting our strategy for preserving the France of our childhoods. Admittedly, the idea of Paul slowly self-destructing did not lack appeal.

People often say I am an insensitive, hardened man. Rather, I am all too susceptible to any issue that might scratch our region's pride, and have long recorded all insults against our Bistronne. My strategy toward the end of the war funneled into this: having guessed Paul's deeds, I thought I should appeal to the glimmer of sensitivity within Arianne. Surely behind her new impersonation of *a harsh woman of the world* must exist a remnant of the softer side I'd glimpsed during our hotel summer.

Certain acts become almost fatally necessary, as my visit to Arianne one fall day was; I thought she would see its greater point. We could not tell what kind of liberation was approaching us, and no one could know what would become of us after. Would we be learning in German in a few years? Unthinkable. English? Even more impossible.

Though I'd been uncertain that she would agree to respond to the card I'd had Odile drop off at the hotel, she sent word via a stuttering boy on a bicycle that I was invited to her new apartments, in the annex to the hotel. These were shadow dwellings she kept in front of the real rooms where I'd learn one day that she and Paul had truly lived. The maid stalled me at the landing, for no apparent reason other than to make me wait, smirking before she ushered me in. As I entered, Arianne failed to rise from her work, too busy knitting little blue booties like some pious mother of the resistance.

"Emile Poulquet," she drew it out as if even my name were a joke. "Emile!"

"I come on official business," I said.

"Emile Poulquet," she repeated, as if now saying something deeper. It is understandable that I stumbled over a low table and upset two crystal figurines. One, if I remember, was of a dancer and the other may have been a model of the Colosseum. But Arianne was not perturbed as the crystal fell to the carpet and I replaced it.

"You didn't break anything," she said, adding, needlessly, "yet." Already my old rage filled me, yet I was forced to apologize. I tried to resume momentum, still standing, hat in hand. I wanted to make sure we were alone, as I'd requested that our meeting be confidential, and so, in roundabout fashion, asked whether or not I might see Paul.

"He's out," she lied. As if on cue, a cough came from the man who would one day lie immortalized as a bronze sculpture on a flatbed driven by me and then by Jacquot. Paul must have sat just beyond the wall.

I tried not to look at her. And yet I could not help observing the face, its brittle collection of smile and affect seducing its audience into a one-shot game. Had I not seen this before? How glaringly clear it became: the woman was barely held together. Like me, a person made of shards. One could enter her face by focusing on its flaw: since the onset of the war, under her eyes, two giant bags had formed, bags with the useful effect of lessening my own shame, pouches the only blemishes in what remained, admittedly, something of a doll's mien, tiny-featured and cheekboned atop a long neck. How her vanity must have hated those pouches, how she must have spent hours studying them, one could tell, how she had the further tic of ducking her head as if to angle the pouches away, a tic I understood, the pouches which seemed to contain all her hypocrisy, her soul's bitterness bulging out.

I looked not into her eyes, therefore, but at the dark pouches and spoke under my breath. "I've heard from various sources that Paul has," how to say it? "turned a bit. He's made certain citizens of Finier, not on anyone's deportation rolls, *flee*."

"Yes?" she said. As if heated, she took off her sweater, revealing her lean frame in its toile shirt. She brushed her fingertips along her neck, edged along her short hair, touched the bones at the base of her throat as if searching for an absent locket before picking up her knitting again.

This was her tactic: to seem an intelligent, decent woman, her words saying one thing and her gestures another, placing the onus on you as her viewer to figure out why your thoughts took such a lecherous spin.

"There have been *activities* in the forest. Perhaps too much of the bottle?" My tones were low, my manner diplomatic.

She took my hand, pulling me to sit next to her on the chaise longue. "Try to be understanding, Emile," she said, palm pulsing into mine. Only now did a trace of anything human enter our conversation, though she denied nothing, surely aware of what had prompted my visit. "Paul has gotten a touch of ergot."

Ergot. Ludicrous. In her cracked voice, enough to seduce a nation of Emiles, she was telling me something about an invisible fungus almost worse than the war, because you could put it on your table and slice it.

Was she after all lying? Many years later, in a Paris café, the memory of her on that day would return, dumbfounding, delivered up to my mind as a poisonous gift. Just as if she sat eternally before me, lithe in her white and blue toile, slippered feet tucked beneath the lower edge of the sofa, anchoring her monster's urge for power. Her scent that day humid and oppressive, not milky at all but a claustrophobia-inducing rosewater. For years, I remembered only the toile and the rosewater, but not what happened next, or how I exited, details which until recently, now that time has become my enemy and memory my deceptive ally, remained as blurry as one of our Finier pewter-gray skies. In fall, we're often gifted with odd vivacity, ill-fitting warmth, and it was on such a day that her words fell on me: *An opportunity to reflect . . . the fungus . . . the sad case of the occupation.*

"I'm sorry," I remember saying, beginning to hate myself, an effect she always exercised on me.

It is her eyes I remember best, pillowed on their pouches, blue and focused on her knitting and then somewhere behind my head as she began to recite, as if a memorized text, her grand Arianne-like justification. Sons and daughters of France had ingested this evil, she was saying, in our nation's greatest food, rationed so rarely, our bread. The war had spoiled our rye flour, used in our region's pain de seigle. Some life-form grew upon the rye if it was left exposed to water, and this life-form could inflict serious damage on the nerves. At least with the war you might see or guess which direction it was heading.

"But ergot—" and again she took my hand, though now her grasp felt parched, a claw, rigor mortis. "Ergot enters the body." Unfortunately, some of my old thrill returned: she had stripped me of speech. Feet tucked, she returned to knitting, lips holding the yarn for a moment, her decorum that of any good housewife. As if she'd never come to sit on my desk and leaned forward, *the same lean forward* as when she'd kissed my hump so many years ago, the same lean forward as at our hotel café table when she'd recited Paul's heroics to adolescent Izzy and me. That day at the prefecture, when she'd wished to humiliate me, leaning from my desk, she'd done what all good monsters do, transforming into what one fears most: Arianne the seductress, spilling *toward*. None of her new yarn-spooling could do away with the central fact. I had waited for her during a night as torturous as her earlier acts, so that room 316 remains a fixture of my most shameful dreams. Meeting in her annex, I had a certain control; I could have claimed my prize, told her outright of her husband's uncertain acts; but I wanted to behave decently, I wanted to rise above a chance to humiliate Arianne, to prove her wrong by an excess of noblesse oblige.

Because, no matter what, she always won. In a tone as dry as her hands, she was prattling on, saying that she considered this ergot problem to be the fault of the prefecture, *my* prefecture, because of the dispensing of tickets: the bad rye had been parlayed by dishonest suppliers to unscrupulous bakers, straight into the gut of people like Paul.

"Others are losing control because of it. Not just him," she said. "People blame it on the war when actually it's our bread!" She tore at a knot in her knitting, as if to say it was *my* bread which had done in Paul. "Our experts found out. Rye flour was kept over the winter. This occupation is killing us!" she said. My old wires were igniting at her every movement. "They're selling the flour five hundred miles from where they store it."

"They?"

"Immigrants," she said, as if this were self-evident. "Tax evaders and petty crooks. Vichy officials." She stopped. "You are prefect and you know nothing."

Then Arianne went into the pinched tenor I'd first heard her use long ago when berating a merchant. "You love medieval history, Emile?" She didn't wait. "You know how people say Saint Anthony's fire was caused by ergot. It makes people think they sprout mushrooms," she said. "They believe their bodies are becoming silver or fire. They think they're molten trees. If it doesn't kill them, it makes them go mad."

She leaned over confidentially, her breath stinging me with some waspish reminder. "Paul must have eaten that bad bread. Others did."

There was no way around it. "Is your Paul killing people?" I half-whispered, all I could manage.

"What did you say?" she said, concentrating on her knitting, newly pious.

"You can't answer me, Arianne."

"Your thoughts are so often deluded, Emile, it amazes me. Sometimes I wonder about our night in Bomont, the promotion, you know. What were we thinking?"

"You haven't answered me."

"Because I don't know how to address your delusions. One never expects them when you blurt your little things. They're funny in a man like you. Not the usual thing. Because you have a certain handsomeness, did I ever tell you that? Asymmetrical, but that chin of yours?" she said, sticking her own out, unfortunately making me blush. "Hard to quantify but it exists. You are, after all, a handsome man, did you know that?" This said within earshot of her husband and therefore all the more intended to humiliate.

"You can't speak straight?" I said.

"It's easy enough to speak straight. I could tell a deluded man no, I could protest, I could say his words are ridiculous, off the scale, but could he hear me? I'd end up tarred by the same brush. Please, don't go, not yet. I'm paying you a compliment, Emile. Your delusions about others haven't taken away from your appeal. You have what people call that ugly beauty. I'm sure it's added to your dignity in your job. I'm sure many people find your dignity appealing."

"We may have to mount an investigation."

"Emile. You haven't heard a word I've said."

It is true that I witnessed Paul's incidents three times after my talk with Arianne. Each time he walked out with a different victim, each time assured that no eyes followed him. True, I watched him on too many occasions for me to declare myself innocent. I should've looked in that shed, but could not bring myself to the act. Instead, I went on my hushed walks, enjoying my careful tread on the slippery stained-glass floor of the forest, damp leaves pressed into the loam. I knew the weekday hour which Paul favored, not long after five on a Friday, when most people concerned themselves with business of the weekend. So there was method to his madness. Each time, seeing Paul reach such an awful terminus, I felt the desire to rush forth and stop him. Yet while I could be methodical in my prefectorial functions, determined with my signature, able to issue orders so that names became like alphabet blocks to me, items to be stacked or eschewed, the satisfaction of order in the signing away of names, in the cross-checking of lists, the tearing-off of the carbon sheet, the procedure we had developed, the inky scent of returned carbon copies, the commendations from Bordeaux and even Vichy, our hay-colored padded envelopes and well-shined filing cabinets all placing me firmly in the center of a certain universe—still, something about these pesky Faurets made me a child all over again. Which is to say that while viewing Paul's disappearance into his shed, I had to hold my hands in place and (as if a chute dropped open beneath, landing me back in the indignities of childhood) I'd occasionally found it hard not to lose control of my bodily functions. "Stop," I'd mutter to myself, hoping Paul wouldn't hear. "Hump," I called myself, to stay in control. "Hump hump hump!"

As Paul and his victim entered the shed those final three times, I found it hard to believe the man's insane determination could solely be the work of bad bread. I hadn't believed Arianne's word. Instead, I tried to list scenarios, to keep myself in order:

1. Perhaps these particular comrades planned to betray Paul's work.
2. Perhaps he had already been betrayed.
3. Worse, perhaps he imagined all his comrades were traitors and had blindly begun to kill random fellows.
4. Perhaps, the worst possibility, he killed no one and merely some trick of my vision insisted on seeing a private conference as murder.

Needless to say, perhaps, the light which has so graced my path as a successful fugitive capable of trusting my instincts was still absent in that era. Not to mention that I also lacked evidence and stamina (or what others would call courage) to investigate and intervene.

The third time that Paul walked a man out of town, three times after my little ergot discussion, I thought at first he had seen me, as his movements were those of a wooden puppet, until, on his return, I saw him sink to his knees on the forest floor and shake his fist up at the trees' canopy. The man was a wretched sort. *Get up you ridiculous creature*, I wanted to shout, *spare your creator the melodrama*. He had won his lady, hadn't he? Though I could not imagine Paul in bed with Arianne. An upright fellow who left their marriage barren, Arianne knitting booties for phantom children. Anything I said to him at that point would have been wrong. My position at the prefecture, as well as what some might call my difficulties with Arianne, had effectively corked me. She must have predicted this. Further, of what matter were these resistance fellows to me? They might as well have been birds in migration, almond blossoms falling, a coffeepot boiling over. I decided I would never again follow him out into the forest.

In my second, janitorial period, I did hint to a fellow plumber at the prefecture that Paul had probably killed fellows who'd been loyal to the resistance. For this sharing of useful information, I was told I was crazy. Apparently, Arianne had been so successful at restoring Paul's honor that, after victory, after the *termination of hostilities*, the entire affair of those heroes who'd gone missing had been hushed up. This is the problem with our war memories: the king is dead or the king goes mad, and then we all have to live in the shadowed eternity of the king was a hero.

DURING THAT BRIEF janitorial phase in Finier, in my heretical glimpses of the Faurets, even apart from the night when he'd fled down the road, I could see that Paul's craziness had flared, surpassing senility. Arianne steered him—a void, burnt man, defeated, held together by invisible wires—by his elbow through the market, bobbing and smiling at everyone. People must have attributed his diminution to valor, Paul smiling and nodding as much as she did, acting very much the part of a beloved, idiot child.

His inner fiber was gone, I could see, and this awareness suffused me with the most expensive sentiment of all: regret. Perhaps it is enough to say that during that janitorial period, I avoided looking into Paul's eyes. Yet perhaps a fortnight after I'd seen him fleeing down the road, he caught me staring at him near the beet-seller's stand, and his eyes brimmed with such warmth and the unspoken, I could do nothing but leave my purchases and find succor at Louis's bar. Paul, the madman, swaying in the sunlight, had recognized me at once. A dimwit could see how much heart had stayed in his gaze.

■ ■ ■

FOR THE MOST PART, Arianne had succeeded in keeping her husband from public gatherings, managing to reconstitute Paul. This was the period in which she was beginning to form what would become the foundation of her society, famous throughout all of France: Arianne Fauret's Society for the Restitution of Memory.

In my fifth week as janitor, soon before my departure from Finier and a day after one of our annual Days of Patrimony, I attended Paul's funeral in my Molton incognito. That is to say, I stood in my own private obsolescence, well hidden on a hill of Esfauret, behind a crusty violinist. For a second, I felt returned to the black earth of our Finier forest, masses of damp leaves beneath me, again unable to stop the man on his strange track of spiting friends or foes.

When I came out of my reverie, spent to nothingness, I believed Arianne was looking straight at me. She gave a nod, as if her head were on a pulley, a nod more about recordkeeping than forgiveness. She knew our accounts. She'd ruled me in the schoolyard and near my house (*one point for Arianne*). During the war, I had tried to rule, but had only halfway succeeded (*one point for each of us*). I had not succeeded in making decisions about her and her hero husband and their entourage of raised-fist rebels. As recompense, however, she had been invested in humiliating me, twice over (*a poorly earned point for Arianne, equivalent to two points for Emile*). So it was that at the funeral of her husband, if she did recognize me, she tried to rise above herself, as funerals enable people to do (*one moral point for Arianne*). But as always, whatever dignity her jerky nod gave me was something that could be revoked, granted solely on her terms. Thus it could not be entered on any private ledger, and did not redeem her soul (*almost a conclusive point for Emile*). We were fairly even, and yet she still managed to play the much-praised lady, all at my expense.

AS FOR A grander point-recording, before the death of one of our presidents, years after my janitorial spell, in a churlish period when our people were claiming that the president had helped the cause of the Nazis and their plunderings, the president—I'll call him F.—had invited his closest advisors and former intimates to a very *bon weekend* indeed: he asked them to visit a remote country retreat for what might be the last of his notoriously grand meals.

And in this remote hamlet, unseen by most of his nation, there sat F., old and diseased, a man in muted shades. His napkin well tucked into his collar, his spirit willing and ready to eat well. The others had finished the white wine while the red waited, breathing from the open mouth of its crystal decanter. Everyone was ready. The president sat with those who had loved and feared him most. Only his young mistress was absent, always an exclamation point at these semi-official occasions.

And then the forbidden meal was shared. The ortolan was eaten. The tiny brown-purple bird which is nearly extinct, which flies over certain corners of France only during six weeks of the year. The ortolan which is delicious. Which one must eat by covering one's head with a large cloth napkin until one crunches and then swallows the entire little bird, including its bones and gristle and feet. For the president, to have a grand chef prepare the ortolan was the ultimate shame and pride, both affirmation and renunciation.

If you can understand how the crunch of the ortolan under the cloth napkin meant that F. still remained part of the esprit de corps of France, you can also understand why those who were invited to the dinner loved that I—demoted by time into a nonentity, a masked one at that, who had fled into anonymous and often demeaning professions, a man to whom the president nonetheless remembered his past loyalty, born from a time when I'd had the power to perform certain wartime and postwar favors for him—did not make myself any more visible that night than what was absolutely necessary.

Very good, I echoed, a person once important, disguised not just by my gray cravat and waistcoat, or the napkin over my head, but also by the intentionally hasty blur of introductions. *Very good*—and I too crunched the ortolan with relish, surprised at my own force.

Along with the best of patriots, unashamed, I swallowed that bird. Please pass the wine, I said to one fellow diner, as if I were a young man opening a delightful door. Here you go, I said, passing the bread to another. What fine foie gras! I exclaimed. I was among them.

At the president's dinner, no one knew me under any of my

aliases. Certainly no one knew my most recent official function had been as janitor of Finier, a man good at discarding documents on behalf of myself and a few well-chosen others, though my current job actually had a far baser price tag on it—their fellow dinner guest being a repairer of tired soles and worn-out heels in an unbeguiling town, as far from Finier's beauty as could be. No, to the diners, despite all the exquisitely mannered flesh on their chattering skeletons, I was one of them, one more skeleton, there with the best and worst of France. Come to think of it, we all might have been in disguise.

Just as none of the shoes' owners in the lackluster town which was then my habitation—I will not name it—knew the high silent cloud of my past life, none of the diners, fellow lovers or killers of France, depending on your version of history, knew my current phlegmatic reality. And all the week following the dinner, as I shined shoes of giggling, sneezing civil servants lacking all bond to me, no one knew what strength it took to avoid hinting that I'd just dined with the president. I was as hungry for those small-town functionaries to recognize me as they were hungry to deride my status, making me part of some normal hierarchy and sequence of events.

That next Friday, however, while shining shoes, I did allow myself to say to the civil servants of the town a single phrase of heresy: *bon weekend*, I said, fully modern, *bon weekend*.

TWENTY-SEVEN

Moses wanted a little lunch but his ladies worked in a pattern, a cosmic message there, he told me: none of them had left him any food. All those cosmic poetry-lovers had disappeared, maybe off to the concert or the rivers or their boutiques. "Whatever," he said. They had forgotten Moses. He surmised that right now they were clutching shawls around their skinny bare arms, watching Jacquot storm the central square in a truck bearing Paul's head. His usual food suppliers gone, however, Moses grew disgusted, the closest I'd seen him come to losing his equanimity. "Where else could we go?" he asked. "You know this place as well as I do, right?" I was flattered that he sensed my intimacy with a town he'd claimed as his own. From what I'd overheard among the reporters, we were down the road from the hall the refugees might have rented, once they'd realized the Arianne-inspired events had to be put on hold, and I mentioned this, though I wasn't sure it would help. Moses lit up with a plan, asking me to wait for him by a plane tree, where my sole entertainment was the fervent labors of potato bugs tunneling in the dirt. He had interpreted my words as a suggestion that he should ask for help from anyone left in the hall.

"Nobody will be there," I pointed out, not liking his plan. "They'll be at the concert." Though I hadn't seen any of them down in the town, I believed that refugees would like to feel cultured and would have slipped inexorably toward the tacky event, despite Arianne's disappearance.

"If they're gone, even better," he said.

But if they're there, you don't understand, I wanted to call to Moses' retreating back, *you're hardly the kind they like to help.*

A happy magician, some five minutes or so later, Moses emerged from the hall with two long sandwiches, one of which he placed on my lap.

"Don't ask." The boy chewed like one of his ravished dogs. "Don't be a fossil, man. You're not hungry?" he said between mouthfuls.

"Nothing fills me anymore," I said, laughing at the hollow music of me.

Inside, on a phonograph, a song had started up. It was a wheezy melody I'd known that summer, working with Izzy, popular at the time. *I will never cry again,* one of the background singers kept insisting.

"You know the song?" Moses asked me, and I realized I was singing under my breath. Sentimental sop but it inflicted itself on me: *I will never cry again, they will never know my heart has stopped, for you I could wait forever.*

"Dark, man. Raoul." He touched my hand. "Eat your food. Stay in the moment."

He was right. On the roof of the hall, I saw a man come out, shambling. A table and chair were set up to look out over the valley, and the man drew up the chair, his back to us, enough so we could see a bit of beard in profile. A man doing nothing grander than setting up to snooze in the fleeting sun. A man wearing huge sunglasses, taking off his jacket, loosening his collar. "You didn't see that guy when you went in?" I asked Moses.

"Why, you know him?" he asked, scratching his head as if a nation of lice had just descended.

I hushed him. "Can we finish up and go?"

He half-laughed at me but not without respect, his strange balance. "Whatever." He grumbled a bit, respecting my silence most of the way back to the manse, heading out through town with its muzzled rooftops, passing the splayed backs of haystacks, the road wound up like the pursing of a giant's mouth. By the time we'd arrived at the manse, he asked again who it was.

"My old best friend."

Moses looked at me, full of sympathy. "I know how *that* goes, man. Too late to patch things up?" He waited. "What were you guys up to? Sorry I asked. We can talk about it later." He was fiddling inexpertly in his pants pocket with what he'd showed to me earlier, a small portable tape recorder he'd said he used for music and meditation chants, but then gave up. "Don't want to talk more, huh?" He was depositing me at the mouth of our habitat, a welcoming place, as far from the mouth of hell as a place could be. Inside was freedom. "Get some sleep, man. No offense but you look awful."

"Where are you going?" I realized how strange it would feel to be back at the manse, swallowed by the universe, alone in the middle of a halfway sunny day not yet on the wane.

"I got to go see about a few things for my custody meeting—you'll walk with me part of the way, right? Tomorrow."

I was struck with a fear of the unknotting of memory that would be mine if Moses left me too long. "You're coming back, right?" Now I wanted to tell him everything, snag his attention, give him trophies, anything to keep him there. "The one you call my old lady, she was the one who married the statue," I said. "The guy who was the model for the statue."

"I get it," he said. He was backing away as if I'd set a large ball tumbling down the hill toward him. "That's heavy. Your old lady was Arianne."

"She's not my old lady," I said. "I mean *wasn't*."

"Still, it's heavy, man. Hey. I can help you find her."

"I'll tell you more if you—" But I couldn't finish the sentence, dissolving.

He continued loping backward, filled with the charisma which could've made the boy a leader had he chosen that route, and it was a sunny, untroubled charm, so different from the snake to which I'd been drawn in all too many people. "I'll be back," he said, fully confident. "You'll wait."

TWENTY-EIGHT

One of the dreams I remember from that afternoon, waiting for Moses, has me in a white sanitary room, waiting, seated, in a line. An official white-cloaked woman calls forth numbers, one by one, summoning people to undergo the tortures of war. One girl sits in front of me, not dissimilar from Arianne when she was still a cruel schoolgirl in black braids. In the dream, however, girl-Arianne chats happily on a portable phone, showing all the glibness she always possessed. At one point she turns around. "Don't worry, Poulquet," she tells me in her unripped young voice, so confident about controlling all of us. "You won't suffer. You picked up enough fallen apples."

"You don't know," I tell Arianne. "I will suffer. I'm a jew now." In the dream I have become the owner of a proud and deep self-pity, I think no one can know the extent of my possible suffering, I'm about to receive the slights of the jews.

She swivels toward me, parting her pale thighs a bit. "Just think!" she leans over to whisper. "You're not Moroccan!"

Just before the white-cloaked woman calls out my number, young girls, all wearing widows' weeds, enter the room, interrupting her. In a Gregorian chant, they sing that the war is over. Actually: that the war has been *rescinded*. Tonsils waving:

The war is now rescinded

The music uplifts me. Arianne places my hand at her crotch. And she croons: "Poulquet, you worrywart! You won't go blind! You made my husband go mad."
"That was not my fault." I whisper to her, confused. "Shouldn't we go in now? Anyway, he was no war hero."
"You're stuck on that detail."
"He went mad without me," I say. I am trying to ignore how she has begun to scissor her legs around my hand. "He started killing people he should not have. You think Paul was a hero but he was bad for all of you in the resistance. If he'd simply collaborated, as I did, fewer people would have suffered."
"You let Paul take over your head. I'm talking about you and me, Emile."
"Paul was worse than I was. He killed innocents but got to die thinking he was a good man."
"Don't delude yourself! He never killed anyone. You shipped jewish jews out. You did things we can't even talk about."
"I'm not a *jewish* jew," I correct her, mistaken myself.
"I'm telling you Paul had ergot. You love to blame everyone else. That little jewess in your bed must have twisted your head. Old man!" winding her legs more tightly around my caught hand. "It's only *unjewish* jews who are free to return to Finier!"

THE NEXT DREAM is no stranger to me; I've had it all too often. In it, I am flying out over an ocean, away from a boardwalk, and far too late I realize an important meeting is due to take place. My attempts to catch the winds back in over the mountains are almost useless, but a sense of duty makes me persevere; I am to preside over the manners of a dinner, to be held in Finier, in our old Hotel Fauret. This will be a dinner attended by all my colleagues and major criminals from the wartime period: yes, my duty is to hold down a table.

But, having arrived, I find myself too paralyzed by excruciating embarrassment to speak. Lapses in protocol abound. One man slurps his soup, thereby stopping all conversation. Another, rather than swirling his wine around in his mouth, gargles and spits back into the bottle. One leans over his seatmate to whisper to a friend, coatsleeve dragging through a perfect circlet of foie gras. Another punctuates a point he makes by sinking his fist deep into a soufflé, forcing out a little sigh. My whole old-man's chest could explode from frustration. I'd decided to come back to Finier. But I needed to find Arianne, soon, before my will to find her collapsed.

TWENTY-NINE

I must have slept through to Monday, butchering a cavalry of hours, highly unusual to sleep so long. When I awoke, Moses hovered over me in morning's light, his eyes like lightning bugs, excited with a promise that he could find some guy who'd help me reach Arianne. He said we should hitchhike down to a meeting place in town, but accepted my desire to walk. "You seem tired though, man," he said, more than once on our journey, "or what's with the brooding?" Our first destination was, I found out, the courtyard just outside the mayor's office, on Finier's broad main tree-flanked avenue, within shouting distance of the prefecture. I was wondering what had happened to Jacquot and the girls storming the musical event, and what the squadron of refugees and reporters might have made of the ruckus, but still a little sleep-logged, I did not feel like questioning much. We sat on the rim of the courtyard's dry fountain and I caught my breath, eyeing my surroundings with distaste. "You don't mind waiting, do you? I have a small errand to run here first," said Moses, a relentless salesman. "After that, we can go find the guy with the goods."

It was almost intolerable, how polite my circumstances forced me to be. Was this scraggly boy really going to lead us to Arianne? I suggested that instead I wait for him across the street, and he grimaced. "Knowing you're here, man, right *here*, it will give me strength."

"I don't like official buildings."

"Okay," he said finally. "Suit yourself."

I crossed the street to a ficus tree in the schoolyard, pretending to be interested in its diseased leaves. The only other occupants of the yard were a bunch of wiggly schoolchildren, struggling to avoid staying in line despite the blandishing inducements of their schoolteacher, a lady in a clumsy gray suit who spoke in a kindly, soft voice no schoolteacher of my era had ever used. However, I was fairly sure that, at one point, while accounting for her rowdy young charges, this teacher raised her head over their wriggling mass to give me the Look. It was insufferable—I had been admiring her—but also unmistakable. I turned back toward the pocked leaves of the ficus as if I were an amateur botanist examining spores, and then immediately pivoted, trying to make my way as quickly as I could out of the yard. Surely it had been a mistake to have come into a schoolyard. I hadn't been thinking clearly. At this point, I thought I might leave word with Moses that I would meet him elsewhere, but my pendulum had taken over: I had an unignorable message from it, like an unshelled mussel throbbing in my pocket.

On the sidewalk, I swung my friend in as hidden a fashion as I could.

IS IT TIME TO LEAVE FINIER? I asked. YES! it answered, with an added inflection of YOU IDIOT.

I thought of leaving Moses a note, I did, I even walked past the guard and into the courtyard. There, through the arch of the inner patio, I saw Moses, talking with two men, one of whose silhouetted bulks was known to me: the man on crutches who'd handed me the newspaper.

Moses may have been asking for directions, or one of the men may have been linked to the official custody hearing, but though the boy surely engaged in benign conversation with these types, I knew the signs were wrong, the embossing of venom.

If I wanted to reach Arianne, I must do it without the cover of these wastrels. The only door open to me with any certainty was that of my doctor friend in Paris. Was it worth going back there, to the rue Luxembourg? Would I be surrounded by angry chanters with their yellow stars, or would my disguise keep? Perhaps it was worth a try; perhaps Paris was where I could better block all efforts to hunt me down. I turned on my heel, meaning to leave Finier.

But Finier itself is so small, jumbled in atop itself on its slight hill, a centrifuge for one's intentions, and there are so few places for someone like me to hide. Even the walk to the train station is somewhat visible from the hotel and the prefecture. As I walked, as quickly as I could, I could hear a mass of people in the square, though now with no music. Finally, at the station, my pacemaker recalibrating itself, I saw the empty platform as a reward, the familiar embrace of an undiscerning, promiscuous mistress. I would wait for the Paris train, only ten minutes away if the posted schedule was accurate.

My luck was not running high, however.

He managed to catch up with me. Panting and heaving, his dogs with sloppy grins behind him. I could not shake Moses; Moses must have been informed of my movements. Or else he'd sighted me and followed me. Or else whatever he called his cosmic rays had alerted him, rays high as birds and keeping track of me. "You can't go," he said. Charmingly in control. "Not yet. Did I say you could?"

I smiled southward, away. The train was due in eight minutes.

"I'll get you to see her," he said. "Whatever. Why'd you spin out? I just asked you to wait." He saw this wasn't enough and that he'd have to strip himself further. "I *need* you, man."

"My apologies," I said. "I don't have it in me to help anyone. You said you were going to get me to see—" He looked away as if I could make him cry. "There's nothing left," I tried to explain to his shoulders, tasting metal as I spoke, as if I had licked a trigger. "Not for you. I don't have anything left in me for anyone anymore."

When he turned back, his face was more composed than I'd imagined. He took out a cigarette from a crushed pack, straightened it before lighting. "Did you ever have anything in you for anyone?" he said.

I chose to ignore this and said I didn't know he was a smoker. A terrible cough was beginning in my chest, irrepressible, and when it came, I tasted blood.

He lit and exhaled pointedly, more on edge than I'd seen him before. "Hey. I need you, man. You've got to be my, um, character reference."

"Why me?" trying to keep from coughing.

"Who else is there for me to use? Cerb-X? *Jacquot?* You know. One look at Jacquot and they'll put me in jail. All you got to do is simple. Say you knew me from Orly. You came down from Orly." He waited for me to stop coughing. "Okay, maybe go part of the way with me? It's a long trek. Or maybe I can get them to interview me in Finier."

I looked into his hazel-green eyes, the dirt-spattered face, the hair wild and sad. I didn't see why I was so important to him, but I wanted him to state it baldly, to get on his knees. "Frankly, you don't think Jacquot might help?"

"He's useless. When it comes to these things," said Moses. "Just come and keep me company. You can tell me about your old-time things if it makes you happy. I'll tell you stuff too. I feel I'm supposed to show you a few things you might not ever see again."

"What are you talking about?" I asked, sharp.

"Hey." He put his hand on my shoulder. "You know better than I do. Old country ways are dying out. Look, this is kind of a plea bargain, all right?"

"Plea bargain?" He wasn't making sense but one wanted to forgive Moses, even though he hadn't told me why he liked me so much. "I'm an old man. You expect a lot from me."

"I don't. What you should realize is I'm trying to give you something. I don't have to but I *want* to."

I was being demanded to be a better person than I was. "Sorry," I said, again the word spiky on my tongue.

"I waited for *you*, you know." He whistled to his two doggy followers. "C'mon," he said, "you'll crash with us tonight. So tomorrow we'll walk a little. You're not that old. I've seen you walk," he said. "Anyway, I got a message to show you things."

"From whom?"

His smile had a sly charm. "My angels. I told you I have a connection with the cosmic rays? They zapped me when I was young." At my stare, he laughed. "Seriously. Right now, while you and I are talking, they're zapping me too. Something heavy. Feel my fingertips." I felt them. They did seem to be trembling, but I could only nod, uncertain about how to judge cosmic rays, conversant only in the ways of my pendulum. "They told me it's okay to play your tour guide for a couple of weeks. Free you of heavy stories. They're zapping me in other places but you don't have to feel them everywhere."

"Not bad," I said.

"My life support. My friends. They're talking. Saying it's only right that we walk tomorrow. Anyway," he said. He was not taking no for an answer. "We'll hang, then I'll go to court. You'll be my moral support. Sort of. Then at night we move the squat. There's been a crackdown."

He told me about some whole EUROPE thing, as he put it, which stood for something like the Establishment of a United Repatriation Organization for Preprofessional Emigrants. "Or whatever. The manse wasn't like forever. We got to move." He scrutinized me again. "Hey, I feel like I haven't seen you. I mean *seen* you. You okay?"

I could not help echoing him. "Sort of." We were already turning back toward Finier.

"You're coming. That's great."

"I told you," I said. When had I assented? I didn't want to lose my patience. "I don't like officials."

"But it's not about officials, man," he said. "It's about me. We'll get you spiffed up." He searched. He dug into his pocket and handed me a lozenge. "All you got to do is say I'm a reliable, safe, honest guy."

THIRTY

That Monday noon, with still no sign of Jacquot and his girls on the streets—had they been arrested for their stunt? Moses hadn't seen them since the previous day—we went into the photo store to take official pictures of Moses. Did it really matter that the storeowner did a double-take when he saw me? Another bitter man, another product of a private history made up of cupboard and bedroom and schoolroom moments. On his wall were pictures of everyone else's grandchildren, smiling, not his own progeny (I asked). On his file cabinet was a single war helmet.

"You know," I said to Moses, "I lost my hat and have to get a new one."

"It's okay," he said. "You don't need one."

Ahead of us, I saw Delhi crouched on a curb and felt unduly excited, going so far as to nudge Moses. Delhi happened to be talking into someone's microphone, and I recognized the bowl-headed reporter, Barbie Rotesc, crouched facing her, who apparently had been persuaded to stay by her own form of professional rays. Clownish, Moses pulled me near enough behind Delhi that we could hear Barbie ask the girl in bad French what it was about living homeless that had motivated Delhi to wage the successful countercultural protest she and her compatriots had accomplished yesterday. Cerb-X faced us, bobbing up and down, trying to get Barbie to listen. Apparently the scene in the square had been a big success. Krenek the composer and the head of Paul, Jacquot and his two ladies, the flatbed truck and the musicians. The tourists had thrilled to it, had thought it all part of a scene, and at least one reporter had sensed a new story about growing anarchy.

"You see yourself taking part in the nascent international struggle against globalization?" the reporter was asking Delhi with her smut-loving nasality. "How do you define your group, that's what I'm asking."

"We're against definition," said Delhi, gold-lit, her smile rippling across at us.

"What's the matter with me, lady?" Cerb-X was whooping it up, bumping close to the mike, jangling her shackles. "I'm too much a hoodlum?"

"Go on," Barbie said to Delhi. "If you were to give yourselves a name, what would it be?"

"New pacifists? Refugees? We were taking advantage of the reunion taking place here in Finier."

Barbie's nod was every bit a professional's. One had to admire her skill, just as one might admire a scythe.

"Even those old-time refugees represent war to us," said Cerb-X.

This last bit stymied Barbie. "I'm not sure I understand. You're protesting the refugees?" she asked Delhi, continuing to ignore Cerb-X.

"Well," said Delhi. "Not protesting." She shot a look of complicity at Cerb-X. "It doesn't make sense if you haven't been involved."

Barbie waved her on, cramming the mouthpiece toward the girl.

"But it's like we think refugees keep the spirit of war alive as much as anyone who hurt them, you know?"

Barbie crossed something out on her pad as if clubbing a small creature. "You advocate amnesia?"

"We're not saying it's bad to keep the spirit of war alive," said

Delhi. "But all we have is this moment." Her face flared with something of Jacquot's regal mania. "You, me. You here interviewing me."

"Don't forget me!" Cerb-X laughed, before performing an exaggerated catwalk away from them.

"Go on?" Barbie's pen was poised midair.

"We think if you crowd the present with the past"—here Delhi again may have been quoting one of Jacquot's epigrams—"what room do you make for the future? That's it," she said, beaming, her excitement probably blinding her to how Barbie folded back into herself. "There's this fetish, you know? In France. We have a fetish with memory. Schools and history, all that. You can say we're trying to clear the present so there's room for a better future. But we're also about reviving the old ways, you know, farming? Stuff like that."

"So what does the statue represent?" asked Barbie. "It was highly fortunate that you were protected from immediate legal action. Did you know that?"

Delhi shook her head.

"You had in your favor that appendix to the statute. About freedom for artistic demonstration in the service of political ideals. That's why none of you were taken in. Were you aware of that?"

"Lucky." Delhi shrugged. "But we believe shame is a big deal here, it's everything, and the law's just one part of it."

"Shame?" Barbie's pen poised in the air.

"Everything wrong and right about our country has to do with shame. That's what we're trying to take away."

"Excuse me—"

"You know, like we're supposed to always speak like relativists, we're not supposed to believe in anything, that's not patriotic, supposedly, but then we're also supposed to be contrarians, we're bred to say no to all values. Then it's also like we make taboos into a shrine. Adultery or whatever. Or we make a fetish out of art. Or the nation, or food. Wine. I'm saying it all has to do with shame. We wish for the moment before shame began."

"Because our parents didn't let us play with our shit!" hooted Cerb-X.

"Even how we say *little* this, *little* that. My little café, my little pen, my little hatmaker's. Everything's little," Delhi was ruminating, more excited than I'd ever seen her. "Have you ever noticed that? We'd be better off if—"

"So you did steal the statue?" Barbie interrupted.

"We got it from the Fauret foundation," said Delhi. "We have it on paper from that Polish guy. He loaned it to us. I think he *wanted* us to make a big protest."

"We were a good distraction, you know? We hid it in the forest," said Cerb-X, flashing her smile. "We're about surprise. We stole it but he was cool. It's a gift. We'll use it again in the future."

Barbie persisted. "But what is it to you? What does it mean?"

Cerb-X shook her head at the woman's ignorance. "The worker. People getting rid of small farms. That statue's just one of our weapons," she said, again quoting Jacquot.

THE REIGN OF JACQUOT could have been a deterrent to my return to Finier, the least of deterrents, however, compared to the hovering figure of Izzy. Many people or places in this town could have been deterrents, keeping me from helping Moses, but I chose to do what I did because of Moses and his yearning face, Moses saying *I need you* at the train station. Moses had brought me back to Finier, and despite everything, I would return the favor by reentering even the prefecture for him, its halls still my halls, probably the same peppermint and animal-fat scent to them, the same eaves if undoubtedly with a new shine off their walls. He'd asked me if I had it in me to help anyone. I would help the boy, I told myself, help reunite a family—what could be better than that?—and it was important that I be here.

Admittedly, the strangeness of reentering my old habitat thrilled me. My pendulum had told me not to, but at this point, I believed the pendulum had taken a perverse turn. Who else did I have to advise me?

We left the girls and the reporter to their discourse and returned to more pressing matters: lunch, for which Moses introduced me to the charms of dumpster-diving, as his ladies had not left him any offerings. Surprised by the insubstantial but tasty bounty we were able to reap from his dives into trash cans, near the Moroccan apartments, the bananas and flat bread heavy as clay, soon after, I headed with him to the prefecture. Yet lunch had helped restore my wits: as we entered, I whispered to Moses that I could serve as his character reference only if a man named Galtimer was not conducting his interview. Moses, used to my sudden balkings, didn't blink.

"Check who's doing it," I suggested. "I'll wait here." I sat near the entrance on one of the stone benches smoothed by centuries of petitioners, my own legs folded, eyes downcast like one of those old-time foreigners, those women swaddled in head-scarves, waiting while Moses blustered down the hall to ascertain his interrogator's identity, braids hopping and skipping down his back in contrast to the lines of the place, as if being at the region's center further electrified his hair.

We were lucky—or were we, after all?—that the interviewer happened to be one of Galtimer's underlings. Moses came back to tell me this. She seemed a fine enough professional woman from the way she ushered us into her office, reminding me of Odile in her deprecating air and smoothness, her sloped, naked shoulders. I wondered if Galtimer was, to use the parlance of the wastrels, *getting it on* with this professional woman.

"How do you know this man?" she began her interrogation of me. I was not happy that she put a tape recorder on as backup to her notes, she said, but then again, I am decent at disguising my voice.

I learned that Moses' real name was François Tyolard. Then I went through the rote, a register deeper than usual, and the woman was satisfied. Steady and crisp, I said I was Raoul Tavelle, and that Moses had been employed for the last few months in a small roadside farm-goods concession I had set up outside Toulouse, but that I'd forgotten to bring my concession license. Using the dialect and grammatical errors of our region's peasantry, I swore over my mother's body that I had never met a more upstanding boy, even if he was a city boy. I will admit that I was gratified by the inventiveness of my performance, the gestures I took on, pulling at my chin, scratching behind my ears, pulling at my collar, just another scruffy salt-of-the-earth farmer: as if the spirit of the deceased Bruno Somport, the old bicyclist, started to move within my bones.

As I continued on, I felt we were all professionals meeting on the solid ground of agreement—the professional lady good at interrogation, Moses a perfect wastrel, and I an artist of camouflage.

Outside, Moses told me I had aced the interview. "You really know how to speak the lingo."

"I'm not without practice, you know."

Yet he was not so ecstatic as I might have expected. "Hey, that was big of you," he said, eluding my grasp, hands shoved so deep into his pockets that his skinny hipbones rose above his pants. "Huge."

"It helped, did it?"

"Now I'll just have to go pick them up from their different homes. Outside Finier, you know, but not that far. It's practically a shoo-in. You're a strange ally, you know?"

You too. Something was troubling him, and I couldn't divine his tone. "You're not sure about taking care of your children now? Is it the responsibility?"

"Something like that." He looked beyond me, clacked his tongue, returned to some invisible box. "You can say that. The responsibility could just about crush you."

THIRTY-ONE

Though I'd been induced back by Moses, *seduced* back really, I hadn't given up my habit of ensuring that I had various backup plans. The truth was that while Moses had provided both protection and interest for old Emile, I wanted to float above Finier, to be many places at once. This final return—I swore it was the last—made me feel gravity-free, like a child who wishes to explore a candy store now known well: I wanted to see the back, front, the peppermint-striped interiors. A strange glee filled me, a certainty about the fulfillment of all I'd wanted on returning to Finier. The lay of the land was known; I'd stared down risk; I had a feeling that Arianne was coming toward me. No matter within which group I waited, whether reporters or refugees, I'd be able to hitch a ride, as it were, ultimately hand off my will. But Moses said he needed me close, in the belly of the wastrels.

In choosing to stay by Moses, I'd told myself I'd spend only another night or two in the manse, away from the hotel which held a greater risk for me, both in terms of vulnerability and its power to make me prey to memory attacks. I also wished to protect the boy—he said he needed me—and didn't want to consult the pendulum on the wisdom of this move. Yet a struggle had taken place.

"Not a struggle," Jacquot corrected us. Monday afternoon found us sitting on the lip of the hill outside the manse. "A conversation. One with consequences."

There were several reasons we had to give up our comfortable habitation. One had to do with some rival tribe. I had never known these scruffy people lived in *competition* with one another, but maybe this was the new shadow order. A different group of squatters was roaming around, truly lawless, drum-beaters united by fervent beliefs and pyromania. The thing was, Jacquot knew these guys and they had it in for him. He sounded almost professionally paranoid. He thought it better that we move closer to the center of town, where there'd be witnesses, where this other tribe would be less likely to set fire to us. Jacquot hadn't seen these guys in a while but he knew about their vicious sock-footed streak. They're sneaky, they'd stoop to nothing, he said, I mean nothing's too little for them. At the same time, the problem with heading to some other squat in the center of the town was that there was the whole EUROPE crackdown. The way Jacquot figured it, functionaries would be more likely to uproot us if we were near their sightlines, at the center of things, near the staid cafés they frequented. But there was another reason we should give up the manse, Jacquot was saying, and it had to do with the place's owner, a crackpot guy who'd assigned a deputy to get his country place prepared immediately, and this guy operated on a schedule beyond tribal competition and government crackdowns.

"The owner wants to be away from gossipers in town," said Jacquot in a tone of false authority. "It was supposed to become a love nest. He may be coming back to it."

I had slept a few nights in someone else's love nest. *The owner*, what I'd never been. My eyelids dead with fatigue, my pendulum insolent, I felt the weight of years, all my unwanted freedom. It may have been true that among them, only Moses was a humanitarian, his consideration like a cozy blanket around my old-man bones. Or to say it in a different way: staying with the wastrels and Moses had started to seem like a perch a falcon would choose, a memoryless, impermanent safety.

"Get moving," said Jacquot. "We have no time to muck around."

BEFORE WE BEGAN the move down the mountain, I couldn't help but study Cerb-X. She said she'd had some work done after her exchange with the reporter, to honor the successful street theater they'd pulled off. Her face was swollen from all the piercings she'd received, tiny golden and silver hoops descending from the tip of her nose in a pagan's straight line. They went all the way down her neck to her sallow clavicle. As we gathered our belongings, I asked her, I thought in a kindly fashion, what the piercings meant.

She at first sneered and then brought herself to answering. It was about seeing if others could deal with their own darkness, she said. "This is a symbol of my ugly side."

"You're hardly an ugly lady," I said, having learned that one shouldn't compliment these ladies too directly.

"Can't you hear me out?" she asked. "If people can be cool with my piercings when they first meet me, I'll know who they are. I'll know they're also cool with their own dark side. It's like hermeneutic magic? Like Sir Isaac Newton? He was an alchemist. And I'm like a witch." For the first time, I saw Cerb-X as a vulnerable girl, a child faltering as she rehearsed lines from a Christmas pageant. "Once they can accept me, then I know we can be part of the same tribe. They don't have to be pierced themselves. They just have to be comfortable with their own inner dark. These are souvenirs of the dark."

I found this to be weirdly eloquent, even if her scowl told me the exact degree of uncool I was to her. I looked at her bad self, parading as a bunch of studs down the front of her face, chastising myself for not having been quick enough to catch all the symbols.

"Will Delhi someday get piercings too?" I asked.

"She already has a nipple ring," said Cerb-X. "And a ring down under, but she won't get any more. I can promise you that. Not if she wants to sleep with you," said Cerb-X, her tone deadpan enough to hide bombs. Back to her usual self, clicking her tongue ring against her front teeth. "Anyway, Delhi is not really into piercing. She likes bloodletting. You know, that whole S & M thing in the cities. Maybe she also likes necrophilia. Or whatever you call that reverse-pedophile thing. You never know with people."

"What?" I asked, and Cerb-X's face loomed into me, fierce with studs, a landslide, far from the vulnerability she'd shown only a second before. Cerb-X loved to shock and she was good at it.

"You're blushing," she told me. "I got the old man to blush," she boomed to the others. For my own part, I turned from her, trying to hide embarrassment by gathering all the paltry tokens of me, my dwindling possessions.

NIGHT WAS COMING and we had to accomplish the move carefully. The realtor's daughter in town had told Moses about the new space, vacated, not far from the prefecture. The daughter was another rich girl but a cool one with a feeling for the people, he told me as we straggled down from the mountains and through the streets. He explained further, with his love of malapropism, that the best formula the wastrels could find was to joke through any upheaval, through all of them, upheaval an element of life, an element nonetheless to be eloquently, scatologically, congradatiously protested.

"Class struggle all over again," Jacquot interrupted his compatriot's rhetoric. Amid our line descending the mountain, the bloodhound could always be counted upon to center himself in anything, even in history, his generation's flaw pure like a jet strip. We numbered a rough nine or so, clutching our bedclothes and belongings. Every now and then Christian let out a little expletive, damning the landlords. I decided to give up questioning whether or not it was good to be among this tribe and just, I kept telling myself, to enter their present tense.

As we walked, for my fortitude in the stream of good times and bad, Jacquot actually tried to pay me some kind of compliment but his words congealed as soon as they were spoken. "When I first saw you, I thought you were a real criminal, no offense."

"No offense."

"I thought you might be the one. To help us, you know—help me out, Max."

Max, eyes unmoving, regarded me. Timid boy, runt of the litter, looking as if he'd been pushed down at the top and sides of his head, hard, until he became more of a plug, neck vying in a thickness contest with the head, yet the eyes an icehound's Nordic blue, capable of frightening one. "I don't know what you're saying, Jacqui. You thought Raoul could—?"

"That he might be a criminal who could—help me out, Max."

"Break into the prefecture?"

"That's it. You could be the one, Raoul. But now that we got to talking, I changed my mind. Now I think you are more. Come on. I think he's—"

"Presentable?" said Max. "Personable?"

"Personable. You're personable." Jacquot had a curious frolic in him, as if he were a loyal person, someone enjoying a practical joke now and again but essentially decent. "You strike me as personable. I mean it. Personable. That's old Raoul Tavelle."

What else was there to do but thank him?

"I mean it, man. You're personable."

I CHOSE TO ignore this and focused instead on descending the mountain, the line of us sometimes bunching together caterpillar-fashion, sometimes stretching, and though Jacquot left me soon enough, behind him jokes and insults clotted, dispersing only after I moved through. That boy was thin and manic, a slingshot of a human, never content unless he hurled action or insult through others. Winding down through the town's night streets, we stretched into a line so the kids became solitary figures, as if on a forced march through a desert of their own regrets, only occasionally springing to life, shouting to one another and the dogs out of an uprising of merriment or previously swallowed words and with such din that the city sparked awake above us, giving taxpaying citizens the opportunity to lean out of upper-crust windows and hiss threats down at lowlifes.

. . .

AS WE NEARED TOWN, past linden trees standing like a rank of flayed bodies against the half-lit sky, Moses tried telling me about how belongings start to own the wealthy rather than the reverse. He said: *Look how the wastrels can move without needing much at all. Here we stay closer to the bleakness, man, the truth of existence.* The only interruption to his words came when little Max had trouble with what I hadn't noticed was his bad leg. First Moses felt compelled to make a joke in what I felt was bad taste, but then he swept the boy onto his back, broad enough for the job.

"Moses is proud!" Jacquot ribbed him. "Strong man, Mister Universe!"

"Shush," said Moses, "leave me alone," neighing like a good stallion and clip-clopping down the road, Max clinging to his back.

At the rear, Cerb-X and Delhi were clinging also but to each other's arms, girlishly, complaining of the cold, wearing a shared quilt which Jacquot kept adjusting around them with a proprietary, gallant-knight mien. In the filtered light, I could make out the ugliness of Cerb-X's extra face rings, barnacles climbing that luminescent skin to clank against one another.

Midnight in the square when we amassed, a few new faces joined us, casual in their greetings, but these defecting-from-the-anarchists wraiths melted away from their greetings, seeming to lack chests, so extreme they could have been stock actors brought in to fill the part of anarchists, their bodies having more to do with jaws and teeth and knees than most people I'd ever seen, clothes like rags draped on hangers. Bright-eyed but ghostly, of a different tenor and tribe. Meanwhile, unfortunately, the new squat which we were to share with them, I realized, was to be next to the old butcher's, or rather, worse, under the shop, facing the annex of the Hotel Fauret, a wartlike bit left untouched after the hotel's remodeling in the seventies. Two alleys squeezed the annex, tighter than a death grip. In the hotel's early days, the annex had been maid quarters. Later it shielded all the myths Arianne kept going around her Paul. Now, in the penury of our times, given the identically rustic lacy curtains hung in the windows, it offered up rooms for everyone, all the indiscriminately chosen visitors to our region's prime hotel.

I did not worry about the centrality of our new squat because I felt protected, whether by Moses—who now hushed us and the dogs, trying the front door of the new squat—or else merely felt part of the forward thrust of a group's survival. If I were a weeper, I might have wept out of perfect criminal hope, an excitement I probably hadn't felt in this exact form since my student days.

I should have left Finier but here I was, given another chance to live closer to the center of things. If Finier is the most determinedly traditional town in France, sophisticated yet honoring its traditions, and France is the most self-consciously traditional country in Europe, and Europe is the most purposefully traditional region in the world, then I was at the very center of things, self-conscious but doing what I could, letting this hodgepodge tribe define the root of a new tradition.

All this pleased me so I didn't mind when Jacquot got perturbed at Moses fussing with the door, nor did I mind the ensuing, spirited parley, during which Moses said the realtor's daughter had promised him it would be open.

The door happened to be all too locked. It is likely we all felt what Jacquot said, a bit *motley* at this first setback. The wastrels turned in on themselves, roaming the square, choosing to discipline their dogs. Some decision had to be made. We were fairly visible, making more upper-story windows light up, or worse, stay dark even as they creaked open. Jacquot's anxiety ticked up a notch. He avowed that we would be pelted soon. To allay that threat, he mounted his own preemptive resistance, hissing up to the dark windows *Bourgeois cake-lickers!* wiggling his middle finger as if struck by chronic St. Vitus' dance affliction.

"Maybe let's axe the door," said one of the girls, out from under their collective cape.

But Moses questioned the axe strategy, thinking it would call too much attention upon us, saying he was not ready for us to get kicked out of Finier. In the middle of this plea, we heard it before we saw it, someone heave-ho'ing toward us. The man on crutches crossing the square, causing a filament of panic to tingle in me. Not so brawny after all but square and tall, and the squareness and cast and the pecking of crutches on cobblestone conspired to render him massive, enough to unite all these scattered wastelings, so that conversations died into the unity of watching him and his bigness approach. This was a hinge moment, the neck-prickling group moment when a decision gets made: a man more religious than I would call it divine intervention. A moment when people move for or against, and I believed we all tasted the potential, whether for good or for violence to erupt.

"I've seen this done," said the big man, "but I'm not promising anything," his breath cigarette smoke and total confidence, already crouching by the girls now seated on the stone stairs. The man showed no recognition of Moses, as if he'd merely asked the boy for directions that morning at the mayor's office. I stayed shadowed by the building, unseen.

"Hello," said Moses, a bit uncertain.

Jacquot was telling the girls to move away, speaking mainly so he could be the one to stay in charge. The big man laid down one of his crutches to take on the project of the door's combination lock, putting his head to it as though listening to a baby's heartbeat, a tenderness so utter I could practically feel it issuing toward myself. When the lock gave, he stood up, dragging the crutch back toward himself. He gave Jacquot, Moses, the girls, and the other new chestless wastrels a mock salute. In his cowboy French: "That should do it."

Jacquot asked the man who he was, but the fellow was lighting a cigarette, inhaling, exhaling, expectorating, then saying he was a *friend*, probably enjoying the role he played, a role about bigness and mystery. He wished us good luck in our new home. Then turned directly toward me, asking whether I'd liked the newspaper he'd given me a few days ago, in the square.

I looked behind me before saying I had (though I'd dumped it immediately), and found myself thanking him as if he'd given me crown jewels. He made a point of saying that I hadn't read it, that I'd thrown it away, and advised me: "Try not doing that again." He'd watched me even after I'd thought he'd gone.

However, he seemed so earnestly disappointed about my dismissal of his gift, I found myself apologizing, telling him I'd save the paper next time. The fellow nodded, took this in before heading off, leaving me smattered with a nervous guilt.

"He's interesting," said Jacquot, still unsure about how to master the situation.

But more urgently, Cerb-X and Delhi were cold under their cape, and made enterprising by this cold already pulled at the liberated door so they might descend inward.

PART THREE

THIRTY-TWO

This is the crawl space that is to become our new home, and as we squeeze into it, dogs tighter around us, no one able to stand up fully, I realize the old manse had spoiled everyone.

"Spoiled," I say into the darkness, knowing no one will answer, too busy claiming territory, undoing paltry sacks within a hush of disappointment about our diminishment, all the zippering and laying out of objects an attempt to antidote unlivability.

And even as I speak, unnerved by the big man on crutches, by everything, I am not sure how long I can stay with this crew, the wastrels and their new wraiths. Though I too mark out territory: near a few eroded angels carved into the wooden frame, close to the cramped crawl space's door, where a strain of butcher's waste lingers, damp paper with an objectionable scent. This is a church desanctified by its tang of entrails, one I will not quantify overmuch, noting only that it is a marvel what one can learn to accommodate.

As if by rote, Jacquot soon spreads out the atmospheric implements, candles, a zither. In defiance of our central location, he begins to hammer and pluck out some cacophony, having found the broken zither after Saturday's market. Yet even he gives up quickly enough, sighing, lying backward into an angular shadow. Apart from him and Moses, everyone pretends to sleep, while I'm still trying to double my bedding, not looking forward to the compacted, damp earth. Delhi has curled up in fetal position, *for warmth*, she said, claiming a spot next to me, though her proximity is hardly my sort of sleep aid.

Now she lies with mouth half-open, forehead a tight surface shining toward me even in this murderous breed of dark.

Moses whispers to me, stretched out on my other side, hands behind his head. "Hey," he says. "Glad you stayed." I wait, having learned this helped the boy follow a thought through to completion. "When you and I hooked up, Saturday?"

"Yes," I whisper.

"I was thinking we should've split. Started a farm together in some other town."

"I have great fondness for this town."

"Yeah, but like a different tribe. In some other town. That could've been good for you, you know?"

He hands me a cracker, some treasure he's secreted away until now, and takes one himself. Two men underground, chewing crackers. And how I enjoy the salty mealy bolus on my tongue, chewing with him, swallowing, offering him water from a battered plastic flask I'd taken from the manse. He accepts, hands me another damp cracker. "Your woman will get out soon," he adds in a lower pitch. "This time it's true, Raoul."

"So she'll be released. Then we'll go work the vineyards?" This had been one of the dreams he'd shared with me on our first walk: his version of the pastoral. "You picture an old mec like me picking grapes?"

"Why not?" says Moses, slamming shut, an easy tone to hear in the semidark. "Anyway, nice to dream about, isn't it? Lots of people at the end of their rope think about things like vineyards."

"But you're not at the end of your rope," I say, and in that candlelight, he gives me that sad raffish smile, effective at closing off anything I might say afterward.

I just swallow this along with the last of his crackers. Probably the boy's one more of those out-of-place humanitarians I've met. There are people you run across who do what they do without hope for any great notice. They don't care to judge you. They simply wish to belong to some great human web. And they have staggered my mind, these mystifiers, even as I've accepted their bounty.

"You're an out-of-place humanitarian," I tell Moses, but he tells me he doesn't like the phrase, says it sounds too much like globalism.

IN THE MIDDLE of the night, a few people awake and enter into a spiraling chat about prospects, choice, meaning, jobs, while behind them Jacquot attempts to make a bit of music. As predicted, I'd been in thrall to my usual insomnia, and perhaps this shading makes me note the group lacks something of the jollity I'd sensed my first night among them. Someone asks Jacquot to stop his music and soon after, perhaps, I succumb to the lure of my nightmares.

Until, unfortunately, I am awakened in the middle of the night by Jacquot, who sounds quite thwarted by the new crawl space. He is going off on a little disquisition about Moses and his love of jews, and how I must be either a former money-grubber or evil. He says evil is a force running through the world entangling bodies. That none of the wastrels had probably ever met someone who was truly evil. That they'd know it if they had, because it is unquestionable when you're in the presence of evil. He says there's a type of evil you find, say, in some person who'd feel no more about snuffing a person than he would about crushing a cockroach. As if this follows, Jacquot then asks Max to read my past from my face and hands. *He's not a party trick* is what I think Delhi murmurs. All of them (but for Moses) decide to drag me outside under the streetlights, holding a candle close enough to my face that I feel its heat and wish to flinch, though I've chosen my sleeping-bear defense, one which has served well in the past. Max does read me, intoning with dreary accuracy about my father and failed romantic past, my fearfully mild habit of voyeurism, until the point that wax drips on my frenulum, between nose and mouth, and I must keep from sneezing. Only Delhi protests, and they finally stop. Before they put me back in my sleeping place, next to Moses, Jacquot says: "Got to give it to him, old Raoul's a kicker. Pretty amazing."

"Why?" asks Max.

"I'm saying this guy could probably sleep through a whole war."

THIRTY-THREE

"C'mon." Moses tugs at my arm. "Wake up. We're diving for food again. Wake up, man." He tugs again. Of course, this had counted as a bad night. After Jacquot had finished toying with me, I'd slept, however imperfectly. I do question myself: had they dragged me outside or had it been another dream?

"Now?" I ask Moses.

He's insistent. "Food for tomorrow." I roll over to follow him outside. On our way crawling out, Jacquot still speaks, in a low but insistent monotone: *There are people who collect evil animals.*

"You mean dogs?" Delhi's voice asks.

"No. There are good people. Or just okay people." Jacquot waits. "But they make the mistake of collecting evil people."

Outside, panting a little, I ask Moses why now. He looks half-asleep himself. "Just help out, man," is all he says, already turning face down in the dumpster. "Hope there'll be something good. It's Monday night."

"Monday's a good night for food?" I wonder if he truly had slept through the near-torture I'd undergone.

He hushes me but it's too late. A light has already gone on in a third-story window above us. "You got to speak more quietly if you don't want someone to rain a bucket on us," he says.

I ask him again why we have to go foraging *now* and he turns on me, eyes livid, braids more wild than usual. "Can't you see when someone's trying to help you?"

I don't see how foraging helps, and say as much. "I'm not exactly starving, Moses."

He holds a can in one hand and a near-empty cracker carton in the other. "Tell me, guy. You crazy? Or do you have zippo idea what protection looks like?"

I say maybe by his definition I don't know what protection looks like. By my definition, however—

"Man. Help me dive a little. Get a little dirt under your nails? Everything comes out." He must regret something in his manner. "Look, we can go to the shelter. Or sneak into a room at the hotel tomorrow."

"I did that once."

"Sure." He pauses. "You ever lose your nerve once you'd signed on for something?"

"No," I lie. "Perhaps." Suddenly I need him to respect my past braveries. I tell him I don't need to change abode, I am actually *happy* to be living at the squat. That I'm not scared of Jacquot. Moses acts uninterested. What am I trying to prove? I am on tiptoes, bending as much as I can into the dumpster, with Moses inside the dumpster, and for this extra effort, we truly gather a bounty. Half-gnawed bones, open bags of chips, crusts of bread. A plastic container of tomato sauce. We stick it all into a canvas bag. When I look up, a broad man, the fellow in the cast, his cigarette lit on a veranda, the man Moses had talked to across the plaza at the mayor's office, the one who'd let us into the squat, salutes us with his crutch and retires back in, closing the terrace window behind him. It is intimidating to be watched, I tell myself, but the guy's infirmity must be what gives him insomnia, a comrade in arms. Strange that when I should be feeling anxiety, I instead feel a certain compassion for someone so lonely and crippled that he must patrol the night from a cockpit.

As we stack our findings, finishing our labors, I find myself mouthing a little plea toward Arianne. *Please just let me get to see you* is what I say toward the North Star, though I've lost my bearing and orientation. Only my origins stick to my ribs, as my purpose has been mixed up by these wastrels, by the superior clarity of Moses' will, by everyone around me. I speak half-aloud, which gets me no favorable dispensation from the heavens, no special disgorgement of light leading directly to the woman, only Moses turning toward me, annoyed.

THIRTY-FOUR

Delhi has a history, like all of us, except I tell her it's clear she wants her history rendered in darkness, like a sixteenth-century etching, using cross-hatched shadows for self-illumination. Tuesday evening at the Bar Central, she hints the darkness has to do with Paris, where she'd been born and continued to pass through; something about not wanting to be too identified with any one place, nation, family. *My essence is movement,* she breathes, and it would strike me as fatuous except for the unbeatable fact that her face glows as she says it, at what is clearly the wastrels' spot in the musty backroom of the Bar Central, close to the pool table. Her particular beauty cued off by a certain downward swoop of the inner eye, spilling across her face from there, all the way to her hands, strangely spatulate for a young lady mainly made up of angles. Have I mentioned that her ears are delicate, or that she incites such odd feeling in me that I see them as sleeping doves?

During these few days among the wastrels, I have spent too many minutes contemplating Delhi's face and its various moods, and find myself speaking warmly with her, late in an especially long day in which we had gone ensemble to a farm nearby, where yet another of the wastrel's farmers had allowed us to glean fallen berries. All day, no one had mentioned Jacquot's nocturnal desire to have my face read, a tact for which I am grateful, though I keep a safe berth away from the brute. I had felt glad to be on a farm, out of the radius of Izzy and Arianne and the reunion of the survivors: it had been like receiving a day's vacation from myself. Talking with Delhi that evening, I am sunburnt but restored by the beer they've brought me, tired but sentimental about her face, as well as about many other aspects of Emile's newly minted life amid this uncertain ensemble, at this table of ours at the Bar Central.

A bar which is, actually, something of a dive, its seediness making me understand better Moses' choice to wait for us in the new squat. He'd said he was trying to turn a new page, trying to keep himself clean. "Go with them," he'd urged me. "I could use a little solo meditation time." And seeing my face, he'd added: "Nothing personal. You'll be okay. You'll have fun." The pendulum had confirmed this direction, and it turns out that Moses was right, I fully enjoy my discourse with Delhi. Only one misstep had occurred, when she'd thought I had placed my hand purposely atop hers, though this had been an accident. But all in all, a terrific evening, though this is a nothing bar, a nowhere place. A bar where Cerb-X and Jacquot like to play pool with people they call rubes fresh off the bus, who are mostly (from what I can see) youth passing through, young kids setting backpacks down like giant turnips made precious by hours of proximity.

The shadow of beauty wings across Delhi's face and because there's a stillness to her—despite her idea that she is movement—for a second it is also the shadow of intimacy which flutters between us. Tonight, for some reason, I find I love all the wastrels, even Jacquot for his familiar brutality, but it is Delhi especially whom I love. What breaks our moment: Cerb-X slams down another shared beer bottle between us, sharing her wins. She has announced that she and Jacquot play the rubes for money, drugs, and beer, in order of descending value. Tonight, she told me, it is beer they are handing off, so though

I'm already sodden, though it is close to midnight, though I've heard from Delhi that the Bar Central will close between three and six in the morning so as to discourage overnight sleeping types waiting for the motors of a morning bus, my veins a giddy buzz, I would avoid sleep forever just because for the first time I feel capable of truly hearing Delhi's story.

Once she'd worked in chemical manufacture with Jacquot and then she'd left that and had gotten involved in other 'scapes until she'd left those too. And she'd worked out an abject little street performance in Paris with her piebald mutt, Lula. That is, until she'd gotten sick of herself and her situation and had gotten on a bus to head south thinking she might find purity, or something close to that, *fundamentals*, and she'd been like these people, the rubes, she too had set down her backpack like a squashed turnip in the bar's corner, thinking she'd wait for the bus for Spain.

But that was when she'd seen him, Jacquot, though he didn't recognize her: she'd chopped her hair off and was probably far skinnier than when he'd worked with her in manufacture. He didn't recognize her to the point that he came over and started to flirt, broadly and badly, challenging her to a pool game, which they'd never played together before.

And she beat him, unrepeatably, and revealed herself to him. That marked the time when the new wastrels started up, because Cerb-X had shown up in Finier only a few days earlier, and had serendipitously found her way to Jacquot up at the manse, and so that was when Jacquot had decided there'd be two ladies among the wastrels, and lucky they took to each other, Cerb-X and Delhi, because otherwise, how would anyone get along?

How long ago was this? I ask about what sounds like an epic biblical origin story.

At least two weeks ago. And Delhi smiles. She further takes my hands, my grizzled old-man hands which have both done and failed to do so much, my hands between hers. Strange hands for such a girl, as I say, yet in her grasp I feel myself cleansed, as if we are playing a children's game of make-believe, freed of risk and consequence, though I fear this may be solely the beer speaking.

Still, something of a special moment, though what happens next is that Jacquot and Cerb-X, ecstatic at having won something that isn't beer, come to swoop Delhi up to one of the landings or vacant rented rooms upstairs. Clearly they're going to share some substance. I wish I could get out of my paralysis and stop this substance-driven activity, help them heed a higher calling, though what that might be escapes me, and moreover my leg seems to have fallen asleep. Clearly, as well, they have their urgent mission, however temporary or based as it might be on self-obliteration. "O, children, come fill the cup—!" I say after their departing backs, quoting some half-remembered poem from my youth.

I'm sitting there in the Bar Central, one of those solitary moments when you become conscious of your station in life, a bushel pinned to his seat by inertia or disappointment, which are often the same thing. I'm watching the bartender rub his sponge on the red and tired fake-leather vinyl tabletop, spreading grease around, and affection for this place fills me. This bar with its unconditional squalor a kindness, the grease of love spread about without many questions. You don't have to ask for a key to use the dirty and frequently unoccupied toilet and the loud video games ping off one another so no one's words or actions have to matter too much. Over all of us hangs a giant unquestioned picture of Brigitte Bardot, framed in a gilded, egg-shaped frame which makes the coquette a saint, and the bartender turns the same dubious look upon all who enter his café, whether they be clean-cut collegians off the buses or scruffy hatless bushels like myself.

I am half of a drunken mind to tell the bartender which elements the Bar Central might seek to conserve, and which it might best dispense with, and how to bring a bit of discernment into the scene, when my three colleagues return to the bar, eyes now pinwheeling.

Delhi comes to sit by me and more quickly than I can understand falls asleep on my shoulder, every so often scratching her wrists, her armpits, and areas from which I avert my eyes. "Relaxed *and* amped," Cerb-X explains, tour guide of the lower depths, "amped *but* relaxed."

■ ■ ■

WE HAVE the long night ahead of us, all of them now poor company, before we—I say we, though naturally I feel excluded—finally drag ourselves back to the squat and find Moses, candlelit in his corner and seated like a buddha. Without glancing our way, he tells us he doesn't look down on us for whatever we've done but he's going to go on meditating. Delhi has been sleepwalking the whole way home, leaning on Jacquot's shoulder, gargling out a nursling's song. Once we come in she stumbles past and falls into what looks like a semi-coma. If Jacquot weren't standing guard, I'd like to help the girl, to see if a spot of water on her face might revive her, especially as Cerb-X is ignoring her friend, trying to tempt Moses out of his trance by offering him some of whatever they'd shared upstairs. "Amp you," croons Cerb-X, next to Moses, stroking him under his blanket, "relax you." She says it several more times until it flows into a song we might have heard back at the bar. *Ampyourelaxyou.*

I am settling down on my pallet too and admittedly at least a few bottles of beer still course through my veins, numbing me from the inside out, and so I find myself shouting, which surprises me probably just as much as it does them, shouting exactly what seems most relevant at that moment, which is this: "You are all in a white cage!" Of course no one pays the old man any mind. The old man is incapable of bothering anyone.

WHEN I WAKE in the middle of the night it is to the sound of a rhythmic pounding which I can't place at first, but also to Moses scratching himself, violently, sitting near the candles, so I get a clear sight of his trousers rolled up to the knee, as if on a fishing expedition, one where the preliminaries require him not to tie worm-bait but rather to gash ankle and calf.

"What are you doing?" I ask, bolting up. Things are starting to look bad, I have to admit that much.

"Can't stop, man," he says, continuing to scratch, "itchy," and now it becomes clear his eyes pinwheel in the same fashion as the rest of them. "Me and her—" and points to Delhi, who has a pair of headphones on and is lying naked, the great tilt of her hipbone near me. Naked, atop her red velvet blanket. An embarrassing delta of straight hair gleaming where her legs join. You'd think she was dead but for her hand, how it lies on her belly twitching, curling and uncurling around a small invisible animal: Delhi in the candlelight a golden idol before sacrifice or degradation, mouth lolling ajar, eyes half-closed.

"Itchy!" Moses exclaims again.

"We've got to cover," I say, already in motion, "cover her." Feeling an abyss of panic that once again, everyone wants to test old Emile.

But Jacquot's voice, from the dark corner, forbids me. "We have other plans," he says. "Horny man! Don't even move," and behind his words, that bleak inscrutability, Cerb-X's laughter.

"Don't move," repeats Cerb-X, druggy queen.

At first I try to do what they say, not move, but then I am struck again by the girl's nakedness, a golden offering, it bothers me, glistening in the center of the squat. I must therefore disobey. I cross over, crossing while taking my own coat off to lay it upon her, and as I do, I glance toward the obscurity where Jacquot sits and that's it, I guess, he takes my move as disobedience, a challenge, makes a little harrumphing rebuke but says nothing more. I figure that whatever token gesture I've done, it's time for me to head out for a little middle-of-the-night walk, the kind of thing for which life has kept me all too ready.

I DO HOWEVER decide to come back in the early morning, feeling an awful dread but needing to reenter, mainly because I realize I'd left both my pendulum and will in a corner of the squat. In the wee hours, I'd tried to fall asleep behind the Ursuline shelter, in a covered area Moses had shown me the dehabited sisters kept, a horse stall laid in with a urine-scented matting of straw, but I'd been unsuccessful and just laid in wait for a benign enough daybreak. A few people, possibly breakfasting survivors in the outdoor café, have watched me head back into the squat, as well as a few of our Finier early-morning marketers. Despite our central location we'd been told to keep our locale secret, and so I feel I have betrayed the wastrels' spot. Yet the right moment to enter seemed impossibly far away, and this shows you again, timing is always the devil's work.

Back inside, oil paper drawn against the cracks, no day intrudes: it's as murky as the inside of a cow's womb. I first make out Max and Christian, still asleep, and Moses a slumbering lump, but luckily no Jacquot. Delhi leans against the wall, dressed but stunned, singing a little song, nodding her head and sputtering an array of phonemes known to me, a rat-a-tat melody and rhythm she may be improvising on the spot. It is unfortunate, but in her melody I seem to detect the names of a few of the camps toward which my deportations headed— Drancy, Vernet, Pithiviers. But I realize this cannot be the case, I've imagined it, she is just sputtering the tune called rap.

"How do you feel?" I ask. "Delhi."

She startles at her name, then returns to the odalisque gaze, out from under puffed lids, saying she just needs someone else to be in charge for a while. To make sure she gets respectful berth.

"Respectful berth," I repeat deferentially.

She asks could I be the one to do that? Be in charge. Could a person trust me?

And not understanding fully, I say yes, of course, I will make sure she gets respectful berth, whatever she wants.

She tells me she is fine but one of my first acts as berth-man is this: I need to make sure people stay cool with her and could I just find out what that terrible pounding is?

I'm sorry, I say, giving her words serious thought, I think the pounding may be in your *head*, and for this minor and easily given help, she blows me a tired kiss and then leans with a crone's fatigue against the wall. Awful how the impulses of youth *age* these youth, I want to tell her.

My voice must have awakened Moses, who rolls to lie on his back, kicking blankets off, legs in the air like an overturned insect, scratching his calves all over again. "Hello," I say, crawling to him, trying to take his hands. "Let's get some air outside? Or water. How about it? Might do you good."

He raises his head, shakes his matted braids, returns to scratching.

"What happened?" I ask Delhi.

She sits up and rubs her eyes. "What time you said?"

"Jacquot gave you something?"

"Cerb-X maybe? Anyway, where's my dog?"

We discover Lula compressed uncomplaining somewhere underneath Moses' hair, and pull the boy up to get her out. The dog is all forgiveness, licking Moses' calves, soothing the distraught.

This is when we hear the clump of Jacquot's jackboots outside, the boy entering like a tyrant in a Greek drama, self-narrating, making a big deal about rolling a cigarette, a giant cornucopian petard with a filter made from a cigarette pack's cardboard. He cuts and mixes the tobacco with what he calls *tickle grass* and places the big cone-shaped thing before Delhi's mouth. Lit, smoky and stale-smelling as she usually likes it, but this time she turns away, spitting.

"Maybe," I say with despicable meekness, Emile Poulquet slow in growing into his role. "That's not giving the lady respectful berth." I will be protector of Delhi, protector of courtesy, protector of all that needs protection.

"Hey, old fart," Jacquot cautions me. Using this name must afford him great pleasure. "She likes it. Delhi?" The girl says nothing so he continues. "Just shut *up*," lilting this last as if a conductor rousing the string section. He turns from me. "Shut the old guy *up*, Moses."

To which Moses grunts, taking a break from his endless scratching before resuming, now hunched over like a rounded potato-bug ball so as to better reach his itchy calves. When I sit by Moses and take his hands in mine, he immediately turns the backs of my hands into paddles to continue this horrendous scratching. I let him use me in this way, though it is awful, and fearing his itchiness may be contagious, at the nearest opportunity I withdraw myself.

ALL THIS DAY I stick around, feeling I am the berth man. None of them are their usual selves, not Delhi and not Moses, or at least not as I have known them. I remain something of a hermit crab myself, waiting, supplying their wants while staying out of the way of Jacquot. I take advantage of the opportunity to change a bit of my will:

To the little girl who happened to choose me, I leave the ~~coffins that have passed through our streets~~ question of the legions of little girls who might have otherwise been chosen by me, and the greater legions of ~~shrouds buried without pomp~~ girls who might otherwise have been spared the consequences arising from just a few of my actions.

Moses doesn't speak, just nodding in and out, scratching, irritable, soothed by evening target practice with bottles and stones by the river, to which Delhi and I have accompanied him, indulging the boy in his avocation. He is not reachable, wishing to remain silent, while Delhi is more voluble but still hard to reach, conversing only in riddles. She has always spoken in questions, but now the trait reaches an acme. When I ask her why she'd been rattling forth all those names of places which presumably she'd never visited, she says that before she'd left Paris she'd been composing a song in her friend's recording studio. "Hip-hop but not?" whatever that means. "You understand?" she asks.

"Sort of," I say in her dialect, watching Moses' stone miss another bottle in the dusk.

ONCE DELHI GETS a little better, Friday morning, she comes close to making a statement. She says she wants to get back to the city eventually, and hints that Cerb-X had slipped her and Moses a drug far beyond what Cerb-X and Jacquot had taken.

"It was for their own good," Cerb-X retorts with some savagery, looking out past all her face-rings when I mount my own investigation. "They went bourgeois. Asking for too much. Gigs. Something."

"Maybe for the better," Delhi whispers to me that evening in the squat, her breath strong upon me. She now believes Cerb-X had given them something *cleansing*. She feels better now, unleashing a little rant on me. Before she'd come to Finier, she'd felt Paris had knocked a few screws loose in her head. She'd wanted to come to Finier, because cities, they sit on one's soul. They're exhausted and exhausting, they're lonely and stuffed with shoulds. Should this, should that. She thought that by coming to the country, she had come to *yes*, a free-flowing *yes*. She'd wanted to live or at least stay awhile in a place where yes could be her dominant mode. She says *no* to nothing, she exhales largely when she says *yes*. Tired and hopeful.

I like Delhi for the world-weariness; it reminds me of an acquaintance I'd admired in my student days, a young man named Georges who'd taught me the uses of the word *jew*. When Georges had been trumped in his first student love, I had tentatively practiced the word's power by calling Georges' rival *a real jew*. For this Georges had flashed me a look of such appreciation that for once I felt capable of saying the right thing, which gave me hope about how to inhabit the administrative role for which I then prepared myself like a scrupulous vestal virgin.

Delhi in her world-weary aspect further volunteers that she'd come to Finier out of the urge to party, that she'd heard there was to be a giant rabble-rousing affair. A real shouette something happening here. In Paris she'd had some trouble with her family, she didn't want to go into it but it had gotten bad. And she'd heard this was the area of France where McDonald's got bombed but not just that. There were said to be a lot of cool farmers out here, and she'd wanted to work with some of the farmers. Then it turned out none would hire her—they couldn't conquer that racist gene in them, you know? This being the first time she has ever mentioned race to me. To my surprise, I hadn't been entirely certain she was of another race. I examine her more closely. Surely, there was after all something generously Asian to her, or meltingly African, hard to say, especially when now ten percent of our population is made up of maghrebins, all our North Africans. It occurs to me that along the road to this moment I may have lost some of the yardsticks of racial discernment which had so helped years ago in my line of work.

"Whatever your blood, you're a beautiful lady," I whisper for the second time in my life.

"You like exotic?" She's turned a little frosty. "Exotic?" shimmying her sad chest at me.

"I'm sorry," I say, palsied in using my new phrase, though the magic of it resonates more than if I had handed her my pendulum: these words relax her a bit.

· · ·

TRUTH IS that I am trying not to worry about Moses, who stays mum, refusing moreover to be taken to a hospital, a decision which privately gladdens me, as I don't wish to be identified, some intake nurse flashing me the Look. Too many near-Looks coming my way. And Moses is taking longer than Delhi to *come down*, as the wastrels keep saying, as if coming down has a predictable arc and trajectory. Delhi says she's sure he'll be out of it by Saturday morning. I tell myself that all of them must have survived such drug-world episodes before. Coming up, coming down, nothing out of the ordinary for them.

"You're all right?" I ask Moses that night, and Jacquot teases me for this.

"The old fart plays at being mother hen!" hooting largely.

So when Moses does return to being Moses, I feel snatched back from loneliness, able to breathe again. In a rather startling manner, he comes back in force, neither irritable nor comatose, not scratching or hankering for target practice, but *back, himself*, Moses again in the chill hours of that Saturday morning when we've had to light a smoky fire from milk cartons.

The chemical smell plays around us, a comforting inkwell scent, the fire a ghastly blue and orange, the night after all so cold. No one had gathered kindling on Friday and a silent collective decision had been made. Especially when, outside, the wind blows hard against our street-level window, making rocks and trash skitter against the walls of our shelter. Enough like the rat-a-tat of a gendarme's baton to set us all a little on edge.

At any moment, Jacquot says, we might be routed by the police, part of the EUROPE effort which we're trying to avoid. I can't help wondering if this EUROPE initiative is the fault of the refugees, who may be, according to Jacquot, establishing permanent quarters in their Finier hall, a base for their operations. For my own good, a measure toward sanity, I've tried to stay away from them.

In the corner, in the blue-orange light, I can see Christian stretched out long behind Cerb-X, his hands creeping around her waist. "Stop," she says, unable to stop laughing. "You're tickling me."

"What did you think I was *trying* to do?" he keeps saying back.

Cerb-X's laugh becomes more and more of a whimper. She starts telling Christian that she can't find her appetite or her sadness, her sadness banished by something she'd smoked and then something else she'd swallowed earlier in the evening, while her appetite had got up and left. She'd announced this last fact to me after I'd remarked on her cheerful aspect. "See? It worked, Papa Raoul," she'd crowed to me, her studs lustrous. "I lost my sadness and then my appetite."

When she likes me, Cerb-X calls me Papa Raoul, and when she doesn't, it is Mister Tavelle this or Old Man that. She hasn't once called me, simply, Raoul, as, say, Delhi does. Delhi has for her part returned into herself, on some temperamental seesaw with Moses, Delhi now *down* and in a mood where you don't get to speak with her unless she first engages with you. Delhi monopolizes the tiny window, her slightness nonetheless useful in blocking the slight draft that comes from its imperfectly sealed top corner. She will not flinch when a stone zings the window, only continuing to nod to herself, half-singing some new song, a song whose words I choose not to hear.

And though Moses now sits up, appearing anchored, he whispers into my ear much as Delhi did when she came down, a flood of things just as if this were a way of picking up a normal conversation.

ONCE HE WAS a baker, he says, or rather, he worked for a baker, he liked it, he woke up early in the mornings, mixed the starter, hands deep in the dough, flour on his dreads. But once, by mistake, as he brushed a last bit of egg white onto the little hopeful buns on their trays, he'd gotten locked in the big wall-to-wall brick oven, he could see the arrow spin toward the red eye, the warning signal, heard the giant *whoosh!* of the fires going up, and there he was surrounded by pan after pan of croissants, telling himself he was going to die if his mind couldn't conquer the heat. He stood with the egg-white brush in his hand while the heat started first under his fingernails, twinging his earlobes, tickling his leg hair and the roots of what he called his *dreads*, the tips already crisping a bit. But he thought that if he could just concentrate on each bit of heat as it snuck into the entity-called-Moses, Moses himself would not suffer, he would sizzle to death burnt but aware, like the monks who set themselves on fire. Then right as the heat slid down the lining of his nose, descending and expanding in his lungs, heavy at the back of his eyes, the head baker had a misgiving about the croissants, enough to rethink the batch: he unlocked the oven and found Moses, saved him, shocked to see his apprentice, the boy hot-faced but not burnt at all, not yet, saved more by his mind than by the baker's afterthought, at least in Moses' version of things.

Moses tells me the tale in such a way that I change my mind, I cannot be fully sure he has come back to himself. He must sense my doubt.

"Look at it this way," Moses says. "We call ourselves wastrels. That's the name we came up with. But we're a tribe, we're the truth of this land." He tells me I have certain choices: I could practically be the tribal elder, I've been more or less accepted, though his tone wavers in saying this.

"Maybe you're recuperating," I tell him.

"What does that mean?" He looks hurt.

"You just went through a tunnel. Your Jacquot wouldn't exactly call me a tribal *elder*. If you want to know, he calls me," I lean close to whisper this, "pardon, *old fart*."

"I told you my story for a purpose, man," he says. "It's not about croissants. It's about what our minds are capable of. Any situation can be changed. Yours could be. You could join us, for example."

I don't understand this *for example*. "Haven't I already?" I ask, humility personified.

"I'm saying we could go. Leave Finier. You and me, Raoul. Maybe a couple of others."

"Why?" The thought's abhorrent. I've taken a week's vacation, essentially, homing in on Arianne, learning how to abide in Finier in this new subterranean way, so that in this moment it appears that if I were to leave, the week would be squandered. All for naught, my investment in learning how to dwell well-disguised among types whose hypervisibility makes them difficult for most citizens to see.

"Out of the oven, man. It's good to be aware and all that. But somewhere else we have a chance of starting fresh. New wastrels, new town. No history." As if that were a tourist attraction in itself: no history.

"History's all I have," I say sadly, and then offer the thing, shrunken to an afterthought. "Also my last will and testament."

"Yeah, right." He waves this away. "You want to get to your old lady." His look hard upon me. "I'm giving you a chance, man." He waits. "Take in what I'm saying. You're no spring chicken. Sorry. But not many second chances come your way. Right?" He scratches his head, changes tactics. "Look what motivates most people."

"Shelter," I say, unsure of the boy's point.

"Shelter. Food. Sex. That covered, we focus our energies on greater things. We leave Finier, see? Meanwhile, we've covered the top three."

"Where exactly is the romantic engagement?" I ask, not meaning to be facetious.

"Ah, Raoul wants sex! The randy bastard!" Jacquot has overheard, unfortunately, putting an untimely end to our conversation. The crackle of the fire is loud enough that I would've hoped Jacquot wouldn't have heard but the man's gifted. "Raoul is randy!" In the half-dark he waves a long stick toward me. Had I not shrunk back, he would have poked my eyes out. "Raoul goes rannnnnndy!"

Delhi rolls herself away from her window to sit in front of me. "Leave him alone, man," says Delhi.

But Jacquot cannot stay in one place. "Fuck," says Jacquot, and says it again. He leans over, as though expecting what happens: his narrow bones jerking, a spasmodic puppet's—a convulsion ripping through him, another wave of horrible jerking, his head whipping back.

"I don't need this," Moses mutters.

"Lay him on his back," says Christian, "hold his mouth closed, get the tongue—" and I am the one who does it, the rest of them struck by that paralysis I know so much about, I the only one among these youngsters who can move fast enough to Jacquot, take the long stick out of his hand, lay him down.

In a second Jacquot is a calm animal again. He looks up at my face, coughs, rolls to one side, sits up, hunches over, spits up, shakes his head. "Too much," he says.

"Jacqui's going buggy." Cerb-X laughs, fully on her own planet.

"Maybe we should put out that fire," says Moses.

Delhi meanwhile has gone over to start pounding Jacquot on his back. She shrugs over at Moses and me. "Too much X in his system. He's tweaked, right? His spinal cord. Or he's an epileptic?"

"Both," says Moses.

She starts to sing a new little song in time with her pounding of his back, so that Jacquot gives out a surprised little cough at the end of each of her lines.

Je ne veux pas travailler!
Je ne veux pas déjeuner!
Je veux seulement oublier!
Et puis je fume!

After a few minutes, Jacquot looks up. "Thanks," he tells Delhi, straightening his shirt, sliding back so that he can get back into his sleeping bag. "Sorry. Low blood sugar. Must have been something. Who knows."

"You bugged," says Moses, half-standing. "You didn't take your epilepsy meds."

Jacquot goes into a little spiel about how he'd given the last of his pills to Cerb-X *to hold for him* but she'd given them to Moses and Delhi, and how the pharmacy guy wouldn't refill Jacquot because Arianne Fauret's commission on vagrant youth had determined you need a whole proof-of-residency runaround bureaucratic-sperm bullshit thing if you were trying just to pick up a prescription.

"That's fine, man," says Moses. "But you were about to poke out Raoul's eyes. Delhi saved you from doing that, man."

"Don't sweat it," says Delhi, first to Jacquot and then to me. "Don't sweat nothing," and eyes me significantly, as if to keep me in place. As if to keep me from saying anything more to rile up Jacquot. Yet as she crawls past, she whispers something so sweet, such a tonic upon my nerves, that it antidotes the ironic whisper of the daughter lawyer in the Paris court. And Delhi says it twice, to make sure I hear: *don't forget we're protecting you, Papa Raoul, you can't leave us.*

WHEN I AM in this mood, the kind that strikes me after Moses' story and Jacquot's little fit, a mood I will call quiescent, I see easily how all of us have arrived at this moment because of Arianne Fauret. Nothing any of us might ever dream of doing in or around Finier would escape the webs spun out from Arianne's shameless, unguilty power. Her idea of herself as martyr, her entitlement. She controls anything that would ever have anything remotely to do not just with me but with this town. Money festering in bank accounts. All the favors people owe the Faurets. All of it. Water rights, baking times, mythology. Jacquot's epilepsy meds, travel, public relations, croissants, crawl spaces, street lamps. Black markets, white markets, sites of the farmers' market, permissions for civic fairs, monuments, fugitives, Izzy, architecture, bridges, schedules. All of it connected to Arianne. That I didn't marry Natalie (her husband, Paul, had avenged himself so cleverly, taking her away, but how do I know Arianne hadn't masterminded it?). Schools, wastrels, squats. Nothing without her touch. No more, nothing, none.

I am struck with two crazy urges, simultaneously:

1. To get these people down on their knees so that together we might *pray to Arianne.*
2. To convince these people to *march with me* to the cell in which she is held, so that we might demand that she be released into the belly of the wastrels.

It is almost visible to me—the whole scenario—how, if I could somehow secret Arianne away, bring her to this warm enveloping body of the wastrels, Arianne and I might come to peace after all these years. She could take the corner spot, sleep when we sleep, roam looking for food when we do, feel what it is to *be glad about relinquishing power*. And finally, in this milieu I would be her master, just by dint of my greater time spent among nomads. Finally she would gain a newfound admiration for my adaptability all this long lonely half-century, surrendering at the same time her puppeting of Emile Poulquet.

Bowing out.

"Give me one of your pills," I whisper to Jacquot.

"You heard the old guy say something?" Jacquot asks Cerb-X. "I'm going deaf."

"He wants a pill," says Cerb-X. "You heard him."

"Don't, Papa Raoul," says Delhi.

But Jacquot is already in my face, undoing the little scrotal leather sack he keeps tied around his neck. "Purples or reds, old man?"

"Reds," I say, for some reason remembering the rose-on-yellow of Arianne's dress at the prefecture. "Reds." In no time at all, my request is met. Jacquot handing me his whiskey-tinged water flask to wash three pills down. It's that simple: in a second, I've swallowed *their* Arianne.

IT IS NOT LONG after this that I find myself running naked along the riverbank, behind the street that curls up from the prefecture. Naked but not cold, bones true to the wind, whooping like a monkey set free, over brambles, over it all. Across the bank, on the highway side, someone shouts to me, a gorgon-headed kid, two kids, a throng of kids with a pastiche of hair alive on their heads trying to get me to settle down man, just come back. But they're on one side of the river and I'm on the prefecture side, and their words (something about clothes, the squat) fade. A throng of kids but only one with a true halo around his head under a bending streetlamp. My young lion, talking in our private dialect.

"Roar!" I say back. "Hey, roar! I can roar too! Roar!" Youth shouldn't be confined to the young, I whisper, but stop, startled to see an appreciative cigarette glowing almost underfoot. It is held by the man with the leg, sitting in the dark along the riverbank benignly, the only one around to appreciate what I have to offer. "Hey!" I don't want to stay near that crutch or cigarette so I pace back and forth along the river, forward and back, and when I trip I get up as quickly as I can, determined not to let naked old age stop me, now a monkey trying to climb up a squat tree. From the lowest branch, I try to explain to the cigarette-man but my tongue's not working all that perfectly, how in my vision, *Arianne* should *join* the wastrels and then do them one better. "Join the animals!" and my tongue gets stuck on this point, repeating it for a bit, each repetition of the phrase meaning something different, along the lines of this: in the animal kingdom, Arianne would discover a new way for the two of us to coexist, on the borders of all human rules about power, tainted power, power which I cannot now in my current circumstances imagine anyone ever holding without sacrificing some integrity. Among the wastrels, Arianne would finally surrender all *her* rules about power, the rules which have set her so far above me (in her mind). "Join the animals!" is what I think my tongue keeps saying. And then a bit of whatever monkey freedom has been granted me is stripped and I see myself as they must, the young halo-headed lion and his coterie now on the street nearby, shouting for me to come down out of the tree, Papa Raoul, come down.

Raoul an older man, naked in a nighttime tree.

Raoul, Emile: whoever he is, Poulquet the pathetic.

THIRTY-FIVE

"That's giving me respectful berth, papa?" Delhi keeps asking, my arm looped around her flat waist. "You got to listen better." We are heading back to the squat, I realize, and I am unable to stop shivering despite the scratchy damp blanket around me. "You promised," she's saying.

"Promised?" I mutter, my tongue flaccid and disobedient, and then manage to get out: "How come you threw me in the river?"

"We didn't," says Delhi. "You jumped out of the tree and then into the river. You don't remember? I got you back. But barely, guy. Barely."

"Because you *get* to be angry," I try to explain, though my words slur so much I'm not sure she understands. "All I get is the chance to be apprehensive."

"That was your way of getting angry?" she says. "No, that was just crazy. Or paranoid. You don't even know what angry looks like, Papa Raoul. You think losing your dignity's the same as getting angry? Anger's way more effective."

. . .

I DON'T LIKE being lectured about whatever had gotten beaten out of me, all the way back to the squat, and it's not pneumonia that has come upon me, I tell myself. Just a spot of coughing and sneezing, my lungs a bit waterlogged. The wastrels grant me the spot next to the fire, everyone but Delhi keen on replaying the latest drama, Delhi making a point of not talking to Jacquot, blaming him for acquiescing to an old man's foolish request for pills. She's placed me under what feels like the weight of ten blankets. "You should be someone's mother," I tell her, but she makes a sour face at this, instead gives me a nip of warmed vodka that tastes like rubbing alcohol, a nip which must be spat out.

After the coughing, the sobriety hurts.

Now I see how they waste their time, and tell Delhi this, though my tongue is still weak, heavy, imperfect. On the one hand, they and I are the same: fleeing the dictates of conventional society. On the other hand, whatever it is that people have said about me, behind everything I have been an idealist, always longing for some better, kinder world in which certain bad choices never get posed one: a world in which one makes no mistakes because certain choices are excluded in advance. Whereas these wastrels, despite their love of tribal affiliation, are individualists, anarchic by disposition and self-promoting by necessity. As much as they parrot idealistic notions, each of their steps removes them from the earthly utopia they imagine, each places them in the empire of aggression and everything warlike. Their love of hierarchy is a constant, numbing form of repression with as much anger in it as anything they accuse my generation of having displayed.

I am half of a mind to organize these wastrels toward better ends, though which those would be, I don't know. They seem like so much loose drift, like consumers of air, space, detritus, language: jittery types who've chosen to be shoved to the place where they can't produce much of anything useful. They hate the government but are on the dole; they loathe their origins but are more tied to them than most of our region's shopkeepers, intoning dreary family histories and lost ambitions as if they're opening-night novice actors, with unmodulated emphasis and false intimacy. They voice their upbringings, whether hardscrabble or bourgeois, with entitlement, bespeaking what seems to be their belief that vociferous self-absorption is a political act done for the good of others.

"Be mellow," says Delhi, but I can't obey her. I am wrought up about their lost fates, and think my own fate must be far more lost than I can comprehend for me to be spending so much time with such types. It is like an unfunny riddle: what happens to the naked monkey who ran along the river? He ends up finding everything damper and colder, including his own paltry version of reality.

THUS, THE NEXT DAY, Saturday, when Moses makes his announcement about wanting to find jobs for all of us, I am more than attentive. I like Delhi well enough but once Moses leaves midday for his harvest reconnaissance—*just a day, man, arrange a gig just beyond the Bistronne. You'll be fine with those guys, just, you know, keep your guard up and whatever you do, man, wait for me, no railroad stunts, right Raoul?*— the truth is I too begin to feel like a consumer of air, space, garbage, lacking a sense of purpose. Or else this is the aftershock of my river extravaganza. What is old monkey Emile doing, Emile the collection of bones, doing hanging around these types? Sitting around, waiting for Arianne to be released, theorizing about power.

I go with Delhi to see if we can collect lunch from some of Moses' posse, but when no food has been set out, I mention that Moses had raided the visiting survivors' rented hall. She decides she'll try her luck; the door is locked, however, with a notice on it stating that the reunion participants have gone on a pleasure-boat outing, on one of our subterranean rivers. Which suggests to me that there has been no progress in Arianne's case, otherwise, would the reunion-makers rest on a Saturday? Although perhaps my assumption is faulty. I investigate other flyers they've posted on the door. They've taken on a name I find rather silly, Stewards of Memory, and now apparently boast a local phone number and mailing address, as if they truly have set up permanent residence in Finier, possessing all sorts of taken-for-granted signs of respectability.

As Delhi and I cannot enter the hall, our situation calls for dumpster-diving. Since we begin our particular itinerary outside Finier's best restaurant, and Delhi proves to be nimble and quick at the art, we don't suffer too much.

The only thing that lifts my heart on this overbright Saturday is a bit of honesty.

I realize, first, that I miss the sight of the refugees' pageantry, and second, that I haven't learned enough about their activities. Couldn't I enjoy their company if from a safe distance? This is Emile Poulquet's tactic, I tell myself: learn about the enemy so as to better outwit him.

THUS, WHEN, that late afternoon, a few survivors return to open the hall, I too have returned, unseen but set up well by a plane tree, behind a windbreak and borderstones on a path above the ancient aquifer which, a century earlier, had become a street. One survivor opens a window, and hence I can hear them quite well, dragging tables and chairs inside the old echoing hall. Soon after, I watch the crowd arriving, sunburnt, exultant. Though many of the war-scarred have gone home, new blood must have arrived, faces I've not seen in town before. Once I think I see the mirage, the curly-haired woman I'd seen on the first day, now in a loose checkered dress, but after she disappears into the hall, I think: wouldn't she be too young to be whomever I keep mistaking her for? She could not be that one.

I have not seen Izzy, glad for it, and end up dozing a bit against the tree. When some music starts up, a not-unfamiliar violin and harp piece, I startle to it, hum along. A woman's voice talks over it on a scratchy microphone, summoning up a rapture about that day's boat trip, their crew's shared survival and adventure. I must admit how left out of their rapidly coalescing group I feel, but surely this is illogical. Another woman takes the stand, evidently introducing the evening's theme, which is what they call the redressing of history, the notation of testimony. Of course, there's a certain entertainment to be had in talking back to her, ridiculing her rickety propaganda within my own private theater, mocking the avowals of those who speak after her. Of course, I'm hoping to overhear some news about Arianne, but I'm not at all unhappy to be there for the ride, to learn what I can.

For example:·I learn that the refugees have officially elected Izzy to be their organizer. So it is that his voice rumbles out again and again over all the others. Gone is my childhood shambler. With a moral weariness, his voice introduces *an honored guest speaker*. And then: *an important filmic record of our lives*. The difference between me and Izzy, as one might understand by this point, undoubtedly, is how smoothly he gets to be the expert, allowed to narrate his era, while they have eternally punished me, forcing me outside the cage of that time and into the cold of our contemporary moment.

They get to play their old films, films with familiar soundtracks and self-important voices, thus granting me a painful, blissful nostalgia. All this hoard must have been the booty the refugees had brought in their twinebound suitcases, film-reels and records to which they now sing along, songs of our era possessing the wistful grandeur our nation once had. Perhaps the pendulum foresaw that, in the absence of Arianne's appearance, I might gain something from this forced escort through memory, and consequently decided I should stay this long in Finier.

It is not given to old Emile to enter the refugee hall.

Most of me understands prudence, and the whole of me stays outside: to this half-bitten dialectic, I owe my continued existence. The crackle of the refugees' films and songs should not continue to startle me so much but it does. If I were to stride into their hall, all those people would probably understand me better than almost anyone else, certainly with greater depth than Delhi and Moses could, and probably with greater breadth than Arianne could summon.

These survivors follow their songs and filmstrips with a heated discussion about communism within and after the resistance. Some speakers seem beholden to others and get silenced easily; some have Spanish accents. Some slur the jews whom they claim always edge in on the reparations owed to the wartime communists. Then another speaker points out that after all it is American jews whose annual contributions keep the refugee society running. Izzy, that shambler, harmonizes them, managing to make peace among these different factions. He lets each speak and then incorporates them into his greater point. I hate to admit that I listen to the old shambler with grudging admiration, though this alone is not enough to get me to stay, despite the particular appeasements I find by eavesdropping. I leave long before the survivors might end their night, heading back to my squat, one fit for dogs.

SUNDAY MORNING begins with Christian on his guitar, spitting a rhythm—of the same spirit as Moses' ka*chung*!—working out chords to one of Delhi's songs, songs with such terrible words. Midmorning Sunday, as a favor to me, Moses not back yet, Delhi enters the fold of the refugees, making a halfhearted search for any news of Arianne among them. As she asks what they've heard, I eavesdrop from my position by the plane tree. Unfortunately, I believe I hear that most of the former refugees are too disturbed by Delhi's appearance to say much.

I'm not wrong; the girl comes out spitting. "Those people are rude!"

"I'm sorry," I say immediately. "Thank you."

"They asked if I knew who'd stolen their notebooks and flags. As if. One guy was nice, another lady was okay, but it was like they were so suspicious of me for asking questions. One lady acted as if she'd like come out of a fancier you-know-what than I had. I mean she'd probably been born with one of those voices designed to make others feel stupid? She said I was asking the wrong people. That their reunion had branched off from the Faurets at this point." This last bit was useful to me. I also realize I must have gotten used to how grimy these wastrel girls are, and no longer see it, sensible only to the beauty behind the grime. After Delhi's experience, I consider going to Bomont to demand of the savvy bartender where he believed Arianne was being held, but don't, telling myself I must stay, halfway content to be held in this strange new cat's-cradle, my filthy life, one in which it takes all I have to keep track of the days. I'd be more content if Moses were among us, but be that as it may.

The way time works within this tribe makes it a stretchable commodity, much like prison time. Outside the usual bounds of society, outside the need to seem like a normal member of society, one floats. As a solitary fugitive who'd followed Honsecker's ideas about how to avoid guilt, I had asked society to regulate me. I had coffee in one place, saw films in another, frequented certain parks, helped certain older people. Now, adrift, it feels as if Moses has been gone forever, though I realize it has been fewer than forty-eight hours.

Before noon, I decide to saunter past the square, now emptied of all but a few pigeons, heading toward the foot of the mountain path that leads to our cross of Saint Finier, a particular walk I favored during my time as prefect. Yet, lacking stamina for the mountain, I stare down its bulk before heading back to the increasingly familiar embrace of the wastrels at the Bar Central, a far more containable choice and knowable algorithm than that of Olivier's café, where, as I pass, the returning survivors congregate again, bulging out into the square, looking worlds more elegant than when I'd first seen them.

In the afternoon, I take my leave of the wastrels at the bar and go have a real nap, away from loud videogames, in the dark hollows of the church (I've vowed to never again enter the Hotel Fauret). As I enter the church, I cannot help looking behind me at the café, and believe I see Izzy lording it over a table of graceful older women. He seems to have developed fully into their leader, and whether this is because his colleagues and survivors defer to his moral authority or his blindness, to his height and bulk or to everything about the antique Izzy that I'd shunned, his shambling self, I can't say. I wish I could get Moses' take on Izzy and this makes me realize how important the boy is to me, but how silly is that? Who is that braided boy to me, who is Emile to him?

WHEN I AWAKE in the church, I must walk past a gauntlet of sniggering little boys and stand in the foyer for a second to smooth my hair. I could use another bath, but what strikes me is the local Toulouse newspaper across from me in its little glassed-in box. Lacking coins to buy the paper, I hunch over, squinting at the headlines. Though voiced by an unaccredited source, the news has it that Arianne will be released in a few days, no later than Saturday. The little boys have followed me outside and imitate me hunched before the news box, turning it into a form of prayer, laughing before they scatter.

That night in the squat, I am adrift, horribly lonely, alone but for the dogs who stir and yawn and gape. Greatly missing Moses, and with the wastrels, including Delhi, off at their nocturnal amusements, I work on my testament, clarifying my legacy by the light of the candle stubs Delhi had gotten from the refuse bin outside the Bar Central.

> I wish to leave, therefore, to Arianne Fauret, the knowledge of all denunciations received even before our true deportations began in the Bistronne, the plethora of folded letters which good citizens brought under cover of night and deposited in secrecy in my prefect's mailbox, speaking of this or that "member of a spiritual community which has always been outside France." Also I wish to leave the memory of such phrases.

I could dissolve in half a moment if anyone apprehended me; I have little crustiness left in me. My will for life, let alone a life of freedom, is dissolving. But having held on for so long, it seems silly to let it all go now. I don't want to succumb yet to what would probably be a bad destiny. Living out the rest of my days in some horrible cell, seeing at most, as my greatest diversion, a garbage truck and its giraffe-neck apparatus entering the prison yard weekly—and emerging from that cell only to see the idiot box blasting dispatches about the extent of my evil and the vices of my colleagues, all from the righteous mouths of those two lady lawyers—this would be a fate worse than death.

THIRTY-SIX

All floating periods have their end. When I wake the next morning, uncustomarily late, I am the only person in the squat and a lady with a familiar voice is talking right outside. I slip on my old boots, which have begun to develop holes so that the day before I had been ever more sensible of which *kind* of Finier terrain I walked over, whether rutted earth, cobblestone, riverbank.

I stoop toward the entrance and through the crack I see Simone, the sullen angel, the lady photographer from my hotel lunch with the reporters. She is talking to Moses while taking unposed photos of him against the burnt outer walls of the church.

In his days on the road he has shaved, so his face looks scalded bare, too young to support all those hairy serpentine braids, tied though they are into one giant ponytail. Too clean, broad-jawed, and sincere as he jokes with her. The two do, however, appear to be enjoying themselves. For a moment I question my right to come out of the squat, yet no one crosses the square; it is a safe enough safari; I might as well take advantage of the relative peace.

So I emerge, blinking as one does, drawing a found raincoat

around me, what I have begun to use as my robe in the squat. I do not look normal anymore, I may have become much more of a bushel, but for the moment, at the sight of Moses, something settles in, as if I'm plugged in again, more comfortable within my skin.

"Hello!" says Moses, his spark back.

Simone pivots toward me, shading her eyes, offering a drowsy smile as I approach. Of course, my mind is almost too busy to take her in, quickly riffling through the possibilities, the particular chess-game involved in admitting that I am in fact working a story as the undercover reporter Liston or Listaing. "You'd like to be in some photos?" she says. "I came wanting to photograph your tribe."

My tribe. She was either putting one on or she didn't recognize me. "Why's that?" I ask, mock casual.

"You know. The pulse of bourgeois society in a place like Finier," she says the town's name with disgust, though I think she too is from the area, "how it pushes so many to the side. You interested me."

"Thank you."

"You sat with the journalists, yes? At the restaurant."

"We met," I say preemptively.

"Yet in town I've seen you with these—"

"Say it," says Moses, "with this scum. She's shocked. You ate at the hotel, Raoul?"

"Last week," I say.

"You never told me that."

"Raoul," Simone says, laughing. "If I may. Here you are, with these people?" This a friendly gibe at Moses. "Excuse us one moment?" She takes my arm, ignoring my raincoat, my dishevelment, walking a few steps away, speaking to me sotto voce. "You're retiring?" Clearly she's a confident woman, one with whom one could not misstep.

"In a sense," I whisper. "Undercover," with false modesty, as if I'm trying to keep this fact from Moses.

"Amazing," she says.

I bow a bit. *Stay calm and natural,* I tell myself. I'd left the pendulum in the squat. *She has not once given you the Look, though she has taken photos. She is merely a newspaper photographer. To her I am merely an old man.*

"So I was curious about you, actually, but your friend here, Moses, took your place," she says in a normal voice.

"Stealing your limelight, man," he jokes.

"Keep it," I say. "I appreciate it. Anyway, isn't it all about how the picture's framed? Does it really matter who you get to be in the picture?"

"That's your credo?" she asks, studying me.

"That's exactly what I'm doing with old Raoul here. Dragging him into the frame!" Moses hoots. I have half an urge to take his hand, to embrace the loud, gauche boy.

"Yes," she says, a bit more primly. "Now you, Mister Listaing, please. After all," and starts to train her camera on me; but I duck, leaning down as if to fix my shoe behind a dumpster.

"Please," I say, avoiding a tone of panic.

I know the important thing is to seem casual, yet, in the presence of Moses, I feel alive. In his absence I'd locked myself down again. I can't help this strange joy of seeing him, but it's dangerous. Such joy could provoke, for example, another riverside craze. I am also, admittedly, hurt—he has been gone longer than promised.

"Simone knows about Finier," says Moses. "You'll see. She can help. She knows way more than I do."

"That's untrue. I'd like to know everything. No one tells me anything." She adjusts her camera to focus on Moses, probably catching me in it at the last moment. Sneaky girl. Then another. And one more to top off those two: a sly female.

"You two are friends?" I ask.

They shrug this off, laugh at me. But I've grown used to this. She then says she saw me yesterday in the vicinity, and asks where I've been staying.

I gesture vaguely toward the squat.

"You don't mind being so near the butcher's?" she says.

"It gives us a feeling of greater life," says Moses. "We dwell near the blood of beasts."

"You're clever," she tells him.

"I'm more than that."

They're flirting! I realize belatedly. The realization comes as if I am from a different species, watching jungle animals making the beast with two backs. Simone must glamorize what she considers the trashy other side of life, I see, much as the vegetarian daughters of the bourgeoisie do, and it becomes wrong for me to stand there. Too conspicuous, and not because of the exigencies of survival: I do not wish to intrude on their love dance. I should leave the two of them, and say as much. However feeble their protest, I tell them I have errands to do.

"Errands?" Moses shouts after me.

"Good to see you back to yourself," I half-shout back.

"I'd like to say that to you, man!" he says. "No riverside dances?"

"Are you clean now?" I ask, using his term.

"Clean." He looks at me and also at Simone. "I was clean for three years. Never touched anything, then I slipped up. That's all. Now I'm getting back to being Mister Clean. You're helping, right, in my rehab?"

"Yes," I say stupidly. "What's rehab?" which makes them giggle.

Moses explains through a big grin. "You'll keep me on the straight and narrow," he says. "Keep those guys from giving me pills. Right?" To Simone he says: "Raoul's my right-hand man. I'm his too."

ONCE I BID THEM ADIEU, heading for my river walk, I think this may be true.

For years I have wandered around, wondering if my trust-broken heart has ever felt love. If what gets sung about and danced about and written about by the monarchy of poets and expressed by every dull or animate person, every quotidian shopkeeper and worry-ridden policeman and squirrel-like functionary, every last schoolgirl and mother and father, everyone else, if love belongs to the category of things which Emile Poulquet doesn't get to feel.

I have known certain things. I'd felt a closeness with our old stablehand. I'd shared a camaraderie with Izzy. A certain intimacy with Natalie. But being around Moses gives me an ease I've never known before, and thus can revise everything. Like the sun dancing golden around one of our Finier squares, outlining our buildings, this brief time with Moses illuminates all those previous moments—with Charlot, Izzy, Natalie—as having also qualified as love.

I had unfortunately long considered Arianne to be the greatest planet in my universe, the sun of affections and afflictions. I'd thought I'd lacked any feeling comparable to the one she'd excited in me: shame, a poor substitute, the chest-tightening thrill which makes one aware of one's contours, which I'd mistaken for love. Having believed the category of anxious sentiment I felt around her trumped all others.

But I love the boy.

And though I've been kept apart from normal human relations—whether because of the hump, or having entered Arianne's sights early in life, or the accidents which history has thrust upon me—though I've been excluded from what others have known, *nonetheless*, my love toward Moses could probably be called fatherly, and though this is different from the romance I'd entertained with Natalie or the affection I'd known as a child toward our stablehand, all these feelings share a common core. With all of them, I had been entrusted with the beloved's stories, whether fairytales or news reports. With all of them, I had been interested in learning more, wanting to breathe the beloved's air and so accrue new stories together. This unlikely Moses is my teacher: Moses with his braids, Moses my son, Moses the one I never had.

THIRTY-SEVEN

Monday, my new penance lights my heart. It doesn't matter what we do, whether it is late that night when we go out foraging for crackers and other goods behind the grocery store, or how gifted we feel when finding something as mundane as canned peaches. You could say I sense that I'm counting down minutes until Arianne's release, and that this acts as a balm. I do not forsake caution, however, keeping to my corner, away from Jacquot. Unfortunately, the squat has become a stinkhole, reeking worse than an old latrine, perhaps because a few mean-spirited dogs have been added to the mix. It is also tighter. Two old-timer wastrels have also joined us, though the chestless wraiths from our first days have vanished, the defecting anarchists, razed and sapped types with whom I never exchanged more than a couple of words. The old-timers scowl noticeably at their change in circumstance, saying hello to nobody. Finally they too leave at the first break of morning Tuesday.

    I wake at their scrabble and clatter, the endless stuffing into and zipping of bags, a field in which these people practically sport degrees of comparative mastery, therefore happening also to see in the pale light Moses getting dressed in a suit, wrinkled and pin-striped, far too big for him, lacking any normal undershirt, so that his tattoos glower under the suit, up and down his chest and waist. Notwithstanding this oddity, he busily knots a skinny purple tie around his bare neck.

"You look like a modern singer," I whisper to him. "A singer of popular songs."

He puts a finger to his lips. "Don't ask," he says.

"Don't tell me, this is for the harvest?" I can't stop myself, a jealous father or worse. "You're not going on another job hunt, are you?" I have been successful at not reproaching him for his long last expedition, when I'd been so alone, and how fruitless it had been: he'd returned lacking any harvest gig.

"I'm begging, Raoul. Don't ask where."

"Fine, you see anyone asking?"

"Just wish me luck."

"Luck," I say, trying hard to return to my new nobility, which would have me want what's best for him. *Even if it intruded on my own well-being.*

"Is that sincere?"

"How could it not be? Good luck," I say again, and for this he gives me a thumbs-up. "For the harvest or anything else." This time I halfway mean it.

ONCE HE LEAVES, Delhi rolls over in my direction. She and Cerb-X slept the previous night flanking Jacquot like guardian angels. But this morning Jacquot is gone and Delhi opens one eye. "Moses is off to see the custody officer again," says Delhi. "He's trying to get control of his kids."

"Good luck," I repeat myself, though Moses has already left.

To this she lets out a long belch which sounds like an animal is caught inside her, complaining of poor treatment. "Amen," she says, rolling away.

■ ■ ■

THAT TUESDAY I sleep late and then spend the remainder of the day pretending to read the newspaper in Olivier's café, having dared to return. I'm eavesdropping on a card-playing group of four friends who, like those I've heard in the hall, have stayed on so as to solidify their survivor activities, but who are also enjoying their vacation, reunited. They josh each other, reminiscing. They are creating a portfolio of all their various destinies, discussing now in the café how to create a *database, a newsletter, an advisory board, an institute for the study of crimes against humanity, a forum for the children and grandchildren, an e-bulletin, a chat room, a listserv*, and various other entities insuperably foreign to me. Yet what is appallingly familiar is their desire for bureaucratic means and ends: they wish to mimic the very apparatus which had ruined their lives. More strikingly, however, I cannot help but note the fact, now unignorable, that these refugees are looking less like some motley collection of big-lipped fish, fish abandoned by a mariner on some lonely shore, that I must now endure *seeing* them: rough-tongued and elegant, proto-bureaucrats or sons and daughters of the earth, lost or found souls, but definitely as individual, quirky, far too human.

So I bide my time listening to their plans and games, which sound to me like feints against the greatest of stinking fish, mortality. Surely some of them must know news of Arianne. Yet the question remains: *do I want to see her now?* Trying to pin myself again to that motive which had seemed so important. The headlines on the paper I've filched are no more helpful, my eyes failing, the fine print swimming before me.

I do feel my time here turning, a slight change in the air, not just my growing nausea about the squat's stench, not merely that hint of cold weather slipping into Finier, a late-August cold fiddling one's skin so suddenly, but just a sense that I will not be able to keep my cover or health much longer, as a certain cough has lingered with me after the riverside extravaganza. Luckily, the four friends don't look up as I cough into my fist. They are too involved with their pasts and legacies. *Too many of us have left*, one with fine features complains, *they really should've stayed if we were going to make a central board, a central organization, have accountability, centrality, people get uncomfortable, don't wish to own the tasks ahead, but we know how to carry on, right?* Eavesdropping only gives me partial knowledge.

When the curly-haired woman in the canadienne enters, one of the friends pulls up a seat for her. *We were just speaking of you*, they say. As she talks through her ill-fitting dentures, it becomes clear how little she resembles the woman I'd first imagined her to be. More than once, however, I have to pinch myself to keep from speaking back to these refugees, important with their futures.

WHEN TUESDAY EVENING starts to pull close, I pay up with one of the few coins Delhi had given me after a good night at the bar, leaving the café to take my usual walk along the river Xerxes, enjoying the possibility of certain old habits returning. Yet in front of the butcher's cave, I see Moses in his big suit, a lost prince, crouched over the guitar, down the alley from the squat. The triangle of bare chest showing at the top of the suit is too vulnerable: the boy is off-kilter. My first thought is that Arianne did something to him, but that makes no sense—the shark is locked up and ostensibly can do nothing.

"Anything wrong?" I ask.

Though still clean-shaven, Moses is wearing huge black eye-surgery sunglasses and shakes his head at me, in time with a nonmusic. Now I'm familiar with these people's ways and means. Pills must have been dispensed.

"You're wrong," he says, turning it into a song.

Screeching *you're wrong to ask, man, wrong to ask*. An upper-story window slams above us and someone shouts down *Get a job!* All this a marker of the extent that lucky, cosmic Moses has been absented from regular Moses.

HE WON'T LET ME budge him, refusing all offers of help, so I finally head into the squat to try to catch a bit of early sleep before the rest of them enter. When I wake, looking out, he has left, and my duty toward him has been forsaken. Instinct is what leads me to the river. I find him at a particular bend where we've gone together, that favored spot where the one-legged man in shadows smoked while looking up at naked monkey me, a place where one can dangle one's feet in the river's tumult. Moses tells me he's gotten cut by brambles and stares up. Without his glasses it becomes quite clear he's on some new dope, as they say, doped and asking if I might be kind enough to clean his wounds.

There are no wounds perceptible in that semidark but though Moses' injuries are invisible, I still make a show of treating them. Making believe, almost as Arianne and Paul must have done when she'd met him in the schoolyard and he'd eaten her mud-crepe. That whole realm of the imagination which had been shut off for me as a child, the game of playing along with one's own fancy, or another's, something highly disobedient to that other realm I'd lived in with all its sepulcher's rules, the congregated might of tradition. Who would have ever thought some years ago that Emile Poulquet would be found in the late summer of 1999, so many years dethroned, wearing a mildewed raincoat, his shoes holey, the former prefect of the Bistronne an eighty-four-year-old shadow behind the centuries-old prefecture, bearing a young prince's head in his lap, mouth open, just as if Emile Poulquet had agreed to play *mother* to the young wild-haired prince?

After a while, the young prince bids me to get myself gone, insisting on being alone. He doesn't want to hear my begging, beseeching him to stay away from the pills—wherever they were, whoever was giving them. "Jacquot likes sharing the wealth," my young prince hints.

"Certain kinds of wealth are awful," I tell him.

He looks at me as if to say I don't get to act unsullied. "He's my friend."

"What kind of friend is that? He wouldn't notice if you weren't there. Would he?" and then I stop, I don't want to be a cruel redeemer. I just follow his bidding, will let him come back, as he requests, in his own sweet time.

■ ■ ■

AT NIGHT, as Moses enters, it sounds like wealth has once again been shared, shared and dispensed, Moses stumbling before falling flat on his face in the center of the squat. He's laughing, seemingly unhurt, unhurtable, yet it takes all my strength to pull him to his padding. Once there, I slap his cheek.

"What are you doing?" he mutters.

"Waking you."

"Who's waking?"

"Let's share stories," I say. The boy looks bewildered but angry, a dog on the foamy edge of rabidity. "Try this," I say, forcing him to drink from his leather water flask. He sputters but takes a swallow. I start in with anything, whispering to him, every now and then prompting him to confirm.

You're listening, Moses? Listening. *Listening now?* Still am, man.

No one else is awake, though Cerb-X talks in her sleep. *I'm old enough to do whatever!* she shouts at one point. To which Delhi lets out a long belch, bass and soprano, a quavering end, and then rolls over. These people are falling apart. I keep my whispering low enough that none of them should hear me, though I'm not wholly successful.

THIRTY-EIGHT

A thick throng of whispers. I tell Moses I understand his suffering. How he might've been so frustrated that he'd needed to collapse inside. If he cannot stop taking pills, I will try to be his balm, giving him a story beyond his tawdry current life. I start with Arianne.

He listens, eyes no longer half-rabid but rapt as a child's, and I tell him about the children from the neighborhood who came to look at me. How they held me down, naked, and peered up at me, between my naked legs.

"Cool," he says, from the depths of his delirium.

"Listen better," I half-beg. "I've never told anyone."

I tell how they prodded me with their sticks, and say nothing about how through it all, I didn't move. How I followed Charlot's long-ago advice about how to respond to adversity.

"You're crying?" he says, reaching up and touching my face. "*Shit.*"

I explain. How I let them do what they wanted and inside, another hemisphere already opened up inside, the cut-off hemisphere, the one on which I would always live.

—The boy's a hump, the others said back then.

—He is *the* Hump, she corrected them. That's his name. The Hump. Use it and you get to look at him for another minute.
—The Hump! they called out, obedient.
—The Hump! proddingly.

And I knew from then on, more than ever before, that my secret—that I was a bad child, *evil*, otherwise no one could have in good conscience done such things to me—had been found out. They had recognized and named me. The Hump was evil; but I could live (with the hump, without it) on my hemisphere, apart from all of them.

"You're not evil," says Moses in his druggy state. "Evil's something else. You're just on your own planet."

I tell him how all her friends from the neighborhood started to call me Hump. It was only through the eyes of Charlot that I felt I was good. The rest of the time I was a child who deserved what that older girl had meted out. This was the world I knew. And though this in itself might excuse nothing of what I may have done in life (for another, it might have been as much correlation as cause), it is an instance of a small, tiny, base power radiating into bad power, a spider plant with many new baby spiders rising and spilling out from it, the whole thing amassing volume; and maybe our problem in France is that we would never call our huge plantlike state touched by evil because it has too much to do with all the tiny pots in our pantries, with what goes on in countless small ways behind our woodpiles and in our linen closets and nurseries and professors' dens, little baby spiders sending an ether of negativity back to the root, the root sending it back, a constant exchange of contrariness in the phloem, apparent in everything—in the overseriousness of diners at dusk spearing raw meat onto their pierrades, our love of creative difficulty, the stickiness of wax seals on our jam jars, the bad ballerinas, the little girl dressed up to be an adult in stiff pinafore and ribbon, checking with her mother that she's not allowed to give a coin to an old bushel in a raincoat, or our almost extinct, crunchy bird, the ortolan, all of it part of the exchange of hardship—I do not call it badness—flowing through the phloem and always back to the root. Delhi called it shame and Jacquot perhaps called it evil but I call it the exchange of hardship and difficulty.

When I had excelled in my studies and received good marks, I thought none of my teachers knew the truth of me, the Hump, depravity stuck in my flesh. So that when I was with Charlot, the stablehand, with whom so few words were ever exchanged, only then had I felt I might end up with a *clean* existence—hunting helped, more than he knew. Birdcalls and every flashing shaft of light down between the trees helped.

"Totally," agrees Moses, nodding in and out of his drugged haze.

I must turn off this desire to tell Moses every last thing, so ask why he'd accepted whatever had been allotted him. I meant his birthright and choice of routine, but he understands me as meaning medication. Moses says what he's into doing *right now* is first taking a bad kind of pill, like he used to, and then taking a good pill to balance it, because the middle way's best, right?

"I understand," I say, half-surrendering to the boy's logic. "The middle." In the end if not the means, he is right. When I still had something of the churchgoing habit, I used to shiver constantly about my inability to live moderately. I felt all condemnations arrowed directly toward me, hence I might as well continue what I even then dimly sensed as a cloistered, selfish, self-protecting existence. Others burnt candles for purity but church only covered me with soot. My best attempt at the middle would only land me in purgatory, which is hardly a static place.

"Shut up, man," says Jacquot, roughly, from the corner.

I startle, as I didn't know Jacquot was awake. I thought I was just whispering to Moses a few of my older stories, the right and wrong turns.

"Shut up again," says Jacquot. "Let me sleep."

Moses takes my hand and in the tone of a confessing child tells me not to worry, Jacquot had slipped him the right pills. This is a good thing, he tells me, though he'd tried hard to stay drug- and alcohol-free for three years. "Now there you go again," he says to the pills or to himself, it's unclear. "Three years all gone."

I will not be silenced by Jacquot. In the spaces left by the different pills I am trying to penetrate Moses' mind, lead him back. And it seems, temporarily, that I succeed, the boy turning cogent enough for me to understand. Apparently, wherever he'd been this morning, in his skinny suit and tie, he'd had an encounter with a character he disturbingly calls Law.

"Law says if I have a fixed domicile, I get to hold on to the children." Moses explains he'd received mail long enough at his grandmother's place, had his name on her bills long enough, that her home counted as Moses' fixed domicile. At noon, Moses was to have met with the custody officer for a second visit, clearing the way for a transfer of custody. His kids would go to him, and the state would put all of them in a luxe government flat. "I won," he says.

"So?" I say, prompting him not to lose the train of his thought.

He says he'd succeeded because the children's mothers had been found unfit for various unsavory reasons. The kids could stay with him and his grandmother, whom he would bring down from Orly. Moses would finally have far more than visiting rights. But before meeting with the social worker, that was when Moses had slipped up. "First time I'd gone in, the officer gave me the creeps," says Moses. "So buttoned-up."

"I'm sorry," I say, genuinely apologizing on behalf of all bad officials.

"Sorry?"

"Sorry the social worker was buttoned-up."

"You would have taken a pill too."

I think about it, remembering my monkey freedom. "I might have," I say.

"Lost my nerve."

"Sorry," I say again, enjoying the word. There's nothing to do for it, it seems, though I am no expert in such matters, but to try keeping Moses awake. His face has become too much a death mask when he goes into his delirious sleep. He keeps asking if I know his children's names: Laïs, Ciel, Gauguin.

"You would like them, Raoul," he says, now alert. "I should have called one Raoul. I say this to you because I trust you. I want to live, make love, eat, shit, learn things from those kids. My son looked at the stars and said *map!* Doesn't that like blow your mind? That wasn't anything I'd taught him. But what I'm saying is I need another chance. Just some goats and land. Okay, we can't do anything about how polluted the rain is. Okay, we could all get cancer tomorrow. But if we live good lives and righteous lives, that's what counts. If I have to go to the store, I want to go in a horse and buggy. Those crazy kids of mine could do anything. They could learn languages or be techno people or whatever. It wouldn't matter. It would all be for the good."

THEN HE GETS caught on the jag of saying *three years gone like that.* This is what he wants to keep saying in between nods. *Three years!* Too much is falling apart in each of his nods. I'm trying to keep him awake with my stories but his nods undo me, a fugitive hitched to a falling star.

THIRTY-NINE

Moses grumbles and sputters, infuriated, tells me to stop harassing everyone, gets to his feet and heads out. I actually follow him but at the door to the squat, he tells me he doesn't want my company. Is it that the threads between us have loosened or only the threads within him?

Not knowing, I stay, trying to ignore the boy's absence, trying to change bits and pieces of my will by the bad light of the last candlestub.

> ~~I leave~~ Leaving ~~to Arianne~~ the success of this resistance ~~of hers~~, which paradoxically made it harder for its leaders to control. Leaving ~~our solution~~ the failure of our solution, which paradoxically made it harder for its ~~participants~~ ~~victims~~ citizens to leave us behind.

The changes which I wish to make to my will have to do with erasing all use of the word *I*: scrabbling old *I* and what it means. *I, Emile Poulquet, being of sound body and mind.* My preference being to use a word like *they*, but who would understand that? Similarly, I wish to avoid naming Arianne, because naming assumes mastery and control of another's massed force. Where, if I avoid naming her, the will has greater truth. This is, therefore, despite my best efforts, a will that keeps erasing itself, no matter my best efforts. Most wills pretend to being birthed in a state of permanence, even as they wish to undo all delusions cherished by the living, whereas mine will be a will commissioned by (the fluctuations of) truth.

MIDDLE OF THE NIGHT, when Jacquot has stretched out into Moses' space, Moses is still out front, humming one of his silly songs, plucking the three-string guitar. Jacquot sits up and sees me working on my document.

"You can't shut your friend up?" says Jacquot. This is half-challenge, half-request. "He's calling too much attention to our squat."

"Me?" I say, though it's clear to whom he speaks. It's not so much that I fear going out into the cold night: I'm afraid of how I will feel if the boy shrugs me off again. So I do what I know how to do, avoid responsibility, blow my candle out. No candle on inside old Emile. Let Jacquot get Moses if he wants.

I must have dozed off again, because I wake with the sense that my damaged-goods soul better at least *try* bringing Moses inside before he catches a cold. So I crawl forward, wrapped in my blanket, creeping over the feet of Delhi, Jacquot, and Cerb-X, finally pushing open the door of our squat.

UNFORTUNATELY, this is when I catch sight of my friend.

His back to me, I can tell from the sound of him that he has returned to himself, his guitar leaned as placeholder against the wall where he'd been sitting, the boy himself across the square, standing like a convivial fellow at a party, chatting it up by the hotel annex, holding onto the grillework of that most suspect veranda, companionably chatting it up with the square man who patrols the night from his station upon the veranda, that man with his leg-cast luminescent and actually hanging through the grille, the crutches stationed above. The two of them smoke together as men do, smoking which should not give one too much fright, men laughing, which is in itself not a bad sign, merely a product of genial discourse: Moses and the man with the cast, the man with his foreigner's way of exhaling smoke. I quite literally bite my tongue, hoping to stay unnoticed, and would know how to comprehend this better, how to make sense of my tangled nerves, were it not that my pendulum itself has turned into an inert tongue, mute and heavy, unchecked for days. I head back in without doing a thing.

PART FOUR

FORTY

Delhi knows I favor the plane tree outside the refugee hall, and the tree quickly begins to mark our new routine. The two of them, Moses and Delhi, arrive at the tree before dinner outside the homes of the bourgeois daughters, before a stint of night work we've obtained, the three of us together as if only good intentions pave the road, mainly because the pendulum has remained obtuse and stubborn, refusing to confirm any direction. On Wednesday, Moses had begged me to take a little night-walk with him, and he'd explained why I must go on staying in Finier. *Stay*, he said. *Implore* would not be too strong a word. He implored me. I did not mention what I'd seen. What I did say was this: *If only I could get to speak to Arianne!*

So much of me had started to flow toward her again, as if she were a cardinal point capable of absorbing all, as if a river could reverse course up a mountain. At one point, days earlier, *seeing Arianne* might have been a more vestigial request: now it felt like an ultimatum.

As we spoke that Wednesday evening, walking and talking, we'd come across what I found rather shocking: a far field outside town, not Bruno Somport's but another's, littered not just with bottle shards and old dark blue cigarette cartons but with small bougies and flambeaus, so that we walked over the kind of shattered glass the two of us had created the first day we'd met, when we'd engaged in that bottle-target practice with stones by the river wall.

In the field we found workers, lit by headlamps and the small traces, all looking like Boris Karloff in an outtake from the kind of horrific film designed to give you frissons, workers digging in orange vests like glowing plankton submerged in the night.

"What's up, man?" asked Moses, oblivious, perhaps, to how his appearance alone was an affront to civil society. One worker shone his headlamp on him.

"We're preparing for the monument," one said. "That's the truth, Jesus."

Moses smiled for a second, distracted. "He calls me Jesus because we used to sell vegetables and he said that I had magic hands, that I could sell boiled beets even to the picky old ladies. Then I also knew how to hide the boiled stuff from the government inspectors. Pretty shouette, no? Cool. A monument going up and down in the dark?"

"Don't listen," said another. "We're digging."

"Whose?" Moses signaled me to step away from a giant hole I hadn't seen.

"The resistance monument. Go to the mayor's office tomorrow if you want. Night work's the best. Tell the short-haired lady at the desk on the right when you come in. Just say *resistance* and put your name on the list. They pay nicely."

Moses watched them, respecting their prowess with shovels. "Why this field?"

They said nothing. The worker held up a small frog, unseated by their work, and held the little thing. It stared out with big eyes over his gloves, having stopped its croaking but unable to stop its breath. "See what we're digging up?"

"They must have found Jacquot's statue of Paul," said Moses.

"Maybe it wasn't the only one," I said. "Maybe someone else was commemorating Paul at the same time. One mold but two statues."

He punched me on my shoulder. "You're good, Raoul. Got a good head for administration. Should apply to do committee work, man."

HE CONVINCED ME to stay, mainly through his promise that he'd rehabbed, as he said, with that combination of boyish earnestness and optimism. I'd told him in so many words that if I was going to stay in that crawl space, I needed a steady anchor in the wastrels, and he promised me he was that anchor. Or what he said was this: "I promise you a gig." I wasn't sure if night work qualified as a better gig for Emile, but why not? What better fate awaited me? I only felt a bit of the peak I'd known when I realized that what I felt for Moses was very much like love, yet couldn't the peak be revisited? In answer to the question SHOULD I BE FOLLOWING MY FEELING FOR THIS BOY AND STAY ON? the pendulum acted frustrated with me for my earlier malfeasance and failed to swing clearly. Perhaps my question had been too ambivalent.

Whatever the case, Thursday morning, Moses at the mayor's office wrote down three names on a foreman's list: Moses, Moisès, and Maises. Under these names, Delhi and I got to work with Moses, all off the same identity card. I tell myself all will be well, and the pendulum, however inert, at least does not say NO. It must have some kind of savoir-faire about my fate, and the boy has pulled himself back together, at least for today, rejecting any pill offered him by Cerb-X or Jacquot.

FROM THE PLANE TREE, near the new memory hall, I can hear the river's lullaby, and over that I can almost hear the crash of the river as young Emile had known it. So it is that on the other side of the aquifer, near the hall, Delhi and Moses come to find me. I have fallen asleep, and when they nudge me awake from my nap, I come to feeling like a harmless collection of bones, an old cat with loose skin and long whiskers.

It is also true that Delhi and I have arrived at a simpatico. She does not talk much, and, like Moses, seems to have forsaken her degrading habits—or has their drug supply just dried up, Jacquot back on his epilepsy medications?—but during that night's work she is a respectful colleague, loaning me her headlamp as I've forgotten mine, picking zones for herself where our Finier sod is hardest, letting me dig the softer ground. *She* is the one granting me respectful berth. She also covers for me when the lady from the mayor's office comes to check up, surprised to find a senior citizen who should not have been allowed to work.

"No, really," Delhi tells her, "our Moisès here," the name that's been given me, "he's fine. Moisès may look old but he's really only middle-aged, Madame." Delhi steps forward, hushing her voice, insinuating I'd suffered a small liver crisis, our most patriotic malady, and that this crisis must have made me look as bad as I do. She accomplishes this in such a proficient manner that the lady from the Mairie ends up being the embarrassed party.

I thank Delhi after work. "You're skillful," I tell her.

"Liver crisis. A good touch, no?" she asks, and I appreciate her wit, having underestimated her initially. "We're both friends of Moses, aren't we?" says Delhi. "Between the two of us, I'm having an affection crisis," she goes on. "I love all of you. Especially Moses." But there is no warning in this, no territoriality, merely a shared appreciation of the boy who, admittedly, leads our faction of the wastrels.

Chatting with Delhi, I am struck again with the shroudlike illusion that I might be understood by someone. The girl may be having the equivalent of our old-time liver crises, an affection crisis as she calls it, but she is not alone. I will say there are moments during this night when again I feel warmish toward Jacquot, if merely for his nameability. And yet, a reminder of the world's leakage of tenderness, when Moses and Delhi and I emerge the next morning in town, turning a corner, I must face down Izzy.

It is not that I don't want to see him—I don't wish to be seen. I say nothing, going dead as shrapnel. Because how blind could a man be? In that early-morning silence, Izzy certainly manages, tottering about a little, cane before him, nose tilted forward as if scenting the future.

If Izzy confronted me, even with my reconstructed face, he would, after a while, despite everything, surely be unable to avoid recognizing at least the outline of his boyhood Emile. Having overheard me talking to the lawyer during the trial's intermission, as the red bear said, Izzy had used my voice alone to identify me, however much others had shredded his testimony.

IN RELATION TO IZZY, I remember in particular a day not long after Sirouve's liver crisis, not long after I had been bumped up two posts, not long after I'd brought Odile along to her higher post (which was, as I consider, one of my best acts accomplished as prefect), quite early into my time with Natalie in my apartment, our habit of list-making still a new one. It is hard to believe that I was such a young man, yet how much I had done, and how much I thought I knew.

Out of habit more than fondness, after student years spent keeping tabs on the other, competitively, while also avoiding each other, Izzy and I had reunited again in Finier, meeting at the train station, Izzy a bit sheepish about his spree in Paris. I assumed he'd been shorn of ambition, having seen that being a working comic actor would not pay his rent. Still, the narrowness of his egoism against the expanse of his ambition gave him great charisma—though now I wonder if part of this charisma was that he already knew he would be hunted down. During our student years together, he had been too quick at his studies for his own good, far more nimble than I. My mistaken sense was that Izzy had turned lazy, and now rued his return to Finier, as it meant he would have to study again to obtain his law degree. I wrongly believed that this difference in our relative positions—student versus prefect—was what led Izzy to tease me. It was not like him, and perhaps his lack of practice made his gibes all the more grating. *Oh, Emile, big man,* he'd greeted me as he first came off the train, an epithet which bothered me despite the triumph I fingered, a slightly cracked trophy on a private shelf. I had an advantage: I'd had my marketing interregnum with Arianne, had learned almost everything about her, our fingernails dirtied with the same earth, and Izzy knew nothing of it.

About a week after he'd arrived, despite the energetic new films being churned out in Paris, he and I'd chosen to see one of the old breed, which had stained our afternoon with melancholy. On the way back to his place, near Abouk's dusty antique store, his mother had accosted us: jaunty, hotel uniform neatly bundled in a woven sack, relieved to be leaving work but a scent of sautéed onions and smoke still upon her like a pledge of fidelity to the hotel, her hat with its long feather touchingly askew. "Where are you boys coming from?" she'd asked, girlish in patting her son's chest. I ached. In the presence of his mother, despite my carapace of new authority, I was stripped of years, a teenager made of earwax and joints and knobs.

She turned us into fools, making us jostle to one-up each other with our wit in describing the movie. In it, ten men in a rural village had struggled to answer for a child's murder, along the way celebrating their brotherhood. In our aped maturity, we raced to explain why the plot was superior to the new films being churned out. It was during this game of commentary that two policemen had walked toward us with no small intent.

His mother hushed into understanding. "Don't say who you are," she whispered to her son. When the gendarmes enunciated her name wrongly, she corrected them. "Madame Horwitz Lisson." Now, as I think of it, I realize how brave this was. Watching the policemen who might as well have had invisible weights hung at the corners of their mouths, who spoke through these heavy mouths at Madame Lisson, I felt myself turn into an inert lump, though my heart sped up, sensing what would happen and oddly curious. People like me probably once filled the gladiator arenas: we feel relieved when seeing others fight out what we would not mention in polite company, when others get stripped down to their most apelike urges.

Yet another factor has become clear with the years. I had been bred by my father to be a polite boy, and times of crisis made me cling to politeness. Even as the police spoke in their rude manner to Madame Horwitz, I mobilized myself, determined to outfinesse the situation—to be so polite that some note of harmony and mastery might be struck. Though my capacities were poor, my intentions were honorable. Emile, so polite, would lead everyone to an escape hatch out of the uncomfortable moment. The policemen would stop themselves, realizing they had trespassed a line of conduct. A line would be redrawn. They would recognize Madame Horwitz's innate grace. Strange as it might sound to contemporary ears, holding back surpassed tact: it was a tactic.

I studied the antique display in the window. When the gendarmes told Madame Horwitz that she'd been registered, that she was to be taken to the station to surrender her house-keys and jewels, but that first she could gather a few things from home, she paused. I held my line of politeness. She looked at her son, at me (I could not avoid her gaze), then appeared to make a decision. She said she would give them no trouble.

"There's been a mistake," Izzy protested. To her, he hissed: "There's no point in being a hero."

"I don't know this man," his mother then stated, a bit too loud. "Officers, these young gentlemen were bothering me prior to your arrival."

Izzy started to say something, and one of the officers, the younger one, showed vigilance. He turned to Izzy, a boy as dark-complexioned and broad-featured as his mother. "You have something you wish to say, sir?"

Izzy glanced sidelong at Madame Horwitz, but now she wouldn't meet his eyes. "It is not that I object," he said. I could see the legal cogs spinning in him, trying to churn up some justification. As I had spent enough time with Izzy, I knew every nuance. He was scratching his nascent beard, a bad sign. He had little idea of how to proceed. Years later in the holding cell, I would recount the scene as if an equation to myself:

	(first) the depth of his desire to protect his mother
(minus)	
	(what followed) his obedience to her command at that moment
(equaling)	his own disingenuous, blameless urge to survive.

Had he truly wished to protect her—

"Excuse me," I interrupted.

They looked at me as if I were an improper species of bug.

"I'm the new prefect, you know."

This attracted the attention of the younger officer but the older one stayed stock-still.

"Who issued this command?" I asked.

"This has little to do with your office," the older one said. He studied a yellow sheet. "We have regional directives. This one was processed by a Mister Sirouve. Are you Sirouve?" I shook my head, my bistronnaise cap slipping off, realizing my youth must have made me seem a liar, deserving a half-response. I did not know these officers; they had been brought into our region. Clearly competent members of the gendarmerie, but whatever my degree of politeness, it was clear that nothing short of an explosion would get them to obey me. I was shorn of tools, lacking my apparatus, my office, the production of exasperation and attrition, all the slow machinery of bureaucratic procedure which I only then was beginning to master. No matter how polite I could have been, or how forceful, I could not muster more than those strategies my office had recently granted me, my tools solely a desk and pen, a wax seal with the state's insignia. Without them I was naked, just a recently promoted young man, a callow youth with a sped-up heart, still in his twenties, mustering his voice. Much like a Scotsman lacking his ceremonial belt, or our ancient Gauls lacking their spears, I would not be obeyed. Let the record stand: I did try.

"I worked with Sirouve. Perhaps you need to double-check the official lists," I said, my voice dry, cracking.

"We have," said the older officer, bored.

"I don't know this man," his mother interrupted, indicating Izzy. "Or his friend. They're impertinent boys. Let's go. Please ignore him." She must have sized up my blundering tone, thinking I would worsen matters.

Izzy stayed soldered into place, suffering from a failure of nerve or clever ideas, even as the police started to escort his mother away— I remember her name as Geraldine, though to me she was always Madame Horwitz. Her feather bounced about, a ridiculous hope atop her head. The look Izzy turned toward me was so ugly, it might as well have blinded me. "Can't you do something?" he asked, as if he already knew what would happen.

"I can't," I said, glancing away, only to find him looming up behind me in the window's reflection. I couldn't say anything. *The directive must have come from above me. Or it came in parallel, through our office but to the police station.* There was nothing I could stop. I hadn't yet been given a full portfolio of wartime affairs, and didn't yet know the worth of declaring a jew to be *interesting* or *useful*. Instead I was made to stand there, pretending interest in a window display. Izzy gave up on me, turned, ran haphazardly after the officers, knock-kneed. His mother's face shot back, a tawny flower. And all the while, the officers' hands had a firm politeness on the mother's elbows, firm and polite in steering her home, Izzy tagging behind, and from there to the unknown place to which polite people were being steered so firmly.

IN MY DEFENSE, as well: he did not answer my doorbell ever.

I accosted him once on the street, a fortnight after that event: I had started to call the event Izzy's *ambiguity*. In a few words, I tried to explain to him that I had not known of the directive. I said that since the *event*, I had retroactively tried to change his mother's status, that he should not have been so law-abiding by having registered her at the station, that who knew if my own later efforts would bear any fruit.

In my words was a halfway truth, as I had found myself somewhat loath to press my mentor. I was new at my job and understandably would not wish to appear partial to any single person's case, even if it was toward the case of Madame Horwitz Lisson. Izzy must have intuited part of this. As I spoke, he had stared through the back of my eyes to whatever he saw writ inside the back of my skull, so that I became uncertain where I myself should place my gaze.

After more than a decade of our grudging friendship, there was no more of anything. I had turned away and now he did the same. He lacked the words to ask me for further help and I must have lacked the ability to offer. Did he know I saw the whole thing as a failure on *his* part? Yet it haunted me, the pesky sense that I might have behaved differently. At least a year after the event, after his *ambiguity*, only a few months after Natalie had disappeared, I'd hesitated when Odile presented me with, on a list, the name of Israel Horwitz Lisson. How to say this? It almost wasn't a question. I wanted to deport him because in this way I wanted to deport our shared ambiguity, when he had obeyed his mother and I had stood by like a dummy, investigating a store's display of antique perfume bottles.

Odile presented me with that day's clipboarded list. She had been rebuffed by Izzy at one point. Her wrists trembled only slightly as she held forth the clipboard. I did not think through the implications of my checkmark. But my pen was capable and confident. *Israel Horwitz Lisson*. I checked it. A single stroke of a pen. √. That was all.

ADMITTEDLY, the *ambiguity* would have been hard for anyone to finesse. Does one obey one's own mother or sacrifice oneself? It came down to betrayal or self-sacrifice. What I'd heard recently from eavesdropping among the reunited refugees was that Izzy had lived a vagabond's life. He'd been entered into the camp where the first moment consisted of being stripped naked: bent over in front of the guards, forced to cough so that any concealed weapons on his person might emerge. Later he was allotted shoelaces and a belt but no necktie, was exposed to tuberculosis but escaped from the camp in Bomont when Paul Fauret's group helped free the deportees. Izzy had clung almost in tetany to the oil-slippery undershaft of a southern-bound train, making it over the mountains into Spain. During the passage, someone had blinded him, but of these circumstances he would not speak. After the war, he'd made his way to America, where he'd stumbled into the good fortune of finding a handful of wealthy, guilt-stricken Christian patrons. One of them paid for the psychologist who told Izzy it was high time for him to give up his crippling guilt. The psychologist told the weeping Izzy that, given the strangeness of wartime, many might have operated, temporarily, out of self-interest. Because Izzy might have done more. Izzy might have attacked the police. Izzy might have disobeyed his mother's demand that he let the police carry out their act. Izzy might have publicly harangued me. Of course, there was a lot more which Izzy could have done.

After the psychologist absolved him of his guilt, however, Izzy thought he had something of a clean slate. He dedicated himself to the field of comedy, succeeding somewhat, becoming what he called a rarity, a blind comedian in Los Angeles, before he moved into his most recent vocation, real estate, from which he'd recently retired.

Until a crisis of conscience must have beset him. I'd heard him say he'd had an awakening, on a day months before I had been dragged out of my Buenos Aires sanctuary. Someone had been driving him down a road he called Pico Boulevard, a hot Los Angeles day falling upon him, rays filtering through what he called the car's *sunroof*, and the urge had struck. He researched the slow arduous briefs the women lawyers were filing against Emile Poulquet, and decided to send them information regarding my late Argentinean mentor, which helped those brittle young policemen to track me down one hot afternoon after the siesta, in the middle of my tango lesson.

I wanted to laugh when I heard the refugees recounting Izzy's story. They all loved to congratulate themselves, but they lacked brilliance. Before Argentina, I had been able to hide many places, but most tellingly, for about a month—and it could have been thirty years, had I been able to tolerate being so near Arianne—in the prefecture of Finier, behind my dusting-feather and broom, my mop and scouring agents. And now I could hide among refugees, wastrels, even reporters: but for how much longer?

Though I don't wish to stray: according to me, Izzy had betrayed his mother, while I had acted in a merely indefinite fashion toward his entire family. That does not mean I have to put myself in his line of fire and let him shame me, or worse, alert the authorities.

ON FRIDAY, feeling my days with the wastrels waning, I stay in the Bar Central with Delhi and Moses, Jacquot occasionally descending upon us. While the wastrels play pool, I share the beer they win. To the disgruntlement of Cerb-X and Delhi, Jacquot has for a healthy sum revealed to the refugees (who've in turn revealed to the mayor's office) where the first Paul statue was to be *found*.

Jacquot is now extolled as rescuer of the original monument. As the reporter Barbie had hinted, a loophole exists, related to artistic expression, another loophole in one of our new regional, civil-liberties statutes, such is the nature of our over-contemporary, conceptual France. Thus, Jacquot does not get charged with theft for having taken public property ransom. The monstrous entity will be carted in on a giant flatbed, Paul Fauret's likeness soon to stare at the Finier mountains. Once the cement is laid in, then Paul will be erected. At this point, I imagine Arianne like a nymph released from prison, coming to ravage herself one midnight at the base of the statue. No more Paul but his memory upheld, some two stories high, Paul Fauret as a new iron and bronze patron saint of the resistance, fist held high in blessing.

Paul Fauret not in his original site.

Not overlooking the camp in which he helped organize his fighters, from which he famously helped all the deportees flee, including Israel Horwitz Lisson.

Not Paul Fauret in Bomont, in the place of his greatest success, on Somport's land, as had been originally planned.

Not Paul Fauret as he was after the deportation of Natalie, when (I believe) he went mad in the worst of ways.

Not Paul Fauret whose wife wanted us to believe he'd gone mad from ergot.

But rather Paul as stand-in for all tall and muscled men we'd ever wished for in our time, Paul frozen in his last years of life, Paul before he went mad, before his final moment, when the weight of past and future must have conspired to crush him and he'd thrown himself into the river, drowned like one of the most noble Redons ever to have been found in Arianne's scrapbook. There is no place for heroes to live eternally but in our imagination. Paul will stand, a stern gravity, representing the mere five percent among all us Frenchmen who actively fought our occupation. And what were the other ninety-five percent doing, I among them? You can say: turned inward upon our own towns, towns as special to each of us as Finier is to me, though perhaps this is too easy to say.

Somewhere in this apparition of eternal Paul is justice, however ironic and violent, and I can't help thinking that once again Arianne has played me for the fool. She has set me down on her chessboard, twiddling me a little to the left and the right, making me witness and participant to this latterday erection of the Paul statue.

And if I am at all a party to justice, in any greater sense of the word, it has nothing to do with Arianne but only with the goodness of Moses, who cannot help but wedge my heart open, such is the nature of a decent boy gone wrong, a boy who expects the wind at his back. A boy who tells me that night at the Bar Central—however drunk he is—that he has wanted, sincerely, to show me a certain life, one based more on ideals of brotherhood than any of those other middling lives in which I have participated.

FORTY-ONE

Saturday morning Moses again wants me to wake earlier than usual, as we have an appointment at the noonday market. When we come to the spot by the beetsellers, where the pianist and her cohort had played that first day, a day already buried in the past, he tells me to wait.

"Where are you going?" I ask, oddly alarmed. "You're not leaving me here?"

"You said if someone gave you the chance, you'd want to go through your old lady's stuff, right? Well. Here's your chance."

"I didn't say *stuff*. I said I wanted to see *her*. You're not leaving again, are you?"

"Just wait for Simone. You know, your pornographer," and gives me a wink.

ONCE HE TURNS the corner of the square, I beseech the pendulum SHOULD I WAIT FOR THESE PEOPLE? and it gives me an unambiguous YES.

The young men who sell beets tolerate my presence. One offers me a bread-crust which I accept, unashamed. It is interesting to look out at life from the perspective of the beetseller. Fussy older men and women approach and finger your goods, yet trust you have something basically decent to offer.

Perhaps a half-hour after Moses has left me, I see the French photographer shopping for vegetables with the American filmmaker, the murderer. They are not quite arm in arm but might as well be. She carries the vegetable basket and he must be holding her camera, as if they share a baby or at least some future they will hold together.

It feels like years since I've seen the American, and I'm surprised he has stayed on so long. He did say he was coming to find out some truth about his origins.

I come at an angle toward them. She lights up, he partly frowns, but hers is a fine face. A strange thing to be taken in by a face which, like Delhi's, reminds me of Natalie, as if Natalieness has become for me a mark of *someone to pay attention to, someone of interest*. As they near, I am not sure for a moment what I'm supposed to offer the American and his Natalie-like escort.

"Hello," I say. "Perhaps we might meet this evening at the base of the mountain?" I find myself saying impulsively to the girl.

"Simone can't," says the American for her, his comprehension as quick as his ingratitude. I shouldn't be surprised.

"Sorry." She shrugs.

"But I'd like you to come with me," he says, presumption clearly his home territory. "If you could stay an hour, I'll take you somewhere. It's a favor. Hey, I'm Rick, by the way."

This is the escort Moses has chosen for me? *I could've turned you in*, I whisper at the departing arrogance of the American's back. *Rick*. Yet the truth is I don't bear anyone great malice. Surrendering to other people can become a restful practice, more than life might prepare one to think.

HE BRINGS ME to an apartment, one I've visited before, and seats me on my own small child's chair, as if he needs a childlike audience. The American works with efficiency and method, strangely certain about how to distribute pieces of a person in small piles.

I'm not sure when to pose the question regarding what we are doing here. There is something bleak in his expression, that of a man who has unwittingly consigned himself to years of service on a penal colony, and now believes it is for the good if he continues his sentence with a show of sportsmanship.

In his yellow T-shirt, actually, he does look like some kind of youthful but fading sports player, conscious of the exact dimensions of his chest, the kind of man eternally on an inhale, shoulders up, chest puffed out. He is a shorter man than one thinks and yet sits for all the world as if he were a minor deity.

Eventually, warming up to his task, he tells me what has happened. He'd found his mother.

Mother.

With some salty taste in my mouth—some wayward tear—I found myself envying anyone who felt close enough to their own mother to say the word with such vigor. Mother. I hadn't said the word forever, it seemed.

Not that he knows her any better now, he says. Merely, for the last week, he has been visiting her. In her sanitarium, where she is being kept before the arraignment *on a charge of insanity*. Because of all this, I forgive him his penal air: it may be the lingering atmosphere of the institution he's been visiting, a noxious air I know so well, one breathed only with difficulty.

AND THEN the pieces come together. So quickly, I don't have time to browbeat myself for my blindness. Because the fellow does look like Arianne after all.

Down to the gap teeth which I'd not remarked before. Gap teeth. Such an insignificant detail, but shouldn't I have recognized it? Recognized him.

Now with a beard and brown mustache, markers that he was a million years younger the day he'd crashed into Somport. Though a younger man had committed the deed, it is not the beard that has aged him.

A great thrill fills me: I am speaking with Arianne's son, part of her body, proof that my pendulum has led me to exactly the right place and time. How fully one *can* see something of a male Arianne in him—a certain beauty, the lustrous hair, the spacing of eyes, the slightly cruel uptilt. He does not want to explain too much about how he came to understanding his mother's identity, but it was partly the French photographer's doing.

Simone, he sighs. "She's a native, you know," he says. "Simone's family goes way back."

Thanks to Simone's *connections*, he intones, to local powers-that-be, given her uncle who was this and that, her mother who was of such-and-such family, Simone first made him aware of his resemblance to a woman his dead father used to tell him, back in Chicago, was not only untraceable but unnameable. Simone as a special favor had helped him look through the archives and birth records of all hospitals south of Toulouse, circa 1939 and on, helping him to find out he'd been born in the small regional hospital of Sacre-Coeur to a young Catholic girl named Arianne Vadet, his Jewish father going unmentioned.

Simone who turned the key. Simone who has had her own losses, who has been especially keen on getting him to be able to meet with Arianne every day since soon after he arrived in Finier. "You knew her?" he asks incuriously. "I sure got more than I bargained for in coming here. You could say we've been making up for lost time." In the meantime, from the institution, considered to be enough in her right mind to do so, Arianne has authorized her attorney to bequeath her old apartment to the prodigal son.

"It's complex," he says with great brashness, unable to wash it off him. "The Polish man she had in charge of her foundation absconded, you heard? Right after the reporters came," he explains. "It's a mess. Funds gone. All that. Some of her holdings taken into escrow by the bank. Liens. Hard to explain. It's fallen to me, you know? I wasn't counting on this *mess*. Helping coordinate the refugees, all that. I can't believe it. I came from her body, you know? And she couldn't be more of a stranger."

■ ■ ■

I WANT TO KNOW what made him want to find me again, as the fellow seems to have a happy explanation for everything: this must be the American trait. I'd heard about it. Everything signed, sealed off. This person good, that one bad, this country evil, that one respectable.

"Simone talked to me, at the reporters' hotel, you know? I told her I was looking for a story about the real France of today. She said I should meet your friend Moses. Then Moses said you had a research project. Hey, what's it you want from my mother exactly?"

"Research is not the word," I say, trying not to sound piqued. "Why'd you seek me out?"

"Hey, didn't I owe you one." Not even a question. As if he were referring to a bottle of beer. *Owe you one.* This his only reference to what had transpired on the road. I have stayed silent on his behalf (and for my own survival, admittedly). I hadn't come forward to free his mother (as she'd done for me, so mystifyingly). Here that all came down to a single tacky phrase. *Owing.* He must trust that I will be stupefied by the coincidence, which is true, I suppose, sitting on a child's painted chair in the apartment in which Arianne had lived with her Paul before he went and drowned himself. Of course, the son doesn't know who I was to his strange-cookie mother, nor who she was to me.

"Well. Happy to be here?" says the American, tired out.

"I don't blame you, you know," I say, still trying to piece it together, drugged merely by the American's confidence. "I understand. If you had come forward," I say.

"You said, right? No good would have come. And she's going to be released anyway. The lady doesn't know what's happening to her. I'm saying two wrongs don't make, you know."

"I understand," I repeat, using the phrase like a battering ram. It is such an ugly phrase in English. *Understand.* While between us hangs a silence dark as the pond separating France from America.

"Okay," says the son. "Got to work. You don't mind."

"No," I say, situating myself by waving my hand grandly. He possesses some of Arianne's controlling nature, and for some reason, this pleases me absurdly, a confirmation of nature, pleasing me almost as much as all those films and songs the stuck-in-the-past refugees insist on playing. The old gas-oven-and-leek-soup scent, one of our eternal

French-apartment stinks, especially strong in Arianne's old home, pleases me further. In point of fact, everything pleases me, a new calm mine for the taking. Everything which ordinarily would shock amuses me, including the orange graffiti I'd seen in the foyer. I suspect it to be the work of Jacquot and his girls; they'd been on a graffiti spree for several days the previous week, orange their color of choice.

FUCK BABIES
THEY HAVE NO INNOCENCE

the foyer below proclaims. A strange access of sympathy floods me, finding myself hoping the slogan will be cleaned before Arianne comes home, released from her sanitarium. At last an answer: she is locatable. Whether to seek her out in such fallen circumstances: this question I will wait upon. I do also find it interesting how Rick the American takes my presence as a given, something bankrolled for me by (this is my guess) Moses' charm, Moses who must have asked something not far from *can an old friend participate in your clean-up effort?*—so I follow suit in casualness, thumbing through an old scrapbook of Arianne's while Rick works. I'd heard about these obituaries that summer in the hotel; now I finger them, her childhood scrawlings, her doggerel next to wrinkled news photographs of men who must have been the Redons, the men who'd worked with her father. Such a long journey she'd made from that girl who'd fantasized about saving the brave. In my case, as far as I can see, she'd instead made at least a partial career of punishing the non-Redons around her. And this is why I have suffered; I must claim my calm again, replacing the scrapbook, closing my eyes against the onslaught of Arianneness.

"HEY," SAYS THE American to me, maybe an hour later. "No offense, but could you, you know, find something else to do? No offense, but stop hovering over my shoulder?" Offering a limp apology: "You see there's a ton of stuff. She kept so much."

He is right. It will appear he has almost gotten through most of it and then he opens up another door only to find yet another cache, another collection in a dusty armoire or creaking closet. And not only is it a bounteous collection, it is *odd*. Folded-up notes, messages about his father, some of which he reads aloud to me. Not to Paul but to another beau she called Roger, Roger the American's father who had returned temporarily to France: theirs a romance in reverse, in soured script. And her oddities on display: that she'd kept the safeties, what foreigners call French letters, stapled and stored with dried bounty all these years, their years labeled. 1967. 1968. 1969. He holds these artifacts up to me: by proxy, I am his fellow archaeologist. Clearly Rick needs someone to share in this weirdness. "My potential siblings. You know, my father never spoke about her. She must have really flipped," he says. "I don't know what she was thinking. The bank is foreclosing and now she asks me to be the one to pack up all this shit. Can't believe it." As if to bring himself back to the living, he takes out his camera and films the room, including me: in my attempt at calm, I find I don't even recoil.

"It must be the ergot," I say. "She had ergot. It makes people go mad."

"How do you know that?" he asks, switching the camera off.

"My dream life."

And he accepts this, the American does, as much as he accepts anything in this scene, equally surreal for the two of us.

"That's it," he mutters, tying up some newspapers with twine. "She must have contracted *something*." He must be aiming to sound matter-of-fact. "She gave me up," he says. "I was her love child. My father was a friend of Paul's even before they married. Saved by America. That's what I heard." He is as straightforward as someone can be, going through his mother's belongings in the old wing of the Hotel Fauret, behind the rooms she'd pretended to live in. They'd existed to hide the truth of her. "I should have been able to tell," he says.

"What's that?" I am stretched out on the couch, watching his industry, trying to make sense of my next move. Could I hitch a ride with the American and go see Arianne in her sanitarium?

"I should have seen from the way she taps her fingers. My mother's an obsessive. It explains everything." He seems satisfied by his diagnosis, closed up and leakproof, and his work takes on the aspect of a moving man, one unrelated to the detritus, a man scarily efficient, humming as he works, occasionally forwarding objects to the old bushel who happens to share breathing space with him. He hands me lists of observations about her various lovers, as if this would be an agreeable diversion for a bushel like me, and further tells me Moses had asked him to be generous toward me.

Anyway, Rick the American says, taking a small risk, he likes to be generous toward someone who sort of saved his life. He grows a bit pensive, showing me a diamond ring which he's found behind the oven. "All these years and before this August, think of it," he says, "I'd never met my own mother."

The American takes the ring back to test the rock's strength, scratching the mirror. It is real enough and he pockets it. But the mirror itself is a strange one on which Arianne had traced, with a waxy crayon, her form as it had changed and mutated all these years: and she'd been careful, in her slanted handwriting, to notate month and year, the exact curve of change, and to remark at times *the same!* to show that in some years, change had overlooked her.

The only hint of this madness, during my month as janitor, had been the odd flung-about dance I'd seen her do at one farmers' dance. As though life had constricted around her and only flung gestures could cut through. After that period, evidently, perhaps even before, she'd been collecting boxes of things, practically palpating in their endlessness, the detritus of a life.

Carefully notated clots of cat hair, hairballs spat up and spun around themselves, cocoonlike, the date marked. This had been Arianne's own private society for memory's restitution. Antiquated larval lamps with stained-glass shades. What kind of life was this? Ashtrays stolen and classified from decades of hotel stays in Zurich, Berlin, Paris, Madrid, Amsterdam. And the task has fallen to her long-lost son, who tells me not only that his mother's young lover, Kosinski, has fled with her foundation's money, but that Rick will pursue the case. To me, the whole place smells not just like leek soup and gas ovens but, as Rick goes through her things, like everything ever lost by all of us, a whole world of regret.

Rick the American doesn't care about any of this. He needs to get to the bottom of things, he says. He would like to stay on here in Finier, right here in her apartment. Maybe get to know his mother, even if she may be a strange cookie. He'll fight the bank, he'll make the place livable, he'll visit her in the sanitarium. He doesn't care. He only shows horror when he unearths a box of hundreds of used pairs of plastic gloves, all in lime-green or yellow. "Is this disgusting or what?" he asks. "Look," he says, opening a new box, urging me to stand up from my repose. "Come here. Test it for me."

I stand on it: a scale so sensitive, one merely twists to make oneself weigh more or less. Watching the numbers run up and down, the two of us start to laugh. The scale makes me wonder what scales themselves weigh, but I have something greater to ask him, the ability to ask another partly a gift from my apprenticeship with Moses. "Is it painful?"

"Not pain," says Rick the American, sitting down. He must be almost done. Surely there can't be all that much more. He stamps one leg then the other on one of the boxes which he's so recently packed.

And then it blurts out of me, the open-faced question: "You told her?"

He sits up, face now a grind of nerves. "Told what?" This may be his first wholly transparent falsehood.

"Between men of honor, surely we can find a way to speak honestly," I say.

"All right," he says. "I did tell." He runs his hands through his hair as if fingertips could script new history into the scalp. "But she didn't believe it. She told me no son of hers would have taken someone's life in such a trivial manner. Then she started with this whole crazy thing about bread and ergot. Exactly what you said. You understand? She said there was this long curse in the Fauret lineage and France and—"

"What?" because he has lost me.

He is leaning forward, touching my knee in a gesture which only a brief while ago might have pricked me with disgust.

"You're not getting it, are you?" he says. "She's crazy. I thought about confessing. I did. Even after you waved me off. The whole way to Finier I thought I'd confess. You meant well," and for a second, he seems able to look out of himself. "You sent me on my way. I know you must have had some kind of connection to *her*," with enough of a quizzical look, I wouldn't mind disappearing back through the pinhole of time, becoming a point which could shrink into the first bit of light which had entered Arianne's eyes and registered itself upon her psyche and brain as *the boy with the hump, Emile Poulquet*.

If only one could go back in time and redirect an impulse in someone else's mind.

"I do have a connection." That's all I want to tell him. "Your mother—we were childhood acquaintances. But so few are left from that time. I'd like to find her. You understand, one gets older—"

We both let this trail off.

"So," he picks up, "here's the thing. I have twin girls at home. Almost teenagers. I'm pretty much responsible for them. One of them's going a little wild, not anything terrible, just you know, adolescents experimenting? She needs me. If I confess, like you said, things could get ugly. My mom's crazy, right? She anyway belongs in a sanitarium. Certain people—"

"Excuse me." I hold up a hand, trying to stop him from himself. "You're sure about what you're saying?"

"I had huge hopes coming here, I did. I was coming to find out about my origins. Look, who wouldn't want to be close to his mother?"

One might think that hearing him would fill me with a sense of justice finally meted out: Arianne getting her comeuppance, a full dose of it. But instead I feel convulsed into rage, one that makes it hard to even grit my teeth, a rage that wants to burst against his logic. His logic which certainly sounds secure and waterproof, weighing one life against another's, contemplating all that he has to offer his daughters as moral exemplar and responsible party.

What I cannot abide is the sneaky sensation of déjà vu: his logic tastes so familiar.

"I want to see her," I say, with all the determination I can muster. "Please. You have the way to bring me, yes?" My time is running out. "Take me to see her."

■ ■ ■

NODDING, unconvincingly, Rick excuses himself. He has to go out, he says, to get more boxes and pick up a couple of sandwiches for us.

"Don't be long," I say. It will be forever before I see her and I try hard as I can to steady my vision, turning away from him, kneeling before a new pile despite a flamelike pain ripping up from my knees.

The American watches me and lets himself out without further word. The pile remains, a welcome place to bury my attention, composed of neatly torn front pages of newspapers, all linking elements unclear, until I notice that the first letter of each first noun in the first headline begins with A. A for Arianne, for the beginning of the alphabet, the aleph of inhalation as a friend in Buenos Aires once told me. Arianne, avancer, arrêter.

Once he has left, I find myself talking to her belongings. "They never knew you," I find myself saying. "None of us did." Arianne now seems no more palpable than a figment of my mind.

BY LATE EVENING, the American and I with him (how could I sit by so uselessly, despite all the fellow's protestations that my presence has been helpful) have Arianne's life wrapped and taped, bagged or twined in our version of order. Some bags will go to charity, some boxes he will keep, the rest he will throw out as waste, the discards of her life. And together, as one man, we put this waste, bags of garbage, all the years of her obsession, out where the collectors will come on Thursday or whenever their most recent strike ends.

BACK IN THE almost bare apartment, we look out the window. It is from there that we see the first of the chestless boys steal forth, one of those wraiths who'd been temporary members of Moses' tribe. I know what this boy is doing: he has come to prowl through the bags. I practically know the inner arcs of his heart, the grasp of his hands, his gut's coil of hunger. He searches for items which might be useful in a nomad's life, showing his own reverse kind of love in how broadly he strews his rejects out over the street, an exhibit of and by the doubly discarded.

FORTY-TWO

Simone has entered, stands behind us, tells me I am lucky, I am witnessing an important moment.

"Witnesses are never lucky," I tell her. I won't meet her eyes, but she gives a disproving laugh. She is a photographer, after all, and has entered the emptied-out apartment to help by documenting the last cleaning-up of Arianne's life. She has brought with her a camera and strong lights which have white umbrellas over them, popping a little explosion as they turn on; and the entire paraphernalia strikes me as funny, turning Arianne's life into a stage set, all of it almost as funny as this newest tribe I find myself a part of—Simone, the American, old Emile still playing Raoul.

Yet the girl's presence is welcome: she speaks as a historian, someone not so connected to this apartment, far more distanced than either the American or I, and this distance helps anchor everyone. There have been, as I've said, so few groups which had invited me in as a child; the war and my position had pushed me into an ill-formed group; and only now in my later years do I seem to be included in groups, or else choose to be in groups, what Moses calls tribes, however multiply forming and radically dispersing they might be.

"Thank you," I say to the lady photographer, who offers me a chair. She gives the air a little schoolgirl kick and pivots around to her camera.

"It's not that I feel shame," Rick is explaining to her, as if she'd asked. "Actually, I feel a bond with my mother. With this place. With Finier. I'd like to raise my daughters here," he proclaims.

"Don't decide too quickly," I advise him. "The place can suck you in."

He looks happy, perhaps as happy as I have felt among the wastrels. "I wouldn't mind being sucked in somewhere."

Simone tells him he's also lucky not to be a native yet. "You will not be blamed for that mess on the street," she says in her English, and at first I think she means something other than what the wraith did with the last of Arianne's detritus. "You are too much the outsider."

"I don't know what you mean," he says, "but it sounds good," before starting to film her again. She must be a magnet for male attention, though this trait had eluded my notice; she wouldn't have been my type exactly, her diffidence too deflective, but she seems to have the same effect on Rick as she did on Moses. The two of them are practically making love, their cameras trained upon each other, until she calls an end to their flirtatious sport.

"Tomorrow." He turns to me. "You can still drive, is that true?" He didn't trust himself yet—I could see that much.

I say I'd try to rise to the occasion. We decide to go in the morning when the light would be better, but the question arises: where to sleep? I can't fathom right now, from within this most recent group, heading back to the squat only to deal with Jacquot and all of them. So it is settled; I take the sofa, the American takes the front room, and Simone heads back to her aunt's place.

■ ■ ■

AT AROUND SEVEN in the morning, the American wakes me. "I want to show you how to work my car," he says. After his offer of bad coffee, I try to arrange my hair into a semblance of order with one of Arianne's old ivory combs. He watches with amusement as I pat a couple of times my pocket where the pendulum and the will are always kept, but who is he to laugh at an elderly man's habits?

We walk out into the morning air where we find, at his Citroën, an older peasant matron with thick mud-caked legs and clogs settling onto his bumper, a woman who has laid her bicycle down so as to set up a temporary fruit-stand on his car's hood, hers a paltry display for early-morning shoppers who, in a marketplace clearly taking place only in her mind, will soon throng around her, craving her dried-up fruit, fruit soon hard as stone.

FORTY-THREE

Driving a tainted car at any age would be hard to do, but how hard it is for me: grip sweaty, pacemaker working double-time every time a truck looms behind us. I often need to pull off to the side of the road, only a few times going into a rut, trying, all the while, to keep my thoughts focused, not wandering toward what I will say to Arianne, what she will say to me, how to identify the right moment in which to hand her the will. "You all right?" the American keeps asking. In between giving driving instructions, he dares to talk, though it should have been clear that I can hear only some of what he says. I muse over the quest he'd kept even from himself. I remembered now his first speech to me on the road, at our first meeting, how he'd said it was his father he'd wanted. In the stench of his gratitude for my silence, now he seems to want to tell me everything.

Both the car and I are reluctant in our southward course, pulling away from the core of Finier. Finally, we chug west, continuing past a boarded-up market, following the river. When the American sees an ancient apple tree spreading on the corner, we are to backtrack, turning left onto a lane flanked by the regal trees I associate more with

Italy than with southern France. This road cannot be separated from its disfigurement: it is both pocked ugliness and wistful loveliness, the cedars tall alongside, the kind of road people think of when they imagine our southwestern slice of the hexagon, a restful country lane with the traffic of centuries embedded in its corrugated mud.

At the end of the drive is a dark wedge of a house and as if it understands that our end is near, the Citroën shows a final burst of enthusiasm. I am squinting out and only at the last moment can say with certainty that we have arrived at some sort of gray country house, settled onto its haunches, open and unguarded, a lemon tree in front, but the over-neat flowerbeds and the walkway make it undeniably an institution.

The proprietor, a matron the American refers to as Chantalle, comes out, a mockery of officialdom in a rumpled gray sheath, wiping her hands on an apron. She leans her sunburnt, garrulous face into the passenger window, already assailing us with speech. "You understand, I take care of the place while the main director is away." The oddness of her face is that one doesn't know which part to believe: the liveliness of her eyes, her quicksilver tongue, or the face with its lines well carved. How could someone look out of such a weathered face with such youthful, curious eyes? I find it disconcerting, as ever unable to see an older woman as my peer. Once she has quite excitedly pointed us toward parking, we follow her to the main house. For all the informality of Chantalle, her manners are refreshingly those of another time. She leads us to a sunroom where she will bring us tea, assuming loudly that we must be tired. Only once does she do a double-take upon my face; then apologizes. "I'm sorry," she says. "At first I thought you looked familiar. Is your name Sal? or Salvatore?"

I am not sure which game I am supposed to be playing. I say Sal suits me fine and it seems she mistakes this for flippancy.

"We must have met," she says, her smile an impetuous young girl's.

"Not impossible, Madame," I say. A couple of years back, I found that accepting the possibility of being known incites less notice than my old habit, a defensive and sarcastic reply. She studies me a half-second longer, but when no further joking comes from old Sal, she puts a finger to her lips, telling us that the half-wit children who also live here are deep in their sleep; we must take care not to wake them, otherwise they'll hang off us the entire visit."

There comes a push in the breeze, a greater insistence. This goes with the matron's tone, forthright like her eyes. Chantalle whispers to the American: "Ah, but the case with your mother. Even for me it's sad. She is succumbing." The word is so forgiving. *Succumbing.* "She may be able to speak to you only from the garden."

She digresses, describes her garden, circling back to what Arianne consents to eat these days. "I'm almost of a mind that you shouldn't see her now," she says, "if you need to see her in her right mind. We've had to give her a veritable bucket of medications." Because Arianne has had a series of bad days. "Now she is propped up mostly by tranquilizers, regrettable—don't you think, sir?—but we've been forced to use them." The patroness says this with the lust of someone denied, shaking her head. "Drugs these days."

"They're useful," I surprise myself by saying.

The son and his mother's keeper slip into a discussion of the relative worth of medications, schedules, intoning words with a chipper scientific cadence, and I can't help but be visited by a shade of Arianne that summer at the old hotel, right before she'd married the son, Arianne who'd kept her mother-in-law hopped up on morphine injections. Already Arianne had been creating a fortress, a privacy which seems to have closed in on her. Has she received her just desserts? Is she another eccentric fulfilling the promise of her earlier idiosyncrasy? *The old become eccentric only if given too much leeway early on*, I say to myself, and then scratch the thought out; I have no clue about the truth of the old, about free or tight rein, I am as eccentric as many, older than most, and have not found a single truth which could explain Emile Poulquet.

As if to shelter myself against the rising wind, and also to give the American privacy, I wander over to the apple tree and lean against its trunk, wondering whether Arianne retained the habit of taking walks leading toward waterways. When I look back the American holds up a finger to me, begging my patience, a sign saying I will understand everything soon enough, but first the son and patroness must confer under the plush shade of a twisted alder tree, emphatic as if engraved within a child's fairy-tale book.

I am so close to seeing Arianne again, the first time since my distanced view of her in the courtroom, but truly, the first time in quite a few years, ever since Paul's funeral and my flight from the janitorial job. It would be the first time we would speak to each other since when I was still prefect Poulquet. I can't keep track of what I'm feeling about this eventuality because by now, son and patroness have exchanged whatever confidences are required and now Chantalle beckons to me, returning to her excitement, turning on me that impetuous young-girl speech, pointing out aspects of her garden, its flaws and potentials, cerisier and lavender, romaron and roses, the sumac californien and pine tree. This is, she says, a garden from which no fruit comes. She hides with a laugh what she says: though none of the women in her family found good husbands, none, all of them have lovely gardens and that has to count for something, does it not, the plants like children, isn't it so, Mister Sal? Finally, she leads me and the son to where we can sit, swinging like fate-driven lovers on the porch swing in a fruitless garden. Behind her, a small boy with a cleft lip and flapping hands has appeared, and as Chantalle takes her leave of us, the boy follows her saying *Romeo? Romeo?* Once she's safely inside the house, we are left stunned by the silence. "Chantalle likes you," says the American, just to break it.

"Ah?"

"It's a good thing," he says. "I haven't met many of these energetic French country women."

"They exist," I say, though since my exile abroad, it has been years since any energetic French country woman has bothered to speak much with me.

The boy with the cleft lip pops his head out of the door, flapping his arms. "She likes you, Romeo," he echoes.

"Go on," says Chantalle. There is a trellis overhung with vines and it makes for a snaggletoothed opening. Beyond sits a white wrought-iron bench on a small, cobbled, sunny clearing. Too much like the gateway to a nightmare, but I approach the opening. There is a half-hidden bench and before it a fountain of a stone maiden in eternal ecstasy, holding her throat, the head in mortal danger of shooting off the top of her body. Chantalle makes a gesture either of impatience or of heaviness, I can't tell the difference, as if shaking an invisible packet. "You just wait. She knows you're here."

AS I SIT on the bench, if I could parse them, the muddle of my thoughts would have something of this melody: a column of figures named yesterday; my drudge of conscience, Arianne, was there ever anything between us? Arianne my relic, dried stains collected and named, hasn't there been a moment, couldn't you admit that in your own seasonless way you loved me? My flesh of thrift, how much better had I lived big and generously like Moses. Your hunger, Arianne, a conversation continuing in me all these years, undoubtedly you will have hardened, Arianne my impotence, once pulling me down in the schoolyard. Cold night, dew frost. Arianne, holding control for so long. Bigger than my nation, Arianne stealing my last free-man's breath. Why did *she* become my referee? My war, ours, did the intimacy of war hold her aloft? Arianne like a blue flame, hunger down to the last bit. So large inside my throat that as janitor, I was unable to speak. That's the burn of it. Arianne my cud, who tore my childhood's skin off and then danced over me. She split me and now I'm more whole, Arianne who knows nothing of my time among the wastrels. Who would find it difficult to admire me. To admit she'd been wrong. About everything. And why the rose dress? My fingers now saying: I had lost the will. No more last will and testament crumpled in my pocket. Where had it gone? Kindling in the crawl space? Arianne who must have known how permanently she would lodge in me. Even without the will, I still had it inside me, I could make her disperse my ashes. Again I'm waiting for the woman. Despite all the life in the interim—my new knowledge, my time with Moses—here I am a naked animal, again fearing her. She has won. Reduced me to this waiting, stripped of will, mind a muddle, gazing up at that open window.

■ ■ ■

BUT THEN the hand creeps out. A thin old-lady's hand, still talonlike, creeping out to bring in a miniature broom left on the veranda. First the broom gets pulled in, then the pot of small pink flowers. Then the hand blindly scrabbles about, searching, finding nothing else to bring in, until it quickly pulls down the white blind behind the curtain.

"She's there," says Chantalle, stating the obvious before heading back into the house by the garden door.

"Arianne!" I say.

"Mom," her American son is saying behind me, his breath foul with anticipation. "Maman." He turns to me. "You want to see her, don't you? You could go upstairs."

I am not sure what I say, all I know is that inside is confusion.

"You want me to get her?" asks the son tenderly; but there's no need for this, as Arianne has come out on the balcony, in a dress of crumpled white linen so thin one can view her body through it.

"That's the delivery boy?" she screeches, her voice more of a smoker's than it had been in the courtroom.

I raise my hand uncertainly, standing to my feet, some ten yards from the house.

"Ah, your posture's the same!" she cries, waving her hands overhead as if I'm a football field away. "You came to pay your respects?" I look to the son but he only shrugs. His mother has sat down on the balcony as if she were a young girl, a wisp of something preserved, swinging her bare legs. "Emile!" laughing as if my name itself were the punchline to a century's joke. "Emile after all!"

"Go on." The son nudges me, whispering. "Maybe she'll be better if you go upstairs."

"Because you know," she says, and her lips are painted a lurid orange, one which reminds me of another sentinel of death. "*I* waited all night for you, Emile!" Here she blows me a kiss in an exaggerated fashion, a lewd gesture, which makes me wonder if her madness is an act, the desperation of someone capable of surviving all of lonely eternity. "All night! Hey, I have gold teeth now!"

"Maybe if we go upstairs," says the American son, but I pay no attention to him, as the face underneath its clown makeup is my conscience; the eyes not just cold marbles but obscene, the shark long gone.

"Oh," I hear, and when I look up to see why the son sounds so distressed, he is also turning away, shielding his sight. Because up there on the veranda, she has lifted her dress so that her pudenda waggles at me, a hairless sex, and she lets out a whoop: this is not conventional warfare.

"Madame!" shouts Chantalle, already running toward the door.

"You thought you'd never see me," says Arianne. To her son, she offers a curt greeting—*hello, egg?*—before lifting the dress fully up over her head. It sounds like she shouts that she's *unscrewing the nameplates*—or is it *how good to see you again!*—from within the folds of her dress.

Yet I'm struck by her power all over: the shivery gift of her nakedness. As if the madness is a cloak. Inside the cloak she finally gives me the gift of honesty, something ultimate, her vulnerability to undo so many years. Admittedly it is perverse for me to find her beautiful, head covered, body bare—I do, all over again.

The American son has taken my arm. "Let's go inside?" he says. "This hasn't happened before. Maybe if we go up, you know, the sitting room or whatever, she'll be calmer?"

But I find I do not want to meet my destination. Not when I'd rather leave it a question whether or not she has gone so fully into the world of the not-intact. I had believed more of her might have remained. Now she may be suffering from a truckload of drugs, like everyone I have met in this past period, no one facing the world without their little helpers. I turn on my heel.

"Spew me out?" it sounds like she yells, dress down. "Don't be unsavory. Emile! Camouflaging!"

And without what she says next, I would have given up hope of being able to reach a sane corner of her mind. There would be no point in recording a testament to give her. But what she ends up saying before returning inside is all too lucid. "We deserved each other, Emile."

"That's a lie," I say, but not too loudly.

"Where are you going?" the American asks me.

I look back to see this, the window upstairs opening a bit more before slamming shut, leaving her alone with the skin and bones of the future.

It doesn't take me long to get in the car. From the house, I see it: a white curtain flutters out like a flag of surrender. Could it be the wind alone?

The American comes running toward me. He jumps into the passenger seat and says *not so fast, can we slow down here?* Yet he chooses to ride with me, shuts the door and sticks his head out of the window too small for his American head. I am turning the car as quickly as I can, but see the female hand, still clawlike, upstairs pulling in whatever has been left outside her window. It pulls in what it can. It pulls in a cane left leaning against the terrace wall. And then there is nothing left for that lady's hand to pull in.

He shouts up to her perhaps the first thing that comes to him.

"We're fine now," he calls in his cowboy French. She might not have heard him over the motor. He repeats it in English. "We're okay, Mom."

The hand raises the blind. Just a bit.

But there is nothing to say. *Romeo*, chirps the boy with the flapping arms, running after the car.

IF I DID have a single thing to say to her, the one who was supposed to finally release me, with her faculties intact, perhaps the truth is that it would have been one sentence: *You lost.*

One might think *you lost* could qualify as triumphal heraldry, the end to our game, a call to go home. But I am shocked that for the very first time I'm having a different thought, which is this: I don't want her to lose. And on the way, trying to drive, calculating the edge of the road, the distances between the cars ahead and the cars behind, my hand almost too tight on the knob to change gears, the car dying only a few times, I find myself thinking this consolation: perhaps her madness is only temporary and drug-induced. When we stop, for the American to settle his stomach, I consult my pendulum, constrained by its annoying black-and-white view of all situations: DO I GIVE UP HOPE?

NO, it says primly.

Yet someone might be deluding himself. She is too far gone. There is little hope that I might pass on my document to her, that her comprehension might be large enough to understand all that has happened since her first sighting of Emile Poulquet.

FORTY-FOUR

Everything has its own private retribution: no one can only win or lose forever.

That Sunday morning, Moses, Delhi and I take our few clothes and go to the laundromat, where a new wealthy old lady in town does her laundry, fulfilling the role our town must require, another woman hiding her wealth in our time-honored habit. I respect her attitude. I also give her as wide a berth as she gives us wastrels. Yet she is the one who mentions to us, as though a kind of hiccough, that it is good we are well-mannered, because there has come down from the mayor's office a straitened municipal injunction against people like us, furthering the powers lent the mayor by the EUROPE ruling. It is a penalty affixed to the EUROPE command: a sentence and fine for people like us, people sans-logements, sans-papiers, sans everything.

· · ·

AND MOSES BELIEVES her immediately, while Delhi is more suspicious. When we discuss it afterward in our cave, our clothes sweet-smelling, enough to make anyone's spirit optimistic, it is Jacquot who, lying awake, having been unable to sleep all night, bug-eyed and twitchy, notices me. I have flinched at a certain phrase. He picks it up, clearly in a mood to insult. He turns to me and asks how does it feel to be Raoul Tavelle, included in this rout?

"There's an injunction against you too. Against people like us. Not allowed to stay. You like that?" saying the phrase again in his most violent manner so that it becomes a cattle-brand. *People like us.*

Delhi believes the lingering, if dwindling, presence of foreign journalists has led to the injunction's severity.

Cerb-X snorts. "You were the one who liked getting publicity, Delhi. Talking to the lady reporter. Your mistake."

Moses thinks otherwise, pointing out that not only have most of the reporters filtered out of Finier, sensing a waning story, but also that journalists don't make the news, they only report it.

Whatever the case, throughout the day we hear the word everywhere. Squatters will be marched out of their homes because of the injunction, which many believe has come down belatedly from the mayor's office so that the entire town will look clean, active, and prosperous for any future arrival of journalists, any future events. Finier, having been in a bit of a depression because of the mean, self-interested international bullies of agribusiness, is now only to summon up, if squalor is present, *a medieval charming squalor*, along with a few men playing boule, since there might be a new influx of journalists once the reunion resumes in full. Which it should, promptly, as Arianne Fauret, involved in this enterprise for at least a decade, will come back to recommence activities!

"Not likely," I say under my breath.

LATER IN THE DAY, I am almost cheered when an old man in a bistronnaise glares at me, followed by his shorter friend. *They have come back after all!* I tell myself, watching the slow start-up to a game of boule. I hear them waxing peevish and petulant about the tardiness of the injunction, and how glad they are that there will be no more disinhabited and homeless maghrebins or French kids playing their guitars with their change caps overturned.

"No more stray dogs," one boule-player says, happily.

I want to ask where the players have been hiding but don't, sitting on a bench until my legs go numb, excited beyond words to see them again. Almost more excited, I realize, than I'd been about the prospect of seeing Arianne when I'd thought she was still wholly intact.

"Get rid of the dogs and we get rid of the wastrels," says another.

WHEN DELHI and Moses and I go to buy bread later in the day, the middle-aged lady baker turns toward me a pitying smile. This woman, who always adds extra buns and loaves for Moses, leans forward to say it might be advisable for us to return to our families, wherever we have people who care.

"You're saying I should go back to my father who left our family?" Delhi asks her. "That's nice. I'll follow him and his new wife around. I'll follow him until he turns around and says *not you again*."

"I'm sorry," says the baker. "Maybe you could go back to your country?"

"This *is* my home," says Delhi. "I was born here, lady."

"She's just trying to be helpful," says Moses, unable to harmonize everyone.

Barely out of the bakery, grabbing an extra bun from Moses, Delhi says: "These people don't have a clue of what they are up against."

So there is an injunction, and what we are up against is this: as we head to the Bar Central, we see them. Workers are sweeping down on the rival tribes. We see groups of civil employees, three or four at a time, knocking on the useless front doors of abandoned buildings. The workers wear natty blue costumes like those our wartime plumbers used to wear, with silver gloves and billed hats, a handsome silver sash wrapped across the chest. We watch two tribes practically marched out of their squats, among them the jawing, wraithlike wonders I'd seen the first night in our new squat. On the chest bands of these modern-day routers, on their silver sashes, a lovely early French script spells out the UNITED EFFORT FOR THE RESETTLING OF THOSE WITHOUT PAPERS OR ESTABLISHED DWELLINGS, explaining what the unfortunate acronym of EUROPE has meant. Moses had misquoted it to me, and the actual idea is uglier than what I've imagined.

I RETREAT back to the crawl space, able to peer at the action through the wall-crack which up until now has been my own little window, covered most nights with a discarded chamois but now unplugged so I can better sight the plombiers, men dispersing across the street with eminent gestures and big flashlights.

According to Jacquot, the survivors' reunion has recommenced on its own, without Arianne's foundation cursing it. The survivors have gone so far as to arrange for their own concert, in a few days, and have independently reinvited journalists to the event.

That this routing by EUROPE should happen as I am recovering from a worsening cough, the malady which has never fully gone away ever since my river adventure, is particularly unlucky. I want to stay in bed, such as it is, a coverlet and matted newspapers under me, just a few more days, at least one solid night, until I get my throat and chest back, since whatever I have caught (and I don't want to blame anyone, not my new friends, not the shock of seeing Arianne lost to herself) could be the start of tuberculosis, though my pendulum refuses to confirm such self-diagnosis.

I cannot help hacking out now and again, doing so just as one of the workers stands outside, nearby, speaking importantly to a neighbor right outside our house about the EUROPE effort. My cough could disclose the entire location and lose us our dwelling. But I have a rampaging beast inside, catching me by its horns, tossing me up, making me unable to stop. Of course I am aware of the need for silence. I certainly do not need Jacquot coming over and almost punching me on the arm to shush me each time I cough, but trying to tell him this makes me only cough more.

I will not stay at room 316 at the Hotel Fauret: yet which is worse, the onslaught of memory or the onslaught of the present? I decide to take a walk by the river, see if the greater humidity cures anything, and return for a regrouping of forces. In all honesty, I cannot believe that Arianne will find her mind enough to *comprehend* what I want to give her.

FORTY-FIVE

On my return, I see Delhi in the square, wearing a long purple jacket and a puffy hat that makes her head into a tall leather soufflé. She is being collared just outside the squat by one of the silver-sashed officials volunteering for EUROPE.

I stop in front of the Café de la Place to understand the scene better. Inside, Olivier leans over a table of prefecture employees, making them laugh. No one sees me as I hug the building near the small fruit shop, sidling toward the corner. The man with his silver sash collaring Delhi is quite old, I can see that much from his hunch. Delhi clearly doesn't want to disclose where the squat is, but inside, a dog, perhaps her Lula recognizing the scent of the beloved, starts to bark out the joy of impatience. I am not thinking as I approach the man.

He presses his stick horizontal against Delhi's forward passage, his voice tired, carrying out orders. "Look, you're going to have to show me an identity card or else leave Finier. Can't you find some other suitable place to live with all your—?" He waves the baton in disgust.

"I have a right to be here, man," Delhi keeps saying, chin out, her tone strained as it had been that morning. "I have as much right to be here as you do."

"Are you a Chinese?" he says, and she says nothing. "Japan lady?" He pulls his eyes long. "I may have to take you in," he says, removing a pager from his belt, starting to dial in a number. "Stay right there," using his stick to block her.

Delhi sees me before the EUROPE router does, but stays fixed on the man, purposely squinting back at him. This is when I move to the side, trying to recognize who possesses such a familiar voice.

Cagnon, gone gray, rumpled and tired-looking, Cagnon the young boy janitor from my first days at the prefecture. Cagnon, routing Delhi, now a volunteer for EUROPE.

I AM NOT thinking as I change my habits, stepping forward, saying hello.

"Shouldn't you be in retirement now?" I ask Cagnon. I see he doesn't recognize me so I say a bit more. "You could be gardening, you know. You used to be so good with uprooting geraniums. With planting nasturtium beds."

And he furrows his brow at me, reassembling my face from bits of memory, seeing the same look in my eyes, perhaps, the same dark hazel eyes which have always been mine, despite the many sculptural alterations to the landscape around them.

"You used to be so good with nasturtiums," I repeat the nonsense. I touch his bar and gently ease it away. "Eh, Cagnon? You were a good janitor. You can let this one go, eh?"

And he does, to my surprise. "Hello," he says. "Good to see you again, sir," fully knowing me as Emile Poulquet before vanishing down the lane toward the main street.

FORTY-SIX

We've been given a final night of work, added on, we're happy about it, having been asked to paint the inside of the decrepit house which will become the temporary memorial museum in honor of Paul and the other resistance fighters. We turn the scratchy radio on low. By just a few of the lights, we jump to action, or, that is to say, Moses does and I, who couldn't even furnish my former apartments, am fairly useless, coughing at the fumes, but I make stabs at painting, a stroke here, a stroke there. Moses, however, is forgiving; he says he will begin with the southern wall and I will take the northern; we'll meet at the western wall and then cross east for detail-work around the windows.

There is something about the mild trance one enters while painting which is probably what makes me say it. "Moses," I tell him, never having used his name so nakedly. "I've gotten used to our life."

"Is that bad?" he asks, without looking at me.

"I just don't know where it will lead."

"Have you ever known where anything leads?"

"I'm uncomfortable around Jacquot."

"Who isn't?" and he continues working. "That's the guy's specialty. He makes people uncomfortable. He gets off on that." After a few minutes, he turns to me. "I really wanted the best for you."

"I can see that."

"Wherever we head, you know that, right?"

"Are you going to some harvest we don't know about?" my voice comes out, a bit weak.

"Not exactly," he says. "Not going anywhere."

"I don't turn my back to Jacquot when I sleep."

"That counts."

"I feel I'm going to be stabbed in the back."

"It's understandable." He puts down his brush. "Actually, it's not. Don't go paranoid on us."

"I'm not going anywhere."

"There's something you want me to do? I mean, about Jacquot?"

"What could you do? You might say something to him, perhaps."

On the radio, a gentle love song of sorts plays. It has turned a bit manic, possessing the sound of a single man in a smoky cabaret.

"I love this singer," says Moses. "Will you listen to this?"

I have holes
Small holes
Small holes des petits trous des petits trous.

After the song is over, we drop mention of Jacquot, or of Moses interceding for me. He asks if I don't mind if he takes a small break. Can he leave me to finish up? He asks if he can take a doze. But will the mayor's office eventually pay us? "Good man," he says. "I forgot. We *were* paid." He presses one hundred francs into my hand. "That's your half," he says. "See how this can go?"

"You're generally the luckiest of people," I say, not meaning it to sound sarcastic.

"It's my attitude," he says. "That's the only difference between us. Attitude is everything."

"So you have the attitude of a lucky boy." I am somewhat vacant, watching him untie his hair. It whorls out in that half-lit room like thousands of snakes alive on his head. He bunches up that hair under his neck as a kind of pillow and lies down on a table in the middle of the room, asking me to wake him when it is all over.

"All over?"

"In the morning." He stretches long on the table. "Your childhood was sad."

"Not sad."

"But you told me about the foxhunts and mushrooms."

"And the stablehand."

"And the stablehand. You make it sound like it was one big cul-de-sac."

"I never told you about the Polish nursemaid."

"Ah, the nursemaid," and he smiles somewhere under his beard. "Is that a joke?"

"Should it be?"

"I had a nursemaid too. You better keep that one private."

"Why do you say cul-de-sac?"

"It just came out."

"Don't you think childhood has that quality? A cul-de-sac? You can't see beyond it. You go around and around, you don't go through. You enter life and it's all set up for you. One big cul-de-sac."

"You're turning obscene, Mister Tavelle," he says. "Get some sleep. You'll need it."

"But the job—"

"Yeah, get the job done first." He is already dozing. "I'm counting on you," he says. "You know me," he says.

I DO KNOW HIM, I think, stroking the paint in long stripes, learning the pleasure of it. As I do what I think is the last of the work, the gold oddly beautiful under the sills, gleaming, thick, the whole room throbbing with life, I have returned to being as happy as I'd been with Natalie. Or does memory of her distort, these days, more each minute, an already fractured glass losing its pattern? Perhaps Natalie and whatever she had been to me was a greater sum than I can now recall, painting and with Moses sleeping behind me. It is hateful how the present forever vanquishes the past, then dares to hoot over its spoils of war. Because caught in my repetitive activity, stroking the paint, forgetful, I am impossibly at peace.

FORTY-SEVEN

"You're still there," says Moses, half-opening one eye. We have been all night inside a room with awful fumes but morning's arrival makes my sojourn worthwhile, raising a sheen on the gold paint. I must have dozed off as well, slumped against the one unpainted door.

After cleaning up, back in the fresh air, the two mutts following us, their tongues affectionate and slobbery after their outside vigil, I am telling Moses something about what I remember about my childhood's Polish nursemaid when he stops me. Not far away, a train whistle blows.

"Hey," he says, stuck in place. "The local stops five hundred meters from here."

"This walk back to Finier is quite enjoyable. I don't mind it, really. We are not so far from—"

"Hey." He takes my hand, looks straight into me. "Remember that other time? You were getting on the train?"

"What's your point," I say, not liking his warm grip.

"Maybe now's the time. You could hop on the local. Hide in the bathroom. Get to Spain and you know."

"Why?" I shake him off, strangely hurt. "You're the one who brought me back to Finier." I walk several paces ahead of him, stiff, wanting to get away.

"I'm trying to say something here," says Moses. "Maybe it was a bad idea for you to meet me."

"You're a wonderful boy," I tell him, "but aren't you hungry as well? Shall we keep going? See if your admirers left anything? A croque monsieur? Rack of lamb in shallot sauce?"

"Listen, Raoul. I'm saying maybe you should get on the train." He hunches down between his dogs. "My leg's cramping up. I'm trying to say it's not comfortable with us. You'd be better off elsewhere."

"Does this have to do with what I said? About Jacquot and his back-stabbing?"

"No," says Moses. "Yes. You'd save your skin if you got on that train. Really," he says. "Jacquot's crazy. This would be good. Please. Just take in what I'm saying."

"Your angels are telling you this?"

He looked at his hands, as if expecting them to tremble. "No," he said. "I can't lie. It's just a feeling. I'm trying to share it."

"You shouldn't pussyfoot," I say, not liking my own trembling voice, a voice which used to carry me through the worst moments but which now springs leaks. "Just say you don't want the old guy around anymore." I'm walking again, as fast as I'm able.

"Shit, would you slow down? My leg's all seized up," says Moses, hobbling only to crouch again.

"I am not sure what you want from me. After all. Why you think you can speak so coarsely. I have the rights of a human being. I can choose to stay elsewhere. Perhaps we've grown too familiar with each other."

He catches up, tottering but fuming, his braids radiating out. "Man, don't go all nuancy. It's not about choice. Listen. Please." His eyes not hazel after all but a hot green, if green could be the color of fire, the dead center of flame. "I'm saying you'd help us both if you'd clear out."

He sees I cannot buy what he offers and kicks the earth, muttering.

"What?" I say.

"Never mind."

I go back to walking, over my shoulder telling him surrender is not in my nature, that it is not as if the earth is going to open up and swallow us if I don't follow his ideas.

"Stop already!" he says, again trying to catch up.

"You said you wanted me to leave," I say.

"Raoul, you high on fumes?"

"I have other places—"

He takes hold of my coat, making me swing around toward him.

"What do you want from me?" I ask.

We are on one of those roads which could be anywhere in the Bistronne, apple blossoms a dried foam atop the grass, smoke rising from a distant hut, the broken clank of cowbells. Exactly the kind of place for which I thirsted during my time of exile.

"You're crazy." He is crying. "I don't know what it takes." And then does the thing, the unspeakable. Sinks his teeth into the flesh of his own arm. Draws beads of blood on the underside. Actually waves the bloodied arm in my face, all while his dogs yelp.

"You shouldn't—" I try to restrain myself but am moved to a terrible sympathy. "Come. Circus tricks won't get me to leave."

"Look. I'm saying." His eyes almost catchable, alive, like those of a passenger on a train one has just missed, intent just before passing on. He arrives at his decision. "Come with me then. It's your own funeral." We are walking again, talking of nothing, Moses limping, holding his arm to staunch the blood. Not quite side by side, not leader and follower, just held in a brace, two men passing through a tunnel of twisted trees. A dog barks far away before he speaks again. "Were you always such a stubborn old goat?"

FORTY-EIGHT

Back at the squat that afternoon, the mood is terrible: not just Jacquot but Delhi as well won't stop badgering me.

My only recourse is succumbing to exhaustion and the codeine medicine Delhi offers me. In the dream, because it is dark I am not sure who they are bringing but when I see her, Moses says: "Go on, you wanted to meet." Far from the facts of who I used to be, I stand trembling, turning away again to find her standing also in the other direction, a slim blur on a leaf-trodden path behind a fence, like the sole picture I retain from our bistronnaise deportation camp, in which a lady not unlike Natalie waits for me. The kerchief she wears makes her eyes huge and glittery, though not mad, calm like a fisherman's night lanterns, the bony figure of death herself.

"We've gotten old," I say to her through the fence. "Did you ever think we'd become so old?"

But it is Arianne Fauret after all, both bully and summer-hotel young lady, laughing sanely, wearing a little-girl dress the white of curtains, lilies, sanitariums. "You don't want to know what I've seen," she says. We find ourselves climbing a mountain together and she asks if it is true, that I have asked them to do me a favor. "What is that favor?" I ask.

"You requested this," she says, insistent as ever. At the top the ground seems holy, waiting for us. "You want to be Saint Simeon Stylites," she says. "Bigger than life. I am sorry. Poor Emile." She is somber now, fittingly grave, handing me an old implement from Charlot's stables, some last sentiment I've salvaged, a horse-brace which, after I fasten it on my torso, hoists me high above the cross and beyond the clouds to some place which will never let me return again to Finier.

FORTY-NINE

Light veins the butcher squat and Delhi tells us she wants to join the EUROPE people. Not that she'll be expelling squatters, nothing like that, she's just heard about some desk job with the EUROPE bureau, open to those without experience. They're offering decent wages, benefits.

"Look, I'm saying it's easier to change the world if you get inside the skin of the enemy," she tells Moses. "Anyway, I can't cut this. It's too unsteady a gig. Working and living here and there. I'm used to a different quality of life. I'm an artist! I used to write songs. Anyway, I *like* working. Hey, Raoul. You should leave here too," she says to me. "You don't really belong."

I try not to flinch: it appears that Delhi is turning something not so different from the Look upon me.

"No?" I say casually. "Where do I belong?"

"You need a garden," she says. "A quiet place to watch flowers. Let bygones be bygones." She holds my gaze and then returns to packing.

Moses sits in his buddha posture without protesting any of this. He actually starts in with his low chant, using that indecipherable eastern language which he employs on such occasions. *Eaumaniepadmieheume.*

"You don't have anything to say, lion man?" She turns on him.

"Hey, your choice," he says. "Just don't report us. We have to stay low. Especially now," raising an eyebrow with uncertain emphasis.

"Hey, I'll help you out," she says.

"Sure," says Moses, returning to his chant.

"Seriously. Who do you think I am? I'll check in on you now and again. Not when I'm in uniform."

"I'm just saying," says Moses. "Be careful not to do anything you wouldn't be proud of."

Cerb-X is in a fine sulk, sliding her nose-ring back and forth through the new hole. "C'mon," says Delhi to her.

Which unleashes Cerb-X's tirade. "I can't hear your bull, Delhi. We were going to get tattooed together, right? Fuck all that stuff about stability. Can you get any more permanent than a tattoo? I was going to get you a line down the back of your legs. Like stockings. I was even going to pay."

"Maybe we could do it still?" says Delhi, to which a thudding silence comes her way. She bundles her belongings into her backpack. "Here," she says, flinging me a pair of men's tennis shoes she's been carrying around. "These don't suit me anymore."

"You have other shoes?" I say, noting the shiny new leather shoes she has on.

Moses stops his low chant, puts his nose close to her feet, apparently in admiration. "You're another rich girl slumming it."

"It doesn't mean I haven't been sincere," she says. "Try the sneakers on, Raoul. What you've been wearing are almost dead. You have small feet, I think."

I try them on, the squat paying uncomfortable attention to me. "Comfortable," I say, embarrassed to have my feet called small. "Springy."

"Will make you a young man again," says Delhi. "More than what I've been able to do."

"This whole thing has been," I say, searching. "Rejuvenation."

"That's what we wanted." Moses with a carnival barker in his voice.

"People come and go but people like you, Raoùl, you are staying by me for the long haul."

"You're always telling me to leave or stay," I say, unable to keep a plaintive note out of my voice. "You don't know what you want."

"No, man. I'm just saying. You can't just *leave*. Not without saying anything, like old Delhi over here. That's our contract," says Moses. "We need you. Hang *out*. Now that old Delhi is betraying us—" and he ducks from a thrown apple core. "We'll be okay. People like us need each other."

FIFTY

After that, I sleep most of the morning, I suppose, using more of the codeine draught to rid myself of my cough, almost successful. When I wake, Moses is coming in from the outside, hair matted down under a new baseball cap. He says we should take the dogs for a walk. "Can't you let me sleep a little more?" I ask, the cough seizing me all over.

"You might be interested," he says. "Your lady's being led into town. The people from the reunion are going to create a little procession behind her as she goes to her arraignment. It's a chance, man. You could give her your little novel. You know, your will."

"I lost it," I say. This is true; I hadn't been able to find it since the previous day.

"But I found it." He waves the will in front of me. "You threw the thing in the *dumpster*, man."

"I don't think I did," I say. "That must have been someone else."

But he doesn't pay attention. "Maybe she'll be more together this time or whatever."

I can't say I'm not interested. Not to mention that I feel happy he'd reclaimed my will, however almost illegible it has become, wrinkled, ketchup-spattered. So I agree, pulling on my raincoat, crawling out into the square. There the refugees are amassing in little groups, politely looking away from such scruffy wonders as Moses and myself.

"She won't be here for a while," he says. "We can get a better view on things if we're not part of the parade. We need to get above it." All of which makes perfect sense.

HE LEADS ME back above town on the old goat-path above the aquifer. The sky has turned a poisonous blue, so rich it is practically pungent, unlikely for this part of France in late summer. It is surely what Moses curses it as being, a sign of an imminent storm, and it probably does have to do with what he calls the freakish melting of the polar ice caps and worse.

"Our imprints are everywhere, it's inescapable," I tell him, "you can't run away from humanity—"

But he doesn't listen. Ahead of us, coming from the rail station, the hubbub approaches. "A real crowd," I say, with some admiration. "She can still get herself a crowd."

We hang back for a moment, sitting down where we are, behind an ancient apple tree on the goat-path, just above the puckered U made by the walls of the aquifer.

The group is determined, pushing forward. The bordering walls along the lane are rounded, the better to contain water and sludge. The result of this is that humans walking on the lane are not tempted to dawdle but move forward with as much lack of questioning as running water, the crowd thus making a formidable onrush. The American is with Arianne—he's holding her arm—startling me. With his shock of hair, for a second he appears like a shade of my prior self. Surely he does not look that dissimilar to how I must have appeared, in front of my mirror at the hotel, back when she burst into my room so many summers ago.

She has pulled herself together, apparently, enough for this walking of the gauntlet. Above on our embankment, a few homes stand, self-enclosed and permanent, their stone boundary fences removed enough from the fray to give us both trees to hide behind and our narrow walkway. It is on this path that we follow the crowd, not far behind Arianne. I could practically reach down and touch the subtle, tantalizing whorl at the top of her head, a now-platinum head: as if she'd used verdigris and flame to burn herself into an idol.

Among the crowd are the few reporters who've stayed on, of both breeds, both the rumpled-bemused and the more avid sort. Those who follow her most closely, however, have greedy faces, and among them I pick out the talkative American named Martin. Also the gum-snapper Barbie Rotesc, who pushes a microphone into Arianne's face. For once I am above all the experts.

Moses nudges me, possessed by some comic urge. "Maybe you should do something really flagrant," he says. "Go visible. Dive into them. Maybe you could make history," he says. "Free us both."

"Too late," I say.

"Come on." He nudges me again. "It would be killer."

"You really want me to jump?"

"Don't take the joke so personally, man."

ARIANNE IN PROFILE after all still has refinement. Dressed again as a proper lady, not so winnowed by the years. There is that same glitter in her eyes as when I'd seen her, but perhaps her craziness had been an act. Should I lean down now and offer her the document? My testament. Will it matter? Or is she still so addled from pills and injections that I could never get her to redeem me?

I'M FINGERING it all over with some nervousness, hating to admit how seeing her hypnotizes me all over again. The lady is sharpened, the collection of all the destinies she claimed to have amassed. And now squinting at the big-boned reporter. "What did you say your name was?" Arianne is acting, her English a stately monotone, that of another age, one which makes it sound as if all folly has been drained out. "Barb Croquette? Or what did you say?"

"Rotesc," Barbie says. "Rotesc. Excuse me, do you have any feelings about being held culpable for two weeks, being released only to be committed to a sanitarium, when some are alleging there have been some behind-the-scene strings pulled at the court? Due to a payoff which brought you a lighter sentence?"

"I am sorry, my dear." Only now do I hear the tinge of drugs. "I am just relieved the ordeal is over."

"She has no comment for you!" says the American, a bearded, defiant son. "She takes the Fifth!"

I LOOK DOWN to study a recent addition I'd made to the will, a third piece of paper I'd added just after my visit to the sanitarium:

> ITEM, therefore, to ~~Arianne Fauret~~ those who can understand, ~~I~~ Leaving all the names I have ever been called. ~~She who~~ Whoever was responsible for my undoing should understand at least this: that perhaps the very first time ~~I~~ we heard jews being called stealers of chickens, stealers of bicycles, the words were soothing, a palliative. Perhaps ~~she~~ such people can sacrifice the ease of the morally righteous, that particular <u>laziness</u> of those who believe themselves to be superior. Perhaps ~~she~~ they can understand how one's spirits can be lifted when the spotlight of being the enemy moves off of oneself and onto others, and what special redemption this can hold.
>
> And ~~I say~~ we say this only now, with a latterday understanding. Back then, ~~I had no understanding of~~ we did not understand the partial suicide which one must commit in order to hate.
>
> While the idea of jews as stealers of chickens did seem fairly based in reality, for the following reason. In our childhood, ~~I had seen with my own eyes~~ we had seen an old man who was poking around ~~my~~ father's chicken coop, a man who fled too quickly for old Charlot to catch him. When asked about the man's identity, Charlot claimed he'd known the man was a jew by the threadbare purple twill jacket he wore. <u>Have you ever seen a real Frenchman wearing such a jacket?</u> Charlot had asked, <u>so ratty?</u> and the question, in its impregnable clarity, made a huge impression. Unlike most ordinary people, jews could be known from their backs.
>
> ~~As for myself, I~~ We knew the jew to be a man apart, someone who strove for things which came more naturally to the native sons of France. And this was a subject one could hear in conversation. It was often those who were perhaps not so well versed in reading and

letters who were best able to assert a certain truth about the people capable of threatening France's very integrity. The jews were a threat contained within, a wind throughout us.

Do you understand that much, ~~Arianne~~? You who heard these conversations as much as ~~I~~ we did. Those who were more enlightened did claim there could be good jews as much as there were bad jews. And the good ones were those who were most like us, that much we understood.

But jews did not go to church. Not that we ever did so much, either, except for midnight mass before Christmas. Nor did jews eat the kind of game we hunted, or at least not much of it. They also controlled banks and newspapers, as well as certain foreign governments; and, so far as ~~I~~ children understood, they used the blood of Christian children to make their communion wafers, which they called dreyfusards. Besides that, they did all kinds of things that set them apart from the truth that ran deep beneath the rocks of our France. You know this as well as ~~I do, Arianne~~ anyone.

So in our childhood we'd wanted to see the ocean or the sea but we were scared of it. Because when we'd asked our grandfathers from where the jews had arisen, we'd heard that they'd come from across the ocean, so we imagined them arriving in constant waves, heaps of purple-clothed people purpling even the tips of the waves. We saw jews arriving on land like wet dogs with their noses long and bloodthirsty, their noses sniffing the earth for a grub totally different from that which we depended on for our own replenishment. They had to grub more than others, that was how it had been explained to me, this was their doom.

And between the jew and my land, there was a link, more than we understood then. Because in our childhood we felt apart from nature—nature was a mediated affair. There were treetops that could be exquisite in one moment, trees that would fall upon you the next. It was not that we did not consider ourselves sons of God, or of history, by being so set apart by such things as a monstrous hump on the face, which delighted ~~you so much Arianne.~~ others. It was that we required an intermediary to reach nature, to explain its ways. Old Charlot our stablehand was that, ~~whom you never met,~~ Charlot a benign priest, his hands and eyes tutored by nature; and it was Charlot who helped us understand what we were really chasing.

By the hunt and the chase, one could better know the vast and unknowable: nature asserted who was on top. Hunt and chase, and you could eventually wolf down the unknowable, assuring your place in a hierarchy, however slippery it could seem. For always there were roofs that could be battered down by our fearsome thunderstorms, or snow that made us housebound for weeks at a time, barely able to find our way in a landscape gone so white, when only tree trunks and shovel handles and paths to the houses made a dark script across our land.

And in just the way that we stayed apart from nature, we found ourselves in society, after we'd had the hump removed, finding a link to the rest of the world by the discreet things one could let slip out about jews. They appeared to be from some unlucky phylum. The bulk of them on this earth were a natural excrescence, something sapping our energy. We did not want to be commingled with them and have our native resources tapped. If they were not always our scapegoat, at least they offered a good subject for complaint. ~~I am sure, Arianne, in the private recesses of your mind, wherever you stay most sane,~~ You too must add to my will this particular legacy: your admission that you too have entertained morally untenable ideas about jews.

"But make a decision," says Moses. "Either jump forward or hang back, man. You're going all visible on me. You don't really want all those reporters in your face, do you?"

"What do you mean?" and I look at him for a moment with some anxiety.

"Nothing. Don't go crazy. I'm just saying."

In the end, I give her nothing, I don't, not with her son behind her, husbanding her with a light hand on her shoulder where the fur of her coat ends and the light cloth begins; she has gone on toward the prefecture, where I assume that there too she will be shocked by the orange graffiti that has appeared there in the last several days.

FIFTY-ONE

(first) I did not know how many would be affected
(second) I did not ask for others to manipulate me as they did
(third) I was young myself

In the Paris cafés, among the red velvet seats and the fringed lamps, the mother and daughter are having an aperitif to celebrate the half-success of their case against eighty-four-year-old Poulquet, who had signed the deportation notices of thousands of jews. Poulquet tried in absentia, Poulquet commissioned to life in prison. But the rascal! Gone, lost, slipped out, nowhere visible, not one to be captured for either his latest trial or sentence. Having fled the well-timed grasp of the lawyers. While they conjecture, mother and daughter, half-congratulatory and mystified, considering the particular legacy of halfness left by a fugitive, who leaves people feeling split around themselves, nodding, jaws tight in their trajectory, knowing, not knowing, filled with self-satisfaction at their mystification, spinning conspiracy theories, geographical theories, folding and unfolding newspapers and maps to help rectify the imbalance, considering one finite act in the great unknowability and miasma, there he is. In an unknown border hotel mocked up to be a Swiss chalet, something undoubtedly attractive to foreign tourists of the discriminating ilk, a hotel overlooking a quiet lake, a simple and neat fact for which no one has to search.

>   (fourth) No one knew what was really going on
>   (fifth) Most of France would have behaved as I did
>   (sixth) It had been encoded in our national ethics as a point of pride, the requirement to be a good bureaucrat
>   (seventh) I had always lacked a clear moral compass, whether in the form of a mentor or a group around me
>   (eighth) the jew Tropied and his case had humiliated the French army and thus contributed to its losing the war

I could be the Poulquet they're looking for, whom they imagine in a room with a white pitcher and basin, a neatly folded towel hanging on the metal rack, so ready and pristine, the glass doors a crack opened onto the veranda from which one can engage in reciprocity: one can take in the breeze and also overlook all the Swiss promenaders. Poulquet himself: freshly shaven, enjoying being clean again, in a hotel again, eyeing the bathers outside. His gray beard and whiskers now clumped in a tiny mountain, a memorial to the previous disguise, a hump on the rim of the white basin. He wears strong eye-surgery sunglasses against the glare entering his room, getting used to the new disguise, but peruses a photo album which he'd not given himself leisure or luxury to peep at earlier, the album he'd smuggled along with him all this time, compiled of old newspaper clippings listing his commendations and exploits.

>   (ninth) My village ran along rules similar to those I used when I had to make my decisions—witness what happened to the family of Luc, the idiot, how his trespasses had been tolerated within the village
>   (tenth) Only later history, rather than the moment in which I made certain admittedly weaker choices, judges me

In the photos I could be Poulquet as full-cheeked adolescent standing before the bridge and the ill-cut boundary fence separating the river from the summer restaurant near where rosemary once grew in profusion, the hotel where the young lady with the gapteeth had once walked in and then backed away, her clawlike hands in protest as if she were more ashamed.

A young boy with a graceful neck after all, dark hazel eyes, a crown of black hair.

> (eleventh) Later in life I became a more self-directed agent
> (twelfth) Who can ever be what they are in any given moment?
> (thirteenth) Toward those I thought I cared for, I was never false
> (fourteenth) Eventually we all die and Natalie as well would have at some point
> (fifteenth) I have neither given nor taken more than was my share
> (fifteenth again) I have no spawn or seed that I know of and hence
> (fifteenth again) I have not polluted the world
> (fifteenth again) I tried to protect Delhi
> (fifteenth again) In one of the cities I stayed in, which will go unremarked here, I cared for an old lady when no one else did, did her shopping and her accounting and took her dead body to the morgue and incanted my own private devotions to her memory
> (fifteenth again) I was never an open manipulator like others I'd known

The priest is a new young fellow, younger than I'd thought, thick-fleeced and too short for his vestments, with a fallen brow and a tendency to blink too much before breaking into a wrecked laugh. I want to care about him as much as he clearly cares about something in his vocation. Sitting in the booth, shadows draw across his face, lending him an approximation of deathliness, but the borrowed dignity fails to open my heart.

"I would like to tell you who I am," I confess. "I came to the church because there's nowhere else for me to go."

"You're always welcome here," he says, the words intoned by

something other than him, enough that he almost looks startled at their close.

"I'm saying I wish there were a way to return toward being a pure soul. I used to hunt as a boy, you know."

"You feel tortured."

"Something *is* torturing me."

"Our being tortured has to do with how we perceive and then treat life's demons. That is why we are both here," says the priest.

I rise in the booth, struck with rage at the priest's platitudes, a rage I've not fully felt since the era of servicing Galtimer. The man has no idea about what it means to desire purity as much as I do, no idea of my copulation with time or history and how bad a marriage it has been. I want to fit both my hands around his sacred priestly throat and shake him until deep in the interstices of his divinely attuned cerebral cortex, he understands this and what it means to have been tortured Emile.

Instead I half-mutter a penance, apologizing. "Forgive me, father," I say. "An emergency has come up."

THAT AFTERNOON, Moses meets me outside the refugees' hall, where I have fallen asleep against my tree. "The seasons practically changed overnight," says Moses. He brushes a leaf off me, tenderly. "Hey. You were shivering. For a long time."

"You were watching me?"

"And you're sitting on pigeon droppings, man. Caked up. Don't you need a jacket?" He himself is bundled up, his hair overflowing over two mismatched jackets of differing lengths so that he looks like an uprooted bit of vegetable matter.

"I need nothing from anyone," I say, unable to stop shivering. But he doesn't take no for an answer, making me put one of his jackets on over my trenchcoat.

Stripped a bit, he still appears larger than life. "You're ready for dinner?" he asks. "You're always so punctual."

"What do you mean? I'm just good at waiting. I thought you were the punctual one."

"No, you're great. You wait at the right time. It's a great habit. I should imitate you." From the twist of his smile, I think this must be some kind of wry joke.

WE HAVE what turns out to be our last meal together. It is one of the most special meals ever had in the history of France. Another meal set out for us by one of the sharp-nosed daughters of the bourgeoisie. Moses is right. I had not fully noticed the emphatic entrance of the cold, but we are entering one of those premature autumns which, at distinct points in our history, have cursed our mountains. From a glass-enclosed balcony, today's particular daughter of the bourgeoisie looks down upon us, a long frame wrapped in a shawl, a small coil radiator near her feet like an eternally spiraled orange snake. Her silhouette waits until we get our two plates, and then she retires inside, the glass doors not fully slamming shut behind.

For his part, Moses sits with me by the dumpster, near the chemical heat exhaled by the bulky-bodied furnace, though my fingers are turning numb and so I must drop the fork sometimes, my trenchcoat still damp from something I must have sat in. Anyone would shiver, not just a bushel like me, ears tingling inward, the cold hungry to enter old Emile's marrow. But we eat off fine china, Moses and I, each of us with a lamb's shankbone infused with wild gamey thyme, and we toast each other, drinking cider à la finierienne from elegant stemware.

I must say it is close to the most enjoyable moment I have ever achieved. I tell Moses this.

Moses listens hard. He draws himself up and then says: "If this is the most enjoyable moment, your memory's short, Emile."

"What do you mean?" I say.

"There's something you got to tell if you really want to get clean." The understanding crawls over me. "You just called me Emile."

"How do you mean?" he says.

"Not Raoul."

"So? Is Emile a pest controller's name or yours?"

"No one said it was my name."

"My mistake."

"Ah."

He leans over, fumbling in the pocket of his topmost layer. "But will you be straight with me? Say it. Is Emile your name?"

It becomes clear what may have happened. A sneaky informer somewhere—or else Moses was better-read than I'd suspected. Two eventualities I had encountered in my years on the run. I had accrued the scent of the too-familiar, the too-easily-identified. The much worse possibility, that Moses had been hired, would never have occurred to me.

Whatever the *why*, now *where to* matters more, and I see my choices split in two, balanced symmetrically on each edge of a double-headed axe. I can flee or confront, take the interrogatory role rather than the defensive, perhaps get him to see that he and I are on the one side. It is not for nothing that in my years on the rise in the prefecture, I was so often called Poulquet the Tactician, the man with a silvery tongue.

Accusatively, then, I say: "I saw you that night."

"Which night?" This is where he pretends to be momentarily more interested in his cider, addressing himself to his glass.

The truth is I don't want to pursue any strategy with Moses. The beauty of our time together has been its lack of strategy. We've had only a bifurcated game of survival and insubstantial pleasure, oiled by a bit of caring, and thus great purity has been ours. Then again, my survivor instincts need no pendulum to tell me to continue with my accusation. "I saw you whispering up to the veranda. Outside the wing of the Hotel Fauret. You also knew Rick, the American. There was your whole thing with that lady reporter. And the other whole thing about meeting Arianne. You knew I—" what *did* he know? "—belonged in her apartment."

Had his hands not raised up, placid and savvy hands, protesting my words, I would have continued. The axe tilting, my whole body constricting into the message *time to flee*.

"You aren't going to admit anything," I say.

"I hooked us up for *you*, man. You wanted to see your old flame."

"There's some organization behind you." This I don't believe, not fully, but I'm accusing him of the moon to get him to admit to the rooftops, to admit whatever lesser knowledge may be skirmishing behind what he cannot hide any longer is the Look. Even now he turns it on me. "You were talking to that guy."

"Which guy?" asks Moses, now avoiding my gaze.

"The big one. The journalist on crutches."

"That's a crime?" He debates tactics inside, I can see it, the boy's motives transparent. "Why won't you just tell me your name? For the two of us. Say it for me. Say *I am Emile*."

"Why does that matter?"

He reaches out to touch my face, the hump removed but the ribboned scar never fully covered over by all the later surgeries. "I am Emile. That's all I'm asking you to say."

"There are those who've called me that."

"You can't answer me," says Moses, as if I'm betraying him.

"It's been too long since that was a name that bore any relevance to my current state."

"You're going against what you always tell me. To clarify myself." He sighs, as if no risk is involved for either of us. "Maybe if you can say it just to me, you'll be free."

"Why should I say a name that no longer belongs?" He will not take this. "When I was young, some people did call me Poulquet the Ugly."

He sets back on his haunches, picks up a glass, replaces it, again debating within himself. "But you can't say it. That's all I'm asking. Say *I am Emile*."

"It's beside the point."

He gives up. Above us on the balcony the young lady comes out again and Moses shouts up *we're all okay*, and she retreats again.

Moses begins again in a quieter voice. "We can't shout," he says. "You have to tell your story."

"Tell my story?"

"Not about foxes. You know what I mean. This is the thing that will free you. You knew all along something like this might happen.

Didn't you? You chose to stay here," and he stamps his mud-caked boot on what for me is the holy ground of Finier. I am sitting on thorns, rocks, weeds, cannot get comfortable and so stand above him.

"But someone convinced me to stay," I say. "You knew all along, Moses—"

"At a certain point, okay, in a certain way. Does it matter?"

I accuse the worst but he is not admitting much. "Who paid you?" What hurts the most is that he fails to defend himself against any of this. "Someone paid you," I repeat, as if a dullard.

He says some awful nonsense regarding the idea that I, with all my expertise, might have guessed there might have been some vested interest. "Especially with your background," he finishes.

I swallow this fact. Leaves skid in drifts down the road, unbearably loud, an insufferably pointed noise, as if amplified over a wireless. I walk from our perch around the small yard, and stop, not seeing the point of walking. A man almost frozen in place, figuring out how to run, but Moses is used to being my travel companion and rises, companionable with me, folding up our napkins and raising a salute up to the window. He puts on his new hat, a ridiculous production, earflaps hanging down over his dreadlocks. "Hey, man," all softness to him. "I wanted to give you a chance. You talk to the reporters and like I'm promising. No one will catch you. Do it for yourself."

I can't even remember what topic he's on. "Let's walk toward the river?" and am so vacated of my usual self, or so filled with self-disgust, that despite the siren call of my instincts to *get out*, *flee*, I want to go toward the terminus of *the story of the boy*, at least halfway toward it. One might say: I want to believe he still has most of my interests at heart.

"You want us to go shoot bottles with stones?" I ask, but he just gives me his miserable grin, lost eyes. "Delivering angel," I think out loud, and then let it go, a bubble into the air. "I'm the package. I'm your goods." The desire to flee has absented my bones, and this alone makes my walk rickety and skeletal, the walk of an old man weighted down by a pendulum, too much love of living. We pass the stores which are closing, a moment of such anticipation in the Finier I once knew that for a second I almost believe this hour of jaundiced light is a good sign, promising some ease.

. . .

WE ARE WALKING the streets without any purpose but his. He is leading me as he has led me, for the most part, from the beginning, leading me past the doors of the hotel, past the English concierge who doesn't even look up, two phones to her ears. Oui madame, non madame, mais oui, madame. He has been leading me all along, to my sorry surprise, fate an awful creature, more crocodile than swan, and we have arrived on the second floor.

It is room number 218, as in the reporters' fables. I might have guessed.

In the corridor, a young man with the air of an undercover bodyguard, a clean-shaven boy with hands folded, looks away as we approach the door. He whistles a tune I almost know, just as if he'd decided to kill a little time hanging about on the hotel's second floor.

"You go in," says Moses. He respects some protocol unknown to me in how he draws out his words. "This is the reporter's room."

I know it but I repeat anyway, the horrific thrill of stepping over the abyss. "The reporter."

"There are a couple of others inside too."

"The reporter." Downstairs someone is playing a sprightly melody on the out-of-tune café piano, tricky and familiar, and my mind falters.

"The one who helped us open up the squat?"

"The guy with crutches. I know who he is." I try to remember the name—the biker, the one worshipped by the reporters. "Essvee?"

"You'll get to tell him the whole story. Certain things need to be recorded. He's good. Like I don't think he's into shaming or anything. You tell him. Then I promise. I think they're even going to give you some good lump sum or something. You'll be free to leave. To go off and hide anywhere you want. You got new skills. No one's going to grab you."

"I'm not interested in absolution," I say and Moses looks as if I had just desecrated the chapel his words have built. "I've done my penances."

"I know—" but not impatiently. A delivering angel is not impatient. "Emile, listen. I chose someone good for you. It's the lesser of two evils, you know? He'll be good to you. Then you can leave." He wants me to believe this, I can see that much, as much as he too wants to believe his own words (I am not unsympathetic to his plight). At this, the undercover bodyguard whistles more loudly, to cover over what must have been a more unscripted moment. "You told me you wanted people to remember things in the right way? Remember when you said that?" I nod, grudgingly. "Your will isn't going to do that for you. You told me you wanted a fancy obituary one day with laurels?" He waits for me to nod again. "All you do is tell your story, then go on your merry way." Again the abyss, again its thrill. "Hey, we can go together. And you'll get money, but you'll be free. You'll tell the whole thing. To someone who can put it forth to people. It'll be way better than your will, Emile. More complete. Then you can take on a disguise in some new place. They'll help you. The guy's a master, Essvee—"

He is daring to insult my last will and testament, this long-torsoed boy crumpled up into himself.

"You didn't read the whole thing I wrote," I tell him. "It got better." But the boy may have a point. "You're saying the fellow just wants the story?" Maybe it could be down, finally, my version, not the experts' version: the coolness of spent emotions, a freedom from my burden. "But what then?" This big-deal reporter was supposed to be good at getting the word of the outlaw down correctly, wasn't that what all those journalists had said? Then it occurs to me there may be another component. "No photos, right? Just the words. No recording devices."

"You have that woman photographer in there too." His voice steady as if he were citing statistics and not detailing a dungeon's entrance. Enough to make one want to believe him.

"I say no more pictures. She's taken enough for a lifetime."

"Okay, you tell her you don't want them—"

"You can't even say her name?" I point out.

He blushes. "Tell Simone no pictures."

"Thank you for some truth around here," and I nod to him before opening the door into a room hot enough to roast the rarest gamebirds of Finier.

PART FIVE

FIFTY-TWO

When I come out, after what feels like a day and a night of telling, I am not unsurprised to find the boy still there, lying on one of the mismatched sofas, looking not quite himself, alone and bereft.

"You feel better?" he asks, sitting up, rubbing his eyes. "Got things off your chest?" But there is some hardness to his gesture, a twist to the jaw, his eyes shut off.

"A world better," I say. "You were right. I had no idea how good it would feel. The full story."

"It felt good." He stands now, awkward, facing me as if awaiting instructions, as if we are two mismatched dancing partners not under the hotel's flickering hall-light but in a ballroom.

"More than good. It became almost bad. For a second." I am studying him but the boy is hard to find, loitering in some vacancy. Stiff, I lower myself onto the sofa. "I still don't understand what you get from having delivered me to these reporters." He looks down upon me, waiting. "What is it you get again? Relax," I say, imitating his speech style. *Sit please* they'd said as I'd entered the hot room.

"Now I'm ready to go find a farm. You young folk can do the harvest jobs," I say. "I'll contemplate fruit. You said you might have some leads? They did give me this," patting the small leather wallet of bills Essvee had pressed into my hand as we'd shaken hands goodbye. "Just like you said. Enough for us for a while. You wanted to leave Finier."

"Well," says Moses, dropping down next to me, making the sofa snarl. The boy hangs his wild dreadlocked head over the edge, making a real warning growl come our way. "That hotel dog on its cushion. The chihuahua's a brat. Hey, settle, boy. Did you see it start to snow?" Moses asks.

"Actually, I did. From that small window, inside—"

"It's supposed to get bad. Freak blizzard for early September. Really unpredictable," Moses tells me, his face pallid. "You know—"

Just then she emerges, big eyes, mouth tight, her hair long and loose, a lady untired by listening, born with an endless capacity for it. Her listening had become a form of talking, a loud and strident listening. In the overheated room I hadn't minded her taking pictures of me—my hand this way, head turned away, none of it bothersome, just because she was such a genius of a listener.

When I lay huddled on the floor, when I could not stop crying, when I took off my coat—she was the one I didn't mind. To them I hadn't mentioned the American on the road, that part I kept under my cloak, but because of this lady, I mentioned just about everything else. The other two had been good enough, but the photographer had been superlative, an eloquent set of ears.

"He's not coming out?" Moses asks the girl, exaggerating the pitch of the question.

"He needs to stay inside."

"Alone?"

"He has endless packs of cigarettes," I answer for her, attempting to resume the camaraderie of the room, dreadfully mild.

"He's finishing up some last taping."

"Taping? The American got it?" Moses asks the girl, his face bloated, picking at his teeth as if unsatisfied with dinner.

"Rick and that Turk or Brit or whoever. They got everything," she says. "We all did."

"What do you mean?"

"Tape, photo, video."

Moses glances at me surprised and says to her: "You must be exhausted."

She gives him a half-petrified smile. Something familiar pricks me, but I tell myself the feeling is out of context, that the two are merely speaking that contemporary dialect expressly meant to exclude the non-young with its vagueness. "I'm okay," she says.

"Super," he tells her. I've never heard him use the word and it jars me, just a little.

"Some game you're playing?" she says.

"No game," he says with full solemnity, cracking a quick half-smile, but I can't understand his cadence, or maybe I'm in an altered state after having spoken for so long. I am waiting for an emblem, a moment's revolution, something to assure me Moses is the same urchin monarch to whom I'd bid adieu before I'd entered the room, but the assurance doesn't come.

She pulls her camera bag on. "I better be off," she says, already heading downstairs.

"Are you being zapped?" I ask Moses.

He stares at me, holds his fingers out. "No." Yet he is working up to something.

I tap Moses' arm. "So you owe me a favor?"

"Listen, man." He stops. "It's going to work out. But first hear me. I told you this was reporters, you know, scooping?"

I don't understand at first. He is gripping my knee as if our sofa is about to break and float free of the hotel and all that will remain solid is the grip. All I want to do is unpry his fingers from my knee. His tone has started to sound a trifle too familiar.

"Listen. Some people came by when you were inside. It's not my fault." Insufferable, recognizable, a plaintive song I know almost as well as my own voice. "Like I didn't plan this part." He wants me to love or forgive, to justify the ways of Moses. I mumble something, sensing it already. Emile useless, going, gone. "That guy Essvee's really powerful, right? But someone else, not him, must have let other people know. It's hard to explain. You won't understand anyway," he says.

But I do, I get it all too well, familiar with the melody of *not my doing*.

"You're turning me in?" I say, my heart high in my throat. "Or you did already?"

He waves his hand, banishing some imaginary moths. He stands up abruptly, sits back down. "Honestly." Too much in my face, his eyes unfixed, actually putting his hands on my gouged-out chest, talking with a lover's urgency. "We had a good time, right? You liked the manse, right, the music. Everywhere we went. You said I re-ju-ve-nated you."

"You can't hear yourself." My voice high too, a fact I cannot help, my knees jumping a bit, this not the ice of panic but the other kind, the panic which turns one amoebic, lacking membrane or will, a creature mobile but without defense. How had I not seen the boy's traitor aspects? There had been fissures in him, sure, but this particular *mush*?

"The night work," the boy's saying. "Delhi, Max, all that. You *told* me—"

"Can't hear yourself!" I need to think. Nowhere to go on that second floor, surely not out the window in the room with the reporters if they too were accomplices. In on it, Emile again *out*. And perhaps my pendulum is lost to me, fallen out of my pocket somewhere en route to this moment. An amputee, I pat my left pocket, can't find it.

"I bargained for extra time. I told him I would keep you here, right? Give you some extra time. But then you'd be free after your story."

"Extra time?" This is an excruciating joke, but a guffaw comes out, out of the mouth I've been stuck with my long existence, the same sorry mouth that sucked too long at the wet-nurse's teat, the same mouth which has taken in thousands of cafés au lait and spoken its directives, a mouth praised for discretion and fluency.

"Tried to give you some happiness, I'm saying. Or like I know it," he says. "You said you'd never seen this side of Finier. Life. You'd never felt so free."

I ask him to stop please. *I don't deserve this.*

"Listen." Taking my hand, voice low and sugared. "I begged you to flee?" He wants me to absorb his lies. "They would have gotten you eventually, right? You were stubborn. It's sort of your fault? You didn't leave. How could I know one of the reporters got linked to the police?"

If you'd cared more.

"They told me they were reporters first and last. Like they signed, man. Signed. No harm to you or me. That was the deal I cut."

"You knew from the second you saw me. You thought you'd get something if you did me in." Half-choking, an old man's throat mine, the boy's hand now viselike on my arm, as if he has become part of my body. Which is the truth: whether or not the floor had fallen through, without his knowledge, a hatch dropping us both into this moment, *he will never be free of Emile.* I want to tell him this but my tongue has died.

"Not from the start, I didn't know who you were, but then he sort of arranged—" He indicates inside room 218 and I know he means the man on crutches. How stupid and unwitting. The discarded newspaper, the locked squat, the day I was a naked river monkey, how I'd just walked into the trap set for me by the master reporter, the one who'd gotten young Moses involved, all cages of strategies leading to further cages, maybe to the end-cage, the law's claws, an inescapable jail cell unto my coffin. "He knew," the boy's saying, as if I really need to know what form his lies will take. "He knew *my* situation. Thought I could be useful. And then he met you the first day you were here." He waits while I realize who that carbuncular man in Olivier's café had been, actually a brilliant disguise, I have to admire it in the flare of this second. "I had a different idea," Moses is saying. "I wanted to show you a few things. I asked for you to get some living in under your belt, you know, when he first approached me. Hey, you're always saying there's no one true history. Of anything." He jerks his head toward the room. "I liked you. You'd already spent a night with us up at the manse."

"You liked me." The most I can manage.

"You can say that. I had my own rescue trip going. I wanted to heal you. Or like teach you something?" The silence after this gets pierced by that strange little animal squeal out from under the couch. We both startle.

"You wanted to teach me?" I say, not understanding. I want to twist his hands in my own with all the unspeakable in me, turn violent, but this is not in my nature, despite whatever childhood flies I might have burnt one by one. He must have bet his life not on my kindness but on my obedience, all past behavior predicting the present.

"Emile. Sorry." His head is ducked in deep study of his boots. "We got to head out quietly. No fuss, I'm saying. The hotel."

The hotel and its walls will close in.

But his words help. This hotel is my hotel, no one else's, its hidden corridors my own. We will head out, a few steps, I'll be nice Emile, compliant Emile, pragmatic Emile; then do what I can, old codger body notwithstanding, use adrenaline and surprise to break away.

"The gendarmes are waiting *outside*," he said. "I asked them to wait out there. Like a courtesy to you?" He must see my blankness. "So we could talk?" His smile not his, only a rusty lower lip, bitten. "But now—"

Strange as it is, rather than wishing to hurt him, I want to bury my nose in the shoulder of his jacket, mildew and stains, hide alongside the boy, *inside*, but he keeps talking. "You'll go. Maybe this trial will work out for the better, man. You never know."

No more trials for Emile. "Yes," I say to the boy's simpers and self-justification.

"You'll get justice? It's probably like false charges, man. We could hook up sometime later. Work the harvest. Wouldn't you feel better not running anymore?"

"No," I say, honestly. "I don't know what not-running is like."

"But," he blew out his lips. "Running's impossible." A maid is hurrying down the stairs now, holding her giant rustic wicker basket before her as if to knock down barbarian hordes. "Salaam," says Moses, genially to her, and back to me. "You understand."

"Moses," I say. "You don't believe a thing you're saying. What did they do to you?"

"Look. You don't want me to suffer, do you? I turn you in, I get my kids. It's about the future, not the past." His last card, playing it fully, his mouth and nose inflaming before me, turning monstrous. "Listen. It's like we have an appointment."

"With what? Destiny? The police?" Now I manage to tell him that of all people he should know. The law is a system of risks and consequences. He could always take the risk of not getting caught. Again he looks me dead in the eyes and then away. Old shell, road companion, faltering Emile.

The same maid ascends the stairs, inspecting us thoughtfully. Apparently clueless, she asks whether we want room 218 to be aired out, and when Moses says the inhabitants aren't ready, she takes that as a cue to start wiping the landing's mirror frame and its small desk, measuring pine oil into a rag, her back to us. This might be code, but it is unlikely, her performance is too unconscious. Then again, what do I know about performance? I have been taken in.

I would like to believe that Moses only learned the truth of the mousetrap while I was inside the room, but first the mouse needs to find a way to escape. Still, I cannot help but sense the bureaucratic ripple out from our moment: if his version is true, one of the reporters had leaked the capture of France's great fugitive, Poulquet of a Thousand Faces, to the local police, which would be a great coup for the locals if they could just deliver perfectly intact their greasy little wartime mouse up to the national police service and the fangs of law and history.

"You tell the police I got away, Moses. Say I escaped. You'll still get custody."

"That won't work. Who'll believe me?"

The maid with her sad-Madonna eyes now turns from her mirror and says, *ah*, did we see the snow? Strange for September, the blizzard coming in, can we see it through the hall window? She has that peasant excitement that makes me believe this to be a sincere response, and my head goes dead, as if it had been unplugged. For the merest second, the three of us look out the window in the way Finier can make even its most jaded denizens do, sighting the plucky cross of

Saint Finier which stays beautiful despite the telephone tower planted down next to it, our unbowed sentinel with bits of confetti swirling around, centering Finier within the whole world.

"Thank you, Mademoiselle," says Moses, and the maid, snubbed by such a shabby boy, makes a show of noisily unlocking the room next to the one in which the others remain, disappearing with waxes and plump brushes inside, where she can eavesdrop in luxury.

"You don't get it," I whisper. "You have my reputation going for you. I'm an escape artist. Guards will vouch for you. I have skills, like you say. I've escaped every trap. I'm Houdini. Everyone knows."

"I'm supposed to—" he says. And takes my hand, as if we are about to commit to an oath. His hand burly, rough, scratched. This is his justice. I told my story; he gives me his. "You said you *wanted* to leave your testament for others."

"That's beside the point. Now you owe me something."

"I'm just a deliverer." He releases my hand. "You called me the package boy?" Tapping his chest as if this alone could release all goblins. "I've been straight with you, right?"

"No." How quickly the boy has learned to lie to himself. This alone could make one wish to cry, were it not for the electric demands of survival. How to finesse the moment?

"I'm saying, Emile, we're going downstairs. You go left and out the door. We'll say goodbye." The slim possibility occurs to me. He may be trying to help me without revealing it to any eavesdropping maids or reporters, but how can I tell? His face has turned into an implacable mask, his gaze battened down. "I'm sorry," he says, which makes me think he won't help me, not one bit.

"Moses," I say. "François." But nothing transforms his expression, not even his real name.

WE BEGIN downstairs, his hand firm on the crook of my elbow. I could escape him if I wanted, but strange as it may seem, I am also compelled to see what the boy is leading me toward. This is partly a fascination with flames but mainly it is fatigue. From the lobby, by the vacated front desk, we see the front door. Beyond, near the small fountain, the silhouettes of two gendarmes, broad backs to the hotel, one pacing and speaking into a radio device, another enjoying his cigarette.

It must be at this moment that the coin spins—one side reality, one side possibility—and Moses comes to his own decision about what role he wishes to play.

FIFTY-THREE

"C'mon," he hisses, grabbing my hand again. We are running backward, my age our impediment, slow man that I am, through the café back into the dining room where lunch is being endlessly prepared, a waiter fixing a display table of fruit, heading back through the swinging metal doors into the kitchen, past all the suited-up sous chefs, out the landing, taking the saggy stairs down and sliding farther down, past the mound of cigarette butts, that steep slope by the river, my knees burning, my hand at the bank grabbed by the boy who says he knows where the Ursulines keep their boat. For a second I think he means the pillars left underwater, pillars used by the medieval nuns who made travelers pay to pass in and out of Finier.

Only in the boat do I have a chance to breathe, to have my pacemaker reset my heart, and yet we are almost across the river. My fingers are numb yet I welcome it; to lose sensation in one's fingers is to be freed of yet another burden. "See my kids. Blame me?" he asks between pulls. "I had no idea they'd call in the police. Where we going anyway?" he asks.

"A driver might help," I say, sighting a big lorry passing on the road. "Get a ride?"

Close to the bank and he jumps out, hand extended to help me out of the boat. "The train to Spain?" His face pure excitement, thinking that we've just gotten away with two scoops of something bad, that both of us can be served, that now we can hightail it to the station or to his mythical grape harvest.

Though I see them before he does.

When he does, his look is so earnest I want to believe it.

"You gotta know," he tells me. "Emile. Believe me. This part I didn't plan. I swear."

We must both catch our breath at the official spectacle of it, the highway blockaded north and south by limousines, long black limos like musical measures squeezed in, like those I traveled about in when on official business years ago. Blackness containing a bevy of disorganized police cars, lights blinking, murderous cave-dwellers brought into the light, the crescendo whir of a helicopter, strange after the softness of our paddling across the river, a giant shadowy presence, a mechanical hummingbird blaspheming the air near our Saint Finier.

IT IS HOW they close in which makes me believe they are wrong. There is no aesthetic to it. Had they wanted to do something a bit more graceful, they'd been given ample opportunity. Many elements to work with: the river, the snow beginning to fall, so much for them to employ more decently. These people specialize in staging their events—I know they do, no one can tell me differently—they are like wastrels wanting to storm the square with the Paul statue—and so it is their manner of closing in with which I take issue. They could have dragged me up the mountain of Finier and manacled me to the cross, next to the ugly telephone tower, could have let me freeze to death in the snow, the scenario consequently far superior. There would have been at least an honesty to the moment and authenticity, some act of self-will on their part and my own before a release into the thing which no one can say frightens me. I'd be granted dignity, would refuse the last unction of the tired priest they'd send uphill. Or: they could have weighted me down with the belongings of the wastrels, Arianne's belongings, any citizen's belongings, could have set me to drown in the river. All more befitting to our Finier and its history.

But barbarians lack a true aesthetic, always seduced by modernity and blinking lights on police cars and the tawdry click of handcuffs controlled by remote devices and the flash of photographers' bulbs. Barbarians chew mints and breathe on your face as they pretend to tell you your rights, meanwhile treating you like some standard-issue pornographer and pedophilic trafficker, barbarians happiest when they cloak their inner natures in the sentimental or at least the black-and-white story.

This exact checkered pattern of my life is what I'm forced to ponder, now, for hours at a time, that tango between barbarity and sweetness, my main companion in such contemplations a cockroach, an ornery one with a crippled back leg whose scrabble across the floor and up the wall would bother a saint, a scritch-scratch no one would welcome, a shuffle into an eternal present tense about which one lacks much choice, but I'm nonetheless loath to kill the bug as his bad dance across the floor remains my sole distraction. If not the ambitious roach, it is this pattern of my life which I must contemplate, the sugar-coated vulgarity of Arianne, perhaps of my family, of all the lawyers and officials and the police who needlessly manhandled their prey as we made our way back north, no one content unless I was held in some properly official embrace of sneering condescension and attentiveness, that unique, toxic combination. No barbarian would rest unless he could drag me back to a summary, cursory judgment in our capital, ensuring that I would reside permanently entombed not in one of our better-known cemeteries but in the heart of our France, the prison itself a former crawl space. Which must be a blessing to my moral development, however blind I am to it, a blessing courtesy of whatever greater wisdom both my pendulum and Moses may have possessed: some destiny they've conspired together to lead me toward, though I'm still waiting to have revealed whatever higher message they wished me to see.

∎ ∎ ∎

MY ONLY VISITOR HERE, apart from my not-so-unfriendly roach, has been Odile, whose loyalty one must admire. One Sunday a month, I'm allowed to receive a visitor, and I have forbidden any of the scrappy lawyers showing up to volunteer to defend me, little bantam cocks popping up so happy to use me, happy to contravene the presiding spirit of their times. I lack any more stomach for their courtroom arguments and counterarguments, for their fake charm and jaw-cracking and knuckle-popping. Perhaps this is the effect of having surrendered my pendulum to the guards, which I'd found en route to the prison caught in my pant-leg, escaped from a pocket. Guards who with the pendulum their ward may feel a new arbitrariness in their decisions.

I have never told anyone this but my hunch is that the pendulum operates free of the usual constraints of time and space: it continues to guide me, though no longer in my possession, as it must have been guiding me even a half-century before I came into its ownership. It guides even those who don't wish to come into its power, those who wish to remain ignorant of its power. Thus I was not wholly sad to relinquish it; the wisdom of age arriving upon me, I knew its clout went beyond being mere property. I do not feel abandoned, as I feel the pendulum may have influenced Arianne to come forward so that even in her, my tyrant, I could spot a bit of humanity. Since I have been in my cell, it has occurred to me for the first time, as if the ghost of a dream, a barely graspable insight that (though I'd spent almost a lifetime in Arianne's thrall, believing I'd seen her from every angle, in every situation, believing I alone contained her both as she had been and wanted to seem) perhaps I'd never really known Arianne. I do occasionally wonder why my old lawyer friend who'd gotten me released before now evidently refuses to touch my case—though, in truth, so little surprises me anymore. What could surprise me? Not the way that Arianne had managed to remain a virgin in the eyes of the law, unsullied by perjury given her alleged *mental instability*, nor the way that poor Odile had passed a fortnight behind bars, scrambling to have a random lawyer mount the same defense on her behalf. Ultimately successful, the papers told me, Odile released to the light, yet assuredly her two weeks in prison endowed her with more of the intricate, tiny scars which ladies like Odile quickly accrue and tend to bear with the silence of heroes.

LITTLE SURPRISES ME, I say, except for this occurrence: once a month, almost without fail, Odile has visited, bearing in her violet satchel reading glasses for me and a newspaper with satisfyingly revanchist editorials, occasionally a not-so-bad cigar which I can at least chew on, sometimes a snifter of port which she has secreted on her spinsterly person and managed to get past the guards, guards who've been given the onerous task of keeping a suicide watch over me. It is tiresome to be watched for signs of suicide, I tell Odile too many times, because it gives one little latitude in terms of what one can show. Too much vitality or lethargy and one receives all sorts of useless attentions, talks with bearded semitic psychiatrists or clean-shaven semitic psychologists or lady doctors of unknown provenance. Never sure what Odile understands, as she is a bit hard of hearing and further possesses the endearing vanity of refusing to wear a hearing aid during her visits, I persist in explaining it to her. None of these doctors can penetrate my core, I say. Only *her* visits seem to matter, though this part I do not confide. We never mention her recent fortnight in prison, nor anything about my case. Rather, what we exchange is a somewhat lopsided but nonetheless agreeable chitchat. She still calls me Mister Poulquet, I call her Odile, and never have we done more than shake hands at the beginning and close of our meetings, though her gifts touch me and I mull over them all month.

The flame she has kept lit in her heart for me all these years would touch any man, as well as her almost perfect regularity. A couple of times she has erred in her pattern, once failing to appear for an almost unbearable two months, and again now, when I have lost count of the months, but these occasions are entirely my fault, my not having learned the lesson which I wanted everyone else to learn: I dragged up the past.

Not long into my stay here—even then I had given up keeping track of time, because early on I believed my roach would outlive me, and the thought was and remains abhorrent, as if I didn't have anything else to get depressed about—while later I tended to believe my roach had already died many times and that the guards merely wished to bedevil me by continually crooking the back leg of some new bug, releasing him into my cell, the endless return of the crippled roach part of their vile humor—not long after my arrival, I asked Odile to seek out Moses, to do what she could to bring him to me. I asked Odile to tell the boy that I would not curse him for what he had done. To say that I believed his story, that the police had come while I was in the reporter's hotel room. To say I understood his wish to see his children and the original deal he had struck with the reporter. That I blamed others more than him, the big reporter as much as the lady photographer—or the American lady reporter—one of whom must have hinted to the police my whereabouts. After my request, Odile stayed away for two months. When I saw her again, she was both empty-handed and more tight-lipped than usual. Your Moses won't see you, she told me. I had to swallow this, knowing that I would have to consider this particular fact—or had she invented it?—during my hours of being watched for suicidal gestures.

He has custody of his children? I asked, mainly to fill the silence.

She told me that he had failed to maintain custody, that he was now stationed in a clinic for rehabilitation, and that they, whoever they were, had told him that "there was hope he might be rehabbed." Hope? What breed of hope might there be for young Moses, twinned forever with his conscience? I swallowed her fable, wondering if some important part of it might be true.

However, though usually I could listen—and attentively—for hours to her prattle about her life, about the new tightfisted grocer down the street, or the neighbor with whom she walked her poodle, not to mention the problems she had with a complaining tenant or the pension office's recalcitrance in addressing certain incorrect figures, on this occasion I heard nothing.

A few months after this incident, it occurred to me that Odile did after all have a certain arthritic perseverance to her sleuthing, and that therefore she might be able to locate someone easier to find.

Izzy? I asked. What about Izzy?

When she returned, again two months later, she had succeeded, nonetheless failing to sound triumphant in her declaration. In the flattest of voices she informed me that my old friend was stationed in the visitors' room, and that he'd said he did not wish to sit in the corridor near me.

That's ridiculous, I said.

Perhaps, but, Mister Poulquet, it is also true.

Here, the guard I liked most reminded us I could only have one visitor at a time. So Izzy it was, with Odile ushered out. Even though my old friend sat far down the hall, he was near enough that I could hear his voice and he could hear mine. I sat in my dark, Izzy in his. Between us a hushed hallway stretched.

Emile, he finally said. You wanted to see me, though I'm not sure why.

I let out a laugh at this. Listening to the burr of his voice, I was not sure myself.

You wanted to be caught, he continued, that was my guess.

I said nothing.

I brought you this, he said.

What followed was a murmured colloquy between the guard and him, ended by the guard finally saying *perhaps it's best that you hand it to him yourself, sir.*

At which Izzy must have made the decision that he could stomach being near me, his vile old friend. I heard the wooden tread on metal as he headed down the corridor toward me, and then the guard must have scraped a different chair than Odile's usual perch into place behind him. Izzy thanked him. He sat in front of the spattered plastic which is my view out into the world, and the narrow meal slot was opened.

This is for you, said Izzy.

He placed in the slot something which, on my side, it took a second to recognize. A bifurcated bit of wood? It bore an ancient, tattered, attenuated rubber flag, and then I recognized its origin. The slingshot I had given Izzy, years ago, when he had first stepped forward to protect me. Cracked but still the same one I'd whittled with Charlot, our family's stablehand.

I can't, I said, feeling the smoothness of the wood. The gift seemed to make me tear up a bit.

You have it, Emile, he said.

Thank you, I said, gripping the toy, lacking speech. We had nothing to say to each other. There was no kind of talk invented to fill the silence between us, as there was a certain kind of palaver possible between, say, Odile and me. I saw him scratch his ear, stretch his jaw, tug at his collar. Soon he would rise. Without thinking, I angled my own hand through the slot, at which I heard the guard's sharp intake of breath. It's okay, sir, said Izzy. Through the slot, I touched his shoulder, a raggy sweater, and traveled down as far as I could on Izzy's arm, managing to pull Izzy's larger hand through the slot. I placed it on my face, pushed the roughness of his fingers over my cheeks, wet enough, and he seemed to understand the moment, traveled my face as only a blind man could, for a second, finding Emile under the sutures, the new nose and cheeks, my sharper chin, memorizing me all over again. But this was a brief span in the eternity of my life. He was soon done, he had his fill of me, his wits about him, his freedom, could return to his banal life, retracting his hand, saying nothing more. Soon—how soon after?—I heard his bulk rising and trying the gate.

Left latch, sir, said the guard.

And that was it, the coda of Izzy, no more of him, only this slingshot which the guards let me hold for an hour but no longer, because after all, it is something of a risky implement for someone under constant suicide watch.

Once he'd gone, Odile rushed in, told me that Izzy felt apologetic, that he didn't mean to do what he'd done.

What had he done? Stop, I was forced to tell her, turning away from the spattered plastic viewing plate. Please. For once I lost my diplomacy toward her. Stop all your old-lady lies! I said. It's as bad as that lilac perfume of yours! Do you know how much I've always hated your lilac scent? It's really quite awful, all these years, I always choke from it!

Then I immediately tried to make up for it by telling her I was tired, but no apology helped: she left soon after. Unfortunately, it is my lot that since my words about her perfume she has stayed away, so that alone with my little scrabbling cellmate, I have again and again regretted my actions, sorely, resolving never again to be rude toward this lady, if she would just give me half a chance. I will tell her that there have been days when I've appreciated her scent, that I was merely discomfited that day, given the pressures upon me: this lady who has kept me alive, in many ways, as long as she has.

In this last period, they have raised my suicide watch to red alert. In fact, it has become their new nickname for me, they call me Mister Suicide, these surly guards meant to keep me from self-harm, and hence these blunted plastic utensils with my tasteless food, insult added to injury of these particular walls which show not a seam, not a splinter. Calling me Mister Suicide must be their attempt at humor, lessening the gravity of their job, but what they don't realize is that there is great power in naming others, and one day I might undo their professional standing, take them up on their gambit, make them all failures at their state-given task of keeping me alive.

I sometimes in these days wake with the illusion that I could just get up and walk outside into the snow-covered bare courtyard which I have glimpsed when they've taken me to be hosed down in the shower, dragging my chains. The illusion is that I could just spend some time by myself in the courtyard, no one watching me, and that Moses might get wind of my new mobility and might after all come pay me a visit. As I see it, the boy will feel offended when I refuse his offer of real escape, and he will leave. Several days might pass and I could continue to sit alone in the cold, unbothered by guards, roaches, urgency, or hunger, the courtyard a tempting freedom in itself, one from which I can hear the road outside. At some point in the reverie, I decide to take advantage of my real powers, powers none of them know about, and I sound a wolf whistle, thereby convening all the prisoners in the courtyard, rightly or wrongly convicted, managing to take them all with me, a tissue of prisoners, one holding on to another's hand, a human kite, together bound and flying free of the courtyard, of the prison, free of the cold of the Paris winter constantly seeping into us despite the old furnace's constant clanking. Having deposited each of the others in their own favored locales, leaving them to their private destinies, I go back to my own hungry ghost view, from atop our mountain of Saint Finier.

Then atop the mountain there will be some time before the fingers, go but after them there will still be the wrists. When these go, there will still be the shoulders. The heart will pound the hardest but the gut will determine everything, the gut which will soon melt into the truth of the head and tongue. And after that will come the kindness of sleep to enter, then the greater pulse of awakening. After the wakefulness there will still be the head and tongue and how reluctant these will be in taking their leave, memory's last stand. But once they surrender, the cold will finish its work, starting in from the edges, tender enough, making all of you soon deep and past.

Made in United States
North Haven, CT
08 January 2022